SWORD SORCERY!

Rehger sensed from the first parry that his opponent was no match for him. It would be an easy fight and, with luck, he would be able to spare his foe's life.

And then chaos claimed Rehger's world. Suddenly he lost control of the sword in his hand. The sword was *alive*. As he raised it, it resisted. It was cold as ice, charged with an energy, a strength that wrestled with his own. Rehger's body broke into a freezing, scalding sweat—not of fear—of pure horror.

Witchcraft! A spell had turned his weapon into a live enemy. In his hand, the grip of the hilt remained, though it rippled with convulsive life. But the full length of the sword had become a serpent, stiffly stretched and writhing to rid itself of the final vestiges of steel. It was the color of milk, the hard scales gleaming like platinum. The eyes stared from its flat head, soulless white. He knew then whose power had formed the spell. It was the Amanackire sorceress, and she meant him to die!

THE WHITE SERPENT

A Novel of Vis

TANITH LEE

DAW BOOKS, INC.

DONALD A. WOLLHEIM, PUBLISHER

1633 Broadway, New York, NY 10019

First Printing, April 1988

1 2 3 4 5 6 7 8 9

PRINTED IN THE U.S.A.

CONTENTS

BOOK ONE

ISCAH

CHAPTER ONE

THE SNOW

In a cone of purple dusk, on the white snow, the young woman stood calling in her husband's dogs. All around, the mountains stared at each other across the valley, colored like the sky and darkening with it, the huge snows caught on them in broad luminous tangles. It was the heart of winter, yet as sometimes happened here in the west, there had been a partial thaw. Panes of ice slipped from the mountain sides and crashed away. A single flower had raised its head against the well—and Tibo plucked it and put it in a crock beside the hearth-fire. Transparent as a ghost it poised there, for Orbin to sneer at. The dog-pack, too, was loosed from its shed and let go up the valley. The dogs might catch a hare or unwary rock-rat out to forage in brief sunshine. By afternoon, however, snow-cloud came down again on the mountain tops and Orbin snarled a command. So Tibo left her pots and went to summon the dogs, with a high-pitched warbling woman's call used the Iscaian uplands over.

Soon, they came trotting out of the mauveness one by one, two by two. She counted each as it passed her, and spoke kindly to it. All had returned empty-mouthed, though maybe they had found something for themselves. When the eighth dog had run by her and into the shed, Tibo scanned the dusk, and presently called out again. Orhn owned nine dogs and one had not come back, the dark bitch, Blackness.

Sometimes tirr prowled through the mountain valleys, if winter had caught them. A dog did not stand much of a chance against tirr venom. Nor against a fresh snowfall. Blackness was valuable, a clever hunt-

11

ress, whose womb made healthy pups. Tibo was concerned for her, and besides would get the blame if any animal were missing. Orbin badly wanted an excuse to give her a thorough beating.

There was perhaps a quarter hour of the twilight left, and new snow had not yet begun to come down. Tibo shut the dogs in. Then she took a lantern from its hook above the dog-shed door, kindled it, and began to walk out carefully across the pasture, calling as she went.

The ground was treacherous, not yet frozen hard again. Tibo knew from years of experience how unevenly the land lay under its disguise of snow. She knew also that a woman's life was cheap, that Orbin hated her and that Orhn—well. There was no point in considering Orhn's opinion on the matter.

She had been wed to him at the age of ten. Her family, a sprawling herd of many rough sons and many slavish daughters, had been no happiness to her, and she was early on acquainted with poverty. Orhn's farm was spoken of with jealousy, his father had had some standing in the village of Ly; even his sons being given the names of Kings. This father was gone by the time of the marriage but the mother still lived, senile, vaguely demented, and chair-bound, for whose every need Tibo must care. Otherwise there were only the brothers to tend. Orbin's two wives were both of them dead and a decline in fortune had, it seemed, prevented him from getting others. Orhn meanwhile, as Tibo discovered, was simple. He treated her gently enough, and in their nuptual bed, the garlands of flowers and vine still on their hair, had pawed and drooled upon her, expending his seed in the first minute, without union, or even an embrace. This had been the format of their coition ever after, though in later years the spark of lust had died in him, except now and then at Zastis. All of which meant, additionally, that Tibo had been some nine years a childless wife, apparently barren, which lowered her value further.

Altogether, she was worth very little, and had better find the dog who, undoubtedly, was worth much more.

*   *   *

A low wall of stones bounded the pasture, where in summer Orhn's blue pigs and whippy-necked fowl rooted and pecked. An open place in the wall, where the dogs had come through, gave on a tumble of rocks, and a few citrus trees, whose leaves the cold had burnt away.

Winter did not always bring snow to the mountains of Iscah, they said, but for as long as she could remember Tibo had seen it. That was the curse of the serpent goddess, they told you.

"Blackness!"

Tibo called by name now. The light was going suddenly fast, as if the fisted cloud squeezed the sky dry of it.

Then, with an almost terrible relief, Tibo heard the bitch-dog begin to whine and croon to her, from somewhere in the jumble of rocks.

"What is it, lass? What have you found?"

Something plainly Blackness would not leave. Or, Cah prevent it, was she lamed?

Holding the lantern high, Tibo moved forward once more. She did not like this place, even in the late summer days, when she came to pick the fruit. In certain parts the farm was hidden from view by the rocks, all of which were faceless now under the snow. She began to think of banaliks, the vampire-demons indigenous, in myth, to mountains.

The dog barked abruptly, very close, to her left. Tibo turned to the sound, and screamed in horror. Something had her by the leg. Hard and cold it gripped her calf just above the cuff of her boot..

"Be quiet," a man's voice said. It was a man's hand that held her.

Her terror subsided to mere fright, and she swung the lantern over, and saw him. He sat between two of the rocks, grasping the dog's muzzle in one hand, to keep her from barking till allowed, while he controlled her powerful body with his thighs. His other hand remained on Tibo. He was clearly very strong, and looked capable of maintaining both holds until they all three, man, dog, girl, froze to stone or starved to bone. Tibo considered crashing the lamp down on his skull. Something must happen then—he would lose his grip on the dog, who might go for his throat, or only of Tibo, who could perhaps get to the farm across the slippery snow before he caught her again.

"Don't," he said, as if he read her mind, as the Serpent People did. "For sure, both of us would be damaged. I don't want to hurt you." No man had ever said such a thing to Tibo. In her experience all men hurt most women, to a greater or lesser degree. Her first memories were of her father's blows. It was the natural order of things.

"I see you are puzzled," the man said. His voice was strange to her, with an alien accent not of Iscah, let alone Ly Village. "I don't mean you any harm. I've already met my share of trouble. Friends of yours, maybe. Bandits—then I wandered. The thaw saved my life. . . . So those prayers to Anack weren't wasted after all. But it's about to snow again. Then I'm finished. All I want is some generous roof—a night or two. And if you've anything to ride—these western snows, poor things, nearly passable. But I suppose a saddle-thoroughbred is too much to dream of. If I could get to Ly Dis, I can reach the capital from there—or somewhere. I'd pay. They didn't find my coins—or couldn't use them. Do you even know money was invented, out here?"

Tibo heard his speech through. For one thing, she would never have interrupted while any man spoke, however formlessly. Even an enemy from whom she must defend herself. But she did not properly understand. The yellow lantern burned on his face, while the world gloomed over. He was young, and handsome, but not in any manner she had ever seen before. The brazen Vis skin came paler in Iscah; his flesh was dark, like that of the men of Dorthar or Alisaar, though not like a black Zakorian's. His hair fell to his shoulders, thick leaden silk—the men of Iscah wore their hair lopped high up the skull, or went shaven in the hot months.

He seemed to be studying her also, with his wide-spaced black eyes.

All at once he let her go, and let go of the dog, too.

Blackness turned at once like a snake against him, snapping, and Tibo reached by him to snatch her away.

"See," he said, "you do like me, despite everything."

Then he shut his eyes and sighed. His head lolled gracefully. Tibo saw he had fainted, and in another moment why, for even in the cold he was bleeding busily and had soaked the dog with his blood, her sable coat hiding it.

"*Cah*," said Tibo, making a little ritualistic gesture to the goddess of her country. The dog crouched growling at her side, and the first snowflake, descending, fell sizzling in the lantern.

Orbin raised his head, sly-eyed, as the door was opened out of the white night.

"Hoh, Tibo," he said softly. "Where is your flower gone, eh? I'll tell you. You were loafing so long out there, we needed another log on the fire. So I put your flower on it instead. Didn't make much of a blaze." He watched, as Tibo glanced at the empty crock, and pointlessly, into the hearth. But Tibo always ultimately disappointed Orbin. She never sniveled, or groveled, as the other women had. Even when he clouted her, she only got up again. And he had to clout her often, for Orhn was too stupid to see to it. Orbin had even had to arrange their marriage, although it was not unusual for the closest male relative of the groom to attend to such things. Due to Orbin's clever management, however, no one had been able to notice just how slow the elder brother was. The farm, and all its stock, belonged to Orhn, who had the name of Alisaarian kings. By law, Orbin belonged to Orhn. That was a fine joke, that. In a practical sense everything actually was Orbin's, in all but name, kingly or otherwise. As for the slut, Orbin could have had her, too. But he never ordinarily saw much in women. During the Red Moon, when the urge was on him, he knew better than to tamper with his brother's legal wife. She might get herself pregnant, and then there could be questions, because the village somewhat suspected Orhn's ability, even while they spoke of Tibo as a barren parasite. Orbin was reverent of Cah and made the goddess regular offerings. He did not want to tell falsehoods before her statue, afraid of what she might then do to him. So he left Tibo alone, and paid to go with the temple's holy-girls, fat lumps good only for such sticking.

On the other hand there was no law, religious or otherwise, against a man thrashing his brother's wife.

"All the dogs?" he asked her now.

"Yes, brother-master." She paused, her eyes lowered respectfully. What else was she waiting to say? Had she lied about the dogs? "Brother-master," she said, "give leave that I speak?"

"What rubbish have you got to say? All right. Babble on. You women, never quiet."

"There's a man. Blackness showed me."

Orbin was alerted.

"What man?"

"A stranger. Robbers set on him. He's bleeding, and may die."

"Then let him," said Orbin.

He watched her covertly, to see what she would do now, but she only went to the fire, and began to put bits of wood on it. The deed woke up Orhn, who had been slumbering on a bench one side of the hearth. The other side the old woman slept on in her chair, dribbling and twitching her blanket. Orhn smiled at Tibo. He reached out and touched one of her slim black braids. She wore her hair parted into twelve of these, each braid hanging to her waist and ending in a copper ring. But the rings were unpolished, she took no pride in them, although they were the mark of her married status. Her hair, though, glistened. She constantly washed and combed and rebraided it. In the same useless way she picked flowers and herbs, and gossiped to the dogs. These practices annoyed Orbin, but they were no real grounds for a complaint. She did not ever neglect her work.

"This man," said Orbin now, as Tibo dragged the iron cauldron from the fire, and returned with it to her pot-scouring. "Where is he?"

"In the yard, Orbin-master."

"The shed—bleeding and dying in Orhn's shed?" (Stirred by his name, Orhn made a sound of mild outrage, copying Orbin. This mimicry, taught him long ago, had often let him pass as normal in Ly.)

Tibo scoured her pots, humble, apologetic. She had some cause to be, having, with Blackness' aid, hauled the semiconscious stranger to shelter. Though treacherous, the glassy ground had taken scarcely any imprint, the falling snow had also helped, obliterating every trace of her connivance. All the time, the man had marveled, dizzily amused, swooning and clinging to her, that her frailty could support him. Of course, she was strong. Fourteen years of fetching and carrying, lugging and straining, had made her so. When she left him in the straw with the surprised dogs all around to warm him, she had been sorry to get him go, his body, its frame and texture and scent, an assemblage she had never before experienced. She had torn his shirt to bind the knife-cut in his arm, not daring to use anything of her own, as yet. And she had worshiped at his flesh, as the old song said Cah did with her lovers. There was no denying it. Never having known such a feeling in her life, Tibo recognized infallibly her desire and hunger.

He should not die. She would not allow it. She knew the properties of herbs. And she had learned in childhood, for self-preservation, how to deceive.

So she went on with the pots, all stupid and careless, until Orbin, having questioned her sharply about the man's story, his garments, his foreignness, pushed her out again shedward, between the curtains of the snow.

By the time the next thaw came, twenty-five days later, the stranger was whole and on his feet, and assisting Orbin about the farm.

Orhn had been very gracious. That was, Orbin had permitted the stranger certain rights and Orhn, standing by smiling, had made appropriate sounds at proper intervals. Having interrogated the stranger, Orbin had asked for his money. If Orhn was to provide the man a roof and nursing, and a share of the food until he recovered, that was only just. Orbin suspected the stranger did not give all his cash, and was correct in this. He instructed Tibo to search the stranger when next she tended him during his fever, and she brought back a handful of small coins. In return, the man lay in the dog-shed, with a brazier for warmth for which Tibo firstly, and he himself when fit, must obtain the kindling. He was also given a piece of bread or slab of black porridge to eat, and a bowl of the evening soup or stew, generally with no meat in it. Tibo's herbal medicines she had prepared in secret.

"He's tough, some mercenary off the roads," said Orbin with lazy contempt, unease and faint envy mixed in his tone. "He'll mend. If we keep him here until Big Thaw he can help with the spring ploughing. Orhn can save on hired men, in that case." (The farm was not rich enough to keep workers over during winter.)

The entire project entailed, of course, trapping the man for as long as possible, and making him pay in any way that was feasible for the privilege. He was an easterner, a Lan, he had said, with a name the Iscaian-Lydian drawl had instantly turned to "Yems." He said, too, he was a soldier, which might be the truth, for he had a fighter's body, trained and tall, and sword calluses on both hands, though he had arrived with only a knife. Even this Orbin confiscated. "You won't be needing that, on Orhn's farm."

Meanwhile, there was no real means for the man to escape their hospitality. Ly village was nearly a day's journey away over the snow, and that was only if you knew the route. Ly Dis, which Yems had stubbornly mentioned more than once in his fever, was seven days distant, unreachable till spring. As for saddle-thoroughbreds, the big animals that, unlike the Dorth-arian chariot teams, could carry a full-grown man on their backs, they were as mythical here in Ly as were the fabled horses from the southern lands.

It was a wonder, in fact, how the fellow had got here himself. He had told Orbin a tale of going to join the Vardish troops over the border, of being diverted west on some other mysterious errand, next falling in with the mountain bandits—who let him go to bleed or freeze to death, having taken his mount, a hardy zeeba, and all baggage and accoutrements.

"Some yarn," said Orbin. "Who cares? We'll work him."

And soon he was up and about and busy, making the repairs Orbin wanted to the ramshackle hovel-buildings of the farm, cleaning out the few thin cattle in their byre, getting and chopping wood—which he even professed himself willing to do, to prevent his arm from stiffening. He made, certainly, no demur about any of it. Probably he had expected no other treatment.

"I'll have to watch you," said lounging Orbin to Tibo, as she bodily lifted the old woman, twittering and feebly fighting, from her chair, "all this help, you'll have nothing to do. Cah knows, I don't want an idle sloven in Orhn's household. Like that old bitch," he added. His senile mother, that Tibo was now spreading gently on her tidied pallet, where she fell again asleep, had not really earned her rest by the laws of the land. She had borne five sons, but only two survived. Her husband was dead, and in the ancient days, she would have been cast out and exposed long ago. But there, she was his mother, rot her. Only look, though, she had wet the chair again. He shouted angrily at Tibo to take the chair outside in the yard and scrub it well with snow.

When Tibo had finished shaking the mattresses and cleaning the chair, she went to see after the three cows in the byre. The afternoon sky was shrilly blue, the pale blue of the cold time, but water dripped from the icicles along the roofs. This thaw might last all of two days.

There were only the cows and dogs to feed in winter, as the fowls and pigs were sold or slaughtered at the summer's end. She did not like the slaughtering, which was brutal and haphazard, but she dealt with the carcasses, hung winter-long in the hut-larder beside the cow-byre, as she dealt with any food. Now going into the dark enclosure, she sorted among the hanged birds, and tore off a meaty plucked wing. This she thrust in the pocket of her apron.

When she entered the byre, the Lan was raking the muck from the mud floor, piling it against one wall. Dried, it would be used for the hearth fire, and to fuel the stranger's brazier in the shed, though Orbin did not know this.

Tibo went straight up to the Lan, and drew out the bird wing, which she handed to him. He took it without a word and stored it under his tunic, wedged inside against the belt.

She had been bringing him illicit food since the onset, also, on occasion, black beer. She had taught him how to get milk from the cow that still had it, jetting the fluid directly down his throat from the yellow teat. She was not amazed he had not known the trick. He was from another world.

She began now to heft the fodder into the trough, and Yems went on raking and piling up the dung. In the beginning, when he had tried to help her move the heavy feed, she had pushed him softly off, liking to touch him. He had had a light fever all one day and night, when he first lay in the dog-shed. He had cried like a child for water, which she had swiftly given him, and she had held his head on her breast, caressing his hair. She had touched most of his body when he slept, later. Though she could not have found words for it, her sexuality and her maternal instinct, both ripe and both equally denied, sought a focus in this male icon.

But now he was recovered, a man, independently apart from her.

She bent to her task, because he had come close.

"Tibo," he said, quietly. He voiced her name a new way, just as she could not pronounce his name in the way he wished. But she liked his altered pronounciation.

"Yes, master?"

"Don't call me that. I'm not some Iscaian clod who'll beat you."

"Yn—" she tried, "Ye—"

"Yennef," he said patiently.

"Yemhz."

He sighed, but it amused him. He always seemed to

do this. She liked the manner in which he noticed and laughed at her.

"Tibo, my dear girl, tomorrow's dawn, I'm off. Do you understand?"

"Ah," she said. She shut her eyes. Suddenly a great well of emptiness opened within her. She had known he would be going, of course. Not so soon.

"Tibo? Those louts can't blame you for that, can they?"

Yes, she thought. But she said, "No."

"Anack," he said. He swore. "I'd take you with me, out of this muddy little hell—but it would be impossible in the snow. Besides, maybe you don't want to leave, I don't know you, do I, only your kindness. And you're clever, aren't you? Telling me how to get to Ly, and about the big dogs the priests use for sleds. And taking my part with that grunting offal when I was sick. Stealing from me with your soft hands—saving me enough cash to live like a king all year in Ly Dis. Clever, wise, sweet Tibo."

She turned her head and stole a look at him, then.

He was a man. Handsome as she had never known a man could be, fined and rare, like the light of a young sun, the carven towers of the mountains—but a man still. Beyond her. Different. Her thoughts or words or wants, to him, like rain falling on air.

So she lowered her eyes again, and put more food in the trough for the cows. Pointing out to him, as she did so, where she had laid his knife in the hay.

There was a winter star which at midnight, on a clear night, shone in through a tiny hole under the roof.

It woke Tibo, pointing down at her with its thin finger of crystal.

In that moment she knew, or recognized her knowledge.

Without hesitation or doubt, she slipped between the covers of the great grass-stuffed mattress where she lay, dark by dark, year by year, with her idiot husband. Orhn did not stir. He would not. Nor Orbin either. As she hurried to make the evening stew, plummy that night with dumplings and livers, she had left out by the hearth two pitchers of beer. She had been taking stock of her jars, and perhaps to leave out the beer in her search was a mistake, for when Orbin saw it he wanted it, and her protest that she had just now meant to set it back had earned her a smack across the head. He uncorked the pitcher and began to drink. Orhn had shared in the drinking, because it was his beer. Both enjoyed the bout. They would sleep deep and late.

Perhaps she had been scheming even then, leaving out the beer.

There was a dull red glow remaining on the hearth. The old woman slept on her pallet, sometimes dreaming and gibbering. Tibo had left the water cauldron over the fire, and the water was still hot. Taking her precious crock of soap from the cubby, Tibo washed herself from head to foot. The temple sold this soap, which Orbin loudly despised, though he preferred it when shaving to bird grease, and so never threw it away. The temple whores washed themselves no doubt with such an unguent. At the passage of the soap, the radiant water, her own hands upon her body, Tibo trembled. The dying red of the fire glowed like smooth mirror on her skin.

When she had dried herself, she drew the marriage rings from her hair and shook it out, waved and springing from its braids, black as night seas she had never looked on.

Presently Tibo lifted her cloak from the nail, and covered herself only with that against the winter night. She closed the door behind her soundlessly, and walked barefoot over the thin gray ice.

A quarter moon stood in the sky, and the stars, to light her path.

Yennef, who had strayed in to Iscah on the wildest quest, Yennef, in whose veins the blood of a king, but a fallen discredited king for all that, wound its way, Yennef had roasted and eaten the piece of fowl, and supped also on the rich stew, and soon stretched out for sleep, since he must be awake very early tomorrow.

He woke silently and totally, tutored to it, long before the dawn began.

The brazier smoldered on with its prohibited kindling. It lit the shed only smudgily, and the mounded backs of the slumbering dogs. But an upright figure slid through the dark, toward him. The slobbering fool, or the ham-brained Orbin, intent on further robbery?

Yennef lay motionless, and waited. He could kill empty-handed, if he had to.

Then the darkness was shuffled off in a single movement, like a breath of wind through a tree. For several seconds he did not know her as Tibo. There was only a naked woman, slender as some Elyrian vase, her body painted by the ruby highlights of low fire, black flames of hair about her, uncanny and beautiful, like the visitation of a Zastis dream, here in the ice-heart of winter—

"Tibo—?"

"Hush," she whispered. Then she kneeled down by him, and he caught from her the savage mingled fragrances, incense-soap, skin and hair, night and desire.

It was so dreamlike even then, there was no need to speculate on what was prudent in this backland midden, what was sensible or kind. And before even he reached out to her, her narrow hands, scarred all over from the misuses of her life, yet tender as the fur of kittens, crept about his neck, and her warm lips sought his own.

He had not had a girl since Xarabiss. He was eager, and she seemed as famished as he was. All the while he stroked her, molded her, she twined him, muttering love-words he could not comprehend. When he met the barrier of her virginity, he was not entirely startled. Iscaian law, the backlands—with a generous impulse to counter his impatience, he took his time to open her, fill her; he owed her boundless thanks, and even his life. To return her a taste of pleasure, obviously what she had trusted him to give, was slight enough. And she responded to his tuition, singing her ecstasy under her breath, gasping, outflung, melting, laving him with brighter darker fires—

"I thought you were your goddess, Cah, there in the shadow," he said to her, a little later. It was a courtesy, an accolade. Perhaps, for a moment, in some way, it had been true. But she made a tiny averting gesture. Blasphemy, to be taken for Cah. And yet, it seemed to Tibo then, lying against him, burned by his heat, her seals broken, her flesh for the first time vital and alive, it seemed to her that maybe Cah had sent him to her, that Cah, in order to enjoy his beauty, had possessed her. Why else the disregard of law and sin, why else the pulsing avalanche of joy?

The sunrise started with a rent of rosy orange, that slowly bled across the straw through all the shed's cracks and crevices.

Accustomed by now to Yennef, as well as to Tibo, the canine pack had paid them small heed, but with the dawn the dogs became restless, aware the thaw held, and anxious for the valley.

"I'll come back for you," he said again. He had said this previously after their third joining, when she had cried out in his arms, trying simultaneously to smother her own delight with her fist—for fear it be heard in the hovel-house. "I can't leave you here. I'll come back, Tibo." But she knew he would not and said nothing in response. She said nothing now. She knows all men, even if not cretins, are bloody liars, he thought, and was glad she knew and that she did not even for a minute believe him. For he would not come here again, of course. A wayside flower, as they said. Not even that. She was braiding her hair, ready for the copper rings. She did not tell him to go or say she loved him, or weep or smile. She simply was as she had been all along. Thank both their gods. It was as if nothing had happened at all.

Despite that, he kissed her at the door, and gave her an Alisaarian drak of gold-bronze—high currency in the towns of Iscah. "I'm not trying to pay you," he said. "Take care. May your goddess stay awake for you."

She lowered her eyes, in the familiar way. As he went, the dogs also crowded out and rushed off over the pasture. Blackness, who, when he lay sick he had deliriously watched licking his own blood from her coat with a gourmet's quantifying attention, now nuzzled his hand as she plunged by.

He looked back only once. The girl was not to be seen.

She had known what she wanted, and asked for and received it. Rather in the way of the white Lowland races, she appeared to look for nothing beyond the measure of each day.

Tibo, the rings on her hair, dressed, aproned and booted, was at the hearth preparing the old woman's gruel, when Orbin entered the room.

His head and belly troubled him after the previous evening's drinking, and he did not notice the easterner had absconded until it was almost noon. Then, too, when the absence was sure, he could not get up much enthusiasm to beat his brother's witless dolt of a wife. He contented himself with hitting her across the head until she fell to the floor—which, at such times, she always did rapidly. Then she would lie for a while, until he cursed her, at which she dragged herself up and went on, unspeaking, with her duties.

Orhn always cried when Orbin repeatedly struck Tibo, and the old woman wailed and rocked herself.

As soon as Orbin had gone off—to search the dogshed in case any Lannic valuable might have been left behind—Tibo comforted the mother and her son.

Though her head still rang, she knew by now how to angle herself to miss most of the violence, and always fell over before much harm had come to her. Orbin had not thought her guilty of any plot, merely negligent; she was a scapegoat for every ill. When the cabbages blighted, he struck her, too.

She did not think particularly of Yennef as she moved about the room and yard. Only in the evening, when the light began to die and the snow-cold breathed down again upon the farm, did she imagine him, in Ly by now, bargaining for temple dogs and sled.

All day, every so often, still hot from the fire of her

womb, the wine of his orgasms ran out between her thighs. It was the only thing he had left her of himself; the rich man's coin did not count. When all his semen had passed from her body, there would be nothing at all.

CHAPTER TWO

THE WILL OF CAH

The temple of Cah, standing on high ground, dominated Ly, which was not difficult. The Big Thaw, snow's end, and the tepid rains which teemed after it, turned the village every year to sludge. Dwellings, shored by earth, came undone and collapsed. The throughfares were brown swirling swamps in which feet and wheels stuck. Everywhere lay drowned rats and the stones of rebuilding. On its central hill, however, the temple squatted above a dressed stone terrace, a pillared box which, even in the rainy cool, smelled of thick perfume and blood.

Cah had created the world. Those who said otherwise were naturally in error. Theology was not worth discussing, it simply *was*. Being female, though, she had made a great many mistakes, and eventually called on the male gods, her lovers, to rule in her stead. She it was who taught women their proper function, which was to grow new men in their bellies. It was well known that Cah also relished the act of conception, and therefore was fond of the male species in general. Worshiped Iscah over, and next door in the land of Corhl, as Corrah, Cah upheld masculine dominion. She had never instituted a matriarchy, as was once the state of affairs with the snake goddess of the pale races.

Every Big Thaw Orbin would set out for Ly to

make his sacrifice to Cah in the temple. Sometimes
Orhn was taken, and less frequently, Tibo—the old
woman then being left to the charge solely of the
fierce dogs. Orbin did not use a cart. They walked to
Ly, over the muddy mountain tracks, starting before
sunup—it took only three or four hours to get there
when the snow was gone—returning just ahead of the
dark. On these excursions nothing had ever beset them.
Bandits seldom came so far north, it was a poor region. By the time of the rains, the more sinister animals had retreated to low country.

This Thaw Orbin nevertheless went to get the
easterner's knife from inside his mattress. Probably he
fancied himself parading through Ly with a steel blade
in his belt. The knife had vanished, however, and Orbin
spent some while hunting for it, concluding at last the
easterner had somehow stolen it back.

Tibo seemed reluctant to make the journey to Ly,
so Orbin told her she would be going. The hopeful
Orhn, he decided conversely, must stay behind to
guard the house. Orhn was crestfallen, and watched
them sadly as they set off into the wet dark morning.

Tibo walked the correct eight to ten paces behind
Orbin, carrying their provisions tied on her back.

Orbin strode ahead. The sun rose. The passes through
these mountains were ramshackle and unsafe, slick
with water now, and here the surest danger lay in
wait. Glissades of melted ice roared down the distances between huge disembodied fanglike crags. Pebbles dashed underfoot and fell over the slopes, sixty
feet or more, to smash on levels beneath. After an
hour the travelers began to descend through the stoops
of broken valleys. Soon the rain began again. Neither
took much notice. This was the way life was.

The robes of the priests of Cah were colorful, the
most colorful things to be seen at Ly, umber reds and
bold ochers, with discs of polished brass, lozenges of
bone and beads of milky resin sewn on. The High
Priest's robe was also trimmed with feathers, and during the mysteries of the temple he wore a mask like a

bird's head. But women were not admitted to the mysteries, saving the temple prostitutes who took part.

Orbin purchased a pig from the temple pen, and went inside to see its throat cut on the altar. Sometimes, after the cold months' long incarceration, Orbin would want to go with one of the holy-girls. Tibo had seen from his demeanor as they passed under the girls' window, where two or three of them always sat on display, that this was the situation now. She stood meekly among the short pillars, while the sacrifice was attended to. It seemed not much more to her than the butchering that went on later in the year. Indeed, the butchers who visited the farms were temple-trained.

When the pig was dead and its blood spilled copiously, Orbin said his prayers, after which he and the priests went away into the shadows beyond the altar. It was now allowable for Tibo to approach the goddess.

The smell of blood was raw. In this place, it did not repel Tibo, for it was the untranslatable symbol of life, as of death.

The girl came to within three feet of the altar, so her boots were in the blood that had overlapped the drain. The carcass itself had been taken off to be portioned. Above the blood-pool Cah was, looking down into Tibo's eyes and heart.

Women could not make sacrifices or offerings. They had no property, and to put anything aside would be considered a theft from their menfolk. All a woman could do to please Cah was to bear children. That was a woman's offering.

The goddess was a smooth stone, that had had, hundreds of years before, a face hewn from it, and breasts. Balms were constantly poured upon her, and blood splashed her and smoke stained her. These things had made her black. Just as belief had made her powerful. Her eyes were somber amber glass. As the incoherent light of the oil lamps caught her, shifting always with the fluctuation of the burning wicks, these eyes seemed full of sight.

Tibo did not say a word. She stood and let Cah gaze into her, and behold. Her thanks were her only offering. The offering itself—her thanks.

For aid, for protection, Tibo did not think to ask. The goddess was Life, and life would protect Tibo, in the same way that it had found her out.

When the passion was complete between herself and Cah, Tibo left the temple and went on to the terrace. She sat down stilly under the low roof, on the other side from the whores' window, and waited for Orbin to come out.

He did so at length, sullen, as the sexual act always made him. He told her he meant to meet some farmers at the drinking-shop. He would be back in time for their daylight departure, he said. "As for you," he added, "go about and see if you can barter those egg-cakes. Sit there and they'll take you for a temple girl. You're getting fat as one, you slug."

He came back from the drinking-shop hours after, and it was darkening as they trudged home, and the rain rang like swords on the rocks. Climbing up to the farm valley, now Tibo had to go first, guiding him with the lantern from her pack. Orbin stumbled, and cursed her.

When they got to the house, Orhn was asleep, and the old woman had wet her chair.

Orbin, sobered on the return trip, became angry. He struck Tibo and ranted about her utter uselessness. He called her a fat moping bitch.

These two occasions, on this day, were the first that he appeared to have seen she had begun to thicken at the waist.

It seemed to her she would carry low, which her mother had said was the sign of a boy.

The year began to turn toward the sun.

Warm days came. Golden light parasoled the valley.

Men, earnest to be hired, had started to arrive and to be taken on, and made an untidy camp for themsleves at the end of the pasture.

A flock of fowl pecked in the yard, unaware that others had done so before them.

The morning of the ploughing, Tibo was up two hours before the sun, to bake bread for the laborers. At dawn Orbin came into the room, and standing

Orhn against one wall, drilled him in the kind of
noises he must make, how to stand and how to walk
over the fields before the men. Initially eager, Orhn
grew frightened.

Tibo set porridge and bread on the table, and Orhn
slunk to eat. As she bent to feed the old woman,
Orbin came hard against Tibo, and slapped her hip.

"What's this?"

Tibo looked at him, then lowered her eyes.

"I said, what is it? Answer me?"

"Orbin-master?"

"That great wodge of flesh. That *belly*."

Tibo resumed calmly the task of spooning gruel into
his mother's withered old mouth. She said, "I'm
childed."

Orbin choked a moment on his wrath. Then he
exclaimed: "Belly-full pregnant are you? How? Let
me guess. Let me guess."

Tibo wiped the old woman's lips.

Orbin caught Tibo by the hair. He wrenched her
about.

"Who did it then, you sinning rotted mare?"

Tibo lifted her eyes. Black Vis-Iscaian eyes, that
had gazed into the gaze of Cah.

"Brother-master," she said, "my husband."

"*Orhn!*" Orbin screamed, ablaze with rage. And
Orhn, picking up the inflection, made a raging sound
of agreement. "*No.* Not Orhn, for the tits of Cah.
Some visitor, eh? Some eastern thing. Not Orhn, eh?"

Tibo met the eyes of Orbin, on and on. He was
unused to it, a woman who looked at him. Even
holy-girls did not.

"Who else?" said Tibo.

"I've said who else."

"That can," said Tibo, "only be you."

He stared. He thought. She saw him do this and was
silent to allow it. Then he blustered a moment or so.
She did not, of course, interrupt. When he stopped,
she said:

"It it isn't Orhn, we'll be questioned. I, and you,
master. You'll swear you never touched me. I shall say
you did. Your brother's wife. I'll be stoned. You'll be

castrated, and may be stoned. The easterner would
never say he'd been here, for fear you had friends at
Ly. There's no other proof. No other man, then, here
with me, but you. And Orhn. I prayed to Cah, and
Cah heard me. Orhn has always lain with me as a man
should. But I was barren. Now Cah has filled my
womb. It's a wonderful thing."

Orbin's mouth fell open.

Tibo lowered her eyes. She had never, in all her
adult life, spoken so many words at a stretch, and she
was rather breathless. Turning, she started again to
feed the old woman.

Orhn tore bread at the table in an outraged manner,
copying Orbin.

Until Orbin sat down at the board, staring blankly
into space.

So the ripe leaves swelled on the citrus trees and the
shoots came up behind the plough. Birds flew over the
valley, free birds with only weather and fate to be
wary of. A pair of black eagles, miles high, day after
day swung from a sky that changed from blue to indigo.

Like the heat and the land, Tibo, blooming and
swelling, the bud of her belly taut with its fruit.

Orhn seemed to have some memory of his mother's
pregnancies. He was interested and encouraging. He
sometimes touched the hill of flesh, delicately, and
made extra room for Tibo in their bed. When the child
began to move, she let him feel it, placing his palm
there. Orhn laughed. Perhaps he believed, if capable of
such logic, that a miracle had indeed occurred, and
that the sowing was his.

Orbin did not often speak to Tibo, never of her.
Only when the hired men were about and she passed
among them, to take them food or on some other errand, Orbin behaved normally. The men congratuledd
Orhn, and Orbin guffawed and nodded and Orhn copied him.

In the house, if he wanted something, Orbin pointed,
or thrust objects under Tibo's nose. When he must
address her, he did so from a great way off, shouting.
He did not even strike her any more. Partly, too, that
was out of caution. If he had been less religious he

would have liked to kick her in the stomach, abort the bitch. But he dared not. Though the law was abused, and though the child, even if a boy, was a half-breed, still any pregnant woman had the mark of Cah on her.

On her side, Tibo continued to serve the household as she had always done. She stinted not at all. If she was tired or in discomfort she never showed it, it did not slow or stay her.

The heat flamed, boiled over. Zastis scalded the night and Orbin was often away. Then Zastis was gone and Orbin back. The year began to yellow.

Harvesting and slaughtering came due, the yard full of cereals, of tubers and cabbage, and then awash with blood.

The slaughterer-priests looked at Tibo. And at Orhn.

"We've made enough offerings," said Orbin. Tibo heard him say it as she drew water from the well. "He's always had his full pleasure, but I reckoned she was wombless. Blessed be Cah, it's good luck." And he gave the priests larger portions than usual of the carcasses, for Cah's temple, to show the family gratitude.

It was a ten-month term for a Vis women, ten wide Vis months. Planted just past one midwinter, the child would be born at the cold season's next commencement.

Tibo thought of that in the fading days of the heat, as she plucked the orange citruses among the rocks.

She might perish, bearing the child. No one would come to her. There were no other capable women at the farm who might assist. She would be alone in labor with two idiots and an enemy.

But these musings seemed irrelevant. She would bear, and live. And Orbin would be afraid to harm her, for a new mother, also, was Cah's.

It was awkward for her, so big now, to gather all the fruit, but she managed it, eventually. In the late sunset she lifted the last baskets, and saw suddenly, between the trees and hard summer rocks, a curious pale runnel in the ground.

She had had such a glimpse before here, once or

twice. The earth was constantly torn open by cold weather, closed again by undergrowth in the heat. Sometimes areas in the soil gave way. Then you saw, deep down, this peculiar underlayer. Some thing lay there, beneath the topsoil, rocks and tree roots. Smooth, like steel, dark white, like ancient porcelain.

Tibo had no wish to learn its nature. She feared it, obsurely.

Soon the storms would come, and then the snow probably, and hide the unordinary from sight.

Taking her baskets of fruit, Tibo turned toward the pasture and the hovel-house, and pushed the memory from her mind by visualizing the changing of the days, copper to bronze, bronze to iron.

It began early.

There had been a flurry of hail, frisking over the valley, the sun a broken egg of light pierced by mountain tops. And as she cracked the skin of ice in the well, a shriek of pain ran through the core of her.

She completed her duties swiftly then, even running, where the ice and pain permitted.

She did not speak to Orbin, but set out the supper, then went away to the dog-shed, where she had already made a birthing bed for herself, catlike, with all the items laid by she would need. It was appropriate that she strive and bear here, where she had taken the child in, and by the glow and warmth of the same brazier.

The dogs, for the most part, ignored her. Blackness and Rag, the two bitches, sensing kinship, came occasionally and stared in her face and licked her wrists.

The pains ran together. She heaved and moaned, gripping in her hands, and pulling against, the rope with which she had circled her lifted waist. As the rope tightened and relaxed with the spasms, its strangling burn momentarily distracted from the tearing pain within: An old Iscaian woman's trick. Cah's teaching.

Once she thought Orbin had come to the shed door and listened.

In her anguish Tibo called aloud the traditional words:

"Cah! Cah, aid me!"

She was safe from Orbin. She was Cah's.

After some hours, her pain burst in and from her. With a scream of terror and agony and release, Tibo watched the head of her baby pushed into the world. When the body came out, Tibo saw she had birthed a perfect living creature. She hastened to cut and knot the cord, to clean the child's mouth and skin. It cried and breathed, blind as a puppy. Blackness came and investigated the baby, thrusting her long nose against the child, and Tibo pushed her away, mildly. Exhausted, she brought her child to her breast. Her invention, he lived, as she did, and was a male as she was not.

CHAPTER THREE

FOUND AND LOST

Katemval Am Alisaar, saddle-sore, snow-sick, shouted his men off the track, in order to make way for a descending funeral.

Traveling as he did, needing travel and yet never hardened to it, Katemval had witnessed a variety of events. He knew, in this instance, how the Iscaians were, and was not amazed to see only women out in the cold; that meant only a woman had died.

It had been audible, the dull resonance of the bronze gongs, from two miles away, in the high clear air.

Then they came down the track, dark on young snow, first fall, and powdery—the snows of the western mountains were nothing, even at their worst, to a winter of the Middle Lands, Dorthar, Xarabiss, let alone Lanelyr in the east.

Some of the men, superstitious, made religious signs.

One, an Iscaian, turned his head and looked aside. It was unfortunate to regard upland feminine rites.

Four women carried the coffin, which was of rough untidy wood and nailed shut. Such biers seldom needed more than four porters for the wretched uplands did not generate plumpness in either sex. Strong though, often, both genders; his reason for being here, the Alisaarian, on his large black thoroughbred—an animal maybe these villagers had never seen. Although they did not glance at it as they went by, walking before and after their dead, banging the gongs with the flats of their narrow gloveless hands.

There was one—the chief mourner, to judge by her position exactly behind the coffin. Katemval's eyes followed her a way along the curve of the slope. Something special there, something that might have been worth going after, twenty years earlier. Too late now. She had been bent and coiled to her existence, as was all humanity, like a vine to a stock. You took them as children if you wanted them formed to a purpose.

The track wound down and away into the white afternoon, and the procession with it, the crags of the Iscah-Zakoris borders a dim shadowy backdrop. The drone of the gongs lingered after the women had vanished.

"Come on," Katemval said, to his five men. "Or do you want to freeze in the saddle?"

It was a joke, of a sort. Save for her northern and eastern hem, Alisaar never knew snow. These effete western-upland colds were horrible to an Alisaarian, or to the man of the Iscaian lowlands, reared under the snow-line.

Katemval rode on, up the track, the thoroughbred treading solidly. He trusted his information was correct. Youth, health, and penury. Or it would be a wasted journey.

By tonight he must be back in Ly, tomorrow they would have to make for Ly Dis (where he had left the other children), then get down to the capital and the ports before the upland weather shut on them. For such a dot of a country, Iscah was tortuous going.

They reached the valley not long after. The farm, if

so it could be named, huddled in the dip. Smudged air crawled from the chimney and dogs barked.

As Katemval rode up, a couple of men emerged, with three big hounds to heel.

"Good day," said Katemval, politely.

"Ah," said the nearer man, shorter and more muscular than the other who stood behind him.

Katemval let them each have a fair long look, at his furs and owar thigh-boots, his men on zeebas, his own riding animal worth more than the whole farm, probably. The fellow at the back seemed silly in the head.

"I'll come straight to it," said Katemval, to the other man with sly pouchy eyes. "I heard there was a child here, one too many, that you'd be happy to be shot of."

They gawped. It was not actually what he had heard at all, only that there was a child. Children were not always a benefit, and from something in the way this one had been gossiped of, it had seemed to fit that category.

"Seven silver Alisaarian draks," said Katemval. "Providing the brat's suitable, of course."

Their women poured babies as their dogs sloughed pups. Too many mouths to feed. And it was easy enough to get more. Then again, sometimes there was an outcry. They yelled about the seed of their loins and set the hounds on you.

Not now, he thought. No.

"Sell you the boy?" said the sly-eyed man. "For what?"

"What do you think? I take for the slave-yards of Alisaar. Not rubbish. Girls for pleasure or show, boys to fight. They live well and sometimes get rich. I don't lie. But it's up to you. How old's this son?"

"Eh? He's—four years."

That was fine, it tallied with the information

"The mother," said Katemval, "where is she?" It was always best to see the sire and dam, too. You learned a lot from that, the sort of clay that had made the child. This man, the father, looked sound enough. The woman was likely healthy—both mother and babe had survived. But then the man said, still hesitating, "She—she's dead."

The funeral—that had been coming from this direction. Hers?

"Then you'll be glad to get the boy off your hands. Bring him out and let me see."

Abruptly the second man at the back started to make low whimperings. The other rounded on him, and said something rapidly in the gutteral gobbling dialect of the region. Alisaarian, accented in its own fashion, was crystal beside this, which had the smear of Zakoris all over it. Only in the Iscaian lowlands could they halfway *speak*, the Alisaarian thought.

But for stamina and looks—the city slums were bred out. Here, on these random dungheaps, among the stillbirths and boobies, sudden wild orchids were started.

The first man was now conducting the simpleton roughly inside the hovel, calling over his shoulder: "Wait. I'll bring him."

So Katemval, the slave-taker, waited.

The old woman had died at some moment during the day, while life went on about her. Her quietus was utterly silent. It was this which had alerted them. She had made noises almost constantly, if senselessly, in her final years. Yet, when Tibo lifted the bony antique body, its sphincters relaxing, the corpse had defiantly wet the chair for the very last time.

A woman's burying was woman's business. Men were not obliged to attend, and male children actively forbidden.

Tibo had not wanted to leave her son, but there was no choice.

Tibo met female neighbors she had not seen for half a year or more, trudging to the nearest farm, a day's traveling, with all her chores either side the trek. In turn, these women informed others. Life was cheap, but death an occasion. After six days, the women arrived at the house. They brought sorrow-gifts for Orhn and Orbin, cakes and beer, and a cask of botched wood for the cadaver—each plank or bit of branch was hammered to another by a different woman. There must be enough women at a funeral to have knocked in each part separately.

There was a burial field just outside Ly Village, and to this the remains of all deceased males of the area were taken, where at all possible.

For the females there was another method.

It moved, the procession, sounding its funeral gongs, through the snow, watching all along the uneven dangerous slopes for an appropriate omen. It might be almost anything, vast or minute.

Tibo, moving in unison, watching, sounding the small gong with her hand, thought of her son. Over and over she thought of him. She had not wanted to leave him. But there was no choice.

For almost four years, he had been scarcely from her sight. He slept in the marriage bed, Orhn had not minded. Indeed, Orhn had liked him from the beginning, playing with him, careful of him. And Orbin for Cah's sake could do nothing, though he set the boy labors almost as soon as he could walk. Orbin had crowed over him, "You'll be a fine lout, won't you? You'll fetch and carry. You'll earn your keep." The child was nimble and quick. He did not resist, nor make any mistakes. Orbin only smote him lightly, and not often. Why damage such a potential treasure? The easterner father had not repayed the farm. His bastard should.

During the second year of the child's life, Zastis came early. In russet moonlight, Orbin pinned Tibo against the wall of the hut-larder. Pulling up her skirt, he rammed himself into her, working and twisting, shaking the flimsy building with his efforts. When he was done, he said to Tibo, "Whenever I want you now I can have you. If you tell tales, so can I. If you get fat in the belly with *my* boy, well then it's Orhn's business again, isn't it?" Tibo straightened her clothes, saying nothing. The next time, it was the same. But Orbin, having made his point, having satisfied himself, and finding even in this way he could not get a response from his brother's wife, raped her infrequently and only then in the months of the Star. Tibo did not conceive. He found, too, in the third year, his member became sore and inflamed after he had been with her. He was afraid the easterner had given her some dormant disease, and when the irritation subsided, left her alone. He had forgotten, or did not associate his condition, with her knowledge of herbs.

Tibo had sinned with a lover. But to sin with Orbin was neither lawful nor the wish of Cah. Orbin did not offer delight, and his seed was impotent.

But the child—

She had called him, not by a king's title, or a hero's, but an old name of the uplands, which dialectically she rendered as *Raier*.

At five, he would become one with the men's side, in the temple. They would mark him in blood. Other things would happen, of which Tibo did not know. She shunned the thought of this fifth year, and welcomed it.

But at the end of his third year she had come on him, free of Orbin for the moment, forming from the rain-wet mud of the pasture slender figurines. Tibo paused, staring, for she had never seen a child do such a thing. The figures were lopsided and bizarre, yet recognizably human or animal, there a pig, and there a woman with breasts and long hair. Humbly, for he was her son, a man, and—she now saw—clever, Tibo collected and brought him tinted stones, to employ as eyes or ornaments. He received them from her patiently, and put them by. He did not need them.

Later Orbin came, struck Raier, stamped on the figures and kicked them over.

The child, like his mother in demeanor as well as looks, walked simply away, and began to clean the yard, unasked.

Oh, the child—

He did resemble her, it was true. But his father more so. Even by the end of his first six months, the length of his legs gave promise of above average height. His hair came and grew silken-thick and black. His eyes, kohled with dark lashes, would rise up like flowers opening.

And he made figures from mud. He sang in a thin bird's voice as he toiled for Orbin, melodies from some place beyond the sky—for he had never heard any song but those his mother had sung him at the breast. Once she saw him, riding on amenable Blackness, through the valley. Something in Tibo's perspective shifted. She beheld a tall man with leaden-blue light on his hair, riding a black beast, a spear in his hand that had been a thistle-stem, and the wind rushed in the mountains like the voice of a colossal crowd.

—She should not have had to leave him.

There were riders on the track, who, apparently understanding custom, removed themselves from the funeral's path. The mounts they rode were zeebas— once or twice Tibo had seen such things at Ly, if never anything like the other beast, coal black, its strange slim head brightly bridled.

But neither Tibo nor the other women looked aside to dwell on the riders and their mounts. For the omen had occurred. The riders were the omen. It might have been a hare, a ray of sun or gust of snow, a tumbled boulder—something in the way, animate or not.

Having found it, they need only proceed to the next steep place, where the rock plunged to some habitationless cold ravine. Familiar with the terrain, each woman was aware they would come to such a prescribed spot in less than an hour, by climbing up a fraction, half a mile off the track. So Cah had been generous, sending the men to make the omen, allowing the rite to conclude so swiftly.

It was still, windless, bitter when they came to it, the ridge above the depth.

The gongs were dumb. The women bore the wooden box to the edge of the slope, and, laying it down, every hand was put to it, every hand that had nailed it up, all but the hand of the kinswoman, Tibo.

Pushed to the brink, then over it, the coffin dropped out into the air, and fell into the frozen channel below. Down and down it went, touching against nothing, until, far beneath, it struck a ledge and shattered away into the exploding snow.

The women stood up, and looked at Tibo. Now she must mourn her loss.

Tibo flung back her head, and howled, to the
blanched, flat sky. The women observed her, braced
to wait, for it should be a prolonged lament; the dead
was Tibo's husband's mother.

And after this, the long route home.

No choice, none.

What, in her absence, would Orbin do?

It was an orchid, then, this time. More, it was a
lion-cub.

Somehow, as it had been more often ten years ago,
Katemval's instinct had drawn him to his goal at the
exact and proper moment. A find.

Yes, he would dismount for this one.

The Alisaarian swung out of his saddle and walked,
stiff from the riding, toward the child. Standing apart
from his oaf father, the boy looked only at the men,
the zeebas, the thoroughbred. As he had been shoved
from the hovel, he had set his fingers briefly, friendly,
on the flank of the dark bitch-dog, taller than he was.
He showed no fear, and no curiosity either. Yet the
black and liquid eyes were intelligent and pure.

"Well, my dear," said Katemval, lowering himself
to gaze into them. He put his hands gently on the boy
and felt him over. He was whole and straight. Even
the feet, when Katemval investigated them through
the sloppy little boots. There was a thread-thin pale
ring of scar on his left wrist, but, whatever had caused
it, clean-healed, and the sinew and muscle unaffected.
"Do you have all your teeth?" The boy nodded, and
permitted Katemval to peer into his mouth. The teeth
were healthy and very white. "Tell me," said Katemval,
"the farthest thing you can see." The boy eyed him,
then the eyes turned away, across the valley. "The
mountains," he said. Katemval followed the dialect
assiduously. "Something smaller," said Katemval. The
boy said, "A bird, on the tree." Katemval glanced
over his shoulder. His own sight was keen. He saw the
bird, far along the valley on a dead seedling cibba
ribbed with snow. "Good," said Katemval. "What's
your name?" "Raier," said the boy. Katemval lifted
his brows, and rose. "He's acceptable," said Katemval.

He gestured to one of the riders to bring him the money bags.

"Just a minute," said the oaf-father. "I didn't—can't be sure—"

"Seven silver draks, I said," said Katemval.

The oaf licked his lips. "Nine."

"No."

The boy, low to the earth, watched them bickering over his head, his destiny weightless as a leaf between them.

"Eight," said the oaf. "Give me eight."

"I will give you seven, as I previously explained. Here." Katemval, undoing the strings, shook seven triangular coins into his palm. New-minted, their edges hard, they glittered in the white light, beautiful and absolute. The man's arm had come out, the hand automatically grasping. Katemval said, "I've registered my dealings with your priesthood at Ly. You comprehend me? This is a legal transaction. Now the child's mine."

The man suddenly grinned. "He owes me," he said. "If I worked the guts out of him, he'd never bring in this amount."

Katemval lost interest in the man. He looked down at the boy again. "You're coming with me. We're going on a journey. I'm taking you across the sea, to a proud land with cities of stone. An adventure. You don't need anything. Is there anything you want to bring with you?" Not an unkind man, Katemval, sentimental maybe.

But the child only gazed up at him. Did he realize what was going on?

Katemval lifted him suddenly and carried him over to the thoroughbred, setting him on the saddle, swinging up again behind him. The child did not seem unnerved, not frightened of the animal or the zeebas, as he had seemed unafraid of the farm dogs.

The oaf was adding up his silver, again and again. He did not or would not oversee their departure. But the dark bitch-hound began to bark, and all at once the boy writhed about and stared back at her, and suddenly, as Katemval put spur to his mount and it broke into a rapid trot, the boy stretched out his arm toward the dog, yearning and desperate, and without a word or a sound, he wept.

"Ssh, little lion, The gods love you. You're going to a better life than starvation in a sty. Trust Katemval. He knows. Glory days, the power of what you are. Don't waste it. Live it. You will."

But something made Katemval hope, for all that, they would not encounter the eerie funeral party on its way back up the slope. He did not know the women had taken a higher track to the ravine, and had as well as hour's keening to accomplish yet.

The twilight was sinking down as Tibo, having parted from the last of the other mourners, came home alone. There had been no chat between the women, it was not seemly, and anyway might delay them. Each of the differing homeward paths was long, and there were dearth and drudgery and hungry fractious men at all their ends.

A wind came with the dark, pummeling against the crags all around, drumming in Tibo's ears. So she did not hear the dog howling until she was very close.

Tibo checked. This was a sound of lament, like the howl she herself constantly had had to give above the ravine, until her throat was incapable of giving more. Yet the dog had not mourned for the old woman.

Tibo ran. Across the jagged rocks, through the soft snow, the shadows, and came to the stone-cold yard, and faltered again. The howling shook the dog-shed, the outcry of Blackness.

Tibo opened the door of the hovel-house.

The room was drenched warm with firelight, Orhn asleep one side of the hearth, the other, Orbin, in the chair that had been his mother's. Warm, but not secure. Things altered. And there, and there, and there— where Raier would be after the coming of night, a vacant space.

"Hoh, Tibo," said Orbin, softly. "While you were out yammering with those women, I got to worrying about this farm. There's no money in it, I thought. But then a man came riding by. Oh, you'd have liked him. A foreigner. You'd have wanted to invite him in. But he wasn't looking for a whore. He was looking for something else to buy. With Alisaarian silver. Look. Shall I tell you, Tibo, what he wanted in exchange?"

The cold months were very hard that year. A period of deadly freezing nothingness. Beasts had died even in their byres. Men had died merely from falling a few yards outside their doors. When the breaking rains began, the snow fell on, mingling in the water, as if they should never be rid of it. But many sought the way into Ly, to sacrifice to Cah for a better year, a chance to abide. Orbin, seeing Orhn had lost two of his cows to the winter, set out on the course as usual, a silver coin in his pocket, leaving the idiot and the slut behind.

The route was doubly unpleasant now, sludge and ice combining, and the snowy downpour pelting over all. Here, with careering descents at regular intervals on either hand, Orbin went slowly, but undeterred. There was the solace of religion, the quick flicker of lust, and some prolonged drinking before him. He might even, rich as he temporarily was, remain the night on a wine-shop pallet. He might even make a special offering to Cah, to appease her, in case appeasement was necessary. He did not think so, really. He had been within his entitlement to sell off an illegal child, as Orhn would have been able to sell his own offspring, or Orbin's, come to that. The slut stayed quiet enough about it. Not a word all winter. Not that one had been anticipated. She knew she had no redress and no say, and that anyway it was her fault. If she had been any use about the place, or any use to Orbin—she did not even know how to enjoy a man—he might have acted differently. Serve her right. Still, he was glad she had spread her legs for the easterner. He liked the silver, and liked telling her what he had done about the brat. Although he had been slightly uncomfortable before and after, wondering how she would take the news. As if she could object, or mattered.

On the viscous track behind him, Orbin detected a

noise, and turned to see what it was. Something quivered grayly in the milky rain—and he thought of demons, banaliks— When he did see, his heart steadying, he was not well-pleased.

"You stupid sow—what're you doing here?"

Tibo did not answer, she only came nearer, her hands extended before her, so he assumed she meant to show him something, and looked at them. But that was not actually her purpose.

He was still berating her and looking to see what she held out to him, when Tibo pushed him with all her force. Orbin was not a small man, but the blow caught him unprepared by the habits of a lifetime, and besides, there was ice underfoot. For a second or so he slithered and scrabbled, yelling, flailing with his arms. Then, as elsewhere and four months earlier his mother's corpse had done, he pitched sidelong off the track and down a rocky little precipice below. Unlike his mother, Orbin screamed as he fell. But not for a great while.

The only problem with a child so handsome was to keep him out of the clutches of brothels. Katemval was well-practiced at eluding them, both the wealthy importunate and the kidnapping scavenger. Nevertheless, it cost him a few pains extra this time, not least in the rat-runs of Ly Dis, and all the other towns, through and including the Iscaian capital, to the port. Altogether, his hunch to delve the uplands, paying off one way in that one child, proved a stumbling block another. Delays and vile weather led to further delays and further, viler weather, culminating at the capital in the words of Katemval's agent: "They say they never had such a sea for tempests. There's not a captain on this coast will put out till the spring."

"Oh, won't they. We'll see what a bribe will do," announced Katemval staunchly, and off they went, to the most southerly port. Where it was discovered that bribes would do nothing. Viewing the enormous raging waters for himself, Katemval was not, at length, disposed to argue.

So there they wintered, he, his men, and two wagon-loads of bought children. Half an inn was required, as well as the services of women to tend the flock. At least, it was warmer.

There was an Alisaarian tower in dock, a ship on which Katemval's agent negotiated first passage out. She would be making for Jow with a cargo of copper and common slaves. Katemval found this traffic disgusting; he himself traded in finer stuff, and for a nicer market.

The children fared very adequately, if the fretful slave-taker did not, kicking heels in Iscah. Blossoming on sufficient decent food, sleep, and care, many had already forgotten or dismissed their origins.

Not the Lydian, though, Katemval surmised. He was after all one of the youngest, and might miss his mother, too. Though death had got her before the Alisaarians took him, maybe the child equated that loss with the other.

The slave-taker was strict with himself, not to make a pet of this single boy. It would be all too easy, and then another parting, distressing for both, perhaps. But on the first sunny morning, when the bloody ocean conceded it might lie down again, Katemval, finding the boy in an upper window of the children's room, pointed out the tower ship to him, lying at anchor, lovely as a toy after her winter cosset.

"That is how we'll go to Alisaar. On that one, there."

"Yes," said the child.

"Tell me, Rehger," said Katemval—for he knew what the boy's name was intended to be, and pronounced it accordingly in spick and span Alisaarian—"What are you going to be, in Alisaar?"

"A man of glory," said Rehger, the words Katemval had taught him to say, and hopefully to credit.

"Always hold to that, my dear," said Katemval. "You are going to be a lion and a lord and a man of fame. Your life will be like a sunburst and your death a thing of drama and beauty. What are you making now?" he added, for he saw the boy's fist curled about something. Whether this inclination for artistry—which sought expression in packed snow, mud, and bits of wood

with a kitchen knife he should never have been given—
would grow up with him or be at all serviceable,
Katemval did not know. But he was intrigued nevertheless. Not hanging back, not hurrying, the boy opened
his hand.

It was the left hand, with that wire of silvery scar
around the wrist. More surprising still, perhaps, what
lay in the palm of it: A triangular blazing coin. Almost
all gold, only enough bronze there to harden the metal.

"Where did you get it, Rehger? Did you steal it?"

"No. My mother gave it me. My father gave it my
mother."

Katemval doubted this. Yet, intuitively, he doubted
also that any theft had been committed by the boy
himself.

"Where do you hide it, then?"

"Here." The boy revealed a tiny leather fragment
around his neck, the sort of thing in which valueless
talismans were retained. All gods, it was worth ten
times over what had been paid for the child.

"Put it back then, Rehger, and don't let anyone else
see. Someone might want it."

"Do you?" said the boy, fist closed again on the
coin, looking at him with utter directness.

Katemval laughed, a little hurt, the kindhearted
taker of slaves.

"Of course not, boy. That's yours, now. Remember
your mother by it."

"Yes," said Rehger.

He had never spoken of his mother, and obviously
would say no more of her now.

But that was as well, under the circumstances.

In five days they might be on the sea. Another
month, and the real life he had been born for, there in
that sty, would begin for Rehger Am Ly Dis.

When the rains paused, three priests of Cah came to
call on Orhn and Tibo.

The priests seldom walked. In the snow they would
have journeyed by dogsled; now the temple's servants
carried them in three litters, up the fearful track, over
the valley, into the farmyard.

Tibo came to the door, kneeled down in the mud and bowed her head.

One by one the three priests were lowered to the ground and emerged, to stand there burning in their red and yellow, brass and beads.

"Get up, woman. Where are your men?"

Tibo got up. Head still bowed, she replied, "My husband Orhn is inside. Shall I fetch him?"

"Where is your husband's brother?" said the priest who had spoken before.

"I don't know, priest-master. Leave to speak?"

"I grant you."

"Days ago, Orbin-master went to Ly, to offer to Cah. He didn't return here. He took money, and maybe is delayed. He spoke of bartering or buying. Orhn lost cows this cold."

"Did no one go to look for Orbin?"

"My husband—he never told me to go. Without his leave, I mustn't. I did go a little way to look, but Orbin wasn't there."

"Enough," said the priest. "I will tell you where Orbin is."

He told her. Tibo listened, head bowed. When he ended, she lifted her bowed head and gave a huge appalling cry, but that was tradition. The priests waited until she stopped ululating, by which juncture Orhn, aroused from sleep and scared, had come to the door also, plucking at her sleeve.

A man of another valley, going over to Ly, had chanced to see Orbin prone at the bottom of a steep rocky ravine. There was no means to get to him, and anyway, the carrion crows of the uplands had already done so, and were feasting—their bustling presence it was which had caused the traveler to look down. The body, what with the depth of the ravine, and the crows, was barely recognizable. But the man, reporting the event in Ly, had thought he knew it by its boots. Then other farmers came to make sacrifice or to drink in the village, and only the regular Orbin did not. So the priests went to visit Orhn's wife. It was true, without her husband's direction, she could not leave the farm's environs to search. Conversely, Orhn

might not have been able to muster such an order.
Orhn, though opinion differed on the extent, was not
quite as he should be. And this in its turn clouded the
death of his brother. That a child had been born here
all Ly knew. That the child had been sold to slave-
takers at the start of the snow, that was general knowledge, too. The Alisaarians had had their camp at Ly,
and come back there with the child, though no one
had seen much of it, wrapped in fur, up on the leader's big black riding-beast. Had Orhn been capable of
the wit to sell his son for cash? Or had Orbin sold the
boy? And did that mean in turn that Orbin, not Orhn,
had unlawfully sired it? And did it mean that Tibo had
run mad and attacked Orbin?

Men did slip and die on the passes, but rarely. They
grew up slogging back and forth along such tracks.
Women, however, now and then lost their minds, a
fault of the inferior stuff from which the goddess had
created them.

"You must come with us," the priest said to Tibo
now, "you must come and be questioned before Cah,
in the temple. But first, bring us beer to drink, and
some sweet cakes."

It was a sin, and she understood it was a sin. As
with the man who had fathered her son, Tibo was
aware of the lawless thing she did. Her thoughts were
transparently ordinary on the day she killed Orbin.
She had meant to see to it all winter, as soon as an
opportunity arrived. An execution. The moment he
had told her what he had done, that instant, she had
known she would have his life. But rationally, she stipu-
lated that it must be a murder the wordly blame for
which she might escape. There was Orhn to tend.
There was the mere fact of living.

But too much had gone on, and they suspected her,
as she had always foreseen was possible. That had
made no change in her resolution when she considered
it beforehand, and she did not alter her vision of the
killing, now. She had needed to kill Orbin.

Yet curiously somehow Tibo had not despaired of
Cah. Even though she had transgressed Cah's supremest

edicts—or had she? It was Orbin who had flouted Cah, ungenerative Orbin, who had given away the born gift of a boy to aliens.

As she walked after the litters, two of the temple servants behind her, Tibo did not tremble or loiter. She did not peer after the spot where Orbin had gone down, nor hang back as they approached it. And when, at long last they came in sight of Ly, Tibo quickened her step.

"Speak freely. Remember you are heard, and seen. Cah hears. Cah sees."

"You birthed a child."

"After many years' barrenness."

The temple was very dark, almost lampless. Perhaps for holiness' sake at this testing, or berhaps because of the lean season and a lack of oil. Out of the dark, velvet-black, the part-seen shape of the goddess, concave face, bulging mammalia. Catching light, the eyes, like lights themselves.

The priests spoke to Tibo in dismembered voices, as she stood by the alter.

They believed she was guilty. They believed that, when this ritual was done, they must throw open the doors and give her to the people of Ly, to be stoned to death.

Even the High Priest had entered the body of the temple, to witness the proceedings, and his head had altered to the mask and beak of a huge predatory bird. A woman became important when she broke the law.

But Cah also was there. Cah's shadow and her eyes, listening, watching.

Cah—

"Woman-Tibo, tell us now, who fathered your child?"

Tibo drew in the solid air of the temple, blood, unguents, smoke—the smell of Cah. Words came: She spoke them.

"The father of my child was the man given to me by Cah."

Tibo waited, an electric tingle on her skin, inside her bones. Was it a lie? By law, Cah had given Tibo Orhn. By magic and desire, Cah had given Tibo

Yems, the stranger. It was what Tibo had always believed. Was a sin still a sin when the goddess offered it? If she was wrong, now Cah would strike Tibo down.

But Cah did not strike Tibo.

There was only the loud silence of the dark and the oil sputter and the breathing of the priests.

"You say you took and bore the child lawfully?"

"I bore him according to Cah's will," Tibo said. Now she *knew* it was so. She said the phrase with triumph and conviction.

"Woman-Tibo," said a priest, (they questioned her or commented, she thought, in turn), "Orbin fell from the mountain and died. What do you know about that?"

"I didn't see it," she said. This was true. She had drawn away and turned her back on him, as he slid and floundered and toppled into space. It was not squeamishness or even superstitious fear that made her do so, but an unwillingness he should behold her face, as if that might somehow help him. But had Cah prompted her, also, then? So that she might declare now *I didn't see?*

"You say you're guiltless of Orbin's death?"

Tibo said, "Masters, I'm only a woman. Orhn had to sell our son, we had no money. Orbin went to get new stock, to sacrifice to Cah so she'd be lenient to us. Now Orbin is dead. All this sorrow."

"But are you *guilty,* woman?"

"Isn't a woman always some way guilty, if trouble comes on her men?"

The words—from Cah. Cah instructed, Cah taught her. There was no need for any confusion. The laws were wrong. Or Cah had made a new law for Tibo, and Tibo performed her will.

The priests murmured and hissed to one another in the dark, and their adornments clicked and rustled. Then the High Priest spoke through the curved beak of the bird.

"Woman, you're obtuse. But you will have to satisfy custom. If you're innocent, put your right hand on the foot of Cah. Otherwise, confess now."

Tibo hesitated. She did not know it, but she had been in a sort of trance more than three months long. It had come on her at the moment Orbin, seated there in the firelight, revealed that he had sold Raier. In this trance, Tibo had gone about her household duties as ever, worked and slaved, eaten her meager share, slept her curtailed sleep. In the trance she had not wept or complained, had not torn out her hair or rent her cheeks with her nails, had not fallen down screaming. No. She had only waited, with the promise of Orbin's slaughter in front of her. And when it was accomplished, still the trance supported her, and did so yet.

However, the clarity of the trance enabled her, additionally, at the High Priest's pronouncement, to recollect a scene of her infancy. She had been taken to Ly and when there, her mother and sisters had mixed themselves amid a crowd under the temple hill. It was a day in the hot months, the sky and the earth blistering. From the temple came a sudden muffled shrieking, and next the doors opened and a woman was dragged out and down the hill by some of the temple's servants. She was an adulteress, Tibo discovered later— for her sisters whispered of the circumstance for years, even dating things by the day of the stoning. As the rocks began to fly, Tibo's mother and sisters slinging their portion determinedly, (though Tibo was too young to join in), Tibo had noticed, without comprehension, that the woman's right hand had been hurt. Even before the stones flailed against her, she kneeled and wailed in agony, though when the onslaught began she had tried to shield herself. Tibo recalled one missle hitting the forehead of the adulteress. Then she fell back and was quiet. The stoning nevertheless did not end until the priests up on the temple terrace, sure the death sentence was complete, gave a signal.

But Tibo was not an adulteress. She had done the will of Cah.

Rather then dismay, the memory energized her. Almost in gladness she turned, her eyes on the amber embers of the goddess' gaze, and set her hand firmly on the base of the image.

Never before, never in all her life normally, would

she have been allowed to touch. How cold the goddess felt, like sheerest snow, yet her eyes were fire. Suddenly an outburst of sweetness rushed through Tibo. Only in the arms of her lover had she felt any comparable emotion. She could not keep back a cry of love and joy.

Then the grip of the priests came, prizing her brutally away. They turned her again, and pulled her right arm out from her body, to look at it. In her whirling ecstasy, for a moment, Tibo was not properly aware. But the peak could not sustain her forever, or she could not suffer it. She sank back into herself, and found she stood alone, the men as before in a circle around her, muttering nervously.

The nasal impeded voice of the High Priest cut through this hoarse soft hubbub.

"A wonder. The goddess."

Some knowledge came to Tibo. She looked down at her hand, still held out before her palm upward. It stung her faintly, as if indeed she had put it on to frozen snow. Even as she saw its unmarked surface and considered the sensitivity, already fading, Tibo felt another thing—a blast of great heat emanating from the statue of Cah behind her.

The image grew hot during a testing. A malefactor, touching Cah, was burned, and so the crime was proved. It was not spontaneous psychic combustion. An oven, set under the altar and the statue, was fired at such times, until the hollow stone of the goddess scorched. When the suspect was thought to be blameless the oven was kept low, and the stone only warmed. When reckoned culpable, they stoked the oven high. Some, usually women, nevertheless tried to keep their hands against the surface.

Today the furnace under Cah was leaping. But Tibo, flesh plastered to the stone, was forced away unburned.

If they were terrified, or only perplexed, still they trusted the power of Cah. The world was simple. Such things could only be accepted.

When Tibo emerged on to the terrace before the temple, she saw people were waiting under the hill. The priest who had come out with her called to the crowd in a high voice: "Cah has judged this one innocent."

Tibo moved down the hill slowly. The hill was muddy and the street more so. Face upon face stared at her, and one of the men snatched up her right hand, and gaped at it, and showed it to others, and let it fall with an oath.

All that remained now was to make the four hours' journey back to the farm.

As she went up out of Ly, rain began to fall again, hard as stones, across Tibo's neck and shoulders.

The fire had perished on their hearth, Orhn, shivering even in his sleep, having forgotten to put on the branches and logs his wife had left ready. Fifty years before, it would have been a tragedy, but in recent times, even to the uplands of Iscah, had come flint and tinder. Tibo brought the fire to being again. The universal symbol of death, a fire gone out, did disturb her. But she was very tired. Tired as never in her life.

She sat at the hearth as the flames bloomed to vitality, and comforted the head of Blackness. She had brought both the bitch-dogs into the house with her. Neither was fecund, after the winter; the warmth of the hovel might bring it on. Orhn would not mind. In his childish way he liked the dogs.

When he woke, her husband, Tibo rose and began to prepare food. Her mind was quite empty, darkened and contained, its vistas closed, like the valley when a deep mist clung on the mountains. If anything had happened, it was over.

"Eat, master," she said to Orhn, setting down the platter.

She would care for him. He was now the only child she had.

BOOK TWO

ALISAAR

PART ONE

CHAPTER FOUR

THE FIRE RIDE

The city skies were filled by the morning hunt of the hawks. They stooped and fell and rose again, broken prey in their grasp, with an unalterable motion.

Until one single hawk stooped, fell, and continued to fall—

Through all the rings of light and color, dawn and distance, it plummeted—into the garbage of an alley.

The man who had come oversea from Vardian Zakoris that morning, was a four-generation mix. His skin was black, his hair light brown, and his eyes, too, had been washed down from the blacks or yellows of his ancestors', to one of the strange occasional grays you saw now in such breeding. He was otherwise unremarkable, a merchant-trader off one of the score of foreign ships in the harbor.

New Alisaar perhaps interested Vardish Zakorians, still themselves under the full sway of blond rule. For New Alisaar, while she paid dues to her Shansar king in the north, was elsewhere solely independent Vis. And of her ruby cities, the port of Saardsinmey was queen. Ninety years had gone into her building, her long boulevards, her teem of alleys, the red tiling that dragonplated her. She flew into the bargain the three-tailed dragon-banner of the former kingdom. As for the northern half of Alisaar, the Shansarian province, they termed it here, with a scathing lightness, Sh'alis.

It was also a propitious time to be in town. This evening would bring Saardsimney's great summer race, the one they called the Fire Ride. The city was a hotbed of wild and spirited gambling, aglow with all the blood-lust and factious rivalry of secondhand danger.

Thinking of this and working at his accounts under the awning on the inn's roof, the mix trader had not neglected his cup, but others had, and now there was a dearth in it. The inn was of the best, far up along Five Mile Street. You expected decent service.

"Hey!" the Var-Zakor shouted, banging his cup on the table.

The noon hour was a busy one, but the three girls catering to roof top custom were not hurrying, rather pausing here and there to chat and flirt. They were thorough Visians, too, oil-black hair and eyes, and firm brazen skins that seemed to invite a caress, a pinch, or a slap. The Var-Zakor took pride in his own elements of pallor, such as they were. As the nearest girl came leisurely toward him, he gave her a glare which, in certain quarters of the homeland, would have made any Vis step lively. But she only stood by, wine-pitcher on hip, and, what was more, raised her smooth-strung brows at him like two black bows.

He thrust his cup forward.

"The jug's empty," she said.

"Then get on and fill it, you lazy cat."

She was well-dressed, with gold on her arms, no less, and a flower in her hair. She looked back at him and she said, "Keep a civil tongue, if you please." Making no move to obey.

"Don't try any of your lip with me," said the mix. "Get about your business, or do you want something to speed you up, sow-face?"

"*You've* got a foul mouth," said she. "I doubt if our wine will wash it out."

At that the mix rose. He brought down his left hand on her shoulder, liking the feel of it even as he drew back his right hand to strike her. To his astonishment— and pain—her knee came up and struck him first in the belly. The trader doubled over, aware even as he coughed for breath that all along the benches customers laughed, thinking it funny. Saardsinmey was a Vis

stronghold, and needed teaching manners. Better start
with her.

She was hastening back toward the stair when the
Var-Zakor caught her. Someone shouted her an amused
warning across the tables, but that was all. The mix
snared her by her Vis hair and pulled her around. She
tried to hit him with the pitcher now, but he pushed
off her arm. This time he landed out with his fists. The
pitcher went flying and was smashed. She gave a faint
scream as she dropped. He had struck her just under
the left eye, she would have a fancy bruise to remind
her of him, but he was not done yet. As he drew back
his foot to gift her a good sound memento of a kick,
someone said to him politely, "Wait a moment." This
checked the mix. He glanced up and noticed a stillness
had come over the inn roof. Suddenly it was so quiet
the rumbling noises of the street below intruded, one
might hear crickets in the creepers and the bells on the
awning in a passing breeze.

A figure was standing a few feet away, having just
come up the stair.

The Var-Zakor beheld the arrival was above average height, and of more than average physique, and
Vis naturally, like nine tenths of the ciy.

Then there was a blur, a surge of motion and heat—in
a terrifying rush the mix found himself high in the
air—he punched feebly, with all his strength, against
the fearsome stamina that held him there so indifferently.

"Listen to Mud-Hair bleat!"

"Throw him off the roof, Lydian."

"Do it, Lydian. We'll say he tripped on his little
dangler."

Roars of mirth and applause were followed by some
hoots of disappointment. For, returning to the stair,
the tall man they had named a Lydian flung his howling burden straight down into the middle courtyard, a
mere dozen steps below. Here the Var-Zakor crashed
among some pots and lay groaning.

There was a general move, beneath and round about,
to observe his condition. But the Lydian had already
set his back to the scene. He was kneeling by the girl,

who, her palm over her injured cheek, had sat up to
lean on his shoulder.

"Let me see, Velva," He turned her face with care,
examining the bruise attentively.

"Has the bastard disfigured me for my life?" she
said fiercely.

"Not at all. Take it from one who knows. Here."
He put money in her hand. "Go to the physician on
Sword Street."

The girl abruptly threw her arms round his neck,
kissing him and shawling him with her beautiful hair.

"Let him alone, Velva," voices cried. "Do you want
his mind on that *before* the race?"

The Lydian now laughed, and gently disengaging
himself from the girl, rose to his feet.

"I love you," she whispered. "It was well worth it,
that pig's fist, to be held in your arms."

"Ah," he said, and shook his head at her, before
walking away across the roof. There was scarcely a
woman in Saardsinmey who had not murmured similar
words to the Lydian, if only in her waking dreams.

From midafternoon, the shops along Five Mile Street
had firmly closed their doors, while quantities of others in adjacent thoroughfares did likewise. Not only
were the usual locks and grills employed: In some
cases boards were being nailed to the facades. After
the Fire Ride there was often fighting in the streets,
and no doubt there would be this year, since three of
the competitors were blond free men from Sh'alis.

By late afternoon, a thick honey light spooned down
on the districts of the city. A peculiar lull had come
with it, the hush before the storm.

From several hundred cornices, balustrades and por-
ticos along the celebrated route, flowers roped and
banners stood flat on the serene hot air. The three-
tailed dragon was out in force, and the blazons of such
innkeepers and merchants whose cash helped mount
the seasonal sports. Mostly the colors of the contes-
tants were on display, in swags and swathes, spilled
from windows, twined in trees and the hair of girls,
the reds of Saardsinmey eclipsing the rest. Luck ban-

ners had been tied to the poles of streetlights or hung across the way from building to building. They depicted the god Daigoth, patron of fighters, acrobats and racers, and, closer to the waterfront and all along the harbor wall, from God's High Gate to the Coast Road, images of the sea deity Rorn.

The spectators had been assembling since midday. As the afternoon wore and flushed, they came in droves, piling up the stairways to their bought benches on rooftops and balconies, and all the upper terraces for the length of fifteen miles.

At the head of Five Mile Street, the vast stadium of Saardsinmey was already packed beyond its limits. There were multitudes who preferred to oversee and make judgments—or merely to emote and scream— along the course. But the rest who could afford the price, high tonight as never elsewhere in the whole year, preferred to witness the birth of glory and its killing finish on the stadium straight, despite the long interim of waiting when all there was to guide them were the flare of distant lights across the city, and far-off shrieking, and occasional panting runners with unreliable bulletins.

By the time the first stars raised their silver torches over New Alisaar, in a clear rouged sky, there was barely a quiet pulse beating in Saardsinmey.

The great mirror of glass, which had once poised in a palace of the old capital, now rested in its clawed frame of gilded ebony in the hall beneath Saardsinmey's stadium. Here men, burnished to the sheen of its gilding, sometimes scarred as its tarnished face, dressed in magnificence to kill or die, would stand a moment, and stare in. It might be the last sight they would ever have of their looks, their wholeness, or their life. It was thought fortunate to touch the mirror as it held you, and to instruct the reflection: *Stay, till I return.*

Usually the mirror was taller than any who gazed into it. One man matched it, height for height. The Lydian.

He wore the charioteer's short open-sided tunic, a garment of linen, ruby-red for Alisaar, strapped with

red-dyed leather cuirass, belted by golden scale-work.
His calves and forearms were also braced by leather,
ringed by gold; his black hair drawn back, for the
chariots, into a tube of hollow gold. He was altogether
a creature of gold as he stood there, of gold and
blood.

The faultless proportions of his body, developed
through practice, since earliest boyhood, of every physical skill of the stadium (in each of which he excelled),
had formed him, *built* him, like the endeavors of
some genius artisan. As indeed they were: He was his
own architect. But the head and face of this man had
also their perfect proportion. Though the immaculate
features were sculpted to strength, it was strength,
too, of mind, and spirit. While the eyes, large and
vividly black, dreamer's eyes, misled opponents long,
long ago, until the pride of jaw and mouth, or of a
simple deadly sword, put them right. There had already been a saying in Saardsinmey, for five or six
years: *As bright as the sun and as handsome as the
Lydian.*

Saardsin professional fighters, whatever their original race or merit, however rich they might become,
however much courted, however many contests won,
or lost, entered these halls as children and remained as
slaves. Barring death, there was no manumission from
the courts of Daigoth. But then, to be slave here, in
this way, was not like the slavery of others.

As for Rehger Am Ly Dis, standing his moment
before the surface that once had mirrored Alisaarian
nobility, he did not seem like any kind of slave. He
looked a king.

Reaching out, the Lydian briefly touched the glass.
"Stay, till I return."

It was a fact, the man who owned one of the finest
seats at the stadium had almost stayed away.

Katemval had had a premonition. If such it could be
called.

Leaving the charming house on Gem-Jewel Street,
he had parted the curtains of his litter, looking along
the avenue in the sunset. Every shop was bolted and

boarded-up as far down as the public fountain, where
a phalanx of the Guardian's soldiery was even now
marching smartly across the intersection. Then something else caught Katemval's eye.

In the warm light and shadow, a cold blank omission.

Katemval turned his head sharply—a woman in a
white mantle gleamed against some garden wall. White
was not the fashion in New Alisaar, its racial connota-
tions were unpleasing. But then Katemval realized
that beneath her white veil, her hair shone paler.

They were past.

Katemval almost shouted for the litter to halt. But
ordinary sense prevented him, and he let the curtain
fall.

Her face had been young—her hair bright with youngness, and she was white-skinned he was sure. Neither
age, nor bleach and cosmetics had made that pallor.
An unmixed Lowlander, then, the plains race of southernmost Vis, they who had tumbled a world. One
heard tell of such albinos, *Amanackire* they were named,
Anackire's Own, the Children of the Serpent Goddess.

Suddenly he plucked the curtain back again and
craned out. But they had turned the angle of the
avenue by the fountain, and that part of the street was
lost to view.

There was something in this incident, small though
it was, that unsettled Katemval. There were certain
legendary traditions in the west that showed death as a
thin colorless ice woman with claws—

Death was always vigilant. She—it—being ultimately
inescapable. So what? How one lived, the gifts of life,
these were the valid matters. Death was the end. No
less, but decidedly nothing more.

He had watched Rehger in combat and competition
at the stadium whenever trade permitted. In recent
years, seldom the traveler now, Katemval had been
there to watch at every event. He saw Rehger fight,
and ride, and strive and win, and fame on him like pure
gold. But death was always there, too, and only a fool
did not know that. Why be troubled now?

At eighteen, Rehger had lost footing in sand slick
with various life-fluids. The sword of the Kandian

youth they had paired with him had cleaved the air in a terrible blaze—cutting home into Rehger's breast, high, against the shoulder. That had nearly been the finish, then. The crowd, Katemval recalled, which had already begun to adore him, becoming one with him as he fought, groaned the sound they termed the death-moan—But Rehger, sashed in his own blood, had steadied himself, and when his adversary came in at him again, returned the blow, this one straight to the Kand's heart. A year later, on the proceeds of a bet laid, in Saardsinmey's most honored manner, upon that fighter one most truly loved, Katemval had bought his house on Gem-Jewel Street.

The pale races existed, and maybe might come to see the boxing and sword-play, and the chariots, in Alisaar. To glut their eyes on the Lydian, too, that Katemval had rescued from the mire of backland Iscah.

Had he not said to him even, at the first, trying to seal the boy's destiny to it—*Grow for glory, glory days, and a death clean and fair—*

Stop thinking of it. Katemval chided himself, superstitious, for the litter was by now forcing through the press of people, toward the stadium gate. It was a lamplit, febrile dusk. And here and there the retired taker of slaves heard the friendly cry, "There goes the Lydian's father!" An old jest, not inapplicable. The father gave life.

"Twenty white pigeons," Katemval muttered under his breath, in his heart, to Daigoth, as the litter went through the gate. "And a two-year bull. And my most cherished wine to quench the burnt offering. If he lives." And added, being now thoroughly a resident of the metropolis, "And *wins.*"

There were ten for the Fire Ride this year. It could accommodate as many as thirteen; often only seven or eight dared it. The prize was weighed on the old measure, twenty bars of gold. But the renown was better.

The slave champions of other places, three long seasons training for it, sponsored and financed by the cities and prospering towns of New Alisaar—and from

everywhere else. There were free men, too, who thought
it no embarrassment to compete with such slaves as
these. Mixes, Vis, the yellow-headed men of the Sister
Continent. Flaunting Karmians, dark or blond, and sly
Xarabs, whose pretty chariots were unloaded from the
ships like courtesans enameled with flowers, the surly
Ommos, Dortharians in their pride, their cars with
black storm emblems and gold-leaf snakes. Men came,
too, from Var-Zakoris, for the Vardian conqueror had
his own customs of such racing, as he had had his own
rules of war. Conqueror Shansars arrived, the charioteers of ships. And Shansars from Sh'alis, riding their
horses overland to be gawped at and envied, though for
this evening's work they had had to learn to manage
the hiddrax, the chariot-animal of the Vis, bred to
race since the times of the All-King Rarnammon.

This night then had brought its usual assortment.

A Thaddrian, a free man and seemingly a bandit-
noble, color brown and ocher. An Ott, free man,
merchant stock but game and wily, color swarthy cream.
A Zakorian, from Free Zakoris, what they called a
fighting-leopard, color applicably black. A man from
Corhl, a petty princeling, color steel.

For Alisaar, a slave racer from Kandis, highly es-
teemed, color Alisaar red with rose. And a Jowan
aristocrat, one of the Jow Guardian's nephews apparently, color Alisaar red with black. Saardsinmey's con-
tender, a slave racer unbeaten in any contest for three
years, but never before drawn in Daigoth's lots for this
one, the Lydian, color red with red.

While from Sh'alis the trouble had come. Two mixes,
both free men, since no man with a touch of fairness
in his pigments might be lawfully a slave. One Shalian
with the color raw yellow, the other yellow with blue.
And last, a Shansarian lord who owned estates in
Sh'alis and in Karmiss, color white.

(*White*. There was the answer to the riddle. In his
box now Katemval, having glanced along the program,
neatly copied and brought him by a stadium scribe,
acknowledged respite. If the Shansar devil could bring
ten horses with him he would not need—he had—why

not an Amanackire mistress with whom to ride after
the Ride?)

It was full night now, the sky above the stadium
deep as a bowl of ink and splashed by stars. Along the
terraces, the lamps were dim, the wicks trimmed purposely low, or capped by smoky vitreous. Tension
close as darkness, waiting for the storm to break.

The stadium trumpets sounded.

A huge single cry went over the stands, and was
echoed all along the wide artery of Five Mile Street.

In the dense torchlight under the stadium, the chariots had been drawn up waiting. The teams of hiddrax,
backed into the shafts one quarter of an hour before,
catching the night's fever, pawed the ground and shook
their long heads, the light flowing over their groomed
and burnished skins, their adornments of metal and
ribbons.

The brass dice of Daigoth had been cast, each position allocated. Now the priests came along the line, to
foreigner, free man and slave alike, the first offering
him the cup of Daigoth, a solitary taste of wine, while
the second priest uttered the ritual sentences before
him.

"You are the god's. Go, be yourself a god."

Rehger, in eighth place, listened to the phrase repeated over and over. The Ott, the Jowan, the
Thaddrian, the Kand and the Free Zakorian, each
drank and accepted. Whatever their personal religion,
tonight they were Daigoth's, tonight they would be
gods. But when the priests reached the color-yellow
Shalian, he interrupted harshly, "No. None of that. I
worship the one true goddess." The priests came away
from him at once, without response. But the Corhlan,
next in the left-hand position to Rehger, laughed loudly.
He said to the man from Sh'alis, "Corrah is the one
true goddess. You mean Corrah?" The Corhl did not
have much of an accent; his comment was quite clear.
The Shalian ignored him. Their teams fidgeted and
shook their tasseled bits, sidling away from each other.
(On the bodywork of the yellow chariot had been
represented the Sh'alis sigil, a staff roped with a golden

snake.) The priests had come to the Corhlan. He drank from Daigoth's cup and received the benison. Then he spoke to the Shalian again: "Corrah will trample your snake-dung of a whore-goddess under these hoofs and wheels." The Shalian stood like stone, holding back his sizzling animals, a smile of fury on his mouth.

The cup had reached Rehger. He bowed his head and drank the thin sugary wine. "You are the god's," said the priest to him. "Go, be yourself a god." Not immune to the galvanic of the incantation, Rehger felt it pierce him through, and closed his eyes a moment, in the verity of its power.

Returning to himself, he was aware of the Shansar next to him on the other side, saying, "I ride for Ashara-Anack. Your Daigoth's a phantom." But the other Shalian, the last of the line, drank from the cup and heard the words without protest. Even in Sh'alis men might worship as they desired, providing they also made offerings to the Shansarians' fish-serpent-woman.

The trumpets shouted up above.

"Corrah," said the Corhl.

Along the line, each side of him, Rehger might glimpse the hands of men quickly marking themselves for their gods, or their fates.

But the ten chariots were already moving. The hiddraxi, glad of mobility, trotted eagerly up the ramp. The gates were grating wide, opening the stadium before them, a mouth darker than the lit cavern they were leaving, which would be appropriate enough for some.

Rehger had no fear of death, only a familiar sense of it. It was integral to the ecstasy. From your earliest adult year in this place, you knew that no sane man took more than the token sips of liquor in the three days before an event. For it was in the very air. The moment you came out on the stadium sand, you were drunker than ten cups of wine could make you.

And they were out. The black huge sky overhead, the oval rings of terraced stone descending from it, crowded with living things, that now welled into an astonishing bellowing thunder—the breaking of the storm.

And over all the cries, the praises and exhortation, a thudding drum beat:

The Lydian! Lydian! Lydian!

So a king must feel, then, when—if ever—he was saluted with such real passion. A man who did not soar, know himself in that hour lord, and god, was a mindless heartless wooden lump—and such did not long make charioteers.

They went down the straight, east to west, took the turn under a rain of banners, ribbons and showering flowers, progressed back again, west to east, toward the Guardian's box.

One saw that important man, the Guardian of the city, often. He liked the stadium sports. Now he was nothing, only part of the vast being of This, part of night and noise and arriving fire.

The young boys were bringing the fire, or its physical emblem. Ten male children of the stadium courts: once Rehger had been such a child, and done this office for others. A million years ago. And a million years from now, one of these would very probably stand where he stood, some other in the future far away, when he and this moment were dust. And a remembered name.

The child held up the burning torch for him. The child's face flamed like the torch.

"Win for your city," said the child, in the ritual, meaning it.

The Lydian laughed.

"Go with me in your heart," he said, and grinned. And having raised the torch high, for men and gods to see, next thrust it down and home into the gilded iron bracket on the chariot's prow. Steeped in fats and resins, even the enormous speed of the racing chariot and the acid salty wind from the sea would not extinguish it.

Then the children ran and were off the straight.

The Guardian nodded. On the stone table below his box they struck the tinder over the oil, and paused, while the world held its breath.

Then let the spark fall.

A blast of scarlet spurted at heaven. The crowd screamed.

Like ten great beasts of fiery night, the chariots sprang forward, neck and neck.

The first three laps, completed in the stadium, would rarely establish subsequent placings. The racing track was firm and clean, blocked only by its central platform that, during other events, was lowered by machinery under the earth. Five Mile Street, similarly, cleared of obstacles and lit by torch-poles, was a smooth dancing floor compared to the swooping coastal road that came next, nearly ten miles of it, revealed only by the lanterns of spectators, stars and the torches of the chariots.

At the first turn, those Daigoth's dice had given the inside positions took the lead, as was inevitable: The Ott and the Jowan burst forward on the straight. But the brown and ocher Thaddrian, third out from the inside, pulling his team of hiddrax around less by skill than main force, drove a diagonal course across the two forward cars, clipping the Ottish chariot so it juddered and banked up on the Kand, who was driving in fast to the rear. A primed racer of Alisaarian Kandis, the red-rose charioteer avoided the mess with nothing more than a restrained sprint, scraping past between the Ott and the central platform, and falling in behind the Thaddrian and Jowan. The yellow Shalian meanwhile, cutting into the Free Zakorian's fifth position, cutting out again in a hurry to miss the sudden huddle of chariots, ran instead against the Zakor's car. This, with a countemptuous slam of its flank, pushed the Shalian sideways and overturned him. The mix from Sh'alis who worshiped the one true goddess, and had made the mistake of losing his temper before the race began, was tipped into the dust. He bolted presently for safety on the platform, to the encouraging jeers of the Vis crowd.

His hiddraxi, writhing and shrieking, anchored to the unyielding mass of the fallen car—which by some miracle had neither felled them nor caught alight from its prow-torch—were abandoned perforce leftward of the center track, the first unstable obstacle of the race.

The remaining chariots had by now reached and taken the second turn at the platform's western end, and were hurtling along the opposite straight. The Jowan and the Thaddrian had the lead, the Ott, discomposed, had reined back and was in third. Behind these, in an almost mathematical line, the Kand, the Zakor, the Corhl and the Lydian, galloped at a loose stretch. While behind these again, the second Shalian, and the white Shansar. To build full speed in the stadium was foolish at the start of a Fire Ride. Not till you were on the street could you afford to do it. Yet every year the unwise and overly-opportunistic angled and snatched and dog-fought for position on the first laps, as the Thaddrian and Jowan did now. As they came around into the eastern turn again, the red and black Jow chariot executed a move known as the Unwilling Girl. Ignoring the favorable inside advantage, the Jowan swerved abruptly outward across the incoming second positon, to throw the Thaddrian wide. The Thaddric car, slapped on the hip, pulled out, her bandit-lord cursing in a dazzle of golden teeth. But as the Jowan wallowed back to grab the turn, the Ott went shooting by on the inside, taking first position once more.

The black Zakorian now broke from line, rattling down the straight behind the three leaders, who, giving it a generous margin, were just past the Shalian chariot wreck.

In the upset, the traces had been snapped from the head-stall of one of the outside animals, leaving it attached only to the crossbar of the yoke-pole. Not everyone had noted this, but it seemed the Zakorian had done so. Spectators, who had observed he had drawn the narrow dagger permitted to a charioteer for his own purposes of survival, began to caw and upbraid him, predicting his move. As he tore by the wreck, leaning from his vehicle—in itself a feat of some daring and expertise—the Zakor slashed the hiddrax's last restraint.

In Old Zakoris, racing had been an art of savagery

and blood for centuries. It was well-known any Free
Zakorian racer kept up these virtues. In Alisaar,
where the animals of sport were pampered, such antics
were not approved.

It was, however, a gambit.

The hiddrax, screaming in hysteria and excitement,
dashed out from the wreck, in the path of the Kand
chariot and the Corhlan.

The Kand split to the left, space to spare, missing
both the animal and the wreckage. The Corhlan, held
off by the presence of the Kand, pressured from the
right by the press of other vehicles, veered crazily as
the untethered hiddrax skipped in a kind of ghastly
dance before him. Then the animal flung itself against
his team, trying to run backward with them. Next
second, the rogue hiddrax had tumbled. The steel-gray
bosses of the Corhlish chariot were seen running up
the air—and grounding down directly into the Shalian
ruin, as, in a terrible cascading bound, the Corhl's
animals went plunging in over the sides of the wreck.

The Corhlan had one chance only, and he took it.
Amid the din of the terraces they heard him sing out
the wild name of Corhl's goddess, and with only mo-
mentum to aid them, he used the whip across the
necks of his team, merciless, not to withdraw, but
driving them on now, and forward, through the panic
and collapse of the dead chariot, its honor splintering
under hoofs and wheels—as he had promised the
Shalian it should do.

Bred for swiftness, the legs of hiddraxi were noto-
riously fragile. Shod and braced by metal, plied by
whip and encroaching fire, they floundered and pranced.
Even as the smashed car gave way under them and
began to burn, they broke out through it, maddened—
whole—slewed around, recovered themselves—*coursed
on*.

A colossal shout was lifted for the Corhlan throughout the stadium, and those with his colors shook them
joyfully. He was the youngest driver in the race, a
handsome boy, and courage and wits were seldom
vaunted without applause in Saardsinmey.

(Trapped on the platform, the yellow Shalian lamented. His chariot burned in great clots of smoke, his team lying broken with it to be consumed.)

The Lydian, glancing over his shoulder, saw beyond the Shansar and the blue-yellow Shalian, the Corhlan pelting after them, silhouetted on the blaze, racing last now, but alive in the palm of his goddess.

When they took the east turn for the third time, elements in the crowd were already yelling: *Doors! Doors!* Commanding that the southern exitway be opened in readiness on the street. As if such a matter might be overlooked.

For the south gate, the benign position was now reversed, being on the outer right-hand side.

Approaching the west turn, the adventurous Ott struck out for the right, premature, and running head-long across the noses of the Jowan and Thaddrian. This foolhardy and clumsily developed measure, not to be mistaken for bravura or dexterity by the seasoned crowd, gained the Ott a precarious minute. The Thaddrian, enraged by the tactic and judging the Jow was about to try something similar, rammed the red and black sidelong, to an overture of hissing and railing from the stands.

The Jowan chariot shuddered but held her course. The Jow, aristocrat or not, might be beheld shouting oaths at the bandit, while the two teams rushed stride for stride. Then the Thaddric chariot seemed to rein up, giving over any hope of advantage. Inevitably, when the Jowan started to pull for the right-hand, the Thaddrian rammed him again. This time, leaning for the crossways cut, the red-black car tilted, skidded on one wheel, curved slowly over and went down. The stands were howling for Alisaarian vengeance. In the dust and spitting crush of light the Jowan seemed gone, ripped away under the hoofs—then he appeared again and the roar of the terraces redoubled. In the Thaddrian's chariot with the Thaddrian, the nephew of the Guardian of Jow was explaining stadium etiquette with his fists. The red and black chariot lay heaped on the track; the brown and ocher car careered across the straight, (the Kand, Zakorian and Lydian breaking to avoid it), to smash against the

terrace barrier, where both men dropped out fighting,
and girl-high the hiddraxi screamed.

The Ott was on the west turn, far right, where the
Zakorian, speed-lifted at the proper instant, passed
him, followed in a graceful in-curling arc by the Kand,
the Lydian, the Shansar. Surprised, the Ott scrambled
in their wake, only the leftover Shalian and the Corhl
all at once behind him.

The southern exit on to Five Mile Street stood properly panting wide. Beyond, the great boulevard, jeweled either side by a watching city—

To a paean of ecstatic frustration the stadium saw
each brilliant fire-strung car complete the turn, hurl
along the ultimate strip of straight, dive in the gateway—
and longed for a means to follow.

The yellow Shalian, the Thaddrian, the Jow were
out, three slaughtered vehicles, slain beasts, living,
bruised, unloving men. On the terraces there were
already wailings and gnashed teeth, and luckless gamblers' talk of suicide in the morning.

The blue-yellow Shalian had twice crowded him on
the track, a thing of no great moment, and mostly lost
on the spectators in the flamboyance of other catastro-
phes. Now, the Shalian was back behind with the
Corhl; it was the Shansar in his gold and white enam-
els who came on, and on.

Rehger spared no second glance for these, or for the
merchanteering Ott, who should have stayed home
with the bales and baskets.

Before, the Kand and the tricky Zakorian leapt
down the road, their dust, with the sparks of his own
fire, in his face.

Five Mile Street was walled by a tall hemmed stitchery
of lights and outcry. The banners and flags poured
past, everything streaming in the gale of the race. This
idle promenade of an hour was a chariot-run of minutes, no more, for the speed was building now, from
the powerhouse of vehicle and team, from the beating
hearts of the animals and the beating heart and brain
of a man, and all the rushing torrent of the night.

The street curved slightly, east to west, an accident—

its straightness had been meant to be the pride of
Saardsinmey. Already, up ahead, there was the dim
straddle of the huge dockside gate, garlanded with
flares. And soon after it, one met the fierce turn to the
right, for on this stretch every turn was set contrary to
the left-hand turnings of the stadium.

The Lydian ran now for Gods' High Gate, letting
the first true escalation mount toward an upsurge of
speed that might slough the Shansar from his shoulder.

And he felt the Shansar fall from him, but not
totally. For the Otherlander, too, had come armed
with knowledge to this fight.

Then the gate rolled over, rang like a giant bell, and
was gone.

The hiddraxi pulled, straining to reach the stars.
The Kandish chariot seemed to flow back toward them.
Vague ghost voices were calling miles away: *The Lydian!
The Lydian!*

Beyond the gate it was darker, a wider mouth of
night, despite the winking windows and the lamps on
the rigging of every ship in the bay. Stiff reek rose
from the shut fish market down below, and the breathing salt of the sea.

The Zakorian folded sideways, a blur of torchfire,
taking the turn, a quarter of a mile ahead now, and
next the Kand went into it and lilted through it beautifully. Rehger met and possessed the turn like a lover,
more beautiful yet, and the disembodied voices laved
him again from their distances. *Win for your city. Go
with me in your heart.*

They were on the Coast Road. Blindfolded, you
would know it, going uphill, all gliding gone, now the
chariot caught the action of steepness, of ruts and
stones, jumping and clacketing. Nor was it a broad
path. Enough room for one chariot to pass another.

The flaming prow-torch spat back at him, flinders of
fire, touching his neck and jaw.

On the stepped heights above and to the right, the
skeins of lamps and beacons continued. But to the left
hand now, for the most part only a frame of ground
pegged with watch towers, that slipped downward to
the ocean. A lit ship or two blazed out on the water as

if she burned, only more motes of arson to one who
ran.

The Kand sank backward into Rehger's arms. A
fume of red and rose, the jingling hustle as one team
briefly companioned and then deserted the other, and
the blare of the second torch whirled behind into the
dark. Up on the heights, the balconies and roofs,
came a screaming of the city's name now, as personi-
fied in one charioteer. And there was the sound of the
Kand, too, trying to regain, to grip and pass—but that
speed, though well judged, not a match for this.
Rehger's hiddraxi, that he had for two years nurtured,
they were in flight, nor were they done flying yet.

The ground, having risen, leveled. The surface of
the road did not.

Only the Zakorian now, in front of him.

(And maybe a mile behind, a bubble crashing as it
burst. The Ott, finally fouled. The Shalian was on his
tail, and had perhaps helped him to it.)

But the fading noise of the Kandish car had ex-
panded. No, it could never be the Kand coming in
again. It was the Shansar, rising now out of the dark
as the Lydian did.

Ahead, the Zakorian looked back. Rehger, closing
the gap, was easily near enough to see the grim flash
of the shadowy face, and the long tongue of the whip
that followed it. To hear the old charioteering shout—
"Ayh! Ayh!"

The Zakor's animals were straining now, not to
catch stars but only in labor. A breakneck swiftness
tugged the black chariot away and away, and Rehger
unfolded the wings of power, unleashed the coiled
spring, held all this while within the hiddraxi, their
hearts, his. "Fly now, my soul—" And though they
had seemed to fly before, now they *flew*—

The night spun off like water. Flame in his face—
The world was cast away.

The Zakorian, sucked up into their vortex, held a
moment, also flung away.

Only the twisting spine of the road before them
now, weirdly splashed with light from the clapping
torch, humped, chattering, made nothing now by the

weightless entity that sped over it. A road that had become a ribbon across the sky.

A lighted tower, its walkway bunched with watchers, jumped from the blackness, bawled for the Lydian, and vanished.

Fireflies unraveled to tiny threads of gold—the lamps above—the ships below.

Yet the Shansar at his back, his white shadow.

Then a white beating wing.

Then on the road, just wide enough, in a speed like stasis, they were side by side.

The Lydian, in his dream of power, turned and stared and saw the face of the Shansar stare back at him, also locked into the magic of the dream. In that split second they were brothers, and like brothers they might kill each other for a birthright.

The Shansar had gained the inside position, against the rising terraces of the land. His onset had been perfectly gauged, and risked, coinciding with those instants when the unevenness of the road had pushed the Lydian's chariot to the outer edge— Now only stumbling rock, the open yawn of night and water walled him in. If the Shansar was treacherous to match his cunning and finesse, here would be the place for it.

As if to illustrate this scenario, there came a sickening noise out of the lost shelves of darkness behind them. The screech of iron on bronze, the clangor of collision and a rippling rush of stones which fell; the dreadful girl-like cries of hiddraxi—it seemed, to tell by the answering crescendo along the watch-posts of the suburbs above, that one of the vehicles had gone to its death over the low cliffs into the bay. And, from the tone of the lament, too, that it was the chariot of Alisaarian Kandis which had been lost.

But that was in another country. In this landscape now, only two chariots existed, the game was only for them.

Neither man now looked at the other. Neither attempted, by ways deft or malign, to shift the other off the road. They raced, and still they were team to team, torched prow to prow, shoulder by shoulder. And when the whips rose now to claw the air high above the animal's necks, they cracked as one. Some god had spoken, Daigoth, Rorn, or the blond man's scale-tailed lady, to link their cars together. Each striving now, thrusting, coaxing, to bring on the last orgasm of pure speed, the severing that would dash the other from him, and mean victory.

The road began to turn with the cliff, swimming to the right, to the northwest. In three minutes, or less, the blocks and walls of the city would gulp them in again. The home stretch then, north and uphill, on the wide byways, all neatly cleared for it, ablaze with smoke and heat and the lather-spume of the animals, between the booming crowds, through on to the outer circle under the stadium's bank, around to the south gate once again, in upon the stadium sand where a third of Saardsinmey would be waiting—

Deep in the night, another voice, not of the sea, not from any mortal throat, spoke out.

The animals shrilled in terror. Even as they shrilled, unflagging, they ran.

Each man, the blond Shansar, the dark Vis, turned, irresistibly, and looked away into the pit of black star-swarmed nothing—

And the voice spoke again.

It was not of, and yet it came from, the ocean, yet also from the vault of atmosphere above, and from the rock beneath their chariot wheels.

A century or more ago, the annals of Alisaar recorded, Rorn himself had stalked these waters. It had been a time of unrest and war. In that era, any great happening was possible. Rorn, striding the waves, touching heaven with his brow, that had been possible—

Aaaurouuu, the voice insisted, a droning, whistling, miaowing howl, parting the night.

Then the earth, like the chariots, began to *run.*

Before, the road had seemed discarded under the hoofs and wheels, but now it pleated itself together, heaved upward, smote them, trying to throw them off.

Rehger heard the Shansar call out, another language, the tongue of his homeland, but the name of the Ashara goddess was decipherable.

The chariots were no longer airborne. They were

earthly things of wood and metal, struggling to keep a purchase. The teams of hiddrax, squealing, bloody foam issuing from their mouths, ran out of rhythm, striking each other with their sides, aliens and team-mates alike.

The night was full of roaring, like the ten-thousandfold throat of the stadium.

A faint hot lightning washed through the sky above the sea, and sudden thunder belled after it, and the other sounds ended, snapped out into silence as if some mighty creature had died there.

The ground shivered and lay down flat. The shock was done. Only stones littered down the slopes, a few trickling off into the air, harmlessly passing as they sought the sea. Somewhere above, in the slanting field by someone's fine house, a dropped lamp had set the trees on fire. This added brightness painted in the deathly face of the Shansar. His dream was over.

Speed-broken, both chariots. Though they still ran, they lumbered.

The Lydian's whip curled out across the sway of necks, not catching them, correcting only with harsh music.

To this accompaniment, Rehger sang to the hiddraxi love words, a litany of pleasures to come.

Overseen by the throng in the burning orchard above, the team skewed, rollicked. Then melted to order like a blessing. He had slept in their stalls, fed them from his hands, gifted them and caressed them.

"*Go*, my soul—"

Above, orchard unheeded, the watchers cheered and stamped.

The Shansar, somehow blundering yet at his side, damned him.

The Lydian, feeling the great surge of speed come back, strong and profound as sex, into the reins, the animals, the vehicle, the world, laughed at him. "Tell them in Shansar-over-the-ocean," he shouted, "Rorn was angry!"

And then they pulled away, as if drawn on a rope of riven fire. And slicing northward quite alone, sprang back into the city, to take the last two miles in a

downpour of petals and screaming, the stadium gate in
an ovation, triumph, gold and glory, within the hour.

It was a sign of Saardsinmey's sporting fervor that
the earthquake, the first to be felt in coastal Alisaar
for eighty years, was almost discounted in the closing
outburst of the race. The shock had been a slender
one, and later, when the tales came in from the watch-
towers and the vineyards above the sea, of the Shansar
chariot speed-smashing at terror of Alisaarian Rorn's
war horns under the water, even that phenomenon of
fear was incorporated in the rejoicing.

The Lydian, winning for Saardsinmey, received the
rich prize, the twenty bars of gold. He scarcely needed
it, since to the Swordsmen of Daigoth everything in
the city came always, in any case, gratis.

Wreathed like a young god in flowers, by firelight in
the stadium, the crowd itself became his team and
dragged his chariot one whole lap, then bore him on
their shoulders. Their love was tangible. And presently, the Saardsin aristocrats, his willing hosts and
companions since he began to fight and win before
them, trooped to admire him, hang their jewels on
him, and their bodies, if he would have them.

The man from Kandis was dead. The had fished him
from the bay. The fly silly Ott would never ride the
chariots again, nor be much use among the ledgers
either, blinded, battered. The Zakorian had been fined
for his conduct, and the crowds of the city, getting
hold of him, partly stoned him, pinned a notice on his
skin that read MURDERER OF KANDS, and sent
him toward Free Zakoris tied upside down on a zeeba.
The Shansar, coming in second, was hooted, and retired from public view. The Corhlan had the third
place, and the rewards youth, bravery and looks might
get him at a time of goodwill. The second Shalian was
fourth, and had nothing.

But that night the Lydian went to dine and drink in
the house of a nobleman on Sword Street, a mansion
with which Rehger was quite familiar. The first wine,
the first spiced food for days. And after it, the first
woman for a month. It was the custom to visit, before

a stadium event, some inn you cared for, and take one token sip of liquor. So that, should you perish, they might say ever after there, *He* drank the last sweet cup of his life with us.

But the girl who lay in his arms that night, and coiled him with strands of rubies red as Zastis, silken hair and limbs, was a princess of the old royal line, and she said to him, "And if you'd died, I might have boasted, might I not, *here* he took also a last sweetness. Do you believe me, I stayed celibate as you did, my beloved? I'm glad you're alive."

Katemval, however, coming from the stone temple where he had filed the tablet of his promised offering to Daigoth, learned he also had received a gift.

Delivered at his house, in his absence, by unseen porters, a plain cibba-wood casket.

Opened by his slave, Katemval found it contained the strangely-embalmed bodies of two birds. A hawk, a shard of flint lodged in its breast, and from whose talons hung a pigeon.

A sheet of reed paper lay beneath them. Which said:

Victory is transient. Since he is, tonight, your city, tell him this.

CHAPTER FIVE

ALISAARIAN NIGHT

"Then, what is it?" Rehger said. He lay on a marble slab of the stadium bathhouse, as the slave kneaded his body with warmed oils. Previously, all day since sunrise, he had been in the courts at exercise with sword, spear and knife, or among the slings and bars of the acrobat's yard. Before that, for two nights and a day, he had been under a nobleman's roof, in bed with a princess.

"Some means to warn you, or more likely threaten you. Go carefully."

"Carefully? This to a winner of the Fire Ride," said Rehger, turning on his back, closing his eyes.

Katemval nodded at the ironic absurdity. His professional gaze—both of slave-taker and of gambling connoisseur—lingered on the young man's nakedness. There was nothing sexual in Katemval's optic possessiveness, possibly not even anything sensual. It was the reverence of life's animal expression, it was the pride of his race, and, even now, of having discovered such a paragon of these things.

Two healed fire-kisses from the chariot-torch temporarily marked Rehger's jaw and throat. There were few scars on his body, nothing to mar it or infer a weakness. No scars on the mind. Rehger had kept his clarity, his primal innocence. *I did that for him. But don't preen,* Katemval thought. *The gods did it first.*

And he remembered the images Rehger had been used to fashion as a child, even into his seventh year. The training of the stadium had already begun for him—it began in certain ways from the very start. Yet in spare moments, the child, allowed clay, had formed these figures, miniature lizards, orynx, little teams of hiddrax—once he had glimpsed them—with tiny men in the tiny, intricate chariots. They had been, his creations, coming to a fineness, perhaps on the verge of beauty—and at that time, all at once, he stopped. Rehger had ceased making external icons and gone to work on himself.

The masseur was finished. Rehger nodded and the man moved away. In the oval bath beyond the arch, other Swordsmen splashed and swam.

Ought one to say more? Katemval considered. But the box of dead birds, the ominous, elegantly-penned script, seemed irrelevant now. Daigoth had taken his offering. The race was won, there would soon be the demands of other events. And Zastis in the sky before this month was through.

Katemval saw that Rehger had fallen asleep. The

high arch of the ribs, the flat belly plated by smooth
muscle, rose and sank evenly. Unimpeded, clear, his
breathing was silent.

That secure in the arms of Mother Alisaar. Well,
then. Let it go.

The fire dancer was black as a Zakor leopard, true
Zakoris, but of an elder or younger strain, for her lips
were full as flowers, her face was sweet.

She stepped between the long tables of the feast, on
to the open mosaic of the floor.

Her arms were ringed by bracelets of white bone.
Aside from these, she was covered, neck to ankles, by
an opaque and many-colored tide of gauze.

The lamps had been dimmed, the room was hushed.

The dancer extended her hands, with a half-con-
temptuous flick of the wrists, and waited for the two
flaming brands to be given her by a steward. She
looked at none of them, the assembly of nobles, their
guests and servants. She looked away into some mysterious inner space, to her gods and her art.

The torches, also braceleted in holders of bone,
were set in her grasp gently, respectfully. Her fingers
closed on them. The steward stepped away. The girl
tossed her head. Her hair was fastened up on it in a
little tower of gold, and let free again from the top like
the tail of a jet-black mare.

Music welled out of the shadows, double pipes, shell
harps and drums.

The dancer moved. She became fluid. She flowed
and coiled, reshaping herself to the pulse of the music.
And the right-hand torch slid down her body—

The gauze, treated with perfumes, lipped by fire,
sent out its incense, the aroma seeming to brim the
room. The girl lifted the torch away, her throat curved
backward and her hair streamed to the floor. She held
the torch toward a ceiling-heaven, rather as they did
before the Fire Ride, then stroked the brand again
downward, to touch her length with flame.

The gauze that covered her sparkled, smoked—a
layer of the fabric dissolved in fire, vanished, then
another and another smoldered away to nothing. In

black moonrise, one bare exquisite night-shade breast
was revealed, tipped with a star of diamond.

The dinner party murmured its susurration of approval.

The dancer neither saw nor heard.

The left-hand torch was gliding about her now, at
her shoulder, her hip. The undulations of her torso
came more quickly, as if to flirt with the fire, or to
seduce it. The floating gauzes lit for a second, now
here, now there, flared, charred, magically disappeared,
each panel of color expending itself into another, and
the perfume coming and going. The drum galloped,
the pipe ran up and down. Fire fastened its teeth into
all her veils, and for a moment she seemed to catch
wholly alight, and some of the watchers, startled, cried
aloud—but the flame, judged to a hair's breadth, scattered from her like burning blossoms. She was bare to
her pelvis now, but for diamonds. Her anointed skin
itself smoldered from the brush of torches. A gem like
a dying coal crackled in her navel. The love affair with
fire began, as if reluctantly, to languish. . . . The dancer
was lethargic, the music altered at her mood, the
drums heavy. . . . She leaned to the fire, swooned
away from it. She drooped, folded herself, lay on the
mosaic and took the ivory fire-spikes from her own
hands, gripping them with her feet. Limpid and slow
as black molasses, she stood upright on her palms.
Her strong legs and narrow feet plied the two fires in
the air, then lowered them teasingly along her spine.
And suddenly she blazed, became a fireball—there was
only fire—out of which there catapulted a somersaulting
wheel of wild lights. It spun and came down and
turned to stone and was a woman.

The dancer stood scatheless before them, diamond-
breasted, diamonds woven at her loins, a garnet in her
belly, clothed otherwise only in faint smoke. The torches
were held outward stiffly from her sides. She was still
as a statue, seeing nothing and no one, as the music
ended.

Acclaim rang through the room. She did not note
the noise, nor stoop for the jewels that were laid—not
thrown—at her feet. Three princes came in turn and

gathered them up on her behalf, while her own slave approached to drape the dancer in a cloak of silk.

"Panduv, I never saw you better. You were embracing the Star itself." The Alisaarian aristocrat bowed to the dancer. Such was the code of Saardsinmey, which revered equally an aristocracy of talent. "Will you come back to my dinner when you've dressed? Say you will."

"I will not," said Panduv, regarding him for the first, and smiling.

"You desolate us."

"I'm expected elsewhere."

"Tomorrow, then?"

"Perhaps."

In the well-lit salon prepared for her convenience, Panduv cleansed her skin and donned her expensive garments. She drew a half-mask of thin hammered gold on to her lower face. It was an affectation, for all the city knew her, or of her, and besides, her covered carriage was always recognizable, Zakorian black, with the Double Moon and Dragon device of the Old Kingdom, once the sigil exclusively of rebels and pirates.

The slave-girl had collected the dancer's fee. As in the case of all the city's entertainer-elite, this was virtually superfluous. Her Swordsmen and charioteers were kings, and her acrobat dancers queens, welcomed and honored everywhere. It was well-documented, and might be seen anyway, any day on Tomb Street, that this fraternity died so rich their burial houses rivaled the sarcophagi of Dorthar's Storm Lords.

Even so, Panduv had not yet reached the pinnacle—to be accorded publicly the name of her birthplace, Hanassor. This recognition—which others, such as the Lydian, had gained—she had sworn to have, on the altar of Zakorian Zarduk, the fire god.

By the gate, the unmistakable carriage stood ready. Panduv entered it, and beheld another was before her.

A woman, mantled and hooded, who surely must have bribed the driver some vast amount, and be besides of high birth. It was almost Zastis. Such things did happen. The Zakorian was not necessarily averse, depending on what was offered when the wrappings came off.

"Good evening, lady," said Panduv, through her own mask. "I've contracted to be at the Guardian's palace before moonset. I can grant you a few minutes."

"Hanassor," said the other woman, softly. "You know nothing of it. Did they never tell you, for example, that the dancer's craft which brings your celebrity here, was reckoned of small worth, there? In the taverns of your Zakorian capital, women burnt their rags from them for a few coppers. It was a commonplace, not especially skilled. The clumsy were frequently scarred. Every such dancer was treated as a harlot. Go to Free Zakoris now, and see the value of a woman."

Panduv held her breath. Her hand slipped to her breast, to the dagger she wore there in a sheath of nacre. The intruder was a telepath. And one who could breach even a Vis mind having itself no such knack.

"Yes," said the hooded woman. "I can speak within. And read you quite well."

"Then you're Shansar." Panduv spoke with all the hauteur of Visian Alisaar.

"No. The Shansarians are not generally so adept. I am Amanackire."

Panduv swore. "A Lowlander."

"Amanackire, I said. There is a difference."

This then explained why the driver had allowed the woman into Panduv's carriage. While the invader-conquerors might occasionally be denied something, one denied nothing to Lowlanders. They could totter cities, the rabble of the serpent witch, and summon gods from under the sea.

"What do you want?" Panduv said. Patently it would not be oneself. Which was lucky, for white flesh repelled her.

"The Lydian," the woman said. "The Children of Daigoth know each other's business. Tell me how he's to be come at."

"You do surprise me," said Panduv. "How should I know? Go to the stadium. Petition him, like the others. Send a gift."

"You misunderstand what I want. To speak with him, privately."

"The stadium. Petition. A gift."

"Zakorian," said the woman. Her soft voice chilled the very air of that hot pre-Zastian night, "my kind are never refused."

"Then he won't refuse you. Why come to me?"

"To ease my path. Yes, now I see it. He's at a supper—will leave shortly, since in four days more he fights in the stadium—how explicit, your mind—And which homeward route will he walk, Panduv Am Hanassor, alone in Alisaarian night?" (Panduv, her inadvertent thoughts rifled, robbed, attempted to wall off her knowledge of the city's avenues. Failed, of course.) And, "Thank you," said this Amanackire bitch, gentle as a killing snow.

Just past midnight, a group of Saardsin Swordsmen came out from under the portico of a mansion of Pillar Square. They were laughing, and a touch drunk, dressed in all the splendor of youth and strength and money. One of their number was Rehger Am Ly Dis.

As they crossed under the columned arcades, moving toward Sword Street, a voice called to the Lydian.

His companions, unheeding, went on. He hesitated, and glanced back. A pale shadow, that of a woman, was framed between two pillars.

"Not tonight, beautiful," he said, already turning from her. "I fight the first day of Zastis."

Then he realized that no one had spoken. His name had been surely uttered, but within his own skull.

All the blond races boasted of their ability to mind-speak. Most unmixed Vis abhorred the notion. Rehger turned again, and went to the woman. A lamp burned near, but it was behind her; he could see nothing of her but the pallor of her cloak. He stood over her, and carefully shut the anger from his face and tone before addressing her.

"That trick could earn you a beating in New Alisaar. Don't do it, even in play." He looked around, and added, "Where's your escort?"

"I have none," she said. She used her real voice now, it was cool, it did not invite.

"That's unwise," he said. "Next time, take your servant or slave."

"Because only a champion is safe on these streets? Even cutthroats follow the races and are gamblers in Saardsinmey."

"No man would try for me," he said. "He knows I could kill him." It was not vanity, only a fact.

But she said, "No man would try for me. That would also mean death."

She took a step away, under the lamp. And as she did so, brushed the hood from her head.

He had never seen such whiteness. Perhaps, in a figurine of marble. Her skin, her hair—there was a trace of shadow on her brows and color at her lips, and maybe that was paint. Her eyes were unhuman, they rasped his senses—the white eyes of a snake—he did not want to look at them, or at any part of her.

All her race were said to be magicians. He supposed he believed it, seeing her.

"Why have you detained me?" he said.

"You acquiesce, then. I may detain any man I wish, roam where I will and as I want? You admit, my people have your people now under the booted heel."

"I'm a Swordsman and charioteer. I know nothing about your people."

"All Vis knows something of us."

"And a slave, the property of this city. My opinion isn't worth anything to you. So much said, lady, excuse me. Good night."

"I don't give you leave to go."

"Madam, with or without your leave, I regret."

He moved away from her and had begun to walk again toward Sword Street, when she said, "A paradox. A slave who is a king. Lydian."

"What do you want?" he said, finding he had stopped after all.

"Come to my house tomorrow evening."

"Again, my apologies. I'm obliged to be somewhere else."

"You can find it with no trouble. Ask on Gem-

Jewel Street. Anyone will tell you where the Amanackire is lodging."

He strode out now, and left her standing under the lamp.

The columns marched by him. Some were scratched with mottoes or poetry, or the names of fêted prostitutes.

He had known this city nearly all his life, been famed and free of it since his nineteenth year. Yet now some drifting memory of the other land, the first, surfaced in his mind. The mountains of Iscah. A woman, whose face he did not remember, only the springing blackness of her hair. He thought of her sometimes, his mother. Sometimes even, in lieu of jewels or the gold chain, he wore in his ear the stud of coin, the drak his father had paid her with for their night. He did not lament or eschew the incoherent past.

He recalled, too, more clearly than faces or words, how in that country one of the men had struck the woman (his mother), continuously. Here and now, no man who was clever lifted his hand to a woman in the Lydian's presence. He had required his preference, confronted by the white-eyed Lowlander. For he had felt in those minutes a thing which only came to him rarely in the stadium, the boiling itch of blood-desire. It seemed to him he had wanted her death.

CHAPTER SIX

CHACOR'S LUCK

The Star ascended, the night burned. From ship to shore, from avenue to promenade, in the sumptuous chambers of palaces, in huts piled up the hill behind the Street of Tombs, lovers loved. But in the courts of Daigoth, those men due to fight tomorrow lay watchful, and hungry. The phallus must become the sword.

The shows were always very good, in the initial days of Zastis.

Before sunrise, before the great hawks, which hunted over the crags of the city, launched themselves into a hollowing sky, fighters were at exercise in the stadium yards.

"The Corhlan is in love with Rehger. The chariots weren't enough for him, he'll be back for more."

"What can dung-heap Corhl offer him? If he can win a bout here, even unowned as he is, he might make some cash."

Boastful, the slave-Swords. Free men were poor things. No one worshiped them enough to keep them. Often they came here, these outsiders, to try the lots, chancing their arm against Saardsinmey heroes. Generally they left the stadium feet-foremost in carts.

Those that sparred with Rehger knew that he, or they, were capable of finishing any Corhlan, if it came to it. This was Zastis, and every man at work here in the dawn mingled words and unspoken concepts of sex with the killer's banter. Not one Saardsin would be drawn against another—that, too, was Daigoth's law. They would be tried on the blades of other cities, other lands. So it was safe to mention death. You did not slay your brothers. And who wanted to grow old?

The sun rose, climbed. The exercise court was empty.

The noise of the morning city came and went. Over the high stadium walls, the sky hammered out its blue.

Slaves appeared with their baskets and scoops of sand. The central platform had been lowered, and the whole great oval stretched flat. The slaves scattered the sand thick and white across it, everywhere, making the stadium into a beach. A sea would break upon this beach, of a sort.

At noon, the gates were thrown open. The crowd crowded in. Colors poured down the terraces. The smell of scent, sweat, and fruit, changed the air into a pomade. But soon there would be, too, the butchery smell of blood, to lay the perfume and the sand.

Because he was a free man and an amateur, not bred and molded to the customs of a stadium, Chacor

the Corhl had spent the foregoing night with two girls.
It had been far from a random tryst. He had sought it
purposely, intending to rid himself of the first need of
Zastis, and leave mind and body clear for the fray.
The idea of starving the need and deploying it as a
weapon was one he would not have entertained. Such
things Zakorian pirates did to their oars-slaves, chain-
ing them during the Red Moon so they could not
even see to themselves, until the act of rowing became
the only release.

Meanwhile, Chacor's luck in surviving the chariot
race had prompted him to display other skills. It was
true, there was nothing much for him at home. He had
come out of Corhl with only his goddess for property.
In little towns of Ott, Iscah, and unfree Vardian
Zakoris, he had beaten the locals at this and that. The
cities of New Alisaar, with their codes of dueling and
betting and their choice of public games, had lured
him on. Perhaps he wanted glory more than wealth,
but pure metal bars and bags of draks were not
uncharming.

He had also, in a young man's way, become ob-
sessed by the Lydian, and wanted to fight him. The
Lydian was a slave, a king, a god, and an older male.
Just as the three-year stallion animal would try to oust
the herd-lord, Chacor longed to challenge him, tussle,
bring him down, or at least to taste the strength of
what bettered him and would not yield. Envy and
admiration mixed in it. Besides, he could not help but
be aware, on some mostly submerged level, that the
Lydian Swordsman, vastly his superior in skill, would
not slay a free man the crowd was partial to. A sense
of the hazard, the mere foolhardiness of the venture,
were not let past the Corhlan's mental doors. Indeed,
he had been praying to Corrah for this chance, to be
drawn in the lots against Saardsinmey's champion.
Obscurely, since Corrah and Cah—the goddess of
Iscah—were one, Chacor imagined she might wish
also to bring both of her sons together, like any primi-
tive mother of the region, to do battle. Not a hundred
years ago, Alisaar's princes fought each other to the
death for the kingship. In Free Zakoris they did it still,

and in several areas of the western lands, many, noble
or peasant, kept the tradition.

Chacor, if his family had retained this method, believed he could have disposed of all his legal brothers,
and so inherited his father's small wooden palace in
the forested swamps of Corhl. But Corrah had instead
meant him for a wanderer. Corrah had brought him
here to match him with the Lydian.

Convinced he could not die, the Corhl thought to
himself, *And if he kills me, that's glory, too.*

The acrobats came out first, clad as characters from
myth, or beasts, and did their tricks, chancy, spectacular and ribald by turns. Then there was a mock race,
spoof of the Fire Ride, teams of waddling orynx drawing flimsy gilded cars. Snorting and defecating in rage,
the orynx soon ran amok and the chariots collided and
collapsed, the charioteers tumbling and diving in all
directions. The winner gained the favors of a promis-
ing maiden, but was only allowed to embrace her
while hung upside down from a pole. After several
attempts, during which the crowd laughed and proffered
instructions, the lady ran off with a monkey.

Following the acrobats, the creatures of the stadium
menagerie were paraded, swamp leopards in jeweled
collars, fighting-bis, plumed and hooded, a pride of
Vardian lions with gold in their ears and manes, Shansar
horses, neighing, brindled kalinx, and apes as tall as a
man.

A selection of these animals might be reared for
combat, but generally they were trained for use in
religious processions, or to spice scenes of terror in the
theaters. The citizens, diverted by a display of their
possessions, always, weighed and measured and evalu-
ated, and threw flowers to the lions.

When the display had finished, and the stadium,
where necessary, had been swept and freshly sanded,
there sounded the blast of brass horns.

It was at that moment, when all eyes were inclined
to fix passionately on the arena, that a slight stir ran
along the eastern tiers. Someone had come late, and
appeared suddenly in one of the boxes to the left of

the Guardian's seat. This was the section reserved for
women of rank. A fringed awning mantled it, and here
and there were screens of pierced stone behind which
the boxes' occupants might modestly conceal themselves, a convention seldom observed. Those female
aristocrats who attended the sports alone, made display, each jamming the box with her retinue and
bodyguard.

There had been a rumor for most of the month that
an Amanackire was in the city. Now, she was here.
Clothed entirely in white, her ice hair lit with silver
ornaments, she entered the box, unguarded, without a
single slave, and sat down there.

The Guardian was absent on political affairs. His
counselor, occupying the center box, angled himself to
favor the white woman with a stare. When she turned,
his nod of courteous deference underlined a plain disapproval, both of her boldness and her life. But her
cold, cold eyes returned him nothing. She looked away
as if she had not seen him, or, seeing him, had not
thought him to matter. She, too, fixed her gaze downward on the stadium floor.

The Swordsmen were coming out on to the sand.
The attention of the eastern tiers refocused itself.

There were eighteen pairs of fighters, eighteen
Saardsins matched with eighteen contenders, slave-
Sword or free, from the rest of Vis. They were strate-
gically spaced around the stadium, to give every part
of the terraces the view of an individual battle, at least
in its commencement. As habitually, the Swordsmen
of whom the most was expected were ranged along the
portion of arena below the Guardian's seat and the
boxes of the rich and royal.

Here, then, the Lydian, with either side, at a distance of some fifteen feet, two Zakor-born champions,
the Ylan, who had only recently earned for himself
recognition by the name of birthplace, and the older
man famous with axe and mallet, nicknamed the Iron
Ox.

The crowd yelled and waved its arms. Flowers fell
for the beauty of dangerous men as for the danger of
beauteous beasts.

Armored at loins, right forearm and calves, heads
helmed and eyes shuttered behind the sealed visors,
already in the drug-dream heat, Zastis, the glare of
the sand, the love-partnership each man with the man
before him, Daigoth's Marriage of the Sword—not
one looked upward to the tiers, or into the boxes.

Chacor had been aggrieved. The lot had not cast
him with the Lydian. He was paired, on the north side
of the stadium, with an Alisaarian-born Sword. Nevertheless, everything was not lost. Overwhelm the
Alisaarian, and Chacor might choose his next "Marriage" from any Saardsin also rendered partnerless by
success. So it would go on, until every man had been
fought out and a majority of one side only, the Swords
of Saardsinmey, or her foreign challengers, were on
their feet. Grueling, this bout, as only Alisaar could
devise. But when the Lydian fought, the city, without
exception, won. He had never left this place other
than on his feet, sometimes bloody, but always unbeaten.

Since his mastery of the chariot race, more than
usual was anticipated from him today, and the betting
had been fraught if biased.

The wise gamblers of the city had seen Regher's
kind before. Like the orchid, they broke quickly to
bloom, and burned in brightest magnificence a handful
of years. Then the gods, sensible men must not rival
them too long, cut the plant to the ground.

The horns brayed, and the Alisaarian's steel came
like a flash of water, to slice Chacor's arm to the bone.
But Chacor was away. He grinned, and slammed back
with a rough crazy stroke, never completed, instead
switched sideways as the Alisaarian moved, disdain-
fully to block it. Chacor's blade, like all the rest burnished to blind, tickled the Alisaarian's ribs into a
thread of blood.

Above, the north tiers, having noted the impudent
Corhlan was returned, gave him a howl of wrath and
glee. He was valued as lucky, and had been bet upon.

The Alisaar, put out to be bleeding, struck back
with his own feint, which Chacor dismissed, catching
the actual blow squarely on the oblong stadium shield.

Then, abruptly tilting the shield, pushed his opponent's sword wide, an equally unpredicted deed the
Alisaar did not care for; he was forced to hurry in his
own shield as Chacor, excited now, drove for his guts.

"Fool," remarked the Alisaarian.

"Accursed-of-Corrah," replied Chacor.

It was a mistake to converse while fighting, but one
commonly made by free men used to backland duels.

"What?" encouraged the Alisaarian.

As Chacor gladly repeated what he had said, with a
jewel or two added, the Alisaarian set his sword glancing, left, right, left—smashing upward as he did so
with the shield. In three seconds Chacor found himself
nipped in the right shoulder, left forearm bruised from
the impact of the brass shield rim. Such injuries, far
from fatal, could nevertheless tell. While anything that
bled shortened a fighter's time on the sand.

A rolling gasp went over the north tiers, ending in
unholy roaring. A man had gone down to the left, not
a Saardsin. (Lost in the universal shouting and clamor,
the fate of the Lydian's partner at the eastern end.)
Chacor, angry at his error, smarting, wished now he
had not ridden with those girls last night. He could
see, from a curious glow in the Alisaar's mask-framed
eyes, that unspent sex might also have its worth.

Then the Alisaar aimed a stroke that almost took
Chacor's arm from his body.

Springing backward, propelled by the instincts of
panic-speed, Chacor's feet slid in wetness. (The Saardsin
leftward had finished his man, blood ran in a river.)
Chacor fell, had fallen. Bloody sand burned his shoulders, and the Alisaar loomed over him, laughing, ready.
Yes, there were frequent kills at Zastis. Chacor had
learned that, from the Alisaar's eyes. Above, the crowd
were moaning and swaying, crying out, caught in Zastian
sex-death-blood-lust.

As the Alisaarian's sword came plunging down,
Chacor brought up his shield with all his strength
behind it. Death-desire met life-wish. The shield's metal
buckled and the wooden frame under the owar-hide
gave way. As the point of the sword tore through,
Chacor rolled aside from it. The Alisaarian, cheated

of murder, only the wrecked shield on his sword,
unbalanced, hung forward in the air. The Corhl came
to his feet, slipping, grasping, deadly silent now, and
slammed into the leaning man. As the Alisaarian went
down, Chacor, who in all his itinerant brawls had
never killed, fell again, astride him, and forced his
sword half its length through flesh, muscle and pounding heart.

The Saardsin died with one orgasmic shudder, giving no audible sound.

Not so, the terraces. Curses and women's scarves
descended on Chacor as he rose up wildly, driven
mad, shieldless—grabbing the Alisaarian's shield—
looking east.

Then, past the couples of fighting men, the length of
the stadium north to east, the Corhlan ran, brandish-
ing the red sword, yelling the name of the one he
wanted.

The Lydian had not killed. The two challengers he
had disposed of he had removed by temporarily crip-
pling them. They lay bleeding and semi-conscious
against the terrace barrier, awaiting perforce the bout's
end to be carried to a surgeon. Killing was another
matter. He did not want it. This might disappoint the
crowd, but the fireworks of his swordsmanship so far
held them cheering him. Though, too, they urged him
to use his genius more cruelly. There had been times
in the stadium, not always at Zastis, when Rehger also
had come to want a man's death. Such occasions were
not predictable. When the prompting took him, he
obeyed. He killed. That was all. He never made a
record of numbers, nor kept count, even, as some did,
of names, countries, dating his life: *That morning I did
for the Istrian; that race when I broke the mix's neck.*

On his left, the Ylan had wounded once, and killed
twice. Rehger had not witnessed it, but heard, on the
edges of awareness, the sea-sound of the crowd shot
up in great waves.

The Iron Ox, to the right, had himself been hurt.
He fought on, dispatched adversaries, but inexorably
slowing. If he had his wits, he would presently sham a

swoon. The crowd liked him; he could afford to skive, and win them back another day.

As the Lydian shed the third man—(unseaming the skin from knee to pectoral, a gaudy wound that, ending just under the nipple, induced fainting swiftly in a tired and unprofessional duelist), someone shouted his name. Not from the stands, which was perpetual, from the arena.

Rehger turned, and found the boy from Corhl before him, sword anointed tip to grip, face insane with the fighter's lust.

From the look he had taken a life, for the first time. Like loss of any virginity, it was significant, that first. He was bleeding himself, a scratch on the right shoulder, not yet impeding him. The Corhlan was untrained, and craving, as they said, to touch the sun.

Fortune had spoiled him, in the race.

Fortune was trustless.

The boy was maybe three or four years Rehger's junior, in other ways younger still. Not done growing yet, he lacked the Lydian's height, but then few men were as tall, and since his twentieth year, he had met none taller.

The Corhlan was smiling, his eyes burning on Rehger. So the hunter might dwell on his prey, so a woman might ponder a man she hoped would possess her.

The tiers had laughed at the boy's headlong stampede, his need to meet the Lydian, and now they were saluting him, his valor and his idiocy. At least, probably, if he fought well, they would not regret watching him spared.

Rehger moved, slowly enough that the boy could see he was accepted and that it had begun.

The Corhlan made one beautiful answer, skimming with the sword—but, instantly checked by Rehger's nearly gentle counterstroke, reacted with a clottish swing. From that, Rehger merely stepped away, as if ignoring a piece of pointless bad manners.

This was how the Corhlan would fight, then. Artist and dolt by turns. Katemval would have said, if he had been child-sold to a stadium something might have

been made of him. But he was free, and it was too late
now.

And then—chaos claimed the world.

It was so ridiculous, so incompatible, that for a
moment Rehger paid no heed to it, only readjusting
his reflexes and his touch as if in response to some
natural happenstance.

It took him a few seconds more to realize that,
although this had taken place, and continued to do so,
it was impossible, and therefore he had no jurisdiction
over it.

He had lost control of the sword in his hand. Lost it
completely. The sword was *alive*. It tugged and pulled
against him, it twisted against his palm. As he raised
it, it resisted, and the length of it thrummed. Cold as
ice, charged with an energy, a strength that wrestled
with his own—

Before his mind had even laid hold of the facts, his
entire body broke into a freezing scalding sweat—not
of fear—of pure horror.

Witchcraft. A spell. Yes, Rehger could credit these.
But whose work? The Corhlan's? The power did not
seem to come from him—

Struggling, a live enemy for a weapon, his actions
suddenly labored and arbitrary, the Lydian strove to
contain the boy's gadfly attack.

(The tiers, supposing their champion taunted the
swingeing young Corhl by mimicry, lovingly chided and
clapped him.)

But the Corhlan was falling back, retreating. Under
the dark Vis tan, his face had paled below the pallor
of excitement. His eyes were on the bewitched sword.

So Rehger had an inch to spare, to glance, to see for
himself.

They called it Shansarian magic. A trick of the
Ashara temples. Katemval, who had beheld it done
often in Sh'alis, had ascribed it to drugged incense and
hallucination, or some odder ability to flex metal.
Snakes became swords, swords were changed to snakes.

In his hand, the grip to the hilt remained, though it
rippled with convulsive life. The hilt had shrunk to a
kind of spine, quivering with the movement of the rest.

Under what was left of the hilt, the full length the sword had been, a *serpent*. Stiffly stretched, it was writhing to rid itself, even as he grasped it, of the final vestiges of the steel. It was the color of milk, the hard clinkered scales gleaming like platinum. The eyes stared from its flat head, soulless white— He knew then whose power had formed the spell.

The impulse was to fling it from him. There was an inherent loathing in the Vis, of snakes, which the people of the snake goddess had fed on and fostered. Real or illusion, to clutch this thing now, as it strove to full animation, turned the stomach, destroyed the will.

It must be she meant him to die. To die in shame, before his hour. He felt her cold eyes on him now.

And then, as if by that recognition of her, as of his fear and anger, he had satisfied the Amanackire sorceress, the sword returned to him. The snake disappeared. There was the flash of metal. Slim and balanced, it filled his hand, his servant, his. For how long? Now he could not rely upon the blade. The steel was a white snake, inside. He had seen it loosed. It might, having learned the truth of its nature, at any moment aspire to it again—

All this had taken only seconds. The crowd had noted nothing, only the Lydian's joke of hamfistedness, the retreat of the Corhlan, the tiny pause that sometimes came in combat before some decisive blow.

Rehger's skull sang. His vision was blurred, and his body too light. Such sensations followed great exertion and bloodloss. They were the prelude to death-danger. You could not stay long on the sand then, you must complete the task.

His hand on the sword felt numb now. The leaden beats of his heart tolled through him. He was past fear and shame, numbed like the sword hand. So it would be, on his death day.

The Corhlan was fighting him, his face full of the terror and fury Rehger had lost. The Corhlan did not understand, but the sorcery had him yet, its teeth in his throat.

Somewhere, the abacus in the Lydian's brain had

kept score, by the noises of the crowd, how many Saardsins had fallen or triumphed, and their popular status, how many men had been discommoded and hacked. Three or four fights still went on and were the last, this being one of them. Then it would be done.

Rehger moved suddenly. As the weakness dragged from him like a cloak, every failure and shadow of his life swept up on him. They were strangers, these emotions, yet they knew him.

He clipped leftward with the serpent sword, and doubled the blow, and the Corhlan's shield clanged down at their feet.

It was not a matter of art any more. A howling mob ran on Rehger's heels.

He saw the young man's eyes, beautiful as a girl's, widen with shock and dismay. Then Rehger brought the sword downward, gods' fire from the sky, and cleaved through him, from the left side of the neck to the breastbone.

The stroke required colossal strength (the clavicle had been shattered), perfect judgment. It was, nonetheless, a butcher's.

The tiers, amazed by rapidity, one falling figure, the abrupt climax, its glamorous awfulness, erupted. Women shrieked. Well, one had known they liked the Corhl.

Regher did not acknowledge them. He stood, the sword ripped from his hand, looking at the unconscious youth dying in front of him.

When the paean of the trumpets rang out, with those who had survived and could, Rehger raised his arm to acknowledge a teem of praise and veils.

He neither searched for the Amanackire among the boxes, nor gazed after the surgeons' carts which were coming up to tidy the corpses and the maimed.

He walked from the stadium, and passing into the rooms below, allowed himself to be stripped of armor and leather. Then, going to the bath, was cleansed in turn of dust and sweat and the blood of others.

A group of noblemen who had come down to laud him, found him stretched along a pallet of the empty upper dormitory, his head on his arms, as if for sleep. "Forgive me," he said. Swordsmen might wax moody after their prettiest battles, it was well-known, nor was the lion-orchid of Ly Dis any exception. They spoke awhile of poets and women, to him, and awarded him their presents, and tossed a garland of golden poppies over his head, before leaving him.

Then, only then, he wept.

The man stood immovably in the entrance of hell.

"I beg your pardon, lady," he said. "You can't come in here."

The torchlit corridor beneath the stadium was very dark, the cavern which opened beyond the man, evilly-lit by braziers, had its own darkness. The woman gleamed between, too white, too ghostly, omen of all things bad.

And now she said, looking in his eyes with her own that were like sightless mirrors, "You see who I am. Stand aside."

"Yes, I see. I'm very respectful, I'm sure. But no woman gets in here. Not even the whores, to say good-bye."

Behind him, emphasizing everything, a man shrieked out in agony. That would be the one the Iron Ox had taken last. It was, altogether, the surgeons' room, no place for the curious, whatever bribe or threat they offered.

"The Corhl," the woman said.

"Oh, yes."

"He's alive," said the woman.

"Somehow. His own gods know how. When they haul the steel out of him he'll hemorrhage and die, anyway."

"Let me by," she said.

The man, like all Vis, knew of the Amanackire, what they were said to be, and to be able to do. But that Yllumite the Iron Ox had filleted, he was screaming now on and on, halting only to get breath. The man in the entrance said to the Amanackire, "Why don't you, lady, go and find your goddess, and when you do, crawl up her hole."

Then something hit him in the chest. Like some beefy fist, it knocked him back, into the upright of the doorway, winded. As he lay on the wall gasping, the Amanackire woman went by him, into the place beyond.

The murky room, stinking of hot metal, blood, offal and medicine, was very busy. The doctors bent to their work beneath the low-slung lamps. A gaggle of boys ran about with boiled water for the implements, the hooks and knives and bone-saws. Another made rounds with a pitcher of wine. He stared at the white being as he went by, and signed himself for divine protection.

The Yllumite had died abruptly and his cries were ended.

The surgeon straightened, washed his hands in the bowl one of the boys had brought. He turned, desultory, to the couch where another casualty lay, a sword wedged among splinters of shattered collarbone, in the meat of shoulder and breast.

The surgeon was anatomically impressed by the force of the blow; perhaps there had already been a weakness in the clavicle. . . .

"That must come out," the surgeon said. "We don't let him die by the long road. There's not much left, but hold him," he added. No one moved. The surgeon looked up and saw the woman who had come to the head of the couch. "Lady, you shouldn't be here. Get out." And heard how the boys muttered with fright that he had so addressed a white Lowlander.

For the woman, she took no notice.

"Lady," he said, "I'm sorry if he was something to you, but he's lost his race. You don't want him to suffer? Go out, or move back. The blood'll splash you."

And he set his grip on the sword.

Before he could do more, one of the woman's slender hands came down on his.

The hand was the color of snow. It repulsed him, its whiteness on his own black-copper—he expected her skin to be cold, but she was warm, as he was.

"I will do it," she said.

"*Daigoth's eyes.* Don't be a fool, woman."

"Stand away," she said.

A silence had fallen over the whole wide room.

To his annoyance, the surgeon discovered he had stepped off as instructed.

Then, while the room watched, the Amanackire drew the sword backward out of the Corhlan's body, as smoothly as from a sheath of silk.

A dew of blood scattered the wounded man's flesh, the cover on the couch. Where the steel had divided him, a ragged purple stripe now crossed the top of his breast, from the base of the neck to just above the center of the rib cage. The woman, letting go of the sword she had extracted, leant forward, and her silver hair rained over him, hiding what she did. When she lifted her hands and her head, there was nothing on the surface of the Corhlan's body at all, save a single bead of blood, which slowly trickled away.

Without another word, the Amanackire returned across the speechless frozen room, passed through its doorway, and was gone.

CHAPTER SEVEN

THE KING'S MARK

The sunset hung like a scarlet awning over the city. The day's stadium events, which had ended with Zakorian wrestling and three nine-lap races, each with a favorite charioteer, had left the gamblers to rejoice or lick their aches.

A bizarre story was going round by lamplighting. The beserk young Corhl, given so obviously to death before the multitude, had been improbably saved by the surgeons.

Of the Lydian, immediately forgiven the Zastis-excess of killing him, there was no special news.

As the sun declined, leaving pools of red along the ground, Rehger was among the stalls of the hiddrax, up behind the stadium on the northwest side. Each racer of worth reckoned to have his own particular team by his twenty-second year, as he would expect his chariots built for him by the best carriage-makers of Alisaar.

Rehger's hiddraxi, who had taken him to the summit of the Fire Ride, now stood kissing his shoulders and receiving fruit from his hands.

But for the humming of the sea-hemmed city, the evening was quiet here. A few grooms went about on their agenda, the hiddrax stirred the straw and ate. North, from the horse stables, there came a vague hubbub. There had been a horse-race, too, this afternoon, and the precious beasts were not yet settled.

"Listen, my soul," said Rehger to the hiddraxi. "Listen to the uproar they're making. And not one to race as you race, like wind and fire. Best on the earth, my loved ones."

A groom came across the court, leading a black saddle thoroughbred, and stopped by the arch, where the team-hiddrax could not see too much of it.

Presently Rehger went out. He was to dine with a merchant-lord, the very one who had gifted him this mount two seasons ago.

As he stood in the rich light, checking the animal's recently shod hoofs, the groom said, "Lydian, you'll want to know. That Corhlan boy, he's alive."

Rehger did not hesitate, picked up another hoof.

"Yes. Not for much longer."

"Something happened. There was a woman, one of the white Lowlanders. But she knew some trick, and they healed him."

"No," said Rehger. He let go the last hoof, straightened, rubbed his fingers along the thoroughbred's neck.

"*Yes*, Lydian. I swear it. The whole stadium knows. Ask anyone."

"Yes," said Rehger.

"There's not even a scar on him."

Rehger mounted, and turned the thoroughbred out through the arch, into the mouth of the sunset, then south down the curve of the high, tree-lined avenue, with its view of the distant ocean, into the city.

*   *   *

It was Zastis after all, Saardsinmey more than usually frenetic. In less than a mile he had been approached more than ten times, always decorously, always part-sensually, to be told the Corhlan lived.

By the hour he rode into New Dagger Lane, he had come to credit it. He had destroyed the Corhlan. There was no chance any man might recover from such a stroke. Rehger had felt an extra guilt that he had not himself withdrawn the sword there and then and, if needful, ended the boy's pain. But Rehger had not been able to take up that sword, that sword which had become a serpent.

A white Lowlander—the groom's words. The sorcery that could accomplish one such trick—why not another? Blade to life, dead to life—

Sinking into the oblivion of fatigue, the victory diadem of poppies yet on his head, Rehger had dreamed the earth shook, columns toppled, and mountains. White seared on redness and rushed into a void of black. The Lowlanders had cast down the ancient capital of Dorthar by an earthquake. They had called gods from the sea.

"Lydian! Lydian!" Young tavern girls in the blushed dusk, gilded bells in their plaited hair. "Oh, Lydian—are you glad or sorry that boy's alive?"

"Is he?"

"Yes, oh, yes."

"Where is he then?" He laughed down at them as they laughed up at him, putting blossoms into the mane of the thoroughbred, touching his ankle or foot shyly, pressing their breasts against the animal, wanting the man.

"With *her*," one said. "The white one. She healed him by Lowland witchcraft. He's her prize then, isn't he. He's handsome, Lydian." She gazed into his eyes, unable to help herself.

He put them softly aside, and rode on, and they let him go, standing to speak of him under one of the night-blooming torch-poles.

Nearly at the merchant's doors, Rehger quickened the thoroughbred into a trot. They went straight by,

down Sword Street, over Pillar Square, and through
the maze of slighter roads that led south.

At the fountain on Gem-Jewel Street, he reined the
beast in. Across the way, on the stair of a prosperous
wine-shop, a man opened wide his arms.

"Thanks for my winnings, Lydian, may your gods
always love you. Will you delight us by drinking here?
Good wine, happy girls."

"Another night," the Lydian said. Then, as she had
told him to, he asked, "The Amanackire woman. She
lodges on this street?"

The man's arms fell, and his face. He looked uncer-
tain, but he said, "By the lacemakers. The tiled house
with the high wall."

The house stood back in the alley that curled behind
the lacemakers. In the wall, a gate of ornamental iron
gave at a thrust. A garden lay there, with trees, and
overgrown by dry grass. Flushed starlight fingered a
choked pool.

The lower floor of the house seemed in disrepair
and unoccupied. In the second story a cluster of windows showed light within their grills.

Rehger, having tethered his animal, went in by the
unlocked entry and ascended to the upper story.

A lit lamp hung over the door, and a bell, in the
Alisaarian manner.

A minute went by, during which he thought of nothing, did nothing. Then, as he reached toward the
bell again, the door was opened. A servant, a tawny
mix girl with those eyes one came to see sometimes
in three or four generation mixes, clear brown as
ale. She said nothing, but stood aside to let him
enter, then led him through the outer chamber into
a salon.

This also was lamplit, the flames under painted glass,
that set the room awash with pale rainbow colors. The
furnishings were simple, not comfortless but with none
of the luxurious clutter Rehger associated with wealth
and women. He scarcely saw any of it. On a table, a
crystal jug and beakers. The servant girl went there
and poured him a drink unrequested. It was yellow

Lowland wine, he had never seen it before, and stared into the cup before motioning her to take it away.

The girl did not argue with him. She replaced the cup upon the table, and went softly from the room.

Rehger stood, waiting, not thinking, clothed in his elegant garments for dining, his fighter's meticulous grace. The Corhlan was not here. He knew that. Only she.

There was a perfume on the air. Not of the usual sort, bottled essences and burning gums.

A curtain drifted. She entered the salon, the Amanackire.

"Be welcome," she said, and bowed to him. Lowland courtesy, meaningless. Or a jibe.

"Thank you. Am I welcome also to lay hands on and kill you?"

"You have done your killing," she said, "in the stadium."

"Yes, and been cheated of it, I heard. Is it a lie? The Corhl stays dead."

"He lives."

"I've only your word for that."

"And the word of the whole city, which brought you here."

"No, madam," he said, "I meant to call on you anyway. You played a game with me today. I didn't care for it."

She watched him across the length of the room, the wavering rainbows of light.

"Why?" he said. His voice had nothing in it, except perplexity. He could not strike her or rage against her. With no woman on earth would he ever do that. So what was left to him? She was not tall for her sex, and slender, a breakable thing that did not even look human. He went toward her because that was all he could do, as if proximity might invite reason.

"Ice in the sun," she said. "You, and all men. This city."

"If you invade my mind," he said, "you'll find nothing of use to you."

"You are too modest."

"Do it then. I can't stop you. But why bother with it, or with the sword? Or to save the boy's life?"

"It was owed to him. It was my fault that you harmed him as you did."

The perfume came from her. It was not perfume. It was the scent of her skin, and hair.

The crown of her head hardly reached his shoulder. And her face was a girl's, she could be no older than the boy she had raised from the dead.

"This is so," she replied, to his thoughts. "Yet I have a power in me and upon me. You never met a man in your arena of blood and steel who had such power. Lydian, I could end your life in moments, by will alone. Do you believe me?"

"Perhaps," he said.

"Look," she said. She raised her hand, and her hand began to blaze. He saw its bones, he saw white fire where flesh should be. Then the blaze went out. Her hand was only white, and the arm, white as lilies, ringed by a bracelet of white enamel darker than her skin. The bracelet was a snake, with tintless zircons for eyes.

"Temple sorcery," he said. "But what's your quarrel with me?"

There were pink pearls in her hair, and a drop of rosy amber, the Lowlanders' sacred resin, depended above and between her brows.

She was beautiful, but not as something born; too beautiful, as something fashioned, sculpted. Yet she was alive, he saw her breathing, and felt the warmth of her, so close now in the heat of night.

There was in fact a depth to her eyes. This near to her, he could not help but see it. A depth without a floor, bottomless.

"Why?" he said to her again. He leaned forward as he spoke, so the word itself should brush her lips. "I seldom fought a man whose name I knew. It's a Swordsman's superstition, you may have heard of it. Are you afraid then, to give me your name?"

"My name is Aztira," she said. "Shall I say yours?"

"Say it."

"*Amrek*," she said. Her voice was a wire of hatred.

"Amrek, the Enemy, branded by the bane of Anackire. Genocide, and monster."

He stood back from her, startled despite everything. He did not know the name, or if he did, it was nothing to him—some king out of history, dead a century or more.

"Your wrist," she said. "What is *that?*

He said, calmly, his heart thundering, "This? A birthmark. I've had it since childhood."

"Yes, birth-marked for sure. Her mark. Her curse on him, on you, son to daughter to son."

Rehger took his eyes with difficulty away from her. He looked at the thin silvery ring around his left wrist, familiar to him, forgotten.

Then he looked again at her.

But all at once she turned from him. As he had done, and with the same recognizable muted violence, she wept.

In his experience, which was limited in such things, women did not weep for any cause. They wept when there was none. Moods of amorous passion or jealousy, to conceal, over little things—the loss of a lover or an earring. In his limited world, no woman had ever shed tears at misery or pain—slave-girls beaten, an old beggar-crone huddled in Iscaian snow. . . . his mother kicked across the dirt floor of the hovel: Dry eyed.

Yet, some inner sense, recognizing her real anguish, for he had been shown something of her strength, moved him to pity.

Almost unremembering their prelude, he took hold of her carefully, quietly, to soothe her. And as against the white silk of her hair and skin he saw the metallic darkness of his hands, bronze on marble, his body, waiting all this while in Zastis cunning, astonished him with a sudden bolt of hungry lust. What he had disliked before, it was this very thing which ravened now through his veins.

He was not amazed that she slid instantly from him. They were cold as they looked, her kind, so it was said.

She had not let him see her tears, only hear them,

and now she moved before a window, her face to the garden shadows, hiding herself still.

"I've been greatly mistaken," she said. "In everything. A blind, meddling child. Go away, Swordsman. Go to your own, of whom you have no fear. For I fear you, and I fear them, your Alisaarians, your peoples of black Vis. And my own kind also, I am afraid of them." She gripped the iron of the grill in both her hands. *Oh, Rehger!* she cried out. "Warn this city! Warn them—tell them—"

She was on her knees beneath the grill, still gripping the iron in her hands as he had seen prisoners do, or men dying in agony. Her weeping now was terrible to hear. Death's music, grief that was triumphant.

To question her, to think that she might be questioned, was impossible. Since he might otherwise only console her in the Zastian mode she would abhor and resist, he did as she said. He went away.

The merchant was cheated of his dinner guest that night. But it was Zastis. Heroes, immune to cutthroats, might yet be waylaid at every corner. . .

He had gone to the inn on Five Mile Street, the drinking-house that he would visit before an event, to taste the "last sweet cup." (One day that would be true.) He had been there the night before. To go back after the stadium was a favor they would value.

He did not climb up to the roof, but sought the smaller court to the building's rear, from which, once in a way, you might catch the sighing of the ocean. It was a spot for trysts, vacant tonight, as he had foreseen, for all the assignations had been made. The Lydian did not want fame or celebration, he did not want to drink.

The girl who came to him through the vine shadows was Velva. Her skin, darkest honey, was as smooth, her face clear of the blow the Var-Zakor mix had given her, for the physician on Sword Street was excellent, even if he could not cure the dead—

She drew in her breath when she saw the man under the vines. The fragrance of her caught in his brain.

Her hair, as his had been, was wreathed by golden poppies.

"What can I bring?" she murmured.

"You." He took coins and put them in her palm, holding her fingers closed upon the money. "If you can, and will."

"Yes—" she said. Her eyes flamed in the light of the Star.

"Not a room here," he said. "Come to the shore with me. Give the cash to him. Tell him I want you for the night."

"No *payment*—not from you— He wouldn't."

"Yes, payment. And more for yourself."

"No." But she ran to take the politeness of the coins to the inn-lord, her anklets ringing.

When she came back, her eyes were lowered. She let him lead her down out of the inn to the yard, and lift her up before him on the black thoroughbred.

Five Mile Street was loud with people and lights. Here and there someone greeted the champion, but soon they turned into the side alleys that ran toward the market.

Near the harbor wall a sentry or two gave them a mild good night. The Guardian's men knew well enough who this rider was, but made no comment. With all the palace and aristocratic liaisons he could choose from, if he wanted to bring a wine-girl to the beach, that was his business. As for such a man being a slave, this sort of slave did not seek to break for liberty. Bred for their destiny, whatever other thing could offer them what slavery gave? The gods of the stadium went where and how they pleased.

As they rode down the path into the vast, plush, reddened black of sea and night, he began to caress her. The entire ride had been a caress, their bodies moving against each other, his arms roping her as he held the reins.

The pleated sea was fired by the Star. The Red Moon scorched behind the heights of the city. Nearest of all to heaven and to Zastis, strangely, the long hill combered by the tombs of the dead—

Under the rock, at the sea's edge, the Lydian lay

over Velva in a bath of satin sand. Her flesh burned
with the light, her breasts tasted of powders and cinnamon, and of the salt of the ocean, budding against,
within his mouth— She could not be still, her hair
furling in inky coils along the dune, her hands polishing his skin, every muscle and tendon waking at her
touch— She fell back dying into ecstasy long before he
had penetrated the sea-cave between her thighs. He
laughed at her rapture, cradling her through the joy,
beginning again to court her even as it ended. When
he took her, she was already crying out, calling thin
and disembodied as a sea-bird— He thrust to the
center of the sweetness, and the fount of life surged
from him, excruciating pleasure, with the misleading
finality in it of death. The poppies of her garland had
been crushed between them.

In the brief hiatus, before the urging of the Star
seized on him again, Rehger heard the waves on the
shores of Alisaar, as he had heard them some eighteen
or nineteen years. Changeless, those waters. Mankind
did not matter. Once could know that at such moments, and not mind.

He had come to this southern city to enable them to
betroth him to a girl he had never seen. She was
apparently most beautiful. That did not encourage
him; his mother was beautiful, the bitch of bitches, a
Dortharian woman who plastered her skin with white.
Why? To be different from every other woman of Vis.
Or for some secret reason beyond him— Unless it was
to turn the knife a little more in his wounds.

From the palace windows, he saw the snow, white
also, lying on the city.

There were Lowlanders in the city. Despite everything he had ordered, every edict. Every terror.

Gloved, held in by cloth and rings, his hand lay out
on the window embrasure before him. He need only
strip the rings, the one great ring on the smallest,
deformed finger, to see the hand as it was. The right
hand, (naked, well-formed, very dark, unflawed), the
right hand moved toward the left, stealing up on it.
Take off the glove, and look. No. No need. He knew.

From childhood, from his first conscious hour. He recalled that once, once only, he had stared very long at the ungloved hand, turning to catch the lamplight of another room, in Koramvis. It had come to him then that the hand was actually a marvelous thing, almost an artifact, for it seemed made of silver, and the fine chiseled scales upon it, marred only by old scarring near the wrist, were perfect as silver discs laid one upon another. The scales, after all, of a dragon, not a serpent. Not the snake-scale curse on him of the Lowland goddess Anackire—

There was rapping on the door. The woman, the mistress of his pleasure-girls. He had told her to go and fetch the one the soldiers had abducted. The Lowland girl-beast.

The door was already opened, and as the slave slipped out, the Lowlander was pushed through, and left to him.

She was terrified, he saw immediately. Good. She was too afraid to see his fear. That was often his means, was it not, the fear of others before a High King, a Storm Lord. They dropped at his feet and did not see him trembling.

He said something to her. What had he said? That she was a Lowlander, was she? Take off her rags then, and let him see the rest.

But she only stood there clutching at the air and gasping.

So he went on talking to her, reviling her, and in the middle of it, as if he could not prevent himself, his own horror filled him and that in turn spoke to her. Was she afraid of his hand, *this* one? Well, that was just. The blasting of her people laid in rape on her.

And he was also horribly aroused by her, her whiteness, her skin like snow, her hair like ice. Revolted and fascinated, sick, and avid— He pulled her to him and pressed the snake-scale hand over her breast and felt the heart leaping like a creature in a net. But then it ceased leaping, there was nothing, under his hand, his mouth. She had died. She was dead. He let her go and looked at her on the floor. A child. A dead child.

He knelt down slowly. He kneeled beside her, wait-

ing for her to live again, for death to be a faint from
which she would recover. He smoothed her face. He
took her hands, and relinquished them. He slapped
her.

He had not meant her to die. That was not fair, on
her or on him. He had meant her to be used. Perhaps
not even that. Only the gods, who hated him, knew
what he had wanted or truly meant to do. But to kill
her—should not have been possible.

Yet it was foolish, for he would not tolerate any of
her race in the world. He would be rid of them. And
this—was one less.

"It was only a dream."

He looked into the girl's dark face, framed by black
hair and night, the Star-burned ocean.

"Yes," Rehger said. "A dream."

But Velva leaned over him still, her eyes wide,
searching his.

He said, "What is it?"

"The Lowland witch," she said, muttering so he
barely heard her. "You were saying, *the Lowlander,
the Lowlander—*"

Red lightning flickered, smiting the southern sea.

Rehger drew her down. "Now I say only 'Velva.' "

He silenced her with kisses. He drew her astride and
let her ride him, helping her with his strength until she
moaned in an agony of delight. But even as his own
body swelled toward its tumult, his mind stood far
away. His mind was in the palace rooms of Koramvis
and Lin Abissa, looking out of the eyes of Amrek,
High King of all Vis, one hundred and thirty years and
more in the past.

In the garden courtyard of the house on Gem-Jewel
Street, Katemval was breakfasting, while his tame water-
birds pecked at crumbs or swam about in the cistern.

When the slave came out, followed by the sun-blazoned
figure of Rehger, a note of keen gratification went
through the older man. It was rarely now that the hero
sought his inventor . . . if the attentions had ever been
frequent, or more than the easy friendly courtesy the

Lydian extended to most of humanity, his fellow Swords,
the city nobles, the drudges of taverns, the gambling
mob. (Yet I'm soothing to him. He knows that. Here he
is now, some enquiry on his lips. He used to ask me
many things, long ago, when I told him the stories of
my travels, other lands, legends. Alisaar's his earth, he
can never go anywhere else, or want to. But my mind-
box is his library. We're to fight Thaddrians, have you
seen Thaddra? I was offered a team of animals from
Dorthar, would they be worth going for?)

"Sit, eat, drink. And ask me," said Katemval.

Rehger smiled. "Is it so obvious?"

Seating himself, then, a dash of sea-sand fell from his
mantle. He was dressed for evening fare, but he had
been on the beach.

"Not the princess, surely," said Katemval.

Rehger glanced at the sand, which some of the water-
birds had come to try. He took one of the little breakfast cakes and broke it for them, stroking their necks of
irridescent indigo as they ate. "No, not a princess.
There was something curious with the sea. At dawn,
when she and I were walking back toward the harbor
wall, the tide had gone farther out than I ever saw. A
couple of ships outside the basin were in difficulties,
they were pulling cargoes off in a hurry. She was afraid
of the sea, she said it meant something bad would
happen. You know what those girls are like sometimes."

"I remember."

"But the fishermen were down the beach, waving
their arms and running about. There were scores of fish
left behind all over the mud. The men said to me Rorn
was thirsty, he was drinking the sea."

"The waters beyond Alisaar were always strange.
Myth used to have it they rolled on into the ocean of
Hell, Aarl, All-Death. Then the traders began going
back and forth to the white men's lands, and Hell had
to move its traps. But you can see sailors, the ones who
stick to the south routes and the west, hair gone gray,
and some of the fishermen and shore-liners get it, as far
up the coast as Hanassor. Bleached by Aarl-salt—and it
turns the brain, too, probably. It'll have been the tremor
on the night of the Fire Ride. The land shudders, then

the sea does flighty things. But that isn't what you came
to ask."

"No, Katemval."

The slave hurried out again with a fresh griddle of
hot cakes, and honey-curd and raisins—and to remove
the milk, regardless of Katemval, which the Children of
Daigoth never drank. Rehger thanked the slave, waiting
till he was gone to say, "Who was Amrek? I mean the
Storm Lord. Do I have the name right?"

"You do. Amrek son of Rehdon, the last Vis High
King. He was the one who said he'd wipe all smudge
of the Lowlanders off life's face. But Rehdon's bastard,
Raldnor—half Vis, half Lowlander, and Anackire In-
carnate for a mother, if you swallow all the tale—Raldnor
made a treaty with the other continent, the blond men
of Vathcri, Vardath and Shansar, and picked up the
Lowlanders and told them they were magicians. And
armed with that, he whipped Amrek into an early grave.
Koramvis city was smashed to bits in the earthquake.
Anackire sat on the mountains and applauded like a
lady at the stadium. Around a hundred years back, it
happened again, another way round. Free Zakoris
wanted war, but the war was stopped. The gods stopped
it. If you believe all that."

"Do you?"

"Well, if I spill the salt I ask the god's pardon like
some up-country wench. And I sacrifice regularly in the
temples. I even make an offering now and again in the
Shalian temple near Tomb Street. To the snake woman.
Just to be on the safe side. But the gods walking the
water—I can never quite credit that. I don't even know
if I credit the gods. May they excuse me."

Rehger laughed softly. But his eyes were distant. His
unleveled beauty, as he sat there at the ordinary sunny
table, filled Katemval with an instantaneous anxiety. It
seemed to provoke fate. The years of fighting and winning, the crown of the great race—and no mark on
him, no disfigurement to appease the envy of perhaps
nonexistent gods.

"But Amrek," said Katemval, "why Amrek?"

Rehger looked down at the ornamental birds. Katemval
looked at them, too, remembering that casket with the

hawk and pigeon in it. Sometimes slum archers bagged
such suppers—the shard of flint in the raptor's breast
seemed to indicate this was their origin. But then some
other one had bought or taken the trophy. They were
not embalmed, as it turned out. The corpses were kept
pristine by some other perturbing method. Flung on the
compost behind the house, even now, the slave said,
they had not decayed. Nor had anything utilized the
carrion.

"Yesterday, it was suggested to me," Rehger said,
"that I come direct from Amrek's line."

"You're Iscaian. There was no look of it, there,"
Katemval said promptly. He was unnerved. He thought,
And every look of it in you. By a pantheon of gods—yes—

"Well, Katemval. My father was just a man who
had my mother, not an Iscaian. He left her that golden
drak, remember. She told me something of how he
looked, tall and strong, and dark. He might have been
rich, once. And he said he was a Lan. Is that possible?
Is there some remnant of Amrek's house in Lan?"

"Now wait—wait—" Katemval tapped the table, so
the raisins jumped in their dish. "Lanelyr— About the
time of that non-war. A priestess who claimed descent
from Amrek Am Dorthar. She married into the royal
house at Amlan. Not to the Lannic throne, you understand, which only goes to brothers and sisters or sons
with mothers, incestuous pairings." Abruptly Katemval
ceased. He sat and looked at Rehger, realizing that
the boy—the man—had never bothered to mention
this vital circumstance of his begetting, all through
their years of friendship—which plainly was not any
kind of friendship at all. Katemval said, in a foolish,
stricken voice, before he could control himself, "Didn't
you trust me, to tell me that? Your mother's honor,
was it?"

Rehger glanced up. His eyes lost for a second the
sheen of distance, they gentled, as Katemval had seen
them do with a woman or a beast. Insulted, Katemval
drew away as Rehger reached out to clasp his arm.
And the gentleness went. Rehger shook his head
impatiently.

"I thought it was unimportant, who he was. I never told you because it meant nothing to me."

"What can it mean now?" Katemval said. "You're a Saardsin Sword."

"A slave, yes," Rehger said, offhandedly. "But I should like to know. If I have a king's blood. If my mother took me from a king's descendant."

"All right," said Katemval. He was brusque. "Stroll along Three Penny Alley and find a soothsayer, or some witch, and ask her to cast it out for you."

"It was a sorceress who told me first," Rehger said.

Katemval thought of a white image by a wall, a message of downfall, of weird rumors concerning a raising of the dead—

"Don't go to her," Katemval said. "If it's the Amanackire woman. *No*."

"It seems I may have to."

"No, I said. Certainly, she is a witch. Without pleasantries, the deadly sort. Like all her race, the white ones. There's a tale they have some colony, in the northwest jungles—oh, beyond Zakoris. They plot there and ferment their cold sickly magics. The written warning I told you of, it has that tone. It must have come from her—"

Rehger's face had acquired a shadow. The prefiguration of the bones within. After all, he had been marked—

"You watched the last combat, Katemval?"

"I can always watch now, when you fight."

"Did I kill the Corhlan?"

"You killed him. And half the city says *she* brought him back. But who's seen the boy? It's an ugly nonsense, but it's compatible with what she is. Oh, they can work magic. Sham or genuine, it's nothing to want to be near."

Rehger came to his feet. He gazed at Katemval, a long, open look, and the shadow was in his eyes now.

"Katemval, I have to be going. I must be in the practice court by midmorning, or put out the fighting-squares."

"Yes," said Katemval. "Go carefully."

He felt old, and sat down as Rehger turned to leave. But then, getting up again, Katemval walked upstairs

to the roof and watched the Lydian riding away along
the avenue on the coal-black thoroughbred. Katemval
watched as far as the fountain, where the road angled.
For the snake witch lived on this very street. In the
dilapidated tiled mansion. Rehger had gone by it without a glance. But neither had he looked back once,
toward Katemval's house.

He might have excluded himself from the practice
court, this one day; the squares would not have been
out, despite what he had said to Katemval, who knew
as much. Champions made their own laws for such
things.

But he had required the fight, the hard exercise. Sex
had not purged him. The sea and the night, disturbed
by red glimmerings, the water plucked away. It was
Zastis. He was of the bloodline of a dead king. And in
his mind, he could recall a white girl lying on a palace
floor, a white girl with her hands locked upon a grill of
iron.

Eight squares, each composed of four men, spaced
two by two, back to back.

The sun streamed down and broiled them, and the
blades, sword and dagger, made lightnings, slammed
together, slithered, grated, shot away.

And the Corhlan. He lived. Did he? Where? Where
would a man go to, who had been slain and restored
inside a day? To the brothels? The temples?

"You're *slow*, Lydian," the Ylan, facing him from
the next square, rhythmically lunged. "Too many *times*,
Rehger, with the one you *had*, Rehger. Last *night*.
Was it *six* times? Or *seven*? Did she go *pale*, then?"

You did not converse while fighting. Except now
and then in the practice court.

"Last night I was *praying*," said Rehger, feinted
almost idly, and thumped the Ylan across his helm
with the sword-flat. The Ylan went down, and the
man back-to-back with him stumbled and cursed.

Rehger thought: *That was word-play, too. Pale. He
meant the Amanackire.*

The trainer ambled up the block of squares. Now he
frowned, now called on Daigoth.

Rehger waited for the Ylan.

"Take off your pathetic rags," he said to the frightened girl, in snow-lapped Xarabiss.

The Ylan was on his feet, shaking his head like a bemused lion.

Amrek. Rehger. A dream, memories carried in his blood—

The Swordsman beside him, a young sturdy Ommos who would be worth watching in a year, if he lived so long, landed a blow upon the Ylan's side-mate. The man swerved, missing the worst of it, and came back to ram the Ommos under the ribs with a dagger hilt. "That's what you like, boy-stitcher." The Ommos sprawled toward Rehger's piece of ground. Rehger sprang away. The Ylan, favoring his dagger now, tried to score under the Lydian's sword. Rehger moved effortlessly beyond the stroke. Bringing up his left hand he took the sword neatly from his right, snatched the dagger right-handed. The showy gambit now brought the sword left-handedly down on the Ylan's blade, and scythed it to the court. The Ylan snarled, his anger was real. Generally they fought in the practice court with blunted iron. Not today. It was Zastis. Tempers and blades were sharp—

The Lydian's sword and dagger re-passed each other, the showy gambit performed twice without a flaw. "Only able three times, then," growled the Ylan. "You saved it for me?"

The Ommos, still rolling on the ground, sank his teeth suddenly in the foot of the man who had felled him.

A howl of laughter and abuse went up.

The trainer groused stamping forward. Dirty fights earned docked privileges. No boys for the Ommos tonight—

What did it matter if you were a king's making? That blood must run thin by now. And he was a slave in Saardsinmey— Careful with the sword. Swords might be snakes in disguise.

"I fear you. Oh, Rehger—warn this city—"

Something was screaming, miles below, loud and sonorous, a mighty creature in the gut of the planet—

Rehger lifted his head—the sun canceled vision. His left arm flew outward for no reason, and he looked and saw the Ylan standing in astonishment there. "You let me cut you."

The blood of a king, it was leaving him now.

The trainer was at the Lydian's elbow, holding the left arm, examining it. The Lydian allowed this. The arm, opened lengthways a hand's breath below the elbow to the wrist, did not belong to him. It belonged to the city.

The other squares fought raggedly on.

"That's deep enough. This old wrist scar here blocked off the stroke. Lucky. Off, out of it. Gods blind me, Lydian, I never saw you take a dolt's bite like that since you were eleven years of age."

He walked away from the court. He held the blood of Amrek inside his arm as best he could, but it spilled between his fingers, to the ground.

The surgeon pointed to the cup of wine.

"Drink that. Keep still."

Unkinder echo of Katemval, this morning.

Rehger did as he was instructed. The surgeon drove his silver needle six times through the skin, tied off the gut-thread and severed it. The wound was bound by an apprentice.

"You won't compete for our city for ten days. You were due two events, they'll pine. I will inform you presently which exercises you may or may not indulge."

When the lecture was done, Rehger said, "Do you know anything about the Corhlan who fought here?"

"I wasn't in attendance yesterday. But I'll tell you, Lydian, I don't know of a single man among all the stadium surgeons who was."

In the under-passages, a pretty harlot, one of scores kept to content the younger Swords, came by the Lydian, slipping her dress from her shoulders and smiling slyly. "They say the Ylan got you—well, and so he did. Well, I know. You let him do it, so you can be with that woman, didn't you? To have your Zastis days and nights alone with her."

*   *   *

On foot, cloaked and hooded, he went there. He even stooped a little; some might know him by his height.

But three torch-lighters, who always greeted him, paid him no attention as they made their way through the main boulevards of Saardsinmey, touching the stalks of light-poles to yellow flower. And the girls did not come up to him, or the shopkeepers and princes who had won.

A couple of riotous dinners were in progress on Gem-Jewel Street, and there was also dancing in the road about the fountain, young women swirling their beads and skirts. Two officers of the Guardian's co-horts, standing to watch, were complaining that word had it the Lydian had been sliced through the arm at practice, and would not fight or race for thirty days, or maybe never again, and how would the bets go now, Daigoth-eat-and-spit-it-forth.

Her house was in darkness.

Even in the garden, no lit window was visible.

He came to the upper entrance, and the lamp there, too, was out. He left the bell and crashed his fist several times on the timbers.

When the mix girl opened the door, he was sorry.

"It's all right, sweetness. I only wanted to be heard."

She said nothing, nor did she try to stay him. She darted away and he was left to enter as he would, closing the door himself.

Everything was shadows, the salon empty. Yet he could smell the perfume of her, faint as fine pollen, everywhere.

He went to the grill, where she had clung lamenting. The garden lay beneath, quite silent. The moon was rising, the Vis moon of Zastis, red as the hair of a red-haired woman—white, in the cold months, as the Amanackire. His arm gnawed and burned. His fingers had stiffened. The surgeon had not told him, since he knew, that even with the utmost care, some malady might set in. The wound could fester. The arm . . . be lost to him. Some chose to sweep the courts then, to clean the privies, to put oil in the bath-house jars. To run errands for the Swords. Some went back into the stadium and soon died there, jeered and pitied, and praised in death. It was the mercy of Daigoth, to kill a crippled man swiftly.

"Aztira," Rehger said to the shadows and the perfumed emptiness. He crossed the salon and tried the doors along the corridor beyond. Each opened. Many of the rooms lacked even furnishings. In some, dim shapes, nothing that was animate.

From a terraced balcony, a stair led up to the roof of the mansion. He climbed it slowly.

I healed before, there have been other wounds.

I was younger. No wound like this.

The roof was garlanded by the garden trees, only on the southwest side partly open to the dancing lights of the street beyond the alley, which seemed remote as fireflies. It occurred to him he glimpsingly heard the sea, as he had at the inn. And on the beach, sheathed in Velva's golden flesh.

Pale on darkness, the Lowland girl was seated at the parapet. Her hair, unbound, with no ornament, hung round her to the roof itself, a waterfall. She did not turn.

"Is your name," he said, "Aztira?"

She did not reply.

"Aztira, you'll have to heal me, as you did the Corhlan. I was cut in the arm today, and it was your fault." He moved toward her, but she did not look about. The moon was in the eastern trees. Not red, as yet, only like the rosy amber she had worn on her forehead. "And then I brought the one clue my father ever left my mother. It's a coin. An adept can read something from a possession. In Alisaar they can, or say they can. I want to ask you about that man. If you take the coin, and tell me. He was called Yennef. My mother could never pronounce it. Nor I, till I came here." He stood by her. All about, the darkness throbbed and whispered. "Aztira? There's also a dream I need you to divine."

She turned then. As she stood, her hair drifted out like silver smoke; her eyes were stars veiled in water. She raised her arms and her fingers touched his shoulders. There was strength in him, fierce and warm as wine. No wound, no trouble. He put his hands on her waist and lifted her and drew her up his body until her silver arms encircled his neck, until her heart smote against his, until their mouths could meet.

BOOK TWO

ALISAAR

PART TWO

CHAPTER EIGHT

SOLD AND BOUGHT

Not the temples. It was the brothels the Corhlan had gone to.

There had been a nightmare, of death. Somewhere. But you need not think of it, here.

He had fought, lost, walked away from the under-rooms of the stadium. To submerge his grievance, he came to this place, near the waterfront. He had had some cash saved, which had not yet run out. When it did, they would throw him on the fish-reeking cobbles, the madam glaring and vituperative, the girls regret-fully sad. Then—then he would devise some other means to get by.

"I'm a prince, in Corhl," he told the girls. They did not care, or believe him. But his healthy limber frame, his handsome face, they liked those. "Come to my palace. Be my queen in Corhl." "Oh, get on with you," they said.

The bed was scattered with the somber marigolds of Alisaar, the pomegranate-color wind-flowers, the speck-led topaz lilies that grew wild on the hills. The estab-lishment servants fed him, and brought wine, and white Karmian spirit that made you think you could fly. ("Fly to Corhl with me." "Oh, get on.")

During the first night, near sunrise, an enormous herd of cattle had woken him, mooing and rumbling under the sea. But cattle did not go about there.

The girl screamed as she lay on his belly, gripping his shoulders. He was finished just before her, and, his eyes clearing, saw through her contorted face into another face, white as a skull. There was a pain in his chest, running down from the neck to the breastbone.

The Lydian had given him a whack with his shield. It had stunned him. Well.

"Now, for me," the other girl said, sliding on to Chacor.

"Corrah, no. I'm dead."

They had heard *those* rumors too, and did not believe them, either, though they did believe otherwise in every manner of miracle, jinx, glamour, ghost and demon.

"Ah, Chacor. The sun's going, the Star's coming up. And look, what's *this?*"

Erect in her canny winsome hands, he surrendered himself. And she buried him in her loins, most marvelously alive.

Wrapped in her cloak of black silk and a great poured collar sewn with jets, Panduv stood and stared.

The man, a mix, poorly dressed in contrast to her opulent slavery, clanked the throats of the bags again.

"Five hundred bars, standard rate. Take and have them weighed, if you wish."

"You're her menial," said Panduv. She snapped her fingers for her girl to go on ahead, through the covered court into the building.

"No. But she can command me, of course. Her kind can always do that."

"So I see. Well. Go back and tell her to—save her money."

The man looked down at the bags.

"They're heavy."

"I cry tears of blood for you."

The man cursed her for a black Zakorian trull, and Panduv stalked by him. She could have killed him with her bare hands or feet, for she was stadium-trained also to fight, like every professional dancer-acrobat of the city. But that was out of bounds. He was, Yasmat snap off his organ, a mix. And an errand-boy for an Amanackire.

Panduv was tiring of that Amanackire. Once had been enough. What next?

Entering the purlieus of the theatre, Panduv discovered.

"She's here."

"Who is here?"

"Your snake woman."

The manager, between contempt and nervousness, peered about the ante-stage, a space just now banked up with properties, and persons who were listening.

"Not mine," said Panduv resolutely.

"I put her in the painters' room. Go and see to her, for the love of the gods."

Panduv left him and went to the painters' room.

"You must be amorous of me," she said to the Amanackire. "May I decline? Those stadium-trained avoid drinking milk."

"I only want what I have told you I want."

"Which you knew I'd refuse, or else why are you here before me, when your groveling money-bags met me outside?"

"Name your own price, Zakorian."

Panduv detained a flock of replies. Curiosity was claiming her, despite everything. The Amanackire had come out tonight mantled in clear colors, a chameleon for once. Her tell-tale hair, and even her face, were veiled in gauze.

"Why do you want to purchase such a thing?" said Panduv.

The Amanackire sighed—for the gauze fluttered. She did nothing else.

Panduv said: "You think you'll need it? And before I shall?"

"Oh, yes."

"I mustn't rejoice. You may strike me down—I've heard your race can kill by lightning from the brain. And then where would you be? But the stone is black, lady."

"The Lowlands use black stone,"

"And burn their dead."

"I'm not among my own kind here. I respect the customs of the lands I visit. I have been influenced."

"Something more," said Panduv. She narrowed her lustrous eyes, toyed with her jet-stone collar nearly as dark.

"What would you have?"

"Say," said Panduv: "Why from me?"

"It has the nature of a balance, Zakorian, which you might not understand. Besides, yours is of the best, the masons boast of it. The most sturdy."

"You fear Saardsins would break in and desecrate?"

By a movement of the face-veil, Panduv saw the Amanackire smiled.

"Before Zastis, you came to me," said Panduv, "asking me about the Lydian."

"It was, if you wish, a prelude to this."

"But you've met him by now. It's all over the stadium, and the Women's House. That you and he fire the Star together. That you hexed him and nearly crippled him in the practice court so you could have him all Zastis to yourself. So why not ask his help with this other problem?"

"He has never bothered with provision. They say it's notable, Panduv. The women, though mostly less exposed to obvious danger, always see to it first." The Amanackire paused. Then she came toward the Zakorian girl, and as she did so lowered the veil from her face. She stood looking up at Panduv. The Lowlanders generally lacked the height of the Vis. But all at once, her slender smallness, the always-unrecollected youth of the white girl, stirred the dancer, sexually and emotively, and, therefore, to an awareness of the human.

"Panduv," she said, "forgive me. My race are arrogant and cruel. I know no better than to demand. Let me crave your pardon, and ask, then. Please, Panduv Am Hanassor, I beg you. Permit me to buy from you your built black tomb on the hill. With the riches I can give you, you can build at once one even finer. Although, I promise you, you won't need it. Your days will be long."

Panduv shivered.

"Not yours? Yes, I see. Why else this hurry."

"You will hear quite soon that I have died. Then rejoice, if you want. Sell the tomb to me. Take my blessing for your curses."

Velva had entered the Salt Quarter, the warren of narrow streets and ruinous lots that lay between the warehouse district and the eastern slums of the city. She had told the inn-lord the Lydian wanted her. Her employer had not argued, or looked for further payment. He had not guessed it was a lie. Would it were not.

There was a thin twisting sooty street that coiled and wriggled through the warren. Though leading nowhere of import, and of revolting appearance, it was well-known in its way, or ill-known, certainly.

Sometimes, from some black crack, a hand reached out and plucked at the girl's cloak, or a face squinted. But they were feeble, indeterminate attentions. Prosaic lust was not what prompted this defile of night.

She passed all the doorways, not looking, and the alley-mouths. She passed the cavelike open entries, shelved with mortal flesh. In this worm-wend, all manner of drugs and essences were sold. Incenses and elixirs, inducements to dream or drown, the recipes of many lands. Here even they sold *Aarl's Kiss*, that had its fame, now, Vis over. It was the juice of a yellow fruit, plucked from a mysterious island that lay at sea beyond the shores of Alisaar, and off the proper routes of the traders. They said the blond Storm Lord, Raldnor, had found the island on his journey of discovery that ended at the Second Continent. The fruit, when eaten, made one drunk. More. In sufficient quantity, the rind and pith mixed in, it made all things beautiful; it opened the portals into the kingdom of the gods. But it also killed, in great pain, and swiftly. Crush the whole fruit, however, distill and dilute the juice, one might imbibe the pleasant drink moderately for some years, knowing something of the ecstasy often. Or, if in haste, much ecstasy and death in a few months. Those that took the juice a decade denied it was an assassin. They loved it as their friend. They tried to hold it off, as a loved friend is held off, and gave in finally, and in the last seasons of addiction, married it. Those that went more quickly acknowledged it was death. What had life, anyway, to offer them, that was delicious as this?

In the deep porch, Velva touched the cord of a bell.

She did not hear it ringing, but the door, after a moment, was opened, two inches.

"What?" said a voice.

"*Aarl's Kiss*."

"Cash? Or do you barter other things?"

"Coins."

"Let's see 'em."

Reared among the tenements of Saardsinmey, she knew to show just one flash of one bright drak. She had saved the Lydian's money, which he had pressed on her, meaning to give it back to him. But he had not sought her again. The witch had ensorcelled him instead.

"Come in," said the unseen one. He held her arm through the door, and she pushed him off.

The darkness stank of sea-damp and filth. A light burned, very low. Neither purveyor nor client wished to be illumined. Velva had slight fear she would be plundered and slain. She would be more profitable alive. For this medicine, she would come back. Taste, and you must return to it.

"How?" said the man she could not see.

"Not the usual mixture. Undistilled. From the pulpings."

Now she was in some unsafety. She had implied she meant this venture to be unique.

"That's not so simple," he said. "Why d'you want it that way?"

Velva turned a fraction, for he was shifting the lamp, trying to spy her better.

"My lover. He's old. Sick. The juice does nothing for him, watered."

"You want him packed off, eh?"

She hid her face in her cloak, and threw weighted dice.

"I need his money. Fill another vial for me—that one distilled."

And the vendor cackled, pleased to be of service. Since, hooked by her elderly paramour, she also was his, and—youthful and hale—might stay so an entire ten years.

It was a winter morning when slave-takers came to the fishing village a mile below Hanassor. Above, the dark conical cliff that held the city, blocked the sun, but the sea was sheened. It was never really cold in Zakoris.

Panduv's aunt-mother—her birth-mother was long dead—was gutting fish and pegging them to dry out on the posts. She was bare-breasted, and big-bellied, always with child, as was the old way, by any one of the village men, who held all their women in common. Other women worked farther along the stony shore, seeing to the nets or the fish the men had brought in just before sunup. Smoke swarmed from the hut-holes.

Panduv, who in those days had been called something in the way of *Palmv*, had also been caught turning cartwheels when supposed at toil with the pots in the water tub. Her aunt-mother had damned her, naming her not only Palmv but the Hated-of-Zarduk. Nearly three years old, eyes wet (for the blows had been harsh), Palmv scoured the clay. She did not know the bruises of those blows would fade in another world.

Zakoris was Vardish, since the Lowland War, over a century: Var-Zakoris. The might of Hanassor was done, and there was a new capital inland with another title. Sometimes pale-skinned men with yellow hair were seen in the village's vicinity. They were not liked, or annoyed. The gods had had their say. Zarduk was chastising his old kingdom. In Free Zakoris, over the mountains, that was where the soul of the land had gone.

Seeing riders coming down on them, Palmv's aunt-mother had called the other women. They spoke of Vardians or Tarabines—but the riders were not white men. Dortharians, then, the lovers of Vardians and Tarabines.

Nor were they Dortharians.

They came along the stones, the zeebas picking a way. The women stood ready to fight if needful. Their men, resting after a night's fishing, were not to be disturbed.

Then a couple of the riders explained what they wanted. Children. Very young. Girls—for boys were not sold at Hanassor. Boys were still considered warriors here, and powerhouses of seed. But girls were expendable. Particularly a girl like Palmv, whose mother had died of childbearing and might have passed this stigma on.

Palmv heard the exchanges. She heard herself offered, for the slavers' price. When they came and looked her over, she barely struggled. No man was consulted. No one knew who her father was, she had never been an asset to the village.

Presently she was carried away to Alisaar.

She thought all this while that it had happened to her because she was inferior. Because she had turned cartwheels. Useless, this was her punishment. It was in the stadium, in the girls' hall, that she learned, gradually, painfully, disbelievingly, that she had been taken for her beauty and her strength, and that her name was Panduv, and she would be a dancer and a princess in glory. When she might otherwise have scratched at pots, dried and pickled fish, and lain with her legs open, either taking men in or pushing them, newborn, out, all her days.

Now Panduv stood on the top-walk of the triple stage, thinking warily of these things. Was it an omen, to consider her start? Had the white woman lied, saying Panduv would not need the tomb and that her life would be long? Was it only that some fate hung over Panduv, a death that was not expected, and would leave nothing to be buried? Obliteration by flames, or water—Panduv felt an instant's awful fear. To the Lowlanders, with their religion of eternal renewings (alien to Panduv as anything of theirs), physical death was nothing. (Why else, that one, so calm in the face of it?) But to a Zakorian, only a holy burning or drowning in sacrifice was valid. The gods provided for all such victims, as for men who fell in war. For the rest of the dead, without the model of their corpse to remember by, the shade would be formless and amnesiac. And if the cadaver was shelterless, how could the shade achieve a refuge? Death was a dim, bleak country anyway. Every aid was needful, there.

The theater was nearly empty, rehearsals concluded. Up in the crimson roof the lamps had been doused by those monkey-boys who could scale the pillars. The poled sections of scenery had been run off along their grooves into the wings—the wheels below, into which the poles were locked, had screeched throughout the rehearsal so the actors laughed and complained and the manager despaired. Behind Panduv, there remained only the great bole, part primeval tree, part column, abandoned on stage until tomorrow. It was a tall drum of solidly carpentered wood, braced with gilded bronze, and painted. Jointed and hinged lengthways, it stood currently wide. The play had a diversion: A manifestation of the love-goddess Yasmat. A magical tree carved into a column was to be split by divine lightning. The goddess would step forth, to be fawned on by leopards and birds. In a dance, she then demonstrated the omnipotence of sexual love. The goddess must at no time speak, that would be blasphemous. She might only be portrayed by perfect beauty and exceptional talent. Panduv had been engaged for the role at a staggering fee. Her worth was further attested by the shockproofed structure of the column, and the cushioning of its interior. However, the cranky crane, having deposited the column-drum, promptly broke down. It had been altogether a disquieting night.

Nor yet over.

The leading actor of the Alisaarian troop appeared on the apron, and came steathily and quickly up the stages to Panduv, taking her into his arms when he reached her.

"Yasmat," he groaned in her ear.

"Delay a while," she said. "We can go to the clothes room."

"No. Let's go in there. Yes, into the column. It's comfortable enough. Black on black, my Yasmat. Oh, don't make me wait any longer—"

It was Zastis, the nerves of both alight. She allowed him to prop her in the dark column and himself against her, pulling shut the hinged sections . . .

Yet even as they clung and plunged, upright and frenzied, in the close-bound, hidden dark, she had an idea they made love in a grave. And that, once all the business of the night was over, she must propitiate

Yasmat for being given, especially flippantly, the goddess' name.

The night ran its course. With accidents and pleasures. With lovemaking and merrymaking. With clandestine messengers bearing deeds, packed harlotries and taverns, street fights near the docks. With a sumptuous dinner in the Guardian's palace, whose guests ranged from indigenous merchant-princes through a pack of nobles from Sh'alis, to charioteers and philosophers.

Toward sunrise, tiring, the night left everything lying, flotsam on a beach, and seeped with Star-set into the west.

The flowerseller moved with earliest morning along Gem-Jewel Street. Few were about but slaves. Women drew water from the fountain. A wine-shop or two had organized its brooms. Hawks sailed high and pigeons fanned their wings on the rooftops.

A snatch of talk came from an upper window.

"The sea's gone out again, the fishmonger said, further than before."

"So. It always comes back. The tides are high."

"And it sings to itself at night. They heard it, as far as the High Gate."

"So. Let the sea do what it wants."

"*Hey, girl!* Give me some flowers. What are you asking for those lilies?"

But the girl shook her hooded head. "Not for sale. Already bought." And went on.

It was true, her flowers were of the best, fresh with dew and dawn, from the hills, doubtless, behind Tomb Street, where the other flower gatherers went.

Why should it occur to anyone the flower seller had not picked a single bloom herself, but paid to take this pannier of lilies, wall-rose and white aloe, from a one-armed woman near the Shalian temple?

She had been industrious, Velva, and extravagant. All her coins were gone now.

Turning into an alley by the lacemakers, she reached the gate of a house wall, and sat down there.

Soon she heard the sound of the zeeba, and the man, calling his wares. Then he had paused on the street to serve customers; then, as Velva had done, turned into the alley. On either side the patient zeeba hung a cibba-wood cask, and through the man's belt was stuck a copper ladle, filmed with white. He was a milk vendor. Since it was possible to learn so much about the habits of the woman who lodged in this house, she being of such interest to all, it was easy to find out that milk was bought here once every three days.

"Clean milk, sweet milk," he called, winking at Velva where she sat with her flowers.

It would be sweet today, wonderfully sweet. Which no one would think odd. In the hot weather, the milk was often sugared or salted against curdling.

"Does the lady take flowers ever?" said Velva, to the milk vendor.

"Well, she might."

Timidly, "Would you let me come in with you, and ask the servant? They're fresh—look—to stand in vases or make garlands."

"Oh, you've heard the Lydian calls here, too."

Velva lowered her eyes. The man stole near and rubbed his hand on her belly. "If I praise you to the servant, and you sell your flowers, what do I get?"

Eyes lowered, Velva said, "What a kind man always gets at Zastis."

When they reached the downstairs entry, the man, having opened the door, hallooed up the steps. The zeeba chewed the long dry grass of the garden, and Velva, pitying it, unseen by the man, fed it two of her precious flowers.

Just so one thing must be devoured to sustain another. It was the gods' law.

Borne to the satin beaches on the black thoroughbred, in the arms of the Lydian, she had exalted and clutched at happiness, knowing it would not last. She had hoped he might want her again, for a while, from time to time. But all the city worshiped him. She was an inn sloven. It might have to do for her lifetime, that one night.

She was resigned, but she loved.

From the vantage of that love, she heard he shared the witch's bed. It was the gossip from one end of the city to the other, tickled and aggravated: That he should be wasted on a Lowlander, that the arrogant Lowland mare should have yearned after him. But she had been his Zastis pairing, it seemed, even before he sought Velva. Yes, he had asked the way to the witch's house . . . but she had been unavailable, and something of less significance was substituted, Velva herself. Next on this knowledge came the story of the sword-wound in the practice court. It informed Velva of a thing already sensed and dreaded. The Lowland woman was Death. As the giant snake would crush, the lesser inject with venom—it was her nature. She would drain him and destroy him, he would perish miserably, before his hour, the mock of men, uncherished by gods.

But not if Velva succeeded at her task today, not then.

There was the quiet noise of sandaled feet on the stair, the servant girl coming down with her pitcher.

The milk vendor said to Velva, jokingly, "You won't get to see *him,* if you were thinking of that. He wasn't with her last night. The Guardian had a dinner for the Lydian. He couldn't say no to it."

Velva had known of the dinner, as she knew that Swordsmen never drank milk.

The mix girl had entered the foyer and the man was ladling into her pitcher. Velva went forward and stood near. The mix did not glance at her. Velva surreptitiously stroked the milkman's side. He smiled.

"My cousin here," he said to the mix. "She's had a bit of bad luck today. Up before dawn getting all those flowers, the first and freshest, for a cow along the street. But the cow's sulking over some tiff with her lover, and won't buy." He hesitated, not yet taking the coins the servant held out to him. He was doing his very best. "I suppose your lady wouldn't care to take some? Do you think you could ask her. It'd be a kindness. I'm sure my girl here wouldn't mind giving you back a bit of what your lady pays . . . if it's enough, of course." His hand shut on his own payment at last.

The mix turned and looked at Velva. Velva hated and was afraid of the yellow-brown color of her eyes, but she said hopefully, "Look, miss, beautiful flowers. These roses—for a love-couch nothing better." The peculiar eyes went on to the flower basket. Velva had begun to tremble. She had an array of gambits, all risky, but was alert to veer in whatever direction she must—even to upsetting the milk pitcher. "Oh, please, miss. Could you perhaps take up the flowers for her to see? She'll like them. And the lilies are good fortune for lovers. Oh, do. I could hold the milk. Here, you just carry up the basket—" And Velva brought the pannier, adrip with water drops and fragrance, against the servant's hands. While, with the dexterity of her trade as wine-girl, Velva laid hold of the pitcher's handle. If the mix refused, something else must be done. But the mix did not refuse. She gave over the pitcher and accepted the flowers, and went away up the stair with them like a doll of clockwork from Xarabiss.

Velva forced herself to turn slowly, friendly, to the milk vendor.

"Yasmat's blessing."

"That's what I trust I'll get."

"Those trees near the gate," Velva said. "It's cool there, and no one can see. Go on, or she may think we're up to something else. I'll meet you in a minute."

"You'd better," he said. But he was deceived. The gods of Vis were helping. He led the zeeba off through the garden. And Velva fumbled the vial of poison from her cloak. Prizing out the stopper, she closed the vial with her finger. Putting her hand down into the milk, she released the poison in its depths.

Her hand was dry again, the milk smooth, when the mix came back. She had no flowers but an array of draks to pay lavishly for them.

"Heaven reward you," said Velva. She pressed two draks, as if ingenuously, on the mix, and then went out to the trees by the gate to let the milk vendor enjoy her. Something must always be rendered for something. That, too, was the gods' law.

The young soldier, part of the Guardian's force, which had a military requirement of a certain height, discovered that the Lydian was still a trace taller. He waited, with the westering sun behind him, and the soldier said, "You can go in, if you want. Shall I tell you the news first? Not good, Lydian."

The Lydian replied that he would hear the news. Accordingly the soldier gave it. "I'm sorry to be the one tells you. Don't curse me for it. Do you still want to go in the house?"

The Lydian said he would, thanked him, and went on through the gate and across the garden.

It was late in the hot afternoon, the sky with a strange glaring light that taxed the eyes. The house was deadened but not refreshed by shade. There were soldiers on the stair. They, too, let the Lydian by, commiserating, one asking after his arm, and, insensitive in embarrassment, when he would fight again. The other said, "The slut's run, a thief, too. There'll be trouble with Sh'alis over it, mark my words."

It seemed she had asked to be shown some lace that day. So the lacemaker and her two girls had come in and found it all, and rushed out shrieking in fright for the watch.

A sheet of lace was strewn on the floor of the salon; they had forgotten it in their panic. It was, too, costly, of gold threads from which the stretched gauze backing was scorched out by a heated iron. Perhaps the lacemaker had thought she would be accused of malice—though who would dare practice against an Amanackire? Somebody, plainly.

Elsewhere chests and cabinets hung open, a jewel-box had been emptied and flung down. The mix girl had robbed her mistress, having, presumably, murdered her. Servants did sometimes turn on their employers. As for Shansarian Alisaar—Sh'alis—always on fire for the honor of Shansar's old ally the Lowlands, they would have to be appeased. It was excellent the villainess was a mix. Nothing else was about to be considered.

She lay on a couch near the window, that window where she had wept. Apart from the fact that the mix had torn the rings from her fingers and the jeweled pin out of her dress, she lay as peacefully as if she slept. Her pale, pale hair glistened in a shaft of sun. Her eyes were closed, her lips slightly parted, fresh, delicately painted as the mouth of an image. Superstition had apparently caused the robber to leave the amber drop on the forehead alone, also the enamel snake on her arm. Its eyes sparkled dully, as Rehger crossed the chamber. But nothing else was stirring.

He had seen death many times, and caused death, and walked with death. But she did not look dead.

Rehger bent over her, and put out the sun from her face.

Yes, this was how she looked in slumber. For he had seen that, too. Serene and still. The dead, despite the words of poets, never looked like this. They looked—vacant, like something sloughed and thrown away. But here she was, poised for life, And no life came.

He would hear, before dusk, for they wanted to tell him all they could, as if details might be of use, that the poison had been identified, in the last of a cup of milk left standing by. Though the scent was very faint, both the physicians sent in by the Guardian had diagnosed the substance, for they had seen men and women depart through its benefits before. She had drained the pitcher; it was thirsty weather. Nothing on earth could have saved her, the medicine being that strong. It was astonishing she looked so quiet, as this way there was firstly euphoria and then terrible pain— And, somehow, obviously realizing her end was on her, she had got out and laid ready the necessary papers to do with her disposal. These also the robber respected.

Although Amanackire, she had at some time decided, with surprising tact, to be buried. The Shalian Ashara temple was to see to the rites. Regarding a tomb, she had recently bought that of Panduv the dancer. Indeed, ominously enough, the documents had only been notarized and sealed the previous night.

From all this one might even suspect a suicide. But the method, if so, was curious; she was young and in the wholeness of health, and of a race thinking itself god-gotten. And she was the doxy of a man any woman, liking men, would have desired.

There was nothing to be spoken to the dead. They would not listen. An inspiration was on him to say her name, *Aztira*. But he did not say it.

In the deep silence, a bird sang in the garden trees.

CHAPTER NINE

THE FALL OF THE HAWK

There was a room which was kept for him above an armorer's shop on Sword Street. It was not quite unusual for Swordsmen, or the dancers of the Women's House, to retain such a bolt-hole. Here they might have a privacy the stadium dormitories did not afford, for lovers, or for mere solitude. Rehger had always thought it proper to pay for the room and its maintenance, his cash rewarded by scrupulous attention from the armorer's cleaner. The whitewashed walls were spotless, the rugs shaken, and the sleeping couch aired and ready. Tonight, for some reason, she had put speckled lilies in a crock under the window. The very same flowers that had clouded up from a figured bowl in the salon of the mansion.

He arrived quietly, ascended the steps behind the shop, and unlocked the door. It was not yet sunset, miles of time between him and a new day. He thought of it in this manner. He did not know what should be done with the night, with Zastis, with all the burden of terrible surprise, of feeling, that had not had the space to become for him recognizable, to fade to an irrelevance, or spur to any height— Dawn, his superstition told him, would wash at least the doubt away. Or night itself, submerging him, would be his teacher. He almost feared to learn. Yet he had come here to aloneness, in order to do so. He had not lived so long in Daigoth's courts through bandaging his eyes.

Rehger had been in the room less than the third of an hour when someone scratched on the door. He supposed the slave had come, or the armorer's wife, to see if he wanted anything brought, supper or wine. Inclined not to answer, he delayed, but to give a churlish response displeased him, so he went to the door and opened it. No one was there. The shadows lay in place along the yard from the well tree and the trellised creepers. While from the yard's far side the hammer and anvil thudded on the forge like an angry heart.

By the room's threshold, a square of reed paper lay, rolled and corded, with a pebble set inside to weigh it down.

Some girl, maybe . . . But the retreats of champions were respected. Love-letters came to the stadium, or the wine-shops.

He took this letter up. Going back inside, he sat, the paper in his hand, looking at the lilies in the final sunlight.

Then he untied the cord.

The stadium educated its children, but there had never been much occasion to read anything. It was often so with the Swords, acrobats and dancers, wedded to the body not the mind. As for love-notes, they were short, or if copious, did not need to be scanned.

The paper was fully covered, by a fine and beautiful script.

It began: "To Rehger Am Ly Dis, son of Yennef son of Yalen: A prince of the Royal House of Lan, and of the bloodline of Amrek, King of Dorthar, Storm Lord of All Vis."

Only one other knew to address him in this way— this extraordinary way. She who had risen in the center of night, leaving his arms to search by sorcery the drak of bronzed gold. She, like an icon of ivory before the one lamp that had not yet burned out, turning the coin, in a while telling him of his mother that she had never seen, of his father that neither she nor he had ever looked on. And of that father's father. Of bastardy and foolishness, of births and wanderings, of a frivolous search she could not properly decipher— She had described the wretched farm at Iscah, and the city of Amlan. She had spoken of a priestess, Amrek's daughter— And in the end he had only left the couch and gone to bring her back against his flesh. It was Zastis. Let the past and future wait.

"Dear Friend," the letter continued, "when this comes to you, I will be dead, and you will know it. I think that you have some care for me, but not enough that this can wound you deeper than a little scratch might do. Salve the hurt, and may it heal swiftly and well. For myself, I loved you, from the moment I saw you I believe. I have never told you of my circumstances, but, like you, I was taken from my kindred early. And so to love, at last, was a gift She gave me. To be requited was not needful.

"She that brought you this, my servant, had disguised herself on my instructions, in the same way that she was instructed to take my jewels. She knows what she must do, though they will hunt her for my murder if they can. She is guiltless, of course. While the one that is culpable will in due season be punished, if even punishment is wanted.

"Only two things more to say, and quickly. By those means you have termed *sorcery*, I can banish pain. But there are not many minutes. A vanity—I refuse to die uncouthly. They will find me lying on the couch composed as if for sleep. And unless some unforeseen mistake occurs, so you will find me also. I regret we had no more together. But since there is no true death, I believe we will meet again.

"Having had communion with the coin, I have, as I cautiously promised you, been able to uncover something further: When you are able to seek your father, you will find him in the Lowland province of Moih. It really asks no larger information. You are, I think, destined to know him. The sons of the hero Raldnor never met their sire; his own was dead at his conception. That which the Vis call Chance, and we, Anackire, tends always to a balance where allowed. It will come at the correct hour, knowledge, and to both. I must be brief—

"Thus. I invite you to my funeral obsequies. Though it is perhaps irksome, nor joyous. To see me to my black stone bed on the hill. The Ashara temple will have charge of me. But I shall lack followers. Do it for kindness' sake, Rehger. I set it on you, that you must.

"And now I shall seek the couch and lie down there.

"Prosper. And, perhaps, remember me sometimes. Or how else will you know me, when next we meet?"

The letter was signed, without any of the flourish which had begun it, *Aztira*.

The madam arrived in person to oust Chacor. Her wide hips filled the doorway and her scent the chamber.

"So soon," he said.

"We're a good-class house, and hygienic. Money goes farther in the stews, but a Corhlish prince wouldn't want *those*."

"And I see I've fallen from favor with my last coin."

"Fallen? Scarcely down than up, from what I heard. And you're pretty enough to ruin all my girls for the other trade. And my best, my Tarla, so taken with you she's left out her petal, and Yasmat knows, now the silly tart's probably womb-full of something the doctor will have to see to. Unless you want it brought up to help you rule Corhl."

"If I had any cash left, I'd give it you in recompense," said Chacor. Cheerfully he placed a squashed marigold in the madam's hand and kissed her well-powdered cheek. "But I've only enough for a cup of bad wine."

He descended the brothel stairs whistling, the girls leaning over the galleries to reprove him for leaving, or for whistling, or to wish him luck.

It was getting dark, and the lane outside was murky. Farther down it forked, plummeting toward the fish market on one hand, up toward Gods' High Gate on the other. He had been thinking a while, once Tarla had gone, (lamenting over the springy "petal" of softened cow gut, that should have been inserted within her before their congress, and which eagerness had made her leave lying in the washbowl. The Way of Women, in rustic Corhl, was normally effected by a leaf pasted over the navel.)

That thing which had happened in the stadium arena—the wild rumors—these were a three-day wonder and would have run themselves out by now. Nevertheless, it was the right moment, maybe, for the rover to be on his way. Corrah showed the path by different means. He had kept enough to buy passage on some roughish ship. Destination was not so important. He would take the fortune of the draw.

Best get round to the harbor, then. Before allnight shut down and the cutthroats came out to pluck the price of supper.

As Chacor started toward the market fork, a woman screamed piercingly not far ahead.

Yells of various sorts were not so uncommon, particularly here. But then, out of the gathering dark, the screamer pelted up the lane toward him. Chacor immediately suspected some thief's trick. He braced himself, but the woman, hair and cloak flapping, rushed past him and was gone. Her eyes had looked properly scared. That established, Chacor now stepped back against a windowless house wall that here fenced in the lane. He expected a gang of men or women to be in pursuit of the first runner. What came, however, was not human.

Initially, he thought it was some evening revel, carrying lamps. But in fact, the lamp was alone, and carried itself.

A pale blue sun, transparent, yet glimmering so fiercely it colored the house wall, and the hand Chacor involuntarily raised to mark himself for Corrah's protection. The ghost-sun drifted up the lane, after the running woman. He watched it come level and go by, and when it had done so put his hand to the knife in his belt. But a knife was no use.

He had been witness to a supernatural thing. For

sure. What had that woman done, to have such bane hounding her?

Bemused, unsettled, Chacor resumed his walk down to the harbor, wondering what to make of this omen. His reflections sent him inward. He did not know, therefore, until he was fairly in the thick of it, that the evening was full of mischief and the waterfront in uproar.

On certain nights, if there had been a great catch, the market lit its torches and stayed open, but the fish by then was singing high. Added to this, now, was the smell of fear, and an electric crackle that made the fires spit. The night was very bright; Chacor thought absently of clear skies for tomorrow's passage out—

But men were running about, and one barged into him.

"What's up?" said Chacor.

"Got no eyes?"

Then Chacor did take notice. The clarity of the night was not due to torches or stars. He thought, *The moon's up early*. No, it was not the moon— It must be a ship on fire down in the basin.

So he went along with the shoving, shouting crowd, to see.

The market ran to a palisade above the harbor wall. Here it was possible to look out at the bay, the beaches shelved away into it, and the curve of the harbor rimmed with watch-turrets. Leftward, a quarter of a mile off under the wall, the smaller craft rocked in their huddles, behind those a wood of spars, galleys, merchantmen and red-eyed towers, at anchor in the basin of Saardsinmey. The activity of the docks seemed also in suspension, or disarray. In one of the huge careening bays, Chacor's keen sight made out men standing on the sides of a landed ship, pointing, or seeming to wrestle with each other in fear. Something was decidedly burning, but it was not a vessel. It was the sea itself.

(You heard, blue fire sometimes lit on the southwestern oceans. At sea, on the passage to the Second Continent, the phenomenon was often spotted. They called it Rorn's Borderings, the fringes of his mantle, harmless, auspicious even.)

But if this was anything of Rorn's it was not convivial to see.

It began just outside the harbor, inside the mouth of the bay, band on band of searing, restless flame, where there should have been only liquid. Now and then, out of the flame, a streamer or ray shot into the sky. This happened as Chacor elbowed a place at the palisade. There were cries of dismay. A big fat man nearby, well-dressed, and with a flower he had forgotten to hold to his nose, said, "I tell you, it's an oil-spillage. Some skimmer's messed on the sea, and it's caught a spark." But no one agreed with him, nor did he seemed convinced.

Then there was another cry. "Look! There it comes again!"

And all the crowd put round its collective head, Chacor's with it. After a moment, he made out two more of the ghostly fireballs flowing across the market. One burst with a sudden implosion, the other vanished into an alleyway.

Thunder rumbled over the sea. Annoyed at the water's antics, heaven was brewing a tempest. The sea began to shine upward on to heaving masses in the air. Lightning, blue or reddish, speared through, broke like an egg, and sizzled down the clouds.

A man beside Chacor said to him, brother in unease, "I know what *I* think. That Amanackire woman. She or her kind, they've sent it, a threat of revenge. Well, it stands to reason. They hate us and we hate them, with their white skins and their stinking snakes. Whoever killed her, no one's sorry. She won't rest quiet till—"

"The Amanackire," said Chacor. "Did you say—?"

"—And they'll bury her tonight. Have to be quick in this heat. But that won't help any."

"You said she died?"

But the man was moving off with his message of doom. The whole crowd, wanting to get away now from the evil spectacle in the bay, to seek advice or consolation, was pushing itself in all directions. A pale red moon stood vaguely gleaming on the horizon, but the moon had not risen yet.

Chacor had a vision of a girl's white face, veiled in silver hair. A silver hand that lay on his shoulder. He was stirring amid some dark that seemed to be inside him. Like a great clock, the essence was dripping out of him, the water level sinking down, and when the weights grounded, the time he would tell would be his death. But the silver hand sent through him a rush of light, and the machinery of life shuddered. The levels gaped wide, and refilled themselves. He rose on the tide, as if the hand drew him, blood drumming, pulses racing—even his loins had answered—and his eyes, from which tears had coursed.

Chacor fell against the palisade. The air flickered and needled. He was not the only one on the verge of fainting—

He knew, now. And knowing, could not return to ignorance.

He had been as close to death as his fingers were to the wooden post he gripped. But she had healed him. The Amanackire. Ah—did they not worship the goddess, too, if wrongly? From the chasm of darkness, she had led him forth. And, while he lay on the girls of the whore-house, proving his life, his guide had herself been cast into the pit of endless night. Poisoned, it seemed, for others were talking of it now, murder and Lowland vengeance.

Chacor worked the iron spike atop the post into his palm, until the pain pulled him together.

As he straightened, the phantom moon went out over the blazing sea.

The Shalian temple stood below Tomb Street, in a grove of cibba trees. Its doors were made of cibba, too, highly polished and inlaid with gilded bronze. The rest was stone, dark, after the habit of Lowland temples, but faced with tawny and white marbles. Though not large it was a costly building, nor easy of entry. Even the colored glass in the high altar-window had a frame of black iron. It showed a bloody cumulus roped and tied by a golden serpent, on a purple base, a motif similar to one of the Lowlander-Dortharian sigils, after Raldnor's sons had come to power.

In the beginning there had been several Shalian fanes in the city, to cater to the several Shansarians. Once Alisaar divided and the south became New, and Vis, only this one place remained, getting its sustenance from Sh'alis, now and then with a slogan scrawled on its marble overnight.

No one was scrawling any now. The discreet convoy sent by the Guardian had come earlier, ten crack guards armed to the ears, a captain, the body in a closed long-litter of the sort awarded the sick, or pregnant women. Thereafter the temple glowed with lights. The birds who nested in the cibba trees might have been forgiven for thinking dawn had come back, but it was the strange glare from the sea which had disturbed them. They had shrieked rather than chirruped, and lifted in a swarm. Most of the birds in Saardsinmey had behaved likewise, it was said. While the populace itself had gone down to the docks to inspect the show. Some were pleased with it. Generally they sought their own altars, where they were now offering and praying.

It was possible to observe the ocean from Tomb Street itself, but not the bay, which the spired bulk of the city hid from view. Along with the glare of mirrored incendiaries, the storm was raging there. No rain fell. And hardly any noise of thunder reached the temple. The air itself seemed dense as water. Only lightnings cleaved through it.

The thoroughbred the guard captain had ridden was restless. The zeebas of his men kicked and shied. The men themselves scratched, sneezed, shuffled.

The Shalian priests, not one of them a Shansarian but all mixes, seemed impervious to the electric tension of the night, and the affair at hand. They saw to the body in a back room. The written instructions she had left had been specific. She had requested only to be tidied. Though refusing fire, she wanted, naturally, no Vis embalming, no sprinkling or perfumes of flowers. No costume save the dress in which she had died. Death would see to her. It was the will of Anackire. And by those words, if by nothing else, she ensured cooperation.

The burial was also to be discreet. One hour before

sunrise. The men the Guardian had conscripted to attend, provision against trouble, expected no one but themselves and the priests to wait on her.

They were therefore somewhat put out, just past midnight, to behold a man walking up through the grove. They did not know it, but later, they would be put out a second time.

Chacor Am Corhl discovered he would be in company with the Lydian after he had paced a little less than three hours in the side court of the temple. He had not wished to be in the fane itself. He disliked the form of Ashara, as he did the form of Anackire—fish or snake, she appalled him, offended him. Though he had had an instant of thinking her some perversion of the Truth, that was not enough to be able to endure proximity. Besides, he had called her names.

Firstly the soldiers had been at him. They frisked him for materials of desecration, and questioned him erratically as to why he was there. Their tempers were short but their tongues were long, and he heard all the story, and all the jumble of suppositions, in exchange for his stubborn: "It's only decent somebody should walk behind the bier." "Well, we know you didn't have her," they said. "Not with the competition." The captain came over and said, "You're the Corhlan. The racer. The one who nearly died. Only that's a lie. Look at you. Some slight wound. I've seen that before. All blood, and no bother. She healed you, didn't she, the witch?" "Yes," he said, and he shook. "Well," said the captain, "you lost a third time, didn't you, if you wanted to thank her Zastis-style?"

They had been asking why he was there, and Chacor did not know, himself. Shaking, angry, he had not grasped now what was meant. (He had misunderstood the laments elsewhere, too, somehow even missed the name. Perhaps not desirous of learning.)

However, lies and slight wound and no bother or not, the guardsmen seemed to become chary of him all at once and let him go on into the temple. Chacor found a priest—Shansarians held to a masculine order, unlike the Lowland sect, which was mingled, female

and male, and the priestesses of some significance.
This priest was a brown mix.

Chacor only inquired for the time of burying. Then
again, what else had there been to ask? He could not
have gone near her body, even if they had let him.
Alive, had he ever properly seen her? That skull-
whiteness, the touch of the hand of light—

There was a small shrine in the court, but delight-
fully lacking any image, only a flame burned there in
glass. It rose very upright, very still. It was Chacor
who moved about. Then he sat on a bench, and fell
asleep. Some noise from the soldiers outside woke
him. Then he got up and paced again.

When someone entered the court behind him he
thought a priest had come to warn him they were
setting out, or even to go away and wait in the grove.
He turned with a snarl ready, his nerves primed high,
and saw the Lydian between two pillars, looking at
him, stock-still as the watch-flame.

In that instant, each seemed to fathom, and to its
depths, why the other was there. Neither spoke. Neither challenged the other on his rights.

The Lydian nodded, as if to a man he knew from
some supper they had both been at, where they had
bartered a few phrases of no import.

Then he crossed to a bench, and seated himself.
He sat in perfect cohesion, expressionless, gracious,
like some carving poured with gold and then for some
reason clad in a good plain mantle.

That man killed me, Chacor thought, *and in there
lies the corpse of the one who brought me back.* He
laughed aloud. Which was, in Corhl, unlawful at a
burial. Then recalled *that,* and laughed harder. And,
*He doesn't care for the Shalian goddess, either, our
hero.*

And Chacor went out, after all, to wait in the cibba
grove, a selected distance from the soldiers.

The statue of Ashara had claimed Rehger's concen-
tration only a handful of moments. He had seen god-
images often, in the city temples. Rorn maned with
black sea-waves, Zarduk with his belly of fire, and

Daigoth in the stadium precinct, the warrior, sword in hand and triumph on his forehead. Occasionally you would also come across tiny effigies of Ashara-Anack, in the bazaar. He knew her shape, and here it was, only a foot or so taller than he. Though her skin was white it did not look like skin. Her hair was yellow-gold, her eyes discs of citrine. Eight-armed, which made the shoulders unwieldy and unreal; the fish-tail of Shansar, yet patterned like snake-scales, and heavily jeweled. . . . She must be worth some sacks of money. She was not, in her way, unbeautiful. But she had for Rehger no look of Being, which the icons of his own race, modeled from men, or women, always had.

Ashara-Anack was not remotely like Aztira.

She had not informed him when her burial was to be. So he had walked up through the city to the Shalian temple and inquired. That done, those miles of time still washing about him, he had returned to the stadium, to pet and feed the team of hiddrax, to toil in the practice court alone. His arm was healing excellently. The wound had entirely sealed itself, and had the healthy dark, ridged color of ten days' renewal. Rehger had not taken it to the surgeon, who would see everything was happening too quickly. Instead, a reliable man on Sword Street removed the stitching only this morning, with no interrogation.

Possessing her had been enough, it seemed. Her loveliness, her love. Unlike the Corhlan's injury, this would leave its scar, seemly, decided. To remember her by.

Finding Chacor in the temple court Rehger had, it seemed to him, understood the cause for being there. Unlike the boy, Rehger did not reveal surprise at unwanted company.

When the Corhl laughed, Rehger, recollecting the chariot race, thought only, *He does that when he's sure of something in the heart of doubt. What has he discovered to be sure of?* (The Corhl had seen the sword become a serpent, in the arena. Had he forgotten? Remembered? Was he laughing at that?)

They had been saying, all along the upper streets, that the sea was burning in the bay. Groups were setting out to look, some with wine-flasks and baskets of food, going to make a night of it on the wall or the beach. Others coming from there looked less happy. Rehger did not pay much attention, having noted the over-radiance of the sky, which obscured even Zastis, and the storm which did not come inland.

When the Corhl had gone, Rehger stood up again. He went to the empty shrine and regarded the flame.

Aztira had presumably worshiped the snake goddess. He touched the flat of the shrine. He said, to the silence: "Be for her what she needs the most. Tomorrow, I'll bring you something, lady. Whatever they give you here. I'll ask, and bring you something fine."

He could not have said it to the statue in the temple. Yet for a second, without the unreality of the image in the way, he did suppose She heard him.

As he turned, a priest appeared between the pillars, and motioned him to follow. It was time.

Across the hill-slopes above the city, the Street of Tombs had gradually wound its way through the years. Richer Saardsins, taking up their abode on it, left orders for paving to be laid and kept in repair. Shade trees and aromatic shrubs were planted, and, between the sepulchers themselves, quantities of which were ornate to the point of jollity, stood altars, statues, and monuments. Meanwhile, on the lower southwestern side, astrologers, diviners, mages, and the practitioners of obscure cults, pitched their tents and cobbled up their mud-brick huts. Death Town throve.

Tomb Street properly began just above the cibba groves. As the funeral ascended on to it, there came the unavoidable impression of entering some benighted aristocratic avenue, mysteriously silent, but not always lightless. Very many of the mausoleums were large, and here and there a lantern shone out from a tall porch, or in some marble hand, for the Street watchmen were paid to effect this service.

The storm had faded at sea. Now and then, seen between trees and stones, lightning fluttered noiselessly far off. The city itself was mostly in deep shadow at last, slipping in her sleep toward the expected sunrise.

Zastis had set. A spangling of lamps along the waterfront and docks gave their usual tokens. An isolated
window or two, torches on the Zarduk temple roof,
were yellowed pearls shaken out on the dark. At the
old capital, Saardos, the beacon fires had burned each
and every night, to warn shipping on the western
ocean to put in for port before Aarl sucked it away.
But Aarl was a legend now, or a condition of the soul.

The night had retained its peculiar stifled stillness.
Some dogs were yowling down the hill, starting off
others elsewhere. But their voices were oddly muffled,
and the chorus did not continue. The night choked it out.

The Shalian priests carried brands, and rang bells
softly. In their midst they bore the long-litter, curtains
drawn. The torches barely smoked. There was no wind.
The Guardian's soldiers, redundant, resentful, but prepared, trudged after, for mounted men were not allowed on this thoroughfare. They had demonstrated
some disapproval of followers, or mourners, especially
that one should be the Lydian. But nevertheless he
and the Corhl walked to the rear, side by side,
unspeaking.

The sarcophagi of the entertainers lay at the topmost stretch of the Street. They had their own quarter, as did all the senseless dwellers in the necropolis.
The painted death-palaces of famous hetairas with
carved roses on their doors, the pavilions of champions, chained chariot wheels and split shields. The chal-
lenging epitaphs caught torchlight under the trees: "*You
live and I am gone, but when I lived my life was
better.*" "*I kissed the sun. It was enough.*" Or, too, the
dulcet, among the blossomy leaves, a dancer's body in
bronze and garlanded with gold, the tablet under her
foot: "*I was loved.*"

Panduv's tomb, far up the incline, and ringed by
flowering aloes, had no inscription. The stone was
black. It was a domed shape reminiscent, to any who
had seen it, of the beehive city in the cliff, Hanassor.

The door of the tomb, thick stone on a grooved
runner, stood open. The priests with the litter paced
inside, the fires and bells.

Over the paved boulevard of the dead, a quietness seemed to descend now like a lid.

For miles, not a sound.

"Trouble, sir."

One of the soldiers spoke abruptly.

Another added, "Yes, someone after us, and mounted up, from the noise of it."

They listened. Out of the night, some distance away along Tomb Street, a suspicion of hiddraxi, even horses, galloping. And some other resonance, as if a heavy thing were being dragged between them.

"Two or three miles, I'd say," said the captain.

His cohort waited, hand to sword, mollified by a chance of action. This was work they knew.

Then, sudden as it had begun, the hoofbeats and the dragging ended. The whole band seemed to have been swallowed into nothingness.

Presently, one of the soldiers swore. He looked at the Lydian, who had won bets for him. "Ghosts, eh?"

They paused there, in limbo. Ten guards, a captain, a prince of Corhl, a hero of the stadium of Saardsinmeny—while from the tomb a muted light stole and the notes of alien prayers.

Then the lawless riders were on the Street of Tombs once more. Pelting headlong toward them all. In three seconds more each man there ascertained some crucial difference. If hoofs, if wagons or chariots, they had come out from the roots of the earth—

And then the ground *rolled*.

Because he was in low spirits, Katemval had been glad to go on a drinking party with old friends. They were men who had made themselves, as he had, through luck and knack, traders and adventurers, in their youth. With the Saardsin grain merchant, he had once hunted wolves. While to the Kandian trapper, Katemval had once stood witness in two legal, savage duels, during which the man won his dead father's goods from five brothers. Only one of the brothers had required killing. He was a plotter who would not have taken to defeat.

Talking of which, and other former days, the out-

ing, litters spurned, roved through a decent inn or
two, ate its supper, and drank its fill. The Star, and
the hot sparks of remembered youngness, sent them
all at last into a house of women, and here they
finished off the night.

They had also, at an earlier juncture, gone to the
harbor wall to look at the ocean. Many people were out
to do the same, some picnicking even on the beach.
But mostly there were long faces. Imbued with the
wisdom of travelers who have gazed on many marvels,
and calmed by wine, the drinking party found the sight
of wet fire interesting but no cause for alarm. They
reassured the timorous on the streets. Some freak
current or outpost of the storm had sent in the fire
unusually close. Oh, yes. As for the flame-balls, that
was something one beheld at sea. Though there were
sailors who swore such things were demons, many tabbed
these random emissions of lightning. With similar facts,
they regaled the uneasy at the emporium of joy.

A while before morning, youth having evaporated,
and the threat of un-well-being upon him, Katemval
hired a boy with a torch, and started for home.

The sea was still giving up to heaven an eerie blur of
light, plainly visible between the tall southern roofs and
garden walls.

Perhaps the gods had been roistering, too. They
lived forever, and must get bored with it. For men,
boredom was normally offset by notions of brevity.
Katemval was not yet to his seventy-sixth year, an
upper path for a Vis. His father had gone to one
hundred and fifteen, but not pleasantly, riddled with
ailments. *Well, my dear,* thought Katemval, following
the bright blot of the torch, *a few more such nights,
and seventy-six should see you out.*

But he did not credit that. Sleep and a posset
would put him right. And there was this breach with
Rehger somehow to be sorted. The witch was dead—so
that at least was seen to.

They had reached Jewel Steps, and were climbing
them, the torch-boy springing ahead, when there came
a sudden tremendous bang, from the waterfront behind.

It rocked the night, a horrible echoing thud, that drove the air deep into the ears.

"Was that the harbor?" exclaimed Katemval. "Some ship's oil-casks have gone up—"

The boy looked frightened, staring back toward the sea that house sides hid from them, the torch dropped to the stair. Katemval had turned also. Below, light was being kindled in a score of windows.

Katemval thought, *No, I won't go to gawp. It's my bed I need—*

Then he was falling.

He could not tell why. He struck the steps, and hit his head, and thought stupidly, *It was aching anyway, where's justice—* But then some rhythm in the stone jounced him on, and he fell farther, and the next blow stunned him, so everything was mazed, a mad misty universe where walls were jumping into the sky, and there was a ghastly mad noise going on, grinding and cracking and splintering, with the strains of bells and screams mixed in.

Since the crane had stayed unrepaired, the column-tree had remained upon the top-walk of the stage. It had been the axis of this evening's discord at the theater, along with the leopards for Yasmat's dance, which were fractious and unbiddable. Panduv herself had unfalteringly performed her routines, her body obedient to her as a black rope. . . . When the rehearsal perished, the night had run nearly into a day. But Panduv's lover among the actors persuaded her to combine with him, again, inside the column-drum. "You never make a sound above a sigh," he complained when they were done. "Don't you like what I do?" Well-mannered to intimates, she was casting about for a reply that would suit his peacock soul, when such things ceased to matter.

"Tits of Death!" the peacock cried, between anger and fear. "Some pig's winching us on that cracked-up crane—trying to kill me—that Epos, he thinks he'll take my place—*Epos!* Damn you into Aarl, you bloody dog!"

The drum flung to and fro. The lovers were tossed

into each others' arms, and away against the cushioning. All at once, the column reeled. Sickeningly, beyond
any command of theirs, they felt it toppling. As in the
other thing, he made more noise than she. The crash
was bruising but not fatal—now they rolled. They were
deafened and buffeted by the tumbling drum. The
actor roared and flailed. "Keep still, brainless," Panduv
spat at him. "Hit me again, I'll tear out your eyes."
"You Zakor sow, don't mark my face with your
talons—" Just then, with a shudder, the column jarred
to a halt.

All of this had lasted less than a minute. Breathless,
and in abject wrath, the actor now scrabbled over
Panduv to release the hinges of the drum. After some
difficulty, he succeeded, and crawled out into the darkened theater. Something crunched under his knee.
With undeductive surprise, he realized it was the piece
of a lamp which seemed to have come down from the
ceiling. Perhaps the column had struck it in the air.

Then, and only then, it came to him the atmosphere
was full of a thick abrasive dust. He began to cough,
cursing the damage to his voice. As he did so, the
second revelation occurred, and on its heels, another.
There was a most bizarre music playing in the city
beyond the theater courts. It had elements of pipes
possibly, a wild wailing song. More than ten thousand
throats seemed to make it up. Instinct caused him to
glance overhead. He saw, through the cloud of ocher,
something flash and flicker in the roof. It was lightning. The roof had become sky—

"Oh, Panduv—" he said, his tone inadvertently laced
with high tragedy, for once genuine.

Then there came a groaning boom. It passed through
the ground beneath and the open sky above. The
world started again to vibrate. The actor sprawled on
his face.

Panduv, in her turn, had been listening to the music
in Saardsinmey. It had held her spellbound on her
belly, shrinking, immobile. And now, while she lay
there still and the earth quaked and thundered a second time, her companion's desperate feet spasmodi-
cally kicked shut the partitions of the column. As all

the tiers of the theater lifted slowly from their beds, and glided down on the stage.

In Velva's tiny cubicle at the inn on Five Mile Street, there was space only for a bed, a slender cabinet, a mirror of bronze upon the wall. No space at all for the earthquake.

Most of the inn had collapsed into the street and surrounding yards. The wing which housed the tavern slaves and girls, only one story high and tucked into rising ground, had largely survived both shocks. But internally it was a shambles, and full of the electrifying sawing wailing sound that now seemed to hang densely on the city as the dust.

Velva had not been sleeping. The deed of the previous morning, the gossip-borne news of its accomplishment, had held her ever since in a kind of paralysis. She performed her tasks in an orderly way, but when the night's service was over, coming into the cubicle, she lay down fully-clothed, straight as a rod, her hands clasped across her waist—the position of one buried.

Neither dread of accusation, nor remorse, had affected her. She had felt herself to be merely an instrument of some great will. Maybe it was in itself this epic picture of the murder that now wrung her out. For sure, she had no thought of elemental punishment. When the earth tilted, throwing her from the bed, and from her apathy, she was only terrified, nothing more.

The first shock tore through the world. And passed. Perhaps thirty seconds elapsed, filled by crashings and subsidences, the human hymn of pain and fear. The aftershock, in itself far less, but needing solely to strum the weakened structures of the city to bring them down, seemed if anything stronger than the first. That too passed.

A beam had dropped from the ceiling and smashed the bed. Had Velva not been ejected, it would have crushed her. But she had no fancy either she had been spared.

*   *   *

The boy had run away. That was not amazing. But he would not have expected it of Rehger. Was the boy Rehger? Rehger was a man, now—Katemval lay on rubble of the Jewel Steps and brooded on these things. Then, his eyes wandering, he saw after all the boy who was not Rehger had also not deserted him. A cascade of stones from a nearby house, covering the steps, had killed him outright. This brought Katemval an instant of extreme grief. Then, his consciousness moving inevitably outward, he realized such motives for sorrow were everywhere around.

Katemval crawled to his knees, and wrapped the edge of his mantle over his lower face, against the smother of stone dust and plaster. He stared in a sort of emotionless acceptance, finding that he could now look out to sea from Jewel Steps, for every wall and building in between seemed to have collapsed.

The dawn was coming, too, carelessly out of the east. It burnished the whirling pillars of the dust, revealing or suggesting distances. Here and there, like lamps underwater, fires had broken out and were burning, attractive sweet colors through the murk, rosy, and soft white— The whole city, on one breath, seemed to scream.

Katemval felt anger then. He looked at the sky, the ghostly sketch of sea. He might have spoken against the gods. But the ground began to shake again. The thundering rumble came from far away, pouring toward him. And like a beaten dog he cowered before the stick.

Then a god rose in front of him, a scarlet blazing tower. Or it was the misplaced sun exploding as it was hurled up from the southern sea, eight miles away, had he known it, turning the sky to blood.

The sea in its sequins had gone this time two miles out. It had run from Saardsinmey as if itself afraid of the quaking of the earth. The water left the ribbed mud behind it, shining still, littered with thrashing sea-life and the slovenly nets of weeds.

The ships in the harbor basin, dashed and buffeted

by the rocking of the world, several alight, were now grounded, ineffectual as huge toys.

Of those people still alive in the vicinity, few paid heed to the sea's escape.

It had waited out its while, a thousand years perhaps, the thing under the ocean. Once or twice, playfully, it had turned in its sleep, and the coasts of Alisaar trembled. Nothing sleeps forever. Feeling its quickening upon it, it woke, and lifted itself into the darkness of the day.

There came then the bellowing crack of doom. Those who could, craning in horror toward it, saw this:

A funnel of brilliant white, a hammerhead of blackness. Then red, red for New Alisaar, the red of roses and fire and blood, bursting, hitting heaven, streaming down.

The landmass seemed lit by it, end to end. The sky recoiled. All hint of sunrise was put out.

Black and red the turmoil now, and through the upsurge, silver snakes that twisted, wreathing the stormclouds, clutching, strangling them, never letting them go.

The submarine volcano, brother or child of countless others located far from shore, south and west, the mountains of fire which had given those oceans their legends of Hell: Its frenzy was flame against flame, so the water, running into it, was gulped and burned away. Steam and magma, liquid rock, salt and boiling smoke, gushed a quarter of a mile into the atmosphere. The volcano raped the sky. The sea churned, caught between waves of moving earth and fire. The sea fell in upon itself, and, repulsed by the phallus of Aarl, turned back for land.

Sixteen years of age, Tarla, her clothes torn, her face freshly painted with dirt, sobbing, framed in the upper window of a room that had no longer any actual walls; Tarla with dead women heaped around her on the cushions and the wreckage, saw—across the flattened chaos of ten thoroughfares, a market, a descending terrace that finished in midair—saw Rorn come out of the sea. Or thought she did.

The towering fire-cloud with its lightning coils of white serpents coming and going, that made no sense to her. Nor had the earthquake done so. It was a nightmare, although she could not surface from it. Only an hour ago, she had been arguing for the hopes of a hypothetical embryo, lodged in her womb by some Corhlan wanderer— Now, those ideas had vanished. She clung to the window-shape. She sobbed, and the red sky heaved and fissured.

Then, Rorn came up from the depths.

He had no form, as in the myths he did. No, he was only water. It piled up on itself, scaling into the sky until the sky was gone. It hid the mountain even, and the mountain's fiery light. The world turned black. Yet the water glowed. It gleamed like bales of silk, up there, stretching to the roof of eternity.

In wonder, the girl had stopped crying. To cry had no meaning.

One moment the ocean was a glittering sheet on its side, distant, unbelievable, and real, and then you saw, too, the curling creamy head of it, pleating over, the breaker, two hundred feet high—

It looked utterly gentle, so smooth now was its passage. And gently, tenderly, it smoothed down the granite palisade of the harbor, the last fifty-foot standing stones. As it came, it drew up the galleys and the merchantmen, the turrets, the basalt slipway itself, in one cupped hand skillful and sure as a mother's—

Tarla saw all things, whole or in portions, gathered to the sky. The needles of a fine spray pierced her face. The breath of Rorn rushed in her mouth, her lungs, as she opened them to call aloud. Then countless tons of water, the tidal wave, combed in across the shore, the street, the city, and her little protest, and silenced every one.

When the ground moved, men fell down as at a magician's mantra in some theatrical comedy. When the ground moved a second time, they fell a second time. Here and there a tree uprooted, leaving behind a perfect impression in the soil. Stones shook out of tombsides, and fifty feet away a lamped statue was smashed in bits, and set the shrubbery in flames.

Farther off, the city had fared much worse. A smother of particles and smokes hazed up from it directly, obscuring and heightening the chaos. Otherwise only noise came out. It rumbled and moaned, and bells jangled—there was a long bass roaring that did not properly end, but seemed to go round and round in circles in the hollow shell of the earth.

Then the gout of bloody matter exploded like a lanced abcess on the horizon of the sea.

As the world flashed red, then darkened to a reborn night, having the clue, even those who had begun to flounder down toward the mass of the ravaged city— checked.

Not one of them had said a coherent sentence all this while. With blasphemies and oaths, pleas and wordless expletives, or total silence, so they had greeted the advent. The Shalian priests, who had scrambled out of the tomb for fear it would come down on them, had done no better than the unenlightened soldiery, the cursing stone-worshiper from Corhl, the Lydian Swordsman fighting, as he usually fought for life, without comment.

Panduv's black tomb, abandoned, had nevertheless withstood both shocks. The quake, spreading from the hell-mouth in the ocean, was lessened here. It had been their fate to survive.

"There're snakes in the sky," said one of the soldiers, softly.

Then they could no longer see them. Something had risen, between the dust-pall of the land and the spasms of the volcano.

They could not make out what it was, this interruption. A couple asked each other. One man said, "I've heard of that—it's water—it's the sea—" And then he screamed and turned and ran away up the street of the dead, stumbling on the upraised paving, clawing through the shattered trees.

The rest stood quietly, looking out toward the curious, shimmering entity that was a wall of water taller than the tallest spire of Saardsinmey.

Chacor said, softly as the other man, "What does it do?"

"Nothing can stop it," said the captain. "Look, it's coming inland."

"But the city—" said another of the soldiers. He added, very low, as if ashamed to tell the secret, "My son's there. And my mother. If she got down into the cellar in time, do you think— No. It'll flood the cellars. It'll break everything above and fill up everything below. No. That can't be. Rorn's stinking guts, it can't be."

Some of the men began to murmur, solemnly, couthly. They stood on, looking out toward death, straight-shouldered, praying. The priests of Ashara were voiceless beside them. They waited also, trying, it would seem, to be faithful to the precepts of Shansar and Lowlander alike: Die well, live forever.

The sound of the water began to come, now. It was like a deep hoarse sigh. All other noise was lost in it, as everything would be lost.

The Lydian spoke behind them.

"There's the tomb. It's solid, and the water has to push uphill, here. A chance."

They turned, not all of them, and gazed at him, surprised he thought to refuse the gods. Chacor said, "He's right. Move, you—" He shoved at the two men next to him. Suddenly the whole group was struggling back to the tomb, the priests coming after.

They got through the tangled aloes. No one properly paused on the threshold. A man hesitated to call after the fellow who had run away, but he was out of sight and did not answer, and the sound of the sea now was very raw and strong.

The last man in, they put muscle to the stone door and thrust it along the runner, closing it fast. Though mysteriously equipped for it, it would be more difficult to open from within. But maybe they would never need to try.

The mausoleum was an oval, divided into an outer and inner place. The priests' torches flowed through ornate carvings, leaves and leopards and laughing moons, which sprawled all about the walls, seeming a sheer insanity at this minute.

Beyond a doorway, the inner tomb held shadows. They did not need to enter it. It was this, the ante-chamber, farthest from the wave, and doubly fenced by walls of stone, which would be the most secure. Nevertheless, the nervous torches spilled into the shadow. There were glimpses of something pale lying on its dais, another madness which they saw and did not see, comprehended and had no time for—

The ground was shaking once again, and fine dark powders sifted down. The noise of the enormous wave had altered to a steady howl—

They heard, through the surge, Rorn's feet upon the hill—

If they noticed each other, or remembered their families or their gods, not one now who displayed it. Each man stood before death, as before death men, though mown down in millions, have always stood, companionless and lonely.

The torches dipped. Night gaped. Thunder. The wheels of giants bore up on them.

Then, shrieking, the water came.

Rehger thought, *I forgot her warning. She was speaking, then, of this. If she knew what she spoke of, that night she cried. And her death brought me here. Not to die. This isn't the unstoppable sword, the broken spine of the chariot's flight. No glory in this, Katemval. And Amrek, where is he? Under what slide of rock and turf, on the plain of Koramvis, listening in your envy to the footfall of men above*—

He half reckoned she whispered to him, the dead girl with the gauze veil across her face, but he could not hear her.

His mother put into his hand a fruit. "Eat, before he sees."

He was riding the dog Blackness, and the crowd cheered. The cheering clove through the stones. The fruit tasted of salt water.

CHAPTER TEN

DISPOSSESSED

Terror, fire, water, and darkness, had bestridden the world. After a short century of obscurity, of thunders and churnings, and a great sweeping away, a slow, uncanny light began to come. And a silence thick as deafness, with, inside itself, the same inexplicable sounds that deafness knows—sudden long whistling notes, sudden inner boomings, a sharp snap like parting bone, a leaden pulse, a rushing sigh—

Miles out, the Aarl-mouth, the volcano, glowed a dark deep red. The huge column of its smoke seemed to stand quite still, though far overhead the cloud had opened into a parasol, magenta in color, and now and then chalked with dim reflected fire. Somewhere, in some other country, the sun had risen; it was noon. The sky here was that of an eternal sunset, all the somber crimsons, thin russets, heavy purples of decay. The sea looked nearly black, but for the streaks on it of the mountain's sinking lamp.

Black rain had trickled over the city, ashes and tears. Dead birds also came down. It was a season of fallings, birds and rain and tiles, and strength. The wave, too, had slipped away. It took with it, back to the ocean, many of the treasures of the city. In return, the wave had sprinkled the land with marine keepsakes. Fish were in the trees. Weeds wrapped the uprights of doors and embraced the legs of arches. But Saardsinmey was no longer a city, a built place. It had become a geography, a place of escarpments and jagged standing stones.

Very occasionally there was the oddest, least conscionable, event. Something living might be seen moving through the city, or heard calling out there. These happenings were infrequent.

Beautiful and pristine, her masts precise, long flanks tidy with oar-ports shut, her prow pointed by a gilded Vardish lion that blazed in the strange light, the ship lay at anchor on the roof of the Zarduk temple, almost forty-five feet in the air.

Below, aside from the massive outer walls, and their girdling pillars the width of ten men around, little of the temple remained. But it was, nevertheless, a marker in a desert, for beneath its stair, strewn with freakish debris, nothing else had stood in a radius of thirty streets.

"The hand of Corrah," said Chacor. "Or some god they offended."

He stared in disbelief and dismay at a dead sea-thing, a dark blue bladder with its eyes sunken in, and half the size of a man's body. It was automatic to measure that, for a man lay beside it, a Zakorian priest of the temple. The wave had broken his arms and squashed out his face with his soul, even as it battered the sea-beast against the pillar.

Chacor was full of horror, and abject depression.

A man darted from the temple. He was wet and filthy and carried a sack. He came at the dead priest like a rat and tried to pull a golden wristlet from him. Chacor struck the looter flat, drawing his dagger as he did so. The Alisaarian looked at Chacor, at the dagger, clearly muddled. "Something to you, was he? That won't help him now. Go on then. You have it." Chacor sprang toward the looter, ready to knife him. The looter, sack held tight, sprinted away, between the hills of patchwork dripping masonry, from which bodies hung, and skeins of hair like weed and weed like hair. . . . How had he survived, that Alisaarian? Corrah knew. Some quirk of destiny, like Chacor's own.

The sea had smitten the tomb of Panduv like a colossal hand, not a fist, a woman's blow, open-palmed.

All light died. That was the augury. One expected to be next.

Flung face down, bruised by those damnable carvings of a dancer's vanity, Chacor heard rather than
saw the walls giving way. The water poured through
and filled his mouth. He thought, formlessly, that this
was a disgusting way to die.

He came to himself, soaked and cold, puking up the
sea, and then to realize someone was helping him, one
of the soldiers. Happiness that another man was alive
with him made Chacor cry. The soldier had the kindness
to pretend that this was only the sickness affecting his
eyes. In Alisaar it was beneath a man to weep. In Corhl,
as in Zakoris, it earned a boy over six years a flogging.

The soldiers, they had all survived, had got out of
the tomb by use of the door mechanism. Three of the
Shalians had been killed. The rest had taken their
bodies away, down to the temple, if anything was left
of it. Everyone else stood on the slope of an alien
land, mud and muck, minced bushes, branches piled
as if for a bonfire, and various rubble. In parts, a tomb
jutted from the unrecognizable vista. Houses of death,
they had weathered death better than fifty thousand
houses of the living.

The light was appropriately hell-light, now scarlet,
now sporadically phased by black clouds and dirty
syrupy rain that had a foul odor. It occluded most
things, and wholly masked the view of the city, a
blessing, perhaps.

The soldiers meant to go down into Saardsinmey—
they still named it that, the havoc below: Report to
barracks. They did not seem to question it would be
there. On the other hand, the Guardian's palace and
adjacent buildings had been erected with much care
and cash. It was impossible to detect anything from up
here. Except look. That was the Zarduk temple, by
Rorn's teeth, drifting in and out of the murk, and
something glinting on the roof—a beacon maybe—

"Where's the Lydian?" said Chacor abruptly.

Some of the men had already gone off to the Shalian
fane, to see if they could find any of their mounts
alive. They were coming back now, mountless, with
grim faces. Chacor had thought the Swordsman might
be with them.

"One court and one wall standing," said the first soldier to reach the captain. "Our Rorn trod on their goddess good and proper. They're making a pyre for their mates, trying to find something dry enough to burn. I said, row out to the fire-mountain. I shouldn't have said it. But Rorn's bleeding guts, there must be thousands dead down there—"

"You can see a bit, from their wall," said another. "It's a shambles."

"The Lydian," said Chacor.

"What? Oh, to the stadium, could be. He's long gone."

Presently the soldiers got themselves into pedantic military order, and marched off, sliding and out of step in the slime. They would be wanted in the city. They had welded themselves to this idea.

But Chacor had no inspiration at all. He decided eventually to start after the Swordsman, or at least in that direction. He did not know why, or ponder why, any more then he knew or pondered why he kept glancing back, through the red-black rain, at the hill and the tomb where the white woman still lay, her bed awash with trapped salt water.

He could not find the stadium. He could not find anything. Enormous stacks of stone and plaster went up, some with caves in them. In the caves were chairs and colonnades, barbers' shops, bread-ovens, gleaming mirrors, dead bodies. Sometimes a tree or pillar had been carried up and pushed through a wall. Sometimes the trees and pillars had stayed put. He saw dogs and hiddrax, and once a horse, hanging by their necks from boughs or high cornices, as if in a knacker's yard. He saw too many such things.

Once he heard, or thought he did, a woman shouting and calling. He tried to reach her but could not shift the mounds of marble, the great fallen arch with its headless statues. And finally anyway, he could not hear her any more.

When he gave up on the stadium, and so on the Lydian, he got to the Zarduk temple and observed religiously the grace of the stranded, crewless ship. For the first time it had occurred to Chacor some god had done all this, and that it would be clever to be gone. The looter, once he had vanished, became unreal. No one else seemed living. A couple of times Chacor was misled—a woman, her hair fluttering in a gust of cindery breeze, the glimpse of light on an ornament . . .

Then suddenly, he found Five Mile Street.

It was easy, in a way, for the sea had cut through it as through a canyon, mostly unimpeded, and so left its wide long shape, the margins only spoiled by debris, pools of water, and fantastic flotsam.

Chacor walked then, looking exactly before him, and climbed up and over where he had to. When he heard things he took no notice. Twice, there were hoofs. They echoed, striking every new hollow, whipping back from a hundred sounding boards, until a phalanx of riders raced through the sky. But there was no point in attending to it. Something seemed to be burning down ahead, near where the docks had been. Probably it was some fire that the wave had not quenched, or a weird reflecton of the volcano, which was now itself barely visible through smoke and umbra. Even so, a few ships might have remained, coasting the wave, as had the vessel on the temple, these with their crews living.

A man moved out from the wreckage on to Five Mile Street, about a hundred yards away. Chacor, fooled too often, would not look. When the man waited, Chacor kept on, although, recollecting the other meeting with the looter, he drew his knife.

In an altered landscape, height was an irrelevance. He did not perceive the other man was the Lydian until he was nearly up to him.

"Where are you going?" the Lydian said. His voice was quiet, lacking the authority with which it had offered twenty men the chance of safety in a tomb.

"The harbor. I thought I saw a beacon." Chacor hesitated. As if the world were after all sane enough for conversation, he added, "You?"

"I went to try to find someone in a street there."

"No luck."

"Well. The house was down. He was always very proud of the house. He got it betting on me."

As rarely in the stadium, the Lydian was dyed by blood. His hands and arms looked as if they had been toiling in the brickwork, veins enameled darkly on the dark gold of the skin. He said nothing more. He seemed sorry rather than anguished, composed, not stunned.

Chacor turned, and the Lydian accompanied him. They went together toward the harbor.

Well, they lived with death. Of course, any day, the end. One forgot, but they were slaves, too, the Sword-Kings of Alisaar's ruby cities. "What will you do?" Chacor said. "Does this make you free?"

"I suppose not," said the Lydian.

They did not run off to liberty. No need. Saardsinmey, perished, offered this one manumission, or disinheritance.

"Go to Kandis. They said you've fought there. And Jow," said Chacor. "Will you? You couldn't go up north and hire to Shansars in Sh'alis."

At the end of the five miles, Gods' High Gate had come down and blocked the road. By the time they had got over it, and all the mess beyond, and were in reach of the harbor, its ruin and smashed ships, Chacor's rogue fire had disappeared. Even the volcano seemed vanquished or asleep. Only the sky of ichor and amber burned on and on and on.

Arn Yr, a ship lord from the Lowland port-city of Moiyah, had taken out his vessel, *Pretty Girl*, a dozen times that summer, with no trouble. This had made him a trifle uneasy, so, a mix, he had offered to Zarok and prayed to Anackire, before again setting sail. Both, it transpired, had been busy with other matters.

No sooner had they begun the crossing through open sea toward northern Alisaar, than the mother of storms hit them.

Pretty Girl was not just a pretty face. Plucky and tough, she took all the weather could give. When the sea calmed, ladled out in an opaque sunrise, they discovered her intact. But they were miles down south, with half the stores gone, and some of the cargo with

them. Arn Yr offered his men the vote, whether to
turn back to Moiyah, or try for the nearer ports of
New Alisaar, where their predominantly yellow hair
might not get them the love they had at home.

The vote went for Alisaar. They said they would
dye their manes black like the hero-god Raldnor, if
necessary, and laughed. Arn Yr, three quarters Lowland, but with an Ommos grandmother, was not too
pleased. But the ships of Moih went by the same
democratic values as her cities. They turned for New
Alisaar.

The overcast and tingling air they took for some
after-aspect of the storm. Then the ship's instruments
began to play up on them, and then the skies grew odd.
In a while, no shore in sight, bereft of moon and stars
and sun, they were lost, and saw themselves in the
hand of the goddess.

Near morning, they made out terrific explosions south
and west.

"Someone's having a fight with someone," said Arn
Yr. He thought he recogized the noise of ballistas
and exploding ships. Nowadays Free Zakorian priates
kept to the north and east. This could only be some
fracas between Shansar and Alisaar, which boded ill
for everyone, let alone poor *Pretty Girl*. Blond or not,
they had begun to trust by now to Saardsinmey's
dockyard and markets.

It was a spectacular dawn, the sky composed of
metals and bloomed with stratos. Birds flew over and
got some applause, for they meant the coast was near.
Some of the birds even settled briefly on the ship, and
were fed as fine omens.

Cautious however, and with no sailing wind, *Pretty
Girl* went to rowers stations and nosed westward, having once more a sun to guide her.

They sighted and identified the coast at sunset. They
would make Saardsinmey inside four hours.

There was no sign of war.

Only, the sunset lingered, its tints growing hotter
. . . After a while, they started to remark on it.

Then the moon came up. It was Zastis, and the
flushed Zastian lunar orb was familiar. But this moon

was not red. On an endless vermilion east it was a disc of molten orange with a purple halo, and it seemed to shift and flicker like a sun.

The west, too, still held the light torch-red, ringing—The ocean soaked the colors up and looked itself on fire.

In the midst of this, they saw the smoke off to larboard, and concluded somebody's fleet had burned. The cloud lay nearly firm as sculptured rock along the water, a large mass slowly gliding west.

Every star in the sky was like a blood drop. Zastis itself was not to be seen. They had now had three hours of sunset.

They rowed on for the Alisaarians' city because it was human, something they understood.

Or so they thought, until they saw it.

The Moiyan ship paused, a mile from land, as they looked on Saardsinmey.

"No Shansarian," murmured Arn Yr's deck master, "no men, no weapon on earth, did that."

"The gods," said Arn Yr, "did that."

And reasoning out at last what might have been the gods' instrument, that tumble of hard black now resting behind them on the sea, still they went in to shore, drawn by horror and compassion, and in case, against all chance, they might render help.

BOOK THREE

ISCAH

CHAPTER ELEVEN

TRUE SLAVERY

She was in the womb of Yasmat, in the hand of fate.
She was in darkness, which rocked her to and fro.

But she discovered a discrepancy in the substance of
the darkness, for half was water, half was not. Then
the dark opened. There was a long horizontal shaft of
burning red. It had the smell of salt and slime and
pitch, yet also a freshness that dizzied her. She gulped
at it thirstily, drinking the air, stretching out her hands
to it—

Perhaps it was this movement, or some upsurge from
beneath, but the great womb which had carried her
turned suddenly over. In that instant of birth, as she
fell into the sea, Panduv's instinctive body flung itself
away, leaping like a black dolphin in a wave of fire.
She did not know why.

Immediately she struck the water she went down. An
entirety of liquid closed over her head and pushed her
under like a hard hand. Beneath her she glimpsed
eternity. But above, the column-tree of the goddess
from which she had been sprung, floating in two hollow halves still joined by hinges.

Raising her arms, Panduv dived toward the surface,
broke the barrier of the sea into the red light, and
pulled herself on to the floating column.

Her body was pulped and battered, as if she had
been beaten by masters of torture. Every part of her
ached and shrilled, even to her teeth and her loins.
She rested face upward on the drum, her arms out-
spread, one hand dangling in the water. Within this
cask of wood and paint and bronze, she had been

catapulted through time and space, and fetched up here on an empty sea of blood.

In a blood-red dream, she lay there.

And, in the dream, she later beheld a purple moon come up, and against its flickering, the image of a ship.

When the hook of the grapple thudded home in the column-drum, Panduv did not raise herself. She did not care.

The ship hauled her in slowly.

Panduv saw, beside her and beneath, in the water, the reflection of the ship, and then, above, the one tall sail. She was a vessel of Sh'alis, mostly Shansarian in design. Over the rail, the faces of men, smudged and staring, and pale of skin, looked down on their catch.

"A black fish of Vis!"

"Or maybe the fires burnt her that color, eh?"

As two of them began to climb down the swaying rope to her, Panduv considered slipping off the column, allowing herself to sink into the eternity under the sea. . . . The life-wish of the stadium-trained kept her where she was.

The men lifted her roughly and handed her up. She was wracked by pain and a sound escaped her.

"You're alive then?"

"Oh, it's alive."

They dropped her on the deck.

The ship lord, the captain, was bending over her. A blond man with black eyes. Not good. Mixes were often the least tolerant.

"You escaped," said the mix captian. "Ashara spared you, Inky. Are you off some other ship?"

She parted her lips to revile him. Perhaps then he would kill her at once. But no, the words would not come. Life-wish, or only that she had forgotten the means of speech.

The captain was indicating his cabin, an uncouth housing amid ships, and they took her there and cast her down by the man's pallet.

Presently he entered, tying the leather door-flaps together, so they were alone.

"Don't fear I'll touch you," said the mix ship-lord.

"I wouldn't dirty myself. But some of them might. They catch Star-itch and go with anything, with each other or the livestock. They're muck. Ashara hear me, this trade is my curse. But you are my slave now. Do you understand?" He peered at her with his Vis eyes set in the filthy, unshaven white face. "Rest up," he said. "Tonight you can eat, and then tell me who you are. You see," he said, bending to her, "if you have a rich family, they'll have to recompense me, to get you back."

Panduv's voice came.

"No family," she said. She smiled a little, which it hurt her to do. "I am a slave of the city of Saardsinmey."

"Not any more," he said. "We went and took a look, after the storm passed. Nothing left of it, your bloody city."

"An earthquake," she said.

"And a great wave from the ocean. Your Rorn spat on your Saard rubbish-tip. So much for you."

"And no ransom for you," she said softly.

"So, I'll sell you when we reach Iscah."

When he left her again, she saw that the sky and the sea were still bright red. Although she had not fathomed what he said about Saardsinmey, an education seemed to be taking place in her mind. On some level, she knew perfectly everything that had happened as, unconscious and absent in the column, it had been rolled and tossed and borne her out to sea in the jaws of the returning ocean. A miraculous deliverance. Yet something also within herself told her that truly, the city was gone, and that therefore she, too, had died, everything of what she had been dashed from her. She had died once before, in Zakoris, on the day she was taken from her village. That first life lost she had never regretted. The life of an empress-slave— already she had passed far beyond it.

She wondered in that case what was left of herself, and who she now was. And searching through herself in the torpor of her physical shock and pain, she found at length the inner place, beyond sight and feeling and thought, and here she enclosed herself, with the peaceful sense that nothing actually mattered, what she had lost, or what had been destroyed, not even her nature and her name.

Panduv slept.

The *Owar* was a ship from the harbors of northern Sh'alis, crewed by the lowest stuff of the northern quays. Sometime trader, and opportune pirate, she mooched about the seaways between the lesser ports of the Shansarian province and Vardish Zakoris, only sometimes venturing south to take in New Alisaar. On a rare commission to carry Alisaarian iron and breeding pigs to Iscah, the storm had caught *Owar* not far from shore. Blown about, she had seen fit, in the unholy sunset which followed, to detour farther southerly, on the lookout for others who had not managed the tempest. Easy booty was often come by after bad weather.

Nevertheless, a glance at the sea and land around the great southern city had turned *Owar* in her tracks. Later that day, sighting intact shipping, they had heard some of the news of a colossal earth tremor, a firemouth gaping in the sea off Saardsinmey, and a wave that had clipped the sky.

"The goddess lost her temper with them at last," said *Owar*'s captain, an irreligious fellow.

That day's sunset was as dire a proposition as the sunset that had attended the storm, and indeed the dawn between. One hour into it, the coast of New Alisaar fading on their right hand, they saw an object in the sea, and hauled it in. It was not much of a treasure, only some upset hollow thing with a black Vis woman on it. She might fetch a coin at Iscah, but frankly speaking, they had gone out of their way for nothing.

She was the captain's handmaiden. He told her, if he had had a choice, she would not have been the fruit of it. *Inky,* he called her. He had an aversion to the touch of her skin, not realizing she was as allergic to his whiteness. To her arrogance and grace he was impervious, did not notice.

The aberration of the sunsets and the dawns grew less. As such evidence dispelled, the events of the

quake and the wave became unreal for the men of
Owar, and might not have happened. Only the Zakorian
girl, who had witnessed less than they, remembered.

Her pride was integral, even though she was no
longer Panduv. (Asked her true name by certain of
the sailors, she replied, deliberately: Palmv. They
found this as difficult on the tongue as once the name
Panduv had been on her own, and clove to *Inky*.)
With the pride, her well-tuned body had also kept its
cravings, for good food and for exercise. That first was
not available to her—or in fact to anyone on *Owar*.
The second, being a possible enticement to the Star-
peppery crew, she kept to a minimum, stretching and
limbering in the bow, before the pen of pigs, when
the last light and most of the ship's activity subsided.
Her hurts healed swiftly. Her body ached now only for
use. She did not sleep well, and insomnia was so new
to her, it did not much distress. In the corner of the
cabin, she listened to the captain, snoring and grunting, and amused herself by facile plans for his murder.
But he was her protector, she could not afford to get
rid of him.

At Iscah she would be sold as a slave.

She neither doubted nor credited this.

She wore a ragged shirt the captain had given her. It
had smelled unclean before she washed it in the sea.
Beneath the shirt, about her neck, the economical
knife stayed undetected in its closet of nacre. Would
there come a time when after all she must use it, on
another, or herself?

The non-physical core, wherein she habited to guide
her body in the dance, to that place she went most
often, out of the world. But otherwise she wondered
sometimes if the battering in the drum had deprived
her of sanity, she was so bland, she cared so little.

The ship came in at last to a shabby port of Iscah.
News of Saardsinmey's fall, garbled and spectacular,
had already got up the coasts, filtered through Sh'alis
on the way. Gossip was off-loaded with the pork and
iron. The yellow mix sailors strutted through the town,

cloaked in the power of Ashara-Anack, glaring down
the dark Iscaians.

"Strip," said the ship lord to Panduv. "You're no
eye-sore here. They'll like you best that way. You can
do your dancing for them. I've seen you at that. Not
bad."

Panduv stirred.

"I will not strip. I will not dance for you or for
them."

The man came and threatened her with his fist. He
did not use it, not wanting to devalue her for the
market.

Through the inner vision of Panduv there chased a
line of scenes. That she might now kill this lout, that
she might flee through the port. That she might find
refuge or a living somewhere. But something restrained
her. Iscah had no love, either, for Zakorians, who had
plundered her when they were able, and were now
accursed of Anack, a goddess recognized as dangerous.

Panduv said to the captain, "You'll manage to sell
me without putting me up naked or performing for
them. They only want a slave to work, in a place like
this."

"Or for bed," he added.

"Or that. So, let them pay you to see and get."

He shrugged. "Undo your hair," he said.

She had worn it plaited and bound on her head by
a thong from the shirt. Now she thought he wanted
her long-haired as an inducement. But when she obliged
him, taking a blade, he cut off her hair just below her
ears. "For the wigmakers," he said, deigning to give
her explanation.

The urge to kill him fell on her again like the wave
upon the city, or, as she had imagined it. The one she
had been was coming back to her.

The slave-market opened in the cool of the evening,
when the more prosperous of the port idled down to
the quay. To Panduv's eyes these had themselves slight
means enough, and would have passed for street-
cleaners in the south. For the slaves, they were a dismal lot, and the captain turned cheerful, seeing his
wares were so superior.

As they waited their turn for a rostrum, a brief
procession parted the crowd. The captain and his second officer each spat on the dusty ground.

"Infidel priests!"

They were the votaries of Cah, identifiable by their
robes of dark red and ocher. Foremost walked the
Chief Priest, shaven hairless, even in the twilight with
a boy to hold aloft a parasol of feathers over the bald
head. A few paces behind this apparition came another, a fat woman swaddled in gauzes, but her lolluping
breasts bare, her arms clattering with bangles. Unmis-
takably, the mistress of the temple brothel.

The captain discussed her demerits with his second.
They laughed, but not too loudly now, for these idola-
trous priests would be venerated here, and even the
fat holy-girls thought worthy.

Torches were being lit. Presently it was Panduv's
turn to mount the rostrum.

She stood there, looking only into the sky beyond
the muddle of lights and roofs. As the stars hardened,
she heard her supposed virtues described. Her strength,
the elasticity of her body, her sterling health.

A flash of brass attracted Panduv's attention, and
her eyes were drawn after all into the crowd. She saw
the blubberous woman, her bracelets colliding, pointing at her. Panduv, too, had made out what the woman
was. There had been, in the courts of Daigoth, a
dancer or two from Iscah.

A priest at the back of the cluster was now approaching the rostrum. He was pointing, in turn, and
offering money. The captain of *Owar* swore. There
could be no haggling with a priest. He snatched the
slave-seller's arm and began to remonstrate, to no
avail. The money had been accepted, the priest already turned away. Panduv realized she was bought by
the local temple. And since no woman was permitted
to serve Cah save as a prostitute, she had been purchased as a whore.

The temple crouched on a platform of stone. Black
trees grew all about it, full of carrion birds by day that

had smelled the offal from the altars. In a precinct behind, the whorehouse of Cah was situated.

The first night they drugged her with a beverage she was too thirsty not to drink. In the morning two young girls, already slopping with loose fat, brought dishes of food.

Panduv ate a little. She did not like the meal. Sweet sticky solid porridges and sweeter leaden breads.

Her abode was a cell, no larger than a latrine. It gave on a yard, or did so when the door was unlocked. She had already noticed temple guards oversaw the outside of the wall, and all the exits from the fane.

At noon, the fat girls came to remove the dishes, bringing more. Panduv asked, seeking to be plain in an approximation of the slur of Iscah, if she might answer the needs of nature. One of the girls, not speaking, indicated a lidded clay vessel in the corner. Not only, it seemed, was the cell the size of a latrine, it was to become one in fact.

Panduv ate no more of the food. She performed certain exercises, raising her feet to the wall, looping her body over—but the space was so confined it frustrated her, as the public jouncing restriction of *Owar*'s deck had done.

In the evening, another meal was served.

As dusk, Star-flushed, began to fill the meshed grating in the door, the holy-mistress came to visit, audible before entry from her bracelets and her heavy, labored breath.

She stood in the doorway, perhaps fearful she would be wedged forever should she enter the narrow cell. She smelled of sweat and perfume and displeasure.

"You must eat," the mistress said to Panduv.

Panduv smiled.

"To increase my weight?"

"Yes, that's so. To make you appealing."

"The men of your town like slugs for women."

The mistress, understanding her, pursed her lips. She was coppery, dark for Iscah, though nothing to Panduv, with tough black hair much-braided and strung with beads. Under the slabs of her porridge-built flesh,

an old beauty peered out bewildered. But her eyes
were flint.

"Who is it you worship?" she inquired.

"Zarduk of fire. Daigoth of the warriors."

"You are Zakr. Free, or under the whites?"

"Neither. I am a slave of Alisaar."

"You know the name of Cah?"

"I have," said Panduv, "no quarrel with Cah."

"Cah has bought you. Cah requires you to serve. To
serve, you must plumpen."

"Your food nauseates me. I can't eat it even if I
would. Look at me. This body is used to exercise. I
was a fire dancer." (The mistress made a little hissing
noise.) "Cage me this way," said Panduv, reasonably,
while her blood roared in her ears, "and I'll become
sick. You'll waste your goddess' money."

"You will grow accustomed to the food. If you'd
gone hungry since your birth, you would be glad of it,
as the other girls. It is an untroubled life."

Panduv could no longer restrain herself—the one
she had been.

"Damn your untrouble, you wallowing sow! Am I
to become a thing like you? I'll starve. I'll die rather.
Take me out and kill me."

She thought then of her beehive tomb she had given
to the white Amanackire bitch. The tomb was swept
to pieces by the wave, no doubt. And the witch-bitch
had promised her long life, that would not need it—

But the fat woman had gone away, her attendant
was closing the door.

Panduv upset the plates of sticky food. (And considered an instant the temple guards, but they were too
many.) She stood on her hands against the wall. She
blazed with futile anger and did everything so poorly
she might as well not have attempted it, finally striking
her head against an uneven place in the plaster. Then
she beat her fists there, and cursed all things.

Later, she flung herself on the pallet. The truth,
reality, had come to her now with a vengeance. She
felt at last the end of Saardsinmey, the loss of what she
had been, at first with raging agony, though this set-

tled gradually through the void of night into a disbelieving despair.

She had no longing for Zakoris, Free or conquered, she had only wanted the Alisaarian fame that to be called the *Hanassian* would have meant. The world was gone which had been hers nearly all her knowing life—but it had *never* been hers, she had been *its*. She belonged nowhere.

Near dawn she slept. She woke and found tears cold on her face. She could not recall the dream which had summoned them. But she considered, belonging nowhere, everywhere had some possibility for her.

She rose, and kicked the spilled dishes aside. She waited for the holy-girls.

Three of them duly arrived, opening the door with caution, looking at her nervously through the kohl on their eyelids.

"Tell the mistress," said Panduv, "I'll make a bargain. I'll eat these messes if she will let me exercise in the yard. Otherwise, I will die."

They gazed at her as if she had spoken in an unknown tongue. Panduv strode forward and thrust all three away from the door. Frightened of her, the caged leopard now loose, they did not resist, only lumbered quickly off, leaving her at large.

The yard was nothing much, a stone space contained by the precinct on two sides, and elsewhere with two high walls covered by yellowish plaster. A few inartistic doodlings in dull pink and gray did the office of patterning, and here and there a pot stood with a flowering shrub. Nevertheless, sunlight lay on the court, and the flowers, freshly watered, gave out a clear and hopeful smell.

Panduv did not linger. She did not know how much time she might have. She began at once to bend and unbend, to stretch and coil and brace herself. Flying into a series of slow cartwheels, she remembered a beating at Hanassor, at childhood's end.

At length, she paused for breath, shaking her shorn hair from her face. And saw all the many rows of doorways about the court fat-full of holy-girls gaping at her, in astonishment. While, on a stair at the precinct's west end, the mistress stood, chewing on a confection, her hard eyes intent.

Panduv grinned, and gave to her the reckless flamboyant salute of the stadium.

"Did they tell you my conditions?"

The mistress said nothing, but after a long stare, she returned up to her apartment, and drew the curtain over with a jangle of its brass-bracelet rings.

None came to usher Panduv back into prison, nor to chastise her.

As for the food, she must make do, eating a modicum, but clearing her plates into the lidded jar, then bearing it to the repository for waste matter. If she ate, or seemed to eat, she might earn alternative foodstuff, especially when they saw she did not after all "plumpen." Panduv lowered herself like a black snake, lifted her feet high, and stalked over the yard on her hands.

By day, when not on duty on the couches over at the temple side of the precinct, the girls would loll about the inner courtyard. Most of them rose late, particularly after a day of service, and the heat of noon generally sent them to a second sleep indoors. Sometimes they employed themselves with sewing, the stringing of beads, or in elaborately arranging their hair. Bowls of candies were continually brought them by the five or six girl children already dedicated; when of age, they, too, were destined for Cah.

In the evening when the temperature lessened, just before the last meal, crickets whirred in the shrubs and the bushes over the wall. The shadows of birds crossed the yard, and the holy-girls often became animated. They lent each other jewelry, put flowers into their coiffures, chattered. They even compared their patrons disparagingly. Cah valued the male ability to give pleasure and so, since this talent was usually absent, her harlots were at liberty to complain. Zastis was the best and worst. The men were in such a hurry, but lust inherent in all and ultimately able to fulfill itself, if perhaps only at the tenth customer.

Panduv, accustomed to the female talk of the stadium-girls' hall, and that in limited quantity, was offended by these costive dialogues.

Nevertheless, she went on with her exercise about the yard, aware that the harlots watched her, openly or under their lids, sullen yet fascinated. In a universe where men were imposed, like the weather, a woman who exhibited the masculine qualities of physical freedom and strength, arrogance and swagger, was an object of awe.

There was one girl whom it suited to be big. Though among the heaviest in the precinct, her large body was firm and she moved with complete gracefulness, looking light as down. Her skin had a luster on it, her huge eyes, on the rare occasions you might meet them, were intelligent. But for two side-plaits ending each in a brass bell, denoting Cah's service, she wore her hair in a beautiful rippling cloud. She was called Selleb.

Selleb was not idle, like the others. In a room beneath the mistress' apartment was a loom with posts, and here she worked away with her feet and her smooth arms, weaving cloth for the temple's winter garments.

Nor, seeing the black leopard enter the loom-chamber, did Selleb stop weaving.

Panduv stood close to Selleb and touched the shining cloud.

"What tresses. The slaver who cut off my hair would have been wild for these."

"When I was brought here," said Selleb placidly, still tending the loom, "my father shore me, too."

"Were you sorry to come to this place?"

"No," said Selleb, "I was starved, at my father's farm. I was born a fleshy child, so they thought they could feed me on crusts and air. My belly was always cramped from hunger."

"Well, you've mended that," said Panduv, and slipped her lean hand down Selleb's succulent shoulder.

Selleb continued to weave.

"But this food," said Panduv, "isn't what I need. You see. I'm as *skinny* as ever."

Selleb smiled, but said nothing.

Panduv raised her brows.

"Meat," said Panduv, "and fruit."

"Every ten days," said Selleb, "there's a dish of meat for us. Fresh fruit may be bought, but the best way is to ask a patron who is regular with you."

"Being too thin to please," said Panduv cryptically, "I have as yet no patrons. You, however, delicious one, must have many who prefer your mattress."

Selleb smiled again.

Panduv ran her arm about Selleb's waist, or at least as far as her arm would reach. Leaning to Selleb's ear, Panduv whispered, "But I must have more meat, too. Is there a chance—something from the altars. I'll have it raw if I must."

"There is a chance, Panoov," said Selleb; she rearranged the Zakorian's name better than the others who had learned it. "Is there to be a return for helping you?"

"I hesitate."

Selleb laughed softly.

Panduv said, "In Alisaar, I learnt several arts of love. I might teach them to you, if you were agreeable. You could then bring them to your service of Cah, to increase your enjoyment and that of your patrons, and so invite the goddess' approval."

The mistress entered the cell of the High Priest and kneeled on the floor, puffing. He sat imperious in his chair until she had got the breath to say: "Leave to speak, High One."

"Do so."

"High One, you may recall an unworthy woman I, in my inferior fashion, chose for the mattresses of Cah."

"The black Zakr."

"As you say, High One. There's some difficulty." The High One waited. The mistress labored, finding her kneeling posture also difficult. "She seems to eat, but never gains weight. Probably she is throwing out her food, or voiding it. In the normal way I'd discipline the girl and force her to swallow her meals before me. But she has been a dancer in Alisaar. It seems she knows tricks for the carnal act and has imparted them to the girls, or to one at least, so that the patrons receive benefit. It's talked of. What shall I do, High One?"

The High Priest pressed his fingers to his shaven chin and looked long and blackly at the wheezing brothel-keeper of Cah.

He spoke.

"Nowhere, woman, in the creed of the goddess, is it suggested that either partner should gain pleasure but in the usual way. The sophistries of Alisaars are their own. Certainly, you chose poorly among the slaves. This Pallnv isn't docile, and forgets the proper place of the female. She can't do any good with the girls. I believe we must be rid of her. At the new moon, we'll sell her for menial work in the port."

The mistress bowed, rose, was breathless.

"One further matter," said the High Priest. "A Watcher is coming from the capital. There's nothing here that may not be seen and reported on to the Mother Temple. But he will arrive before Zastis is done. Make sure your charges are groomed and at their best, he may want use of some of them."

Among the girls of Cah, once the news of the Watcher had been given them, there began some excitement. Such a priest was of importance, but often young—since the traveling required of him might be taxing. He went about from place to place, inspecting the fanes of the goddess, seeing the rituals were correctly kept, and the other temple business, such as slaughtering and usury, properly in hand. Revenues were sent from all the towns and larger villages of Iscah to the Mother Temple in Iscah's capital, but it was a haphazard affair. The land was not known for its riches, one did not expect too much blood from a stone.

"There has been no Watcher here for three generations," the girls told each other, their sleepy sulky voices brighter and more wakeful. They ate heartily, washed and rubbed and oiled their bodies and their

hair continuously, lying out in the sunlight like sleek
fat cats with glistening fur.

"So he's powerful, this priest?" said Panduv to Selleb,
as they lay side by side at midnight.

"You're wondering what can be made of that,"
murmured Selleb.

"And you are too clever," said Panduv. "Why aren't
you a porridge-brain like the others?"

"I have heard, he must go on a journey up into the
mountains. A town or village there has come to the
attention of the Mother Temple. I've heard, he likes
women very much."

"Then he'll likely have women with him, don't you
think?"

"No. He tired of them and left them or sold them
for funds."

"Yes," said Panduv, "I, too, have used lovers
casually."

Arud, Cah's Watcher, entered a minor port of Iscah
to which his duty had taken him, in the last phase of
Zastis, and the heat of late afternoon. He had been
three days on winding trails, in the dust, without a
woman or a bath. He was saddle-stiff, since the munif-
icence of the capital ran to zeebas, sore from the
stings of insects, red-eyed and ill-tempered. His mood
was not eased, moreover, by knowing that the road
from this wretched haven would be longer, drier, dustier
and more difficult, and end at an anthill even less
prepossessing.

The port—shoddy—did not attract Arud's attention.
His mount clumped through, the four outriders and
baggage trundling after, while the people in the streets
made way and offered pious obeisance. The temple,
its pillars unpainted and crows sitting in the trees
around, was much as he had expected. He had seen
five such already on his trek.

The High Priest came out to greet Arud, then there
followed a ceremony in the temple, before the High
Altar. (Arud would gladly have dispensed with it, but
one could not insult Cah.) Thereafter a room was
provided in which to steam, and a tepid sluice, and a

couch in an odd triangular chamber. To this you were
driven. To find relief in such small things.

Exhausted, longing to sleep, Arud lay on the bed
and could not close his eyes. He was thinking resent-
fully of the jealousy of others in the Mother Temple
which had sent him on this mission. Ostensibly it was
to show him off, and win him a promotion, maybe.
But frankly such Watcher jaunts were the traditional
way of being rid of an unpopular and ambitious brat.
The five temples already visited, and this, were routine matters enough. But the expedition to come, up
into the mountain valleys, to a town not even paying
revenue more than once in ten years, would prove
irksome and arduous. There had been rumors of curious goings-on there, trickling out with roving traders,
bandits. Doubtless these tales were no more than nonsense, but the Watcher had been asked to investigate.
They had dispatched him miles down to the coast
firstly, to irritate him properly before the worst part of
the journey should begin. It had already been half a
month's excursion. The uphill work would take longer.

With an oath, Arud turned on his stomach. (He was
a comely young man, with an unshaven shock of springing hair.) Cah confound his envious detractors! And it
was still Zastis— He quietened his fretfulness. There
were girls here, big soft pillows of feminine compliance. He would be offered comforts. He could throw
his weight about, for if he spoke poorly of them to the
capital, Cah rescue them.

Forget the damnable journey and the bump of mud
town on its mountain climb ahead.

He thought, as sleep began to come, of his father's
pride which had put the second eldest son into the
temple. He thought of Cah, in whom he believed, but
in an aloof, mathematical way. Arud was of a new
persuasion. Not a heretic certainly, but a seeker after
truth. Cah was an ultimate symbol, her rituals the
correct reverence that an ultimate anything should
command. Before the black stones of the Cahs Arud
bowed down, but he did not reckon Cah was especially in them. Cah was everywhere, and everything,

the principle of life. . . . As for mountain miracles—no. There were things explicable and there were lies.

Arud slept. The bed became a woman.

After the evening meal, which was served early, the holy-girls trooped out of the yard and up an inner stair that led into the temple section of the precinct. Timing perfect, the brothel had been closed to ordinary patrons since the previous sunset. Each girl was cleansed and fresh, burnished and perfumed, with brass, copper and enamel glinting and clicking upon her.

Panduv, having no appropriate ornaments, and only the colorless gauze shift the mistress had awarded her, begged no bauble and made no show. Nevertheless, her fall of jetty hair had swiftly grown in confinement, and swung beneath her shoulders now. She had roped her waist with some twisted red cord found discarded by Selleb's loom. Panduv was so unlike the other women, holding herself so straight, so black, so supple and so slender, she made a show regardless. Indeed, she moved one or two of the sisterhood to spite, to pinch her slim flesh and remark that she had better stand under a lamp, or she would never be seen at all.

They entered the corridor in which these whores stood or sat by day, to be chosen. Each girl took up a familiar position, leaning this way, or that, her hand on her swelling hip, or toying with her plaits and curls. Lamps of oil with two or three wicks shone with a dark fluttering glow.

Then footsteps approached, and great shadows rushed along the tunnel of women and lights, making all totter and fragment, as if shattered, falsely.

The mistress came first, slapping down her flat feet. She carried a rod of office tipped by a phallic copper bud. She looked expressionless on her holy-girls. Behind her walked the Watcher, the High Priest at his side, the Watcher inspecting the line of whores. They, since he was a man, lowered their eyes from his face. Panduv did not lower her eyes. The High Priest met the bold gaze with affront and some startlement, for he had not expected her inclusion in the line of choice—

she had never been offered previously, being unacceptable. The Watcher, however, had hesitated.

Arud also was taken aback to find a black Zakorian before him, there among the soft pigeons, her eyes staring openly into his.

Panduv meanwhile had surprised herself. She had put herself into the line without the order of the mistress. Her plan was mostly formless and had nothing to do with sex. But it was still Zastis, and her preference being for men, Selleb had not sated her. This Watcher priest was young, and handsome, and though his body did not have the honed edge of Daigoth's courts, he was only soft in the way her actor-lover had been, or the princes she had favored. She felt, in fact, a brilliance of desire. Holding his eyes, she partly veiled her own with the long black lashes, not subservience, the play of a fan, to let him see her awareness of him, as a man.

Next moment he was moving on along the line of cinnamon flesh. He continued to the corridor's end, paused, and, in conversation now with the High Priest, went away. The mistress, informed of his selection, came back down the corridor, tapping the rod upon her hand.

She stopped before Panduv and said, coldly, "Go to the three-sided chamber. Serve Cah, and please him."

And reaching past her, tapped the rod on the shoulder of Selleb.

A gentle scratching at the door in the hour before sunrise, did not rouse Panduv. She was already wide awake. The pettiness of her own anger at a backland priestling's refusal had kept her primed all night.

Yet, as Selleb slipped into the room, Panduv made pretence of awakening. This, too, was petty.

"Well, did you *please?*" she said.

"Greatly."

"Did he please you?"

"Ah," said Selleb, "the touch of men means very little to me. Before Cah, I make believe." She added, "He's to be here another night."

"Has he the sense to call you back, or will he want one of those lumps?"

"He was very taken with my skills. I told him who it was I learned them from."

"What?" said Panduv.

"His appetite was still strong. The more I spoke of you, Panoov, and what you'd taught me, the stronger it became. He said you weren't like a woman, and if it were left to him, you should be punished for looking at him the way you did."

Panduv chuckled. Her tension left her. Another began.

"And he would like to see to it personally?" She stretched, and caught a handful of Selleb's hair. "In Saardsinmey I wouldn't have glanced twice at him. He would have had to woo me. He would have needed to be rich, clever, a wit, a poet. How low Zarduk casts the proud, into very pits."

When Selleb was gone, the first milky hollowness had started in the sky. *Don't wait all day upon a call which may not come.*

But there was nothing else to do with the Iscaian day but wait.

In any case, the call came at midafternoon.

The mistress waddled into the yard, and beckoned Panduv from the shade of her doorway.

"Wash and prepare yourself."

The blood glittered in the black girl's veins.

"Why?"

"You're to go to the couch of the Watcher."

"I?" said Panduv, "skinny and unlovely and *Zakr* that I am?"

"No insolence. I'll have you beaten. It should have been done long ago. Make the most of Cah's service. The High One means to sell you as a menial at the new moon."

Panduv did not answer, but went to prepare herself for Cah's service.

One of the little girls guided the Zakorian to that three-sided chamber where the guest was housed. The daylight, though mostly obscured in the furtive temple by ways, was broadening. It was the time sometimes called by poets in Alisaar, the Hour of Gold.

The little girl indicated the door, then ran away. Her mother, a whore, had told her the Zakorian was a demon—like all her race—and would, if the child were unwary, bite off her half-grown breasts.

Panduv rapped on a door panel.

"*In.*" The cry was peremptory, but mostly eager.

Panduv grimaced, composed herself, and opened the door. She stepped into golden space—a wealth of full light through a large latticed window. The patterns of the iron lattice fell upon everything, and now upon herself, and she was struck again by this image of broken lights—as in the lamplit corridor—half wondering what it might portend. Then she looked at Arud, lying on the couch. He wore a long loose shirt of linen, nothing more, but for a wristlet of silver, some prize of his that probably he never took off. Panduv, upon whom jewels and precious metal had showered, noted the vanity. But more than this, the flat belly and well-formed legs. It was a meaty body and would run to flesh, but had not yet done so. She felt again the hunger of desire, and gave him, across the gilded air, one intent gaze. Then, like a proper temple harlot, lowered her eyes. At the same moment she dropped from her shoulders Selleb's borrowed mantle. Under it Panduv was naked, but for that emphasis of the red cord girdle, tied now upon ebony skin.

She heard him breathing. He was some while, eyeing her. Then he said, the slur of Iscah pronounced, "Come here."

Panduv went to him, stepping meekly, not lifting her lids.

When she was close enough, he reached out both hands and took hold of her, pulled her down beside him.

"They've instructed you how to look at a man now, have they?"

He combed her hair with his fingers, his mouth on her breasts planting starving kisses, then one hand was under her buttocks and the other between her thighs. He rolled on top of her and entered her at once. He did not force, but neither did he attend. After a few thrusts he growled and collapsed on her, shuddering and done.

Panduv lay on her back. She waited. Presently he said to her, "I heard there were tricks you know. But you don't know enough to give thanks to Cah."

"You mean, to offer her my pleasure?"

He grunted.

"I had none," said Panduv. "Or very little. Do you think it happens by magic? Is that the mystery?"

"You look too boldly and talk too much."

"How can I teach you my tricks if I have to remain dumb?"

"You can show me. In a minute or so."

"Then you must obey me."

"*Obey*—" he raised his head, ridiculous and very handsome in astonishment.

"I must instruct you," said Panduv. "You also cheat Cah of your pleasure. Do you think that thing you do, over in less than a minute, is worth anything to her?"

"Blasphemy now," said the Watcher priest. But he observed her, and when she looked into his face, he grinned. "You're so black I can hardly see any features. Only your eyes, and your lips, polished with gold."

She drew his head down and kissed him, stroking his body now, taking time over it, so that he began to like the procedure. Even very ordinary love-modes of the ruby city would be new to him.

It was not a great while before he was aroused and wanted her again. But he was already more malleable, curious and lazy together. He let her lie down on him, and when she took him in, steadying his tempo with her dancer's pelvis, she worked for him, bringing him by stages to the pitch of uncontrollable excitement at which she lost him. On this occasion, he shouted aloud.

The light was reddening and Zastis no doubt on the rim of the east when they joined for the third time. He was much slower now. He lay back under her minis-trations, gasping, and sometimes laughing in a way that pleased her: Beneath his hide he had some sense of the absurd. By now her own lust was at its wits' ends. No sooner had they amalgamanted than she found release. Remembering the dictates of Cah, she

expressed herself in groans and sighs. Left to himself he
followed her swiftly, and more noisily, and falling
back, put an arm over her waist.

Later, food was brought to the door. Arud shared
the supper with his bedmate, baked fish and cheese,
figs and wine. She might have fought him for it otherwise, and perhaps he saw that, too, in her eyes.

When calm, his accent was nearly shot of the Iscaian
blur. So there was no doubt when he told her she
must stay with him for the night.

She had expected that. To make him want her for
longer would be more chancy.

Even so, she had begun to have faith in him. She
lavished on him a tenderness she had never felt for
any man but sometimes pretended to out of affection.
She played his body like an instrument—it was greedy
but not insensitive. She offered him the bed-games of
dancers and warriors and the slight but inventive
perversions of the Saardsin court. He gulped all down.
He was a pleasure-lover, and, too, teachable. He did
not, of course, want to know anything about her.

At last he slept heavily. She lay beside him, pondering the temple, how it left him alone and shut in with a
vicious Zakr slave. But she was only a woman. She
would not, for all her foul blood, be able to overcome
the power of Cah, the omnipotence of men. Possibly,
that would prove true.

When she was dozing, near morning, she felt him
wake. He went to the vessel to urinate. Returned to
the bed, she knew he lay a while in turn, looking at
her. She could tell it was not only desire, now, but
what else it was, she was unable to guess.

She acted an awakening. He put his hand on her,
and caressed her lightly. And then he spoke the perfect words.

"Cah's womb, but I'd like to take this with me."

"Do it," said Panduv. "They daren't refuse you,
here." He was paying little attention. She continued
carefully, "They said you have a long tour before you,
through the mountains. The women there will be nothing. Thin as sticks—worse than I am. And not half so
wise. No other holy-girl would have the stamina to

make the journey with you. But I'm strong. My body is used to grueling exercise.'' Then, Panduv made her voice velvet, she called him love-names, and kneeling, pressed herself to him, and murmured into his ear, ''I love you. Cah's stricken me. Let me be your property. Don't leave me here to joy common louts. My flesh has known your flesh. After all, if you turn sick of me, if I offend you—you can sell me on the road.''

She could not see his face but she was able to picture it when suddenly he said, ''You're a liar, black girl, and a rotten one. Sell you on the road—if you don't make off first. Do you know the reward given runaway slaves? For runaways from a temple? For those who annoy a priest of the goddess?''

Panduv drew back from him. She sat on her heels and gave him stare for stare.

''So you value yourself so slightly you reckon no woman could love you?''

''Women's love—what's that matter? Rubbish, nothing.''

Panduv said cunningly, ''You offend Cah, to whom a mother is sacred. Didn't even your mother love you?''

He opened his mouth—then laughed again. Lifting his hand he struck her glancingly across the cheek. Panduv leapt to the floor, her hand after the nacre sheath—her knife—which she had luckily removed before coming to him. Her eyes were for sure a leopard's. She could kill him with her body alone. And then the temple guards would intercept her and do to her whatever they did do to slaves who annoyed the priests of Cah.

As for Watcher Arud, he was all agog. She should have been prone, entreating forgiveness. But this creature would not do that. She was a compendium—a swamp-cat, a devil, and a lean beautiful boy with breasts. His muscles still sang from what she had done to them. He already wanted her again.

''You lawless thing,'' he said. ''Cah didn't create you. Were you even born?'' He waved her to him. It was evident why.

Recovering herself, Panduv said, ''I won't lie with

you again, unless you promise me, in Cah's name, to take me with you."

"I can have you anyway."

"Try," she said. She thought, in that hot second, it might even be worth a death, to get her vengeance on him, for the temple and the temple food, for the Shansarian slaver and the wave that destroyed the city.

"Yes," he said abruptly, lying back. "Get out then. Tell the mistress to send me in another girl."

Panduv shrugged. She was no longer heated. She came to the couch and slid herself upon it. She lowered her head until the silk of her hair flowed over his belly and his thighs. It was the gambit of story and legend, but by Yasmat's lilies, in such naive circumstances, a hope.

When he was writhing and arching beneath her, she pulled herself away from him.

"Promise me, and by Cah."

"You—bitch— No."

"You must finish yourself then."

He lay helpless with fury, weak with interrupted lust, gathering himself.

"I'll have them flay you."

"You must still finish yourself."

It was the absurdist in him that won her day for her. She saw the amusement struggling in his inflamed face. He gave a roar and bawled at her: "You'll come with me, to the mud-nest up the mountain. Miles without number—You'll walk every step. You'll have zeeba rations. If you become a burden I'll sell you, or push you off a cliff. This I swear, by Cah. May she oversee my words. Now—"

She returned docilely, and gave him all he wanted. The rush of his orgasm, the sea wave . . . She had bought a potential liberation. With her body. The first time she had ever had so to use herself. In a night of bargains, she had become what she was meant to be, here, in Cah's brothel.

CHAPTER TWELVE

FALSE MAGIC

Zastis vanished on the first lap of the journey. Arud told her in the tent that night he would slough her at the next village prosperous enough to buy. "You'll be able to escape from such a spot with ease."

"Where should I go," she said, "in this rocky dust-platter of a land?"

"Better now than later. The villages and the rocks are worse where I'm going."

"Why not manumit me?" said Panduv, teasingly. "You paid the temple nothing for me."

"No, you haven't walked sufficient miles over the stones. I vowed it to Cah, to punish you. And you know if you run away from *me,* those outriders will soon get you back. They'd enjoy it. And then—"

"I adore you," said Panduv. "I would never run away from you."

Both of them laughed. It was a malign game, perilous—to Arud much more than to his slave. For there were chances now, to cut his throat in the darkness, to sprint away before the hue and cry was up. But, as she said, the land did not invite. Its tracks were channels of powder and its rivers thin runnels of spit. Ahead, the mountains were now in view, static brown upheavals going to distant mauve. She had exchanged one prison for another, but this at least was in the open air. Walking much of the day—despite his words, he afforded her now and then use of a zeeba, to the outriders' disapproval—was exercise she valued. At their halts, too, she exercised and sometimes she danced for him, once even with a pair of lighted torches, though naked, for her clothing was a utility, not to be burnt. Arud marveled. He would not, being a son of Iscah, praise her, but he called on Cah over and over. Despite this, Panduv found herself rusty, her genius already withering. She had expected nothing else. Even so, it made her rage. It was a stormy session that night upon his blanket.

Before his servants, and in the villages, she adopted the decreed stance of the Iscaian female. She did not want to exacerbate him. Besides, coming to a mild fondness for him, she did not, either, wish to cause him embarrassment.

On her freedom, she had developed some awkwardness of thinking. She never had been free, she must acknowledge that. Perhaps slavery, although she had never formerly thought herself a slave, was now ingrained. If she ran from Arud, as she had said, to what should she run? It was more simple to remain with him. Too simple, maybe. But eventually life itself would show her the way. He would sell her, or dismiss her—at liberty. Or his enthrallment would go on, she would accompany him through the mountains and back down again, to the capital. And then, surely, something must occur, to wrench her loose, to employ her.

She would never move in the verity of the fire dance again.

She would never be "the Hanassian."

Meticulous in diet and exercise, in the city she had had five or six or seven flawless years before her as a dancer, even more if her well-tuned body kept faith with her training. After that, obviously, decline would have come. She would then have been a valued instructress of the stadium, a courtesan if she chose, (as unlike a holy-girl as orchid to weed.) This existence might not have suited her either. She might have preferred suicide to ease and envy and regret, and not been the first. Yet that time was far off. Far, far and far.

But her body, agile, fluid and lovely, had already succumbed, betrayed her, in the foolish dance in the grove before lascivious Arud. He had thought her talent wonderful. She could have wept.

Late at night, Arud sleeping deep, when she might

have got away, she had gone out among the trees and set up a small altar of stones, and burned some oil there. One of the outriders came to see what she was at, but finding her praying, left her alone.

She had given back her life's reason to Zarduk, for to attempt any more the dance would be an insult to the god. She asked for some other thing to fill the gaping crevice in her spirit.

They climbed the paths into the mountains of Iscah. It was a thankless business. Up and down, down and up, the heights and the valleys, wading in the dust.

He took her less often now the Star was gone. But he liked the way she tended his hair, and massaged his body after the day's fatigue. Hardly knowing he did so, he had begun to talk to her. In an unwary moment he remarked he was glad she was with him. She hid her eyes Iscaian fashion, covering her contempt. Probably that was the origin of the ritual. For if the women here showed what they thought of their men, doubtless the men would slaughter them at once.

There came a morning, when she was walking behind his zeeba, that he called to her.

"I suppose you believe in magic and miracles?" he said.

It was the first time he had asked her opinion.

She was not misled into thinking he wanted it.

"In what way do you mean?"

"This dung-heap I'm to go to, there's been a rumor—Things that can't happen do so, allegedly."

Panduv was silent, attentive, respectful, striding by the zeeba. (Involved in an art form, she was no longer appalled at the act.)

Arud, who had never inquired even to that minute anything about her, taking it for granted presumably she came from Var-Zakoris, said, "This town, it's not so far from the border. Have you heard anything of it? A welt called Ly Dis."

Panduv felt a start of unnamable emotion. She went on striding, but her body seemed internally scalded.

"I've heard of Ly Dis. I knew a man born there, a village there."

Abruptly, Arud was glaring down at her.

"Your lover?"

At last, a personal question. Panduv might have been tickled. He was put out at the idea of her having been selected by another man, in the days of her freedom.

"No. Not a lover." She visualized Rehger Am Ly Dis. *As bright as the sun, handsome as the Lydian.* . . . She had not known him well, not as a man. He was one of the heroes, as she was. Her brother from the courts, child of her huge family.

"What's the matter?" said Arud. "'If he wasn't a lover.'"

But he did not wish to hear her history. And she did not wish to offer it. Rehger must have perished. With all the rest, he had been smashed and swept away. He, like herself, had died before his time.

They reached Ly Dis in a summer storm, dry, blustering with thunder, dust and wind. Bone-naked lightnings tore about the mountainheads above. They were so tall, those upper pinnacles, they had seemed, since appearing, to invite an aerial attack. Ly Dis town lay in a cradle of the lower crags, on whose levels the travelers had been for forty days of their monotonous ascending and descending. (The routes were easier and quicker from the capital—Arud had never ceased telling her.) The valley-cradle was untidy, and the town, blathered by the storm, like a heap of stones.

Only a handful of beggars were on the dirt streets, huddled in what purported to be doorways. The temple, with the house of the local tyrant, abutted on a single paved square, with a well and a scaffold in close proximity.

The temple was a condensed replica of the fane at the port. The smell at Ly Dis, however, was larger. It stank, of blood, oil, incense, an overpowering odor that dashed at them with the wind.

Arud pulled a face. But he had also been telling Panduv for hundreds of miles that he expected the worst.

Word had been sent ahead long since, of the Watcher's advent, but it might never have arrived. Certainly, no one came to welcome him. Arud sent one of the outriders into the temple to announce him, and sat his zeeba under the terrace, in the dust-storm, his panoply of baggage, attendants, and jet-black harlot about him, to get his dues.

The High Priest received Arud in a bare stone chamber. The old man—he seemed and moved as if he were ninety—wore his ceremonial regalia, a robe sewn with metal discs and black feathers, and a bird's mask. Arud, who owed the Priest's position unstinting reverence, bowed and genuflected, leering with scorn. The least acolyte in the capital, to Arud's mind, was worth more.

No refreshments were offered, neither any ritual at the altar. They hugged Cah close up here, and their victuals tighter.

When the politenesses were done, it became apparent the High One was in some concern lest the visitor be after revenues. Arud must explain such accounts were nothing to do with him. He then coughed, and asked for water to moisten the dust from his throat. (And water was precisely what they brought him, murky at that.)

"It's this other affair," said Arud. The bird's eyes goggled glassily. "Fabrications of wild magic. Healings. Conjurings."

The High Priest did not move. The bird's head did not. Outside the lightning cracked like a whip.

"It has come to the capital in the form of gossip and stories. Nevertheless, it was deemed serious, by the Highest One. I'm here to question you about it."

Another silence.

"I would like," said Arud, "to have a word from you, Father."

The bird's beak went down. It angled at the floor, and the gnarled old hands gripped the arms of the chair.

"We do not speak much of it."

"Thinking it beneath your notice?"

"To make it so."

The rejoinder brought Arud up short.

"That won't do, High One. You must speak out now, to me. And I shall want to question any of those involved. And the woman." He had kept himself till now from saying that: *The woman.* The admission that the tales centered on a female. There were sometimes witches, but they kept to the feminine side, practicing on or against their own sex. It was unlawful but not unholy. This woman, however, was reported to have power over the being of men. Arud credited none of it. He, too, would have preferred not to speak of it, to ignore it and let the falsehoods fade on their own. But the Mother Temple had sent him here to do the opposite. So he lectured the old High Priest for a while on the dreadfulness of not speaking and of striving to ignore, ending with: "And is it a fact? Not that she has any abilities, patently she could not. But that all this concerns a female?"

"So it seems."

"Seems isn't good enough, Father. No. You must send for this woman immediately. Have her brought. And perhaps, before I see her I might bathe and—"

"Not here," said the High Priest, with a twinkle of malice. "I mean that the woman isn't in this town. In these areas, there is often confusion, the names of places—it's the village of Ly, that is where the woman is."

Arud quivered with dire foreknowing. He choked on dust and muddy water, cleared his throat and snarled, "How far is it and where?"

The High Priest pointed upward.

"Five or six days up the mountain. You've come at a lucky time. In winter, or during the rains, it would take you much longer."

The climb took seven days. The air was thinner. Shards and pebbles fell from the passes. The storm came and went. It needed only to rain to wash them away, back down to the heaped stones and the square. But there was no rain. The taller mountains screened the sky, like scored red-bronze in the sunsets.

At the night halts, Arud lay trembling with ire and

slight fever, while Panduv bathed his forehead, massaged his feet. Her constitution was more robust than his, and she saw she had started to be indispensable.

The dwellings of Ly were in their cracked summer wholeness, the refuse mounds fermenting at their doors. On high ground, Cah's house, smaller even than the temple in the town but smelling as greatly, dominated the prospect.

Only the zeebas and Zakorian Panduv attracted attention on the streets. Filthy and unshaven, Arud, his clothing now totally defaced by the journey, escorted by outriders no better off—and also dwindled, two having gone missing at Ly Dis—might have been any itinerant nobody.

The temple servants who came out to accost Arud on the terrace top were inclined to dismiss his claims. He was driven to giving them secret signs of the religion.

When, finally, he had been taken away into the inner rooms, the outriders, grown desperate, gathered the animals and made for a crude drinking-shop they had seen. Panduv was left with the baggage on the terrace. Glancing up, she saw a square window, with two faceless creatures in it, peering at her: Holy-girls. Seeing her look at them in turn, they averted their eyes, and made superstitious signs. *Zakr.* Perhaps only to outrage and amaze them further, Panduv walked into the body of the reeking temple.

There were short thick pillars to sustain the roof; they loomed grotesquely, for it was very dark. At the port, she had never entered the temple hall, never observed any sacrament before the altar.

That was quickly come on, here. It was a butcher's block, still steaming from a recent sacrifice, while blood had overflowed the drain below. Above all this, the statue, if it could even be enhanced with such a name.

Cah was black, as Panduv, but nearly shapeless. Bulges of breasts, and a bulge that was the face, for two amber eyes were set into it.

Something strange suggested itself to Panduv. What was it? These eyes—*yellow* eyes. Eyes for snakes, or Lowlanders.

A draft caught the meager lamps. The quarter light wavered, and the amber Lowlander eyes seemed to blink and steady upon Panduv.

Did the beautiless hump have some life? Was their goddess present in it—would she deign to be? The stone was very old.

Panduv made a gesture of politeness to a foreign deity.

The eyes went on, *boring* into her.

"What's your riddle, lady?" murmured Panduv. "Do you want something?"

A man shouted harshly from the shadows.

"Back you! Zakr sow—stand *off*. You'll defile the altar."

"But I forgot," said Panduv to the stone, "you hate your own sex, don't you, *lady*."

She bowed her head in suitable abnegation and stepped away among the columns.

The shouter did not pursue her. Very tired now, Panduv slipped down a pillar, to sit with her back against it, on the floor. She let her eyelids fall. She began to dream she was in Saardsinmey, inside the theater. The white Amanackire woman stood in front of her.

Panduv said, "You think you'll need my tomb before I shall?"

"Oh, yes."

She had unveiled. Her pallor was exquisite after all, her eyes like bright silver. She said, "And did I not say, Panduv, you would not need the tomb?"

"I'm dead. I'll never dance again, with the fire."

"Life is the Fire," said the Amanackire. "We dance with it constantly, and burn off with it the draperies of blindness. It scorches us, till we learn, how to dance, the meaning of the dance."

"He was your lover," said Panduv, "Rehger. I'm at his birthplace. But he's dead."

"No," said the girl. "He lives. I gave myself to death. He followed me in the death procession, up into your well-built, obdurate tomb. There he was, Panduv, when the wave broke Saardsinmey. The tomb withstood the water, as I knew it must. But what a terrible thing. I should have saved that city. I could rescue only the man I loved. A woman's foible, Panduv."

Panduv shook herself and opened her eyes wide.

Someone was standing over her. The shouting fellow again? No, it was a young woman, her own age, or a very little older.

Panduv was puzzled by an awareness of seeing someone that she recognized, had known at least by sight for many years. But she did not know this woman. She was an Iscaian, a wife who wore her hair in the ordained way, twelve plaits ending in copper rings. Her garment was darned and patched all over, her feet were bare and smeared with the dust.

But her beauty, that was another thing. Coming after the white girl's glamour, so sharply recaptured in the dream, it needed to be of a fabulous sort. And so it was. The eyes that were the fulcrum of the beauty looked down on Panduv, as if questioning her state of heart or health.

"Don't be afraid," said Panduv. "I'm the body-slave of the Watcher priest. Quite tame." And with a feral smile denied the sentence instantly.

But the Iscaian wife did not flinch, she only *looked* another second or so. Then she turned and walked to the bloody altar.

She stayed there some time, her back to the hall, her face turned up now to the shadow-face of the Cah.

Panduv watched intently. It seemed to her, from what she had heard and seen, even Iscaian women were not normally allowed so near the goddess. But no one shouted.

Presently the Iscaian left the altar. She crossed back over the temple hall, looking neither left nor right, and went out of the doorway.

Panduv came to her feet. For some reason she was going to follow the Iscaian. She did not know why.

As she emerged on the terrace, Panduv spotted her again immediately. The Iscaian was on the sun-baked mud of the street, walking slowly along, her hands loose at her sides. That in itself was unusual. Every other woman who went by, even to children of six

years, ported something, baskets, jars, or bundles. As
for the other persons on the street, they were aware of
the girl. They did not stare at her, greet her, avoid or
make way for her—but their actions became somehow
self-conscious in her vicinity. They were like bad actors playing a scene in which one of their number goes
among them supposedly invisible.

Then a man, a burly brute, stepped into the girl's
path. She halted, and all around the bustle of the
street stilled. *Now* they could see her. *Now* they could
stare. It was so quiet the chirrup of birds and insects
might be heard, and the voice of the big man carried.

"Cut my hand. Won't close."

And he thrust before the girl-wife a great wodge of
paw and dirty bandage.

"Your leave to see, master?" said the girl. Her
voice was soft. It was the Iscaian tone, pleading to be
unvaluably of assistance.

Involuntarily, Panduv clenched her fists. Unclenched
them. They all went on that way here, and she, too,
when she was sensible.

The girl was unwrapping the bandage. Her movements were deft. She had been honored and must now
take care to show herself worthy.

Panduv could not make out what she did, with the
hand, the wound. It happened in a few seconds. The
man gave a snort. Then he threw up his arm, over his
head, flexing the hand. With the other he gave the
girl-wife a light push. "Ah," he said. "Cah be praised."
The raised-up hand had a blemish on the palm, a
bluish ridge like a clean ten-day-old healing.

In the fever Arud had mentioned sorcery repeatedly. He had even once called the sorcerer *she*.

The girl was walking on, and the crowd pleated
round her. Panduv after all stood rooted. Was this
deceit? She herself had not been able to see the open
cut. The man was merrily elbowing away to the tavern. Perhaps Arud's outriders would hear his summary
over their cups.

A knot of women meanwhile was just below the
temple terrace, and they were muttering together, looking off now where the girl had gone.

Panduv ran lightly down to them. She touched one on the shoulder. The whole group cowered away from her, disliking, nearly showing their teeth.

"Who was that?" said Panduv, slurring her words forcibly, to offer them a nice homely sound.

"Who?" said one of the women.

The rest were speechless.

"The healer," said Panduv.

The woman who had spoken shook her head. She, too, was a wife, all of them were, and the twelve rings on her hair clashed together.

"Yes. I saw her do it. If it wasn't faked."

The peripheral women were beginning to slink away. Two ran off suddenly. Panduv reached out and got hold of the one who had spoken. Panduv said, "My master is a Watcher of Cah. He's in the temple now, with the High One. He wants to know the name of that woman. Dare deny *him*?"

A second woman spoke now.

"Her name is Thioo."

"And she lives here, in your village?"

No answer, which meant she did not.

Precisely then Arud came out on the terrace, announcing himself by ranting: "Panv!" (Definitely agitated). "'Here, you bitch!"

Which scattered the women like terrified beetles.

Panduv went back to him.

"He denies it all," cried Arud in boiling passion, dignity superfluous. "The old imbecile in his stenchful bird-head. There is no witch. Nothing happens here."

"Oh, master," said Panduv, "I have just seen it happen."

"What?" said Arud. His face collapsed.

"I was questioning those women, when you spoilt my luck by bawling and scaring them off. But I've seen her at her work, your sorcery-maker." Arud was speechless. As an Iscaian woman with a man, she hung on her words. And, having divined its form, since one of the Iscaian acrobat-girls had had a lost sister of the same name, Panduv concluded, in the clear accents of Alisaar, "She's called Tibo. She lives outside the village. But then again, if you go to the wine-shop, I can point out to you her victim, the man she cured."

Arud exclaimed, then excused himself to the goddess.

Panduv was dismayed to find herself content at this miniscule victory, over a man.

No women were allowed in the wine-shop. Small boys did the serving. Panduv waited doglike at the door, under the shade of the tattered awning which comprised the roof.

There was no necessity for anyone to point out the cut-cured man, for he was noisy in his relief, and the two outriders had bought him a jug of drink.

Having been convinced Arud was a Watcher priest, the man divulged that the woman Thioo would already have gone home to her husband's farm. She came in early to sell vegetables: She saw to the women. Panduv heard Arud say, "And to you."

"I let her, yes. My woman's useless, can get nothing right. I'll smack her hard when I get home. I've got a good firm palm now to do it." (Panduv gazed on the dust and wished the whole arm might drop off there.)

"Are you perhaps," said Arud, "in league with the woman Thioo, to make a mockery of the temple?"

The man was shocked, infuriated, and frightened by this accusation. He was devout. He had made sacrifice to Cah only two days ago, which was why he was here. As for being in league with a woman—what man could be? He might as well plot with his cow. But Cah had given the sloven power that she might be of use to Ly. Cah cared for the men of Ly. They were lusty. She favored them.

"When did all this begin?" Arud interrupted eventually.

None of the men in the wine-shop was positive. Years gone. In the long snow. At the time of the disastrous harvests—hadn't she stopped the fire, then? The woman had been thought an adulteress once, but that was previously. One of her men, her husband's brother, had fallen off a pass in the rains. But Cah had proved the woman was dutiful. Maybe five years after that, at Big Thaw— Now certainly that was the month she saved a neighbor's son, when the mother was killing him, trying to birth him out feet first.

Thioo's own son had been sold, did you remember that? The slave-takers came. Alisaarians. So poor, Orhn's farm then, he had had to give his own boy. And Orhn was never much of a man, as a man should be. And the woman was barren again, after that.

(Panduv, at the door, had locked herself against the upright. Something was amiss in this tale—)

Arud said, "Well, then, let's date this from when the slave-takers came."

"Twenty summers, or more." "More, more."

"This woman isn't young, then?"

No, they said. But nubile, still.

(In those mountain valleys a woman of thirty could look like a city woman of sixty. The woman Thioo— Tibo—had been near to Panduv's age. She *was* young. Yet if she had borne the child the slavers took for Alisaar—Panduv realized, not the wonder of Tibo's youth, but the aspect of the information from which she had been thoughtlessly advancing. She knew then why Tibo had seemed familiar. Tibo was the mother of Rehger.)

Arud was exasperated. His voice was full of high blood and Panduv could hear him banging on a table.

"You will all of you be questioned, at the temple, before the Cah." A desperate silence fell. "Meanwhile I'll want directions to the farm of this man Orhn, the woman's husband."

When he came out, Arud said to Panduv, "Another curse of a ride. But I'll sleep before I do it. I *vow* that, Panuv. I'll go tomorrow. She and her witchcraft can wait."

Panduv walked the expected number of paces behind him to the temple.

She would have to walk behind the zeeba to the farm. Arud might not want her company. She must explain how useful she would be, to wash his feet and ease his back at the ride's end. He might be forced to remain overnight at the farm. He must have a handmaiden, not trust to the domesticity of the witch.

Panduv had a violent need, a yearning, to see Tibo

again. It was like love. How strange that now this unknown Iscaian woman should be the only link, the last representation, of Saardsinmey and the days of life.

CHAPTER THIRTEEN

THE WITCH

Up and down the tracks went, down and up. It had become the only mode of travel. The passes were tortuous and unsafe. The crags across the border stood northward like transparent paper. Beyond— Zakoris, and Panduv never gave it a thought.

The farm lodged in a valley, in a bowl of mountains, under a sky wheeling with three black eagles.

The poverty and ugliness of the place were almost dreamlike. Nevertheless, there were fowl in the yard, a cow or two on the pasture, and beyond these a rocky upcrop with a thick plantation of citrus trees already in young orange fruit. There seemed another low building in among them, something that shone pale through the rocks and trunks. Could anything to do with the farm have a sheen on it?

In the yard, a healthy-looking oldish man sat on a bench, with an elderly black dog at his feet. Both were asleep in the sun. As the travelers drew nearer, the dog heard them, lifted its head and began to bark. The man also woke up and made a flurry, waving his arms, and next running into the hovel.

"Cah bless us, a bloody ninny" said Arud. "The cup of plenty spills."

He rode down into the yard, the one outrider (who had lost on the throw of the dice) behind him, and Panduv some three or four paces to the rear. The dog flattened itself growling, hackles high, to maintain the house door. But just then the girl came out.

"Hush, Blackness, hush. So," she said. The dog hushed.

Arud had claimed from the temple a coarse-woven, poorly dyed, cack-handedly-stitched fresh robe. Seeing it was not only a man but a priest who had arrived, Tibo kneeled among the fowl, bowing her head.

Aarl's night, thought Panduv. *If she has any power. Why kneel?*

Arud was dismounting.

"Get up," he said to Tibo. "You are the woman Thioo?"

"Yes, priest-master."

"That Thioo who claims to be a witch?"

Tibo waited, her eyes down on the pecking fowl.

"Answer," said Arud. "Do you?"

"No, priest-master."

"But you healed a man yesterday of a cut hand." Another pause. "Do you deny it?"

Then Tibo raised her eyes, only to Arud's sparkling-new-shaven chin, nevertheless, that high.

"It is the will of Cah."

"You add to your crimes the crime of blasphemy."

"If I blaspheme, may she blast me."

They stood half a minute at attention, as if for a volley of lightning.

"I won't say," said Arud, "that you are a liar and a cheat. I'll ask you only how you, a female, came by such gifts as they say you have, of healing and conjuration. Well? Do you dare tell me the goddess visited you?"

Arud had been questioning the villagers all morning, in the temple. He did not put them to any trial, but their terror was apparent, and they babbled. The witch could stop an outbreak of fire in the fields with a word. She could summon it, too, into a lamp or on a hearth. She had caused various animals to drop double sets of twins. Women in childbirth, or the sick, always wanted her. Barren women turned fertile at her handling. (Interesting, there, she could not see to herself.) She could send away storms and call the rain. She—

"I'll say again, and you'll answer me, woman: Did Cah visit you?"

"No, master. But once I was questioned before Cah. They let me lay my hand on her. I've guessed it started then."

She belives that. Panduv, ferociously. *She thinks that the stone passed magic into her, and that all is well in this land. She consents to kneel to the male priest, and to serve that witless one as if he were a king, since he must be her husband. She isn't much like Rehger. The eyes.* And then Panduv, thinking of Rehger, visualized the firm gentleness behind his fierce barbaric strength, the curious innocence she had once or twice noted in his beautiful face. Nothing foolish; more—profound. The eyes of a child several hundred years old, who has been able to unlearn the cleverness of his younger seniority. Tibo had a look of that.

"I'd take you to your temple to be questioned again," said Arud, "but *not yet*. Cah, let me rest. Watch that dog and keep it off me. Give some water to the beasts."

He went into the hovel with a proprietary but hopeless air, plainly pondering fleas and insalubrious meat and bitter beer.

The girl Tibo remained at the door until he and the outrider passed through. The zeebas had been tied to a post. Tibo drew water at the well, and took it to them in a bucket. She promised them fodder, Panduv heard her, talking in a secret friend's voice at their ears.

Toward Panduv Tibo made no display of recognition.

Yet, she must truly have some sorcery. She knew, without knowing it or me, that I had some significance for her. I saw her son in his glory.

One large room, the hovel was divided from its main area at the back by two wooden walls. These created two sleeping cells, out of the larger of which into the smaller Tibo lugged a mattress. It was clean, fragrant even with herbs and the scent of soap. This bed was Tibo's own it would seem. Her half-wit husband slumbered by her in the same room, but on another couch.

Tonight husband and wife, if needful, would share, in order the priest should have good rest.

Arud left his instructions. The outrider was to guard the entry to his sleeping-place for three hours, then wake him. The outrider sat by the entry, and, as promptly as Arud, fell asleep.

The husband had been reassured and gone out for a constitutional with the black dog. From the hovel yard they were visible in the valley, playing with a stick.

Tibo went on with her chores, now doubled by guests. She offered Panduv nothing, nor refused her anything. Panduv in turn drew water and drank two cups. Then she watched Tibo. In the end, Panduv spoke to Tibo.

"Are you afraid? I mean of this questioning at the temple. Arud is persistent."

"I'm not afraid," said Tibo.

She went into a hut and returned with fodder for the zeebas.

"Witches are stoned, aren't they?" said Panduv.

"Yes."

"But you're not a witch."

"I obey Cah."

"Why," said Panduv, "did you look so long at me in the temple?"

"Your black skin," said the Iscaian.

Panduv checked. Perhaps it had been only that.

She followed Tibo back into the house and observed her making dough at the hearth. Panduv sat down opposite to her.

"I can't help you with your wifely tasks. You see, I was never trained to them."

Tibo made no comment. But suddenly she said, "Your master the priest has a fever. I grow an herb here that will cool it."

"He's not my master. He may try to think so. Nevertheless, little Iscaian wifeling, he's useful to me. I'm not about to let you poison him."

Tibo made no comment. And this time offered nothing else.

Tight-strung, Panduv said harshly, "They tell in Ly

your son was sold to slavers some twenty years ago. I know the name of your son." She hesitated, to equip herself with the essential, recognizable slur. "Raier."

Tibo's hands turned to stones in the midst of the dough. The hearth fire's glow flickered against her face, its lovely youngness and veiled eyes.

"But he wasn't yours. You're no older than he would be."

Tibo said, "Yes, but he was my son."

The air tingled. This was like some duel, but not between enemies, not even sisters at practice.

"I have known him," said Panduv. "He and I were starry lights of the arena at Saardsinmey, in Alisaar. His light was the greater. They called him Rehger the Lydian. He was a famous swordsman and charioteer, the best of them, gorgeous as a god—"

Tibo lifted her head. She looked at Panduv with great eyes full of ancient, worn and uncomplaining hurt, and sudden lashing anger. The power that came from her made Panduv start. In another moment, the Iscaian had controlled it, her emotion, the power. She soothed them down, like her dog at the door. Then she gazed far away, beyond Panduv, the hovel, the valley, and said, "Not now. Later. If you want, speak to me then. First I must answer to your master."

Vastly disconcerted, Panduv could only rasp, "I told you, he isn't my master."

"What does it matter?" said the Iscaian, her eyes on other worlds. "Nothing matters. Here we are. Here, it's the custom."

"Your custom. That pie-brain up the valley—your lordly, masterful husband—does he give you Cah's pleasure? I doubt if he fathered Rehger. What's he worth?"

"While I'm married to Orhn, I needn't take another man."

"You could geld every man in the village with your magic. By the Fire, I felt it, just now, what *you* could do. You *are* a sorceress. Why be a slave?"

But Tibo was busy again with the hospitable dough.

*   *   *

It was quickly over, in the eventuality.

Arud wakened near sunset, in a foul temper, berated the snoring outrider, said to Panduv, "My head aches—it's the stink here—" which was wrong, for the hovel was kept fastidiously and did not stink—and called for beer and food.

Tibo served a savory stew, into which he would do no more than dip a chunk of bread. He was suspicious of venoms, or only of eating up some intrinsic element, and thus being warped to the witch's charms. Panduv, having offered to act as his taster, did have a plate of the stew. It was delicious, and the hot cakes tasty. The fever was still on Arud, as Tibo had said. He drank cup after cup of "Orhn's" beer, to quench the fever's thirst.

The idiot husband ate farther along the board, sometimes feeding the black dog. She was a bitch, full of age, yet despite the gray on her muzzle, clear-eyed and alert. She had been ready to go for their throats at the door. Tibo's youth, while it had not infused the dog, had still kept her in health. Panduv remembered how the idiot had played with the dog. He could not be blamed for anything. He looked at Tibo with unIscaian, unmanly love and admiration. She was now his mother.

Arud pushed away from the table, and called for more beer. He went over and sat in a wooden chair by the hearth, the fever making him want the warmth one minute, then draw off in a sweat.

Tibo filled his cup as he demanded. Suddenly he rose and caught her wrist.

The idiot whined, and the dog rumbled.

Tibo, not resisting, said back to them, "It's well. Hush."

"No," said Arud, "it isn't well. How will *he* manage after they stone you?"

It was then that Tibo lifted up her eyes to his. It was only for two or three seconds, enough, it seemed. In the beginning, Arud had sometimes struck Panduv, weightless puppy blows, and she had been able—after that first occasion—to contain herself. Later there was no aggression of this kind. Now his hand went whirling back, gathering up all the strength of his arm, to bring a blow on Tibo that could have broken her jaw. Panduv, who had been trained to know the measure of such things, sprang straight for him. She snatched his arm on its backswing, and hauled. The Watcher priest went toppling over, on his spine on the dirt floor. He took a pot with him, which smashed. He lay there in the debris, cursing and sprawling, his eyes madly upon Panduv, while the outrider, pulling a knife, made as if to come at her. Panduv flung up her hand, holding the outrider off with her dramatic gesture. To Arud she said, "Master, you *mustn't* strike her. Before Cah. *No*."

Arud gabbled, struggling to sit up. The outrider, in a dilemma (Panduv had cowed him), hurried to assist.

"Master," wheedled Panduv, hating him, "I thought only to save you. If Cah truly *is* with her, you daren't raise your hand against the goddess."

"Cah—" Arud panted, his head swimming, blundering to his feet, "there's no goddess—Cah is only life—"

"Close your ears," Panduv said severely to the outrider, who was now blinking indeed, and making signs over himself. "You misunderstand his words."

"Life—embodied in the *symbol* of Cah—" cried Arud, striving to teach them.

Panduv thrust him down into the wooden chair. She shut his mouth by putting her hand on it (scandalous). When she moved away, it was to balance on the soles of her feet, fighter's stance, at the room's center. She looked about. Everyone waited, even the idiot hiding behind a bench, and the rumbling dog.

"There's only one means to see if this woman is a cheat," said Panduv, "or sacred. You can do it here and now, lord Watcher. This man and I will witness. Tell her to demonstrate her abilities." And turning, Panduv glared at Tibo. "Tell her to call fire."

Arud was regaining some sense. Shivering, but coherent, he snapped at the outrider to refill his cup.

The dog had stopped growling. Everything was very still. The hearthwood crackled, the beer sounded as it ran into the cup,

Tibo stood with her eyes lowered. She was waiting.

She would have done nothing—nothing—until the priest should require it of her.

Arud said, "All right. Let's see you do that. Bring the fire, as they say you do." And he drank noisily.

After which it was the quiet again, thick as syrup in the hovel room, the crackle of the hearth absorbed away into it. And then they heard Tibo breathing, audibly, deep, catching breaths—like a woman with her lover—

She will do this. It's impossible and it will be done, Panduv thought. *No trickery, a truth. The Fire of Zarduk.*

Tibo extended her left arm. Her eyes were up-turned, the whites visible. All at once the sound of her breathing stopped.

The Zakorian saw Tibo's left breast gleaming like a lamp through the thin stuff of her garment. The light spread, into the shoulder, the upper arm. The forearm bloomed red as roses—it was the blood inside the skin—and the bones showed black. Then the left hand of Tibo became a torch, and from the four fingers and the thumb there pierced five spurts of living fire.

The outrider yelled. Arud had dropped the cup, for Panduv heard it rolling. The idiot and the dog, they only looked on, interested, accustomed, without a trace of fear. (The dog even wagged her tail.)

The flames, hitting the floor, leapt and twined. A fire dance. Then Tibo sighed. She began to breathe again, and her arm, shoulder and breast abruptly darkened like a dying coal.

Arud came plunging forward.

"It isn't real. Illusion—ah!" He drew out singed fingers, beat at his smoking robe.

Tibo gazed down upon the fire.

"Hush," she murmured. "So."

And the fire went out.

Arud said, "It burned me."

Between them, Panduv and the outrider caught him this time as he fell.

"He's sleeping most serenely. What herb was that?"
"It has an upland name. But I could show you."

Panduv had administered the drink to Arud. For half an hour after swallowing it, he sweated profusely, and then sank back into a level slumber. The outrider stationed at the entry of the sleeping-place was by contrast wide awake, his teeth gritted and the knife lying across his knees.

Panduv and Tibo returned to the hearth. Orhn also slept on the bench, the dog dozing with her head in his lap.

"This life suits you then," said Panduv presently.

"To what other life should I go?"

Panduv examined the words. They applied in due course to herself. She had already said them. Besides, she had tonight, even loathing his actions, defended Arud. She discovered in herself a tug toward him, a deep-seated moderating attachment. She had already tutored him in many ways. There was much that might be done—not to change him, but to allow him to be the man she had once or twice glimpsed under the flaccidity, the bludgeoning nonsense. This was rather dismal, that she had come to have such feelings for an Iscaian priest. But this was what fate had given her, and the gods. And Zarduk, whom she had worshiped in the tall temple at Saardsinmey, here he had let fall the bane-benison of his fire on an outlander who did not even honor him.

"However," said Panduv, "we were going to talk of your son, Rehger. That was how the name was spoken, in Alisaar. Come now, your Orhn wasn't his father."

Tibo looked into the common flames of the hearth which she had summoned with flint and tinder.

"A man came here, once."

"Your lover."

"For a night. Cah sent him to me. I thought he'd leave me nothing. But I was childed by him."

Panduv stayed silent, but Tibo said nothing else. So then Panduv recounted the youth and manhood of a Swordsman, of Rehger, in the courts of Daigoth. At first the story was objective. Then it became mixed with her own, the training which she had undergone— Next, the enormous sealed vista of that lost world

opened before Panduv, and she flung it out before
Tibo in turn, in the hearthlight, like a carpet of many
colors. Woven there, the trials and failures, the excel-
lences and the rewards. Woven there the city, its squares
and avenues, the adulation of the crowds, and the
ringing of the sea. The markers of the festivals, she
related, the seasons of its calendar. The night of the
Fire Ride, and how Rehger had won it. She conjured
Rehger, as if she, too, were a witch, there into the
hovel, and caused him to stand before his mother, in
beauty and pride. Panduv herself hung the last garland
on his golden brow: She made him from the night, as
he had partly been, the cipher for Saardsinmey.

And after that, when the hearthlight guttered—she
had talked for more than an hour—it came time to tell
of the end of the city and of Rehger's death. And only
then, Panduv recalled the dream she had been having,
in the Cah temple of Ly. The Amanackire girl who
said to her: "Your well-built, obdurate tomb. There
he was—when the wave broke." And the Zakorian,
explaining the destruction she had never seen, of her
city which was not hers, to a woman who surely could
not, being ignorant for all her sorcery, comprehend
half of that which Panduv specified—Panduv found
herself saying, "But someone assured me, Tibo, that
your son survived the cataclysm. It may not be a fact.
You're a witch, perhaps you can divine. If he's alive."

But Tibo was looking away and away into and beyond
the ashes on the hearth. In the new silence, Panduv
felt her own exhaustion. She was wrung out. She had
made confession and she was purged, she was empty.
She could have wept at last, but she scorned tears, the
Zakorian. *Fire* not water.

When Tibo rose, Panduv looked up at her in a
vague surprise.

"Consent to come with me. There's something I'll
show you," said Tibo.

Not a whisper about her son, not a glimmer of that
hurt and cruel fury that had been in her face before.
Nothing. Had she even heard, this Iscaian drab, even
noticed the jewelry carpet of a city laid before her?

Panduv got to her feet.

"What is it?"

"Outside, a little way."

Panduv's instinct verged on distrust, but she said, "If you like."

They stole out of the house, and by the door Tibo took a lantern, and with the flint she lighted it. Panduv said scathingly, "The god will be glad you don't waste his fire." But Tibo, of course, did not reply.

They walked through the summer night, across the pasture where the cows lay like boulders under a slender tree. A stone wall had mostly come down, and over it they went into the citrus trees and the standing rocks.

The beacon of the lantern disorganized rather than assisted vision. When it smote on the dome, this seemed an error of the eyes. Then the light steadied. It hardened into being.

"What is that?" Panduv recollected now having sighted the shining top of this object as Arud approached the farm.

Tibo said quietly, "It was always there, underneath. But the trees grew bigger, the roots pushed off the soil. Last summer, the earth shook and lifted it up." At her words, Panduv envisaged the pale smooth thing, rising like a fish, through the tide of the earth-tremor. It did not seem to be all above ground even now, but wedged into a socket of stone. The form of it was nonetheless like the shape of the fish of her imagery. The material of which it was made appeared metallic, but there was not a scratch or pock upon it. No mark at all.

"When you go near enough," said Tibo, "an opening comes."

They went forward, very slowly, the lantern engorging everything before them, putting out the rest of the valley.

And, as predicted, a door-opening evolved in the side of the fish-shape mound. Such mechanisms were not unknown. The modern temples of the snake goddess, Panduv had heard, were frequently so equipped. Yet the manner in which the door made itself bewil-

dered her, happening not with an upward, downward
or sideways motion, but in a kind of swirling. . . .

Within the door, was only darkness.

"Have you gone inside, Tibo?"

"Never."

"Afraid to."

"Yes. Here always, I never like to be here."

"You're a sensitive. It must be a bad place, then."

Panduv took the lantern from her, and, going closer
to the opening, let the light press on the darkness.

It was an oval chamber without corners, and again
she thought of the white races, tales of the round halls
in their ruined city in the southern Plains. Instantly
the lantern found a confirmation. There on a featureless wall, what she took for a carving. A coiled, unmistakable snake, white on white.

The Zakorian moved back, so the darkness possessed the hole again.

"It's a temple. The Plains People had them everywhere, scattered, even in the land of Dorthar. This
must be old as the mountains."

She felt that she was shaking. It was not fear. There
was a current of energy in the vicinity of the snake
temple, a supernatural force to be avoided, as Tibo
said she inclined to. Panduv backed farther and the
electric awareness was less. She said, "Why bring me
here?"

Tibo said, "Cah is here."

The Zakorian swore. "No. Cah is a goddess for the
Vis. Yours. Mine, maybe. That thing, there, that's the
yellowhairs' magic. Their goddess, the Lady of Snakes,
Anack."

Tibo said, "Cah forgave my sins. Each month, her
hand was on me. When this thing came out of the
earth, it was full of Cah. I'm afraid here. Fear doesn't
matter. This place is why I heal and how I bring the
fire. I've told no one else. It's Cah's place."

"It's *theirs*," said Panduv. She was angry. Stupidly
she thought of athletic contests between the dancers of
the city and blonde girls of Sh'alis. Inappropriate, yet
total—the racial unmeeting, the fight, the war going
on in small ways or large. Would Sh'alis not have

sung over the battering of Free Alisaar by a white, screaming wave?

Panduv shut her eyes and saw a star dashing, flaming, from the sky. It crashed against the bosom of the earth, seared and split the land, driving a channel, burying itself deep. As the patchy clouds and cinders settled, the star lay smoldering in its ditch, in a valley between mountains.

"There," said Tibo, as she put her hand on Panduv's shoulder. "You saw the star? I've seen it, too. Cah's sky-chariot falling. It remembers."

"Lowland magic, the power of flight," muttered Panduv. Tibo had taken her hand, and was leading her away from the shining domed mound, temple, fallen star, time-fish, between the citrus trees, into the commonplace pasture where the cows still lay peaceably chewing.

Panduv's limbs were water. She sat herself on the rough grass before she should stagger. "I don't like that, it isn't for me," she said. She shivered. "But for certain, it had some meaning."

Tibo loitered patiently until the Zakorian got up again. They returned into the hovel. They did not speak to each other any more.

Lying by Arud on Tibo's mattress, Panduv dreamed of Saardsinmey after the wave.

She saw initially from high up, as if she flew winged above the wreck. Far below, the landscape was a desert, with jagged monoliths and fanged ravines of masonry. She would not have known it for a city, except she had come there in the dream armed with its former name.

Circling, as once the hunting hawks had done, she descended through the bruised air.

She was impartial, the winged Panduv, in the dream. It did not tear her heart or consiousness, how it was, the sights of it.

On the roof of the Zarduk temple, whose entrails had been wrenched out, a ship rested. She flew by the ship, circling the pillars, and away. Above, there lay the stadium, which, with almost everything, had been

obliterated. There was only an abysm—the arena, piled
by tumbled things.

North and west, a metropolis of ruins, clung with
seaweed, with bits of shells on their stairs and roofs
and floors, and dotted with all the feasible remnants of
a human society suddenly vanquished.

A wind was blowing. It was clearing off the blots
and stains of the atmosphere, and Panduv was blown
to earth by it, and alighted, still high over the city,
where she might have expected to, on the Street of
Tombs.

Everything was mud. The marble seemed mostly to
have been turned to mud. And here, too, as she had
dimly noted in the shattered ruins beneath, tiny groups
of men and women were picking about, like beggars in
a gutter after a coin.

Panduv, invisible, poised among the mud hills, and
looked at them with mild pity, but no sense of kinship.
They were distant in all ways. There, where a white
stone had protruded from the clotted slime, someone
was grubbing, trying to pull out a corpse by its legs.
But there another only sat, and did nothing.

The soul of Panduv—so she supposed it was—began
to drift again. It came along a rise, to the sarcophagi
of kings and queens, the entertainers. On the incline
above rose the black beehive of her own tomb, washed
up amid the aloes.

The door stood open on its runner. She recalled . . .
Rehger, maybe others, had found shelter there. One
of these persons, seemingly left behind, now stepped
from the doorway, white out of black.

Panduv was not alone in seeing the phenomenon.
Two women a short way down the slope had stopped
in their grim pottering. They appeared terrified, as if
by an apparition, not realizing that this was only some
survivor of the wave like themselves.

The figure was not intrinsically alarming. It was that
of a girl, wearing a white dress, her head also veiled
by white. She did not stay to gaze about her, but went
on, up the incline, away from the black tomb. On the
crest of the slope, however, she did hesitate, and

next looked back, as if she had become aware of another watcher—Panduv.

The white of her clothing blended subtly with that of her skin and hair. The survivor out of the tomb was the Amanackire.

In the dream Panduv experienced no shred of wrongness. On the eve of nemesis, avoiding the gossip of the theater, she had never heard of the Lowlander's poisoning, while her actor-lover had been too busy with other commerce to tempt her ears with it. Panduv had not known of the murder, the burial, until that other dream in Ly's temple. *I gave myself to death—* The former dreaming, recaptured in this, conveyed only utter correctness.

The Amanckire had died, and by her death, ensured that Rehger might find shelter from destruction. Some days had passed, and Rehger, too, was gone. And rising up in the shadow, healed and whole, the white girl moved out into the world.

Now, drawing her veil over her face, she walked on across the rim of the hill and disappeared from view.

Winged, incorporeal, still Panduv did not follow her.

Instead she woke with a dreadful violence, jammed back into her body, not knowing where she was or what had happened to her. And in the intuitive battle to reclaim her memory and herself, for her heart to beat and her lungs to breathe, this dream, like the other, came undone and flowed away, down again into the sea-depths within her, out of sight and out of mind.

"What am I to tell them, that they could accept, at the Mother Temple?"

Arud voiced his distress twelve days later, when they had got beyond the crow's nest of Ly Dis, among the enduring sameness of the mountains.

Now, he is actually asking me.

"There is a course."

"Yes? Well? *Well?*"

"Inform them the rumors were grossly overblown. She's a healer who sees to women's complaints. She has the antique art of making fire with two pieces of wood. She does nothing, meanwhile, without invoking Cah, and her temple finds her virtuous. Besides, she's married, and her husband wouldn't permit her to do anything unlawful."

"Falsehoods, woman. I'm to condemn myself before the goddess by lying?"

"Cah is only an idea . . . the embodiment and symbol of life." (The two outriders were some way behind them, out of earshot. The other absconding pair had vanished even from the town.)

Arud did not chide Panduv. Conceivably he recalled how she had defended his feverish avowals to the world at large. How she had mentioned, too, the outrider's extreme unreliable drunkenness on the night in question. Should it ever be of use.

At last Arud said, humble before the infinite, "There are some who think in that way. Not gods, but their essence. In the capital, provided a man's discreet . . . Even the Highest One—Cah is All. Everything. The fount of existence. Not simply a stone with breasts."

"The Lowlanders, I hear, speak that way about snaky Anack."

Arud frowned. "Cah is the one true goddess."

"Then credit that the little Iscaian wife acts only in her name. Tibo's a devout believer. Let her alone. What does your temple care? And you. You only want to be home."

"Yes," he said. He heaved a sigh. "I've a house, on a hill. Breeze-fanned in summer. Flowering vines. A fish pond. Blue walls. You'll like my house."

So, I am to be in his house.

She thought of his love-making of recent nights, changed and passionate, and very deft. The dance of fire was over. She had become after all an instructress and courtesan.

Besides, she had not been able to safeguard herself. Or perhaps she should not have asked her own gods to fill the void in her days. Jokingly, Yasmat had intervened.

"Arud," she said, for he was learning, too, that in private he would be addressed by his name.

"What is it now?"

"I'm carrying your son."

He seemed to consider this. Some minutes passed.

"Well, how do you know it'll be a boy?"

"I know."

That would have been her role in Zakoris, in the sea village. To take men in, to thrust men forth. But she was fit and vital. A pregnancy would not quell her. It would be a child of late spring or early summer.

Yes, she was strong. The strength of any partner would be superfluous to her. Her lovers, whatever their reverence for a dancer's genius, or their titles or intellectual knowledge of songs or stars, they had, none of them, been her spirit's match.

And a warrior needed wars. Iscah would be one long campaign. She laughed aloud, and Arud said, "You're glad then, you Zakr girl, to be filled with my son?"

"Only delighted to delight you, master."

"You'll be mistress of my house. Have no worries on that front."

One must not employ irony. Be generous and lesson in generosity. At least, keep quiet.

He glanced down and saw her, striding by him, straight and royal, black as night, her long hair like a banner—having no past, for *he* had given her reality. He stopped his zeeba. He took her up before him. It was not Iscaian, and the outriders stared.

BOOK FOUR

MOIH

CHAPTER FOURTEEN

A MOIYAN WEDDING

Unlike the nuptuals of most of Vis, the marriages of Lowlanders were not concerned with the Red Star. It was well-known, Vis over, the Plains Race was immune to Zastis. For the mixed blood, and the Dortharians, Xarabs, and others who interwed on the Plains, they did not seem to mind too much not waiting on into the hot months. The first of summer, after the rains, before the deluge of the heat, that was the favored time, in the southern south.

In the province of Moih, the dual city-state of coastal Moiyah and the inland metropolis of Hibrel, a thriving culture had for some sixty years been growing up. Giving fealty direct to the Storm Lords of Dorthar, the cities and towns of Moih were democratically governed by their elected councils, enriched by their merchant fleets and traders' guilds, tolerant in the extreme of all gods, while cleaving themselves proudly always to Anackire, Lady of Snakes. There was neither racial, religious nor class stricture in the mores and legalities of Moih. Theoretically, there, you might befriend and worship whom you chose, and rise to whatever position you were capable of. Out of the melting pot of persecution, off the anvil of two famous wars, Moih had emerged, splitting herself free of the Lowland Way. Not for her the passive and unorganized fatalism still current in the southernmost Plains. Nor the xenophobia of the purist Amanackire, one of whose strongholds, the city of Hamos, lay four days' ride from Hibrel's outskirt, behind a barricade of ethnic ice. Correspondingly, as the frigid zealots had gathered to their own, into bustling Moih flocked the makers and doers of the Lowland people, along with representatives of almost every Vis-Plains mixture possible.

The wedding customs of Moih, therefore, tended somewhat to variety.

Upon this, one particular bridegroom was not pondering, late in the day in Moiyah.

Attired like a peacock for the event, it was nevertheless obvious that the good-looking young man was himself no son of the Plains. His hair and eyes were blackest black, his skin boldly metallic. Indeed, against the darkness of him, his Moiyan marriage clothes of white and gilt looked especially well.

She had seen him in something less elegant, the first time.

The bridegroom smiled. He was exhilarated, and a very little nervous, for this sunset's rituals were alien, and he meant to present them faultlessly. For her sake, of course.

If it came to that, what had he thought of *her,* at the first sighting? He had been half-blinded still by what had led up to it, and coming into the bay of Moiyah, among all the creamy shipping, the painted walls above with the golden Anackire perched there, and then beholding the flaxen throng in the port—he felt a sort of fear or disgust. Xenophobia was his portion, too. The ship had been difficult enough. Something in him was starving for the multitudes of his own kind— And in and out of the jostling crowd along the quayside, had come the two daughters of Arn Yr, with their maid.

Annah, the elder, was also the taller of the two, with a dainty porcelain head bound and wound with hair like ripened wheat. News had already run east, of the Aarl-mouth, the great wave, and their outflanking tempests. There had been unearthly dawns and sunfalls, too, at Moiyah. Arn's ship, *Pretty Girl,* was anxiously looked for. Getting word from the agent that she was approaching the bay, his daughters hurried down to make sure of their father. But Elissi had seen the ship-lord first. Arn himself, enthusiastically waving in return, pointed out both girls to his passengers.

Elissi was slight and small, fair-skinned but summer tanned. Her hair was so light that the sunshine sent it up like a scarf of white fire. But she had remembered her Ommish granddam. Elissi's eyes, like the eyes of Ommos, and of Alisaar, and of Corhl, were jets.

Maybe Chacor had been consoled by her black eyes. When, later, he came to look into them.

He had meant to go away quickly. Up into Zarabiss, to Dorthar, or to the homeland, like a frightened dog. The kindness and the openheartedness of Moih he accepted, and was prepared to repay if he could, like provisions bought on credit. He knew these people were alive, had characters and minds, even souls perhaps, as he did. But they were nevertheless dream-people.

Of the daunting telepathy of the Plains there was not much overt evidence. The Amanackire prided themselves on their secret inner speaking, but in the mercantile peoples of Moih the art had been restricted, from craft, or common politeness, more to the family circle. On *Pretty Girl* they had seemed to take care not to bother their Vis passengers with displays of minds in dialogue. In Arn Yr's house, though it was sometimes apparent a thought had passed between the kindred, they saved their wordless discussions for the private rooms.

However, out in the city, mind speech was sometimes observable. More often, and worse, with the very children playing in the public gardens, their delighted shrieks suddenly stilled as they stood together in complete dumbness, planning the next stage of their game.

As for those Vis Chacor saw on the streets—a handful of Lans, amiable Dortharians in from the fort up the coast, Xarabian merchants, one Elyrian astrologer in a shop near the quay—even Annah's betrothed, a mix so nearly Vis in looks it came as a jolt to hear his Vathcrian twang—they only disconcerted Chacor, put him out. There were not enough of them. It was foolish to be there at all.

Arn Yr's unfailing charity and humor had been evident on the ship. The vessel had got a battering and enough cargo had been lost she must go home without profit to repair, but he had not bemoaned misfortune, and once in port spent less time with his agents than in showing Chacor the city. Chacor had long since found Rehger valueless as a companion. There was an Arms Academy at Moiyah. Rising early, Rehger would be gone, to utilize the services of the gymnasium. He sold the gold on his wrists and off his belt to pay, and to recompense Arn Yr, who, with his wife, had made such a fuss of refusal it developed into a one-sided row—Chacor had scarcely any money and nothing to sell, apart from himself. But to take work in Moiyah seemed to imply remaining in Moiyah, and he did not want to do it. No one gave cash to see acrobatic street brawls, and most of the bets in Moih inclined to archery contests and Shansar horse-races. On the fifth day Arn Yr, who had shown Chacor the markets and the guild halls, the exterior of the gold-roofed Anackire temple and the race-track, led him into Moiyah's Street of Gods.

Chacor looked about in earnest dismay, seeing represented on every side, among the groves of yellow-flowered sintal trees, most of the foremost deities of Vis. There the temple of the Ommish fire god, cheek by jowl with his brother of Zakoris, and there the pavilion of the Xarabian Yasmis, furled with incense. Farther along, obsidian dragons marked a shrine to Dorthar's mysterious storm gods, where two or three Dortharian soldiers were playing dice familiarly on the steps. Even Rorn, blue-bearded, loomed on a plinth.

Chacor muttered. He asked Arn Yr, if the Lowlanders were so devout, so given to Anack, why this sacrilege under her nose. Arn Yr explained the ethics of tolerance. He himself did not neglect Zarok.

"Then," said Chacor, "where is Corrah?"

Arn Yr, who had possibly been waiting for this, indicated a lane. Unconvinced the Corhlan turned into it, and soon found the house of Corrah, and the house of Cah, neighboring each other. He went in at the Corhlish entrance, and gave one of his last coins to make an offering of balm, had no comfort, wanted to ask the goddess what she was doing there.

That evening, Rehger achieved gainful employment in Moih. The ship lord's domicile, partial to dinner parties, had given one. Loath and uneasy you might be, but you found yourself nonetheless in yet more borrowed garments, spruce and garlanded, at a snowy-draped, belilied table with the family, and eight of its intimates. Nor were you churlish, but did your best to behave for your generous hosts. For some reason it was very bright before Chacor, the image of Arn Yr's ship emerging from the bloody fog beyond Saardsinmey's shore, (only, quite incredibly, a month ago.) Who had Arn Yr been that day, coming toward them over the ruin of the beach, the red froth of the fouled black sea about his boots? And the blond men of his crew, shaking their heads, giving wine, going into the wreck of the city . . . returning silent in the scarlet dawn that seemed ready never to conclude— A man, Arn Yr, and other men, fellow humans in the world's night.

To Chacor's left, the younger daughter, Elissi, offered a segment of candied citrus to a late arrival, an impeccable small silver monkey. Eating graciously, the monkey reviewed the table with indigo eyes.

"Ah, the monkey-princess," said the man seated on the left hand of Arn Yr's wife. "I hope she is well?"

The monkey twittered.

The man said, "Alas. She tells me she's had something of a cough this summer. But how is it now, my dear?"

The monkey flirted, taking her tail in her hands and veiling with it her lower countenance.

"She says, she supposes if she were not treated so uncaringly, she would do better."

There was some laughter.

"How cruel," said Elissi now to the princess. "To say such untruths, and before everybody, you ungrateful, furry thing. Besides, you ate the pearl out of my earring. That was the cause of your cough!"

The man who had spoken for the monkey, previously introduced as Master Vanek, was himself a small, grisled individual, of the Guild of Artisans and Stone-Workers. He commented now that the pearl-eater was a paragon, and outlined the vices of another of her tribe, taken to his studio on Marble Street for the purpose of being drawn, who ate her cage bars, and thereafter a bar of casting wax, some sticks of paint, and a wig from the store room.

Then, turning eyes on Rehger, who sat opposite to him, Vanek added, "But it's a fact, we are always in need of sound models."

Rehger smiled gravely.

"I won't boast," said Vanek, "as the boaster always *will* say. But the three sons of a lesser Dortharian prince have modeled for my sculptors. It's well known."

"The frieze of the warriors on the great library," said Arn Yr. "Yes, everyone knows. They, too, boasted about it. Your studio's reputed."

"My father," said Vanek to Rehger, "was a herder on the plains under Hibrel. We do what we like here, what we're good at. This is a virtue of Moih. Nor is any man ashamed to tell another his price." Vanek took a grape and toyed with it. "We are about to engage on an epic venture: A *Raldnor,* a statue of the hero-god. It's commissioned in Xarabiss, for the king's own winter palace. We must *not* go wrong, you will agree." Another pause, and anyone who did not guess what was up, unless it were the monkey, must be the biggest fool in the south. "Well, now, I promise to you, Rehger Am Alisaar, sixty ankars in gold, Moih-Xarabiss guild-weight, if you'll take on the job."

The amount, which was impressive, caused a hush.

Then Rehger said, presumably playfully, "Do you mean, sir, the job of sculpting it or of modeling for it?"

The table laughed again. Vanek only looked crafty, intrigued. "To sculpt would bring rather more, but my man already has the commission. I meant, to model."

And then, another diversion. Rehger said, gently:

"But I heard the face of the messiah-king Raldnor is commemorated. I'm not like him, surely."

"That may be a subject for debate. The likenesses we have vary, as do the likenesses of his ancestor, Rarnammon, and even of Raldnor's son, the second Rarnammon, though he's only dead some twenty-five years. I don't mean to embarrass you, young man, but

great handsomeness *is* required, of physiognomy and
of body. And some endurance also, the stance and the
hours are not easy. You were a gladiator in Alisaar, I
believe."

"I was a slave there," said Rehger.

Vanek said, briskly now, "Moih doesn't recognize
slavery. Any slave who can gain our borders is reckoned a free man, as are all men in the sight of the
goddess. Aside from that, do you accept?"

"Yes," said Rehger. "And my thanks."

"Thank me when we're done. And now, Elissi, let
me embrace the monkey-princess. I must be going,
Arn my friend, ladies, pardon me. You know my
routine. The studio begins labor at first light, Rehger."

Rehger nodded. His face, as his voice, had not
changed.

Annah and her Vis-Vathcrian were discreetly canoodling
in the vine arbor, and so Chacor cut down the other
garden path through the sintal trees.

Rehger was sitting beside the water tank. The moon
had risen, and the fish in the tank, by day golden as
Lowland eyes, were rising to the surface to see it.

Enclosing the garden's stillness was the breathing
lull of a late city night. The dark beyond the walls was
sparingly patched with glowing windows. Now and
then a strain of music might be sounded, or mellow
voices on the streets below. Sometimes even there
rose the murmur of the sea. It was not an hour or a
spot for altercation. And, despite any likenesses, it
was not Saardsinmey.

"So, you're to stay here and be a Moiyan."

Rehger looked up, and another fish broke the moon
on the tank, or it might have been this time one of the
sintal flowers, falling down there.

"Vanek's proposal meets a need, I think."

"And was arranged beforehand, *I* think."

"Yes," said Rehger. "As we've noticed, Arn Yr's a
generous man."

They had conversed, the Lydian and the Corhl, only
rarely on the ship. It was not that Rehger pushed him
off, avoided him—it was that Rehger gave him attent-

ion—yet did not seek any response in turn. There was
none of the comradeship of survival that Chacor anticipated. Rehger did not confide. He listened and replied, and was often alone. And as they went away
perforce to the pale shores of the foreigners' country,
Chacor missed, and wanted, *something*. He had, from
the beginning, wanted something of Rehger. To best
him, or be bested. To vaunt, to copy, the polish of
abrasion. Events had made them reluctant sharers,
or—*she* had done so.

They had walked, each of them, behind her bier.
They had taken shelter in her tomb. Together they
had escaped.

Chacor said suddenly, "Was it true?"

Rehger did not say *What do you mean?* He seemed
only to consider how the fish rose and the flowers
fell, and the moon, breaking and reforming, shattered
and born. Then: "I believed I'd killed you. That horri-
fied me. I'd never killed in that way. You know why it
happened? It occurred to me you saw."

"The Anack priest-trick, sword to snake." (Something else hers, shared.)

Chacor leaned on a tree. It no longer seemed to be
anything to do with him, the death-blow, the healing.
Could his indifference be sane, or wise? Better to
suppose, maybe, his memory was at fault. When he
spoke of it, it was as if he forced himself to do it, not
in terror, but out of courtesy to some nameless element
of his physical personality, or some aspect of his goddess. (He should make Corrah a decent offering. If
anyone had saved him, it was Corrah.) After all, the
Amanackire had died herself.

As though there had been some clamor, now stillness returned, the living stillness of garden and night.
In the vine arbor, if they spoke, it was without any
words.

"Before she died," Rehger said, "Aztira told me I'd
meet my father in Moih. When the time came due.
I've never known my father. For several reasons, I'm
curious about him."

Because Rehger had not said previously *What do*

you mean? Chacor, now, did not blurt out, *Oh, was that how she was called, the Lowland witch—Aztira?*

"Would she be accurate about a thing like that?"

"I think so."

They had been lovers (Something *not* shared.)

"I intend," said Chacor, "to go north. Xarabiss sounds a likely venue. Or Dorthar. I gather Ommos stinks. But I regret I'm in his debt, our ship lord."

"I don't imagine Arn's much of a man for keeping tally of debts."

A fish, larger than the rest, leapt through the reflection of the moon. The continual breaking of the light . . . It was destroyed, it could not *be* destroyed.

"Well, I'll look for your Raldnor statue, coming into Xarabiss, on a car of gold, with trumpets," said Chacor.

Walking along Amber Street half an hour later, Chacor heard a wolfish step pacing to catch up to him. You did not expect footpads in Moiyah, but that was not to say they were absent. Chacor, knife most ready, turned about and found Annah's betrothed on his heels.

"You handle yourself like a fighter," said the latter. "Not ready for sleep? Listen, excuse my frankness, but do you want a girl? There's a very appealing house I can recommend. They used to know me there, before I cast myself at Annah's feet. Quite a few of the officers go there. The girls are mostly Xarabians; winsome. Don't worry about money. I can cover that."

"Why?" said Chacor belligerenty.

Annah's betrothed shrugged. "Why not? I'm happy tonight."

His proper name was Jerish. He was the captian of one hundred men of the Mioyah garrison. The curl in his accent came from his father's being a Vathcrian, and the tongue of the other continent the first language at home. He had once observed in Chacor's hearing that his father accused him of speaking his Vathcrian conversely in the accents of Vis.

"You know what's wrong with your Moiyan city?" said Chacor.

"No, what?"

"You *give* too much."

They began to stroll northwest, into the streets behind the race-track. Moiyah was never dark, painted all over and well-lit at night by street lamps. Where they burned closest to the sintal trees, with which every park and garden of the city seemed planted, a warm fragrance wafted out that filled the avenues.

"My pack are starting for the fort in two days. You could travel with us if you want. Save you the chance of robbers on the border."

"And if I like, you'll help me get into the army, which is always in need of fit and healthy men, regardless of race or religion."

"That's true. I tell you, we still get reavers on our bit of sea. And we like to show New Alisaar fair will and a firm face."

"But as luck has it, you can now forget Saardsinmey."

They parted near the cattle market, from which a faint shifting and lowing mocked Chacor as he strode off.

Passing back again by the race-track, he took unfriendly note of tomorrow's races pinned up on the gate.

Even Anack gave.

At noon the next day, plunged from a sleepless bed, he had put put the ultimate scrap of his financial hide upon a black Shansar racer, and won twenty silver parings, Moih rate.

Then when he reached the Corrah temple, he saw Elissi passing in under the porch and petrified, thinking he had gone mad.

But no, there was the little maid against a pillar, rocking the pet monkey like a baby.

Chacor stationed himself in the doorway of the shrine opposite, and waited, in a bemused fury. After perhaps the third of an hour, Elissi came out of the temple. There was a brilliant flush in the clear honey of her cheeks which, as Chacor arrived in her path, faded into pallor.

"What were you doing in *there?*" said Chacor. When

Elissi only stared at him, he said, "Do you go there regularly, you pious ones, to spit on the altar?"

"No."

"What then?"

Elissi ran suddenly from guilty shame to annoyance.

"What do you think? To make an offering."

"What? The worshiper of Anack the Serpent goes to the dirt-heap of the unbeliever to *offer?"* (He had chosen to forget Arn and the fire god.) In her face then he saw a struggle to be serene, as when dealing with an irrational, fractious child. This caused him to burst out loudly, "And won't the snake woman enviously strike at you for it?"

People turned to glance their way, good-humoredly, not catching the gist, probably guessing here were two lovers quarreling.

Elissi blushed now with embarrassment, but raising her head, faced him out, as if across a shield rim. "Anackire has no jealousy. Anackire is everything," she told him stingingly. "Anackire is the name we give the State of Life, of existence, body and soul, earth and eternity. But you give it the name *Corrah.* And so I came to your *Corrah,* and made an offering to your *Corrah,* since we seldom offer to Anackire, and Anackire isn't yours."

Chacor could only glare at her. Her flaming black jets of eyes glared back.

At last, "Why?" he said again.

"That the sympathy should pass directly to you, if able. As I'd speak where I could to a man in a language he knew. I asked that she might give you peace of mind."

He missed that and grated, "But to you and yours, Corrah doesn't exist."

"All things exist. Look at that pebble lying there. You might call it *um* and I might call it *oom.* Isn't it still a pebble, and lying there?"

An abrupt wave of relaxation swept over Chacor, stunning him. The girls of Moih were well-schooled in the means of debate. And how lovely this one was, summer-brown as a girl of Iscah, her color coming and

going and her eyes on fire and her hair not like hair at
all but a sheet of hot white light.

"Respite," said Chacor, a term he had picked up
from the dueling etiquette of Alisaar. "Put down your
sword, lady. You've won. My apologies. Your father
sacrifices to Zarok, too, doesn't he?"

Then she laughed. And then he remembered why
she had made the offering.

Presently they were in a public garden under the
yellow boughs, the princess climbing a tree, and the
maid gone away to buy the juice of berries.

They were speaking of ordinary things, not even
religion, and he had not questioned her again about
the offering. Elissi had become a real person. Suddenly it came to him that she loved him. Though not
in the normal headlong and demanding way to which
his travels among young women had accustomed him.

He found it difficult thereafter not to flaunt him-
self, to make himself grand and beautiful in her eyes.
But he must be cautious. There was jeopardy in this.
She was not a flower of the wayside, but the protected
daughter of a man who had himself lavished upon
Chacor great kindnesses.

So, he restrained himself somewhat. But even so, he
did tell her his beginnings, that he was a prince, and
Corhl was far behind him. He did sit there with her
under the trees and speak of the end of Saardsinmey.
He let her see, not meaning to, not evading, the
impress that had since then been upon him, as if the
death cry of a million despairing hearts had darkened
his own.

The afternoon tilted away toward sunset. A bloom
dropped from the trees upon his hand. (Summer was
going, too, toward its set.) He put the bloom in her
hair. He had now been silent a long while, she with
him. Looking at them, the passersby would think, perhaps, Chacor had some Lowland blood, and that they
spoke within.

"The sintal grew in the old city of the south," she
said. "There was an elder language, then. *Sintal.* It
means *goddess-hair.*"

"Like yours," he said, and wondered if he should bite out his tongue.

But Elissi only told him, "We say, we, too, are Anackire, for Anackire is all things, and all things one thing. Each of us has God within him, *is* God, Chacor."

"You credit that souls come back to be born again; death doesn't count."

"Even if," she said, "that weren't so, the terror and anguish of Saardsinmey is over. The pain is done, for them. And if the pain goes on for you, then let it be a part of you, Chacor. But not, Chacor Am Corhl, you a part of *it*."

They walked back in the youthful evening, one pair among scores of couples, drinking chilled fruit juice, praising the monkey as she walked daintily by their side on her long leash. The maid had found her own young man, a carter from Marble Street, and been allowed to run away until the dinner hour.

He permitted himself no familiarity. He did not even take her hand.

At dinner, he spoke to Jerish, accepting the company of the soldiers going toward Xarabiss, and asking after a zeeba he could now afford to hire. On Arn Yr he next attempted to leave ten silver parings, and was refused.

Later, looking for Elissi in the garden, Chacor did not find her. He was sorry and relieved.

Somewhere on the two-and-a-half-day ride up to the fort, Jerish and his sergeant sold Chacor the soldier's life. Partly it was done, he thought in confusion soon after, by inquiring what he meant to aim for in Xarabiss, or Dorthar? Then he as well would have to inquire into his prospects. He had always been a drifter, taking up brawling as a trade, but, in Alisaar, he had learnt something of chariots, of hiddraxi and zeebas, and of the methods of the sword. Now soldiering seemed to present itself as this same trade and learning, in better harness. He had begun to get on with Jerish and his officers, and the mixed "pack," which called itself the Plains Wolves, were a lively bunch, three-quarters yellow Moiyan and a quarter everything else under the sun. Black-bronze skin did not debar from command, either, Jerish was proof. While the Dortharian captain who was to govern the Dortharian peacetime battalion in the fort, was a white blond.

Besides, after this paid brawl got stale, Chacor could opt out of it. As Jerish assured him, provided he gave due warning of intended departure, and providing New Alisaar or Ommos were not actually training ballistas on the city, there would be no checks.

Once he was in, and the cut and dried rigmarole of military training started, Chacor wished himself off and away. But it was too late then. Moih's new recruits received two months' pay in advance. Thereafter, they kept an eye on you.

Then, he began not to mind it so much.

He began to discover brothers, against whom he could try his strength and his fighting wiles as much as he wanted, and still go drinking with them in the village under the walls at night.

The city he returned to for his leaves, or more usually went up across the border into windy Xarabian Sar, from which Raldnor the hero had claimed false derivation. Rehger Chacor had lost touch with. Jerish said the Lydian was still employed by Vanek. Arn Yr, intent once more on profitable voyaging, beyond one visit Chacor avoided. (He did not see her, either.)

Just before the winter closed down, in the interim of thaw, there was a tirr hunt. The filthy beasts had been massing in the area, their castings and stench marking the tracks and trails, and there were stories of gypsies and village children poisoned by their claws. Tirr were hated worse than any wolves. Chacor, who had hunted them in Corhl, had some tips to offer which proved effective. They wiped out three nests, and brought home one whole flat-skulled jutting earless head and flange of talons, carefully unvenomed, to set by stealth on the officers' supper dish.

Winter was bleak, and they damned it extravagantly, always ritualistically complaining about the weather, the difficulty of getting to Moiyah and Xarabiss. The fires blazed high in the mess. On sentry-go you might watch the stars Elyrian fashion, in the winter clarity of

sky above the turrets by night. Beneath, the bay had
frozen and the sea was plates of ice. The white fields
stretched off from the fort the other side. Chacor
favored a mix-Sarish girl, but she was like all the other
free girls he had gone with. By the time of the thaw
rains, they had even-temperedly done with each other.

It was Jerish and Annah's wedding that spring. The
Plains Wolves were heading back to the city garrison.
Chacor had for three months been moving upward,
and was now offered the rank of division sergeant
under a Moiyan captain. It meant another stint at the
fort. But with hunting weather returning and the leave-
route open again to Xarabiss, he was not unwilling to
stay. Best of all, there were tales not merely of tirr
but of bandits in force on the border. It was in Chacor
yet, the viral restlessness that sought release in combat.

He did go to the wedding. He was chosen by Jerish
in fact to be one of the Raiding Party—a custom of the
wedding—along with Vathcrian cousins and boyhood
friends from the army. He could not have said no.

In the uproar and festivity he did not properly see
Elissi until the dancing began. Moih had a form of
dance not yet popular in Vis lands. Here the sexes
mingled, hand-locked, man with girl, in long lines.
Elissi came by with a soldier of the Wild Cats. She
looked still and smiling, but her face was not viva-
cious, as Chacor remembered. Mostly he saw how the
winter had paled her skin. What had been Iscaian
honey was now Amanackire snow.

They spoke some words to each other during the
evening, wishing the bridal couple well.

He had long since made his own offering to Corrah,
precious oil and wine. Blood sacrifice was not the vogue
in Moih for any of the gods, except at certain seasons
when the carcasses were immediately portioned and dis-
tributed to the needy. They never sacrificed to Anackire.
So far as he knew they never gave her anything.

In the morning, he rode out again for the fort,
soldierly and somewhat admired on the streets.

Then, in Sheep Lane, at a silversmith's, he saw
Elissi, perhaps a foot high and made of silver, standing
in the shop-front.

He stopped his mount and stared. In the end, he walked into the shop. A curlicued Xarab came out at him, and Chacor, aggrieved, pointed at the statuette.

"You wish to buy?" The Xarab seemed dubious. "This isn't cheap."

"Who made it?"

"I see you are a connoisseur. I will be honest with you." (Dishonesty shone radiant from his brow). "Not a master. An apprentice, but of a reputable studio, the worthy Vanek's. Obviously a pupil of mighty promise, you will agree? Would I, indeed, accept an inferior cast?"

A strange suspicion made Chacor say slowly, "An Alisaarian."

"So I am led to believe. From that tragic city torn by the hell mountain last year."

Looking more closely, Chacor saw the resemblance to Elissi was fleeting. Some memory had lodged, or else the model was a girl rather like her, but only in build and style of hair.

"Very fine," said Chacor, dazed.

He went out of the shop, nothing bought, and the Xarab bowed to him in such a way that adjacent booths began to chortle, but Chacor did not hear.

The bandit, whose other choice was an escort to Sar, elected to betray his leader's hideout. Moiyah was reckoned lenient to criminals; she fined or imprisoned them. Xarabian-Dortharian Sar, on the other hand, tended to maim or crucify them on the terrace under the altar of the wind gods.

Of Chacor's detachment, twenty-five men, he sent five back to the fort with their debilitated captives. The engagement, an ambush in a stony defile, Chacor had foreseen. It was not too difficult, for the terrain begged for something of the sort. The dead robbers they buried; Moih, who burned her own dead Lowlander-wise, gave specific instructions.

So far the fort had not lost a man on this expedition. The local bandit population had been decimated. Chacor was justly not displeased, and his men were positively jolly, although the Moiyans tended to crow less over killing.

The fort meanwhile was now some days behind them. The mission had sent them northeastward. Technically they were out of Moih, on the map of the Plains, and that evening they made camp on a low eminence with a view of the Xarabian border. The hideaway should be a task for the morning, but Chacor fancied a night attack, which he was keeping from any of the bandit king's spies who might be about.

As the cook-fires sent up lazy smoke, Chacor's scout noticed a movement three miles off, over the barren folds of landscape. The sun-blushed dust was skirling there, intermittently, but only in one generalized spot.

"Dust devils?" said Chacor, who was not yet properly used to the Plains.

"No sir. Not really late enough in the year. Not enough dust."

"You joke with me," said Chacor. Like the scout, he was powdered head to foot.

The scout grinned. "Unless I have it wrong, sir, that's the Dragon Gate smack against the border, where that dust dance is."

Chacor had seen the Gate several times by now, going up and down to and from Sar. It gave him an eerie sensation that caused him to invoke Corrah, but that was all. He said, they had better go and see, put the camp on dignified alert not to excite possible watchers, and with three men galloped off northward, with the sun in a sinking rage on the left hand.

As he rode along then, Chacor came to feel that there was something uncanny about the evening. It was nothing he could put a hand on—maybe only the red sideways light, the success of the jaunt, the little command he now had going to his head, in the warrior fellowship of fighting shoulder to shoulder. Or maybe it was something in the weather. They had been hearing of summer hail and flash-floods farther north, and that a series of earth tremors in Dorthar, where they had become a triviality and were mostly ignored, had nonetheless created enough damage to send the population to its temples. Yet, he was not uneasy, merely

sensitized. Even if the moving dust were a ploy of the
bandit lord's—which he doubted—four armed men,
mailed, on cavalry zeebas, would be a match for it.

As they crossed the last mile, and the dim shape of
the pillars of the Gate came visible like ghosts through
the dust, Chacor's skin prickled. It was the sensation a
Lowlander would have called flatly *Anackire*—their
label it seemed to him for any random otherness.

Then he heard the shouting. It was human, both
irate and desperate. And then, the long-drawn, gut-
twisting screech of tirr.

Two of the three men he had brought along were
expert javelineers. As he gave them the word, they
were already reaching, ready.

They sprinted through the dust.

It was almost a tableau. A slope with boulders and a
stand of sunburnt trees. A wagon with empty shafts,
now and then slipping and bucking on the slope, hitting the dust up in spouts. Two men were on the
wagon, trying to hold it, and at the same moment
whirling a staff apiece—torches, smoking and invisibly
flaring in the sunset. Six tirr crouching, mauling the
wagon sides. Abruptly one beast, two, springing, meeting fire and slewing aside.

"Anack!" swore the mix javelineer.

No one waited. Next instant two of the tirr were
pinned by iron. A third spun and came at them. Chacor
kicked his zeeba, leaned forward and rode straight at
the tirr, seeing only the death-ripe claws, the red coins
of the eyes, swerving, and his sword coming edgeways
down across the mangey neck. The beast collapsed
and he jerked his mount away from the death throe
and the talons— Looked up and saw a third javelin
had done its work, and the third man had another tirr
on its back, not yet risking pulling out his sword. That
one was a female with sallow furrowed nipples—she
had been suckling young not long before.

The last of the creatures crouched hesitating, vicious, unnerved. Once you had hunted them, you
knew they were inclined more to kill than to preserve
themselves. Gaining some fluke of escape, often they
would not take it if they might inflict another wound.

Full grown men seldom survived a single scratch, unless cauterized within five minutes. A slender woman or a child—it was hopeless.

Chacor sat there staring into the red eyes. The hiatus was unnatural. Were they considering, he and his men, they would spare the brute?

Suddenly Chacor was thinking of a name. It was the name by which Rehger had called his lover, the Amanackire—*Aztira*. This had a likeness to the other name—*tirr*. The notion was irrelevant, disquieting.

"Finish!" Chacor shouted.

A fourth javelin went over. The tirr seemed to leap snapping toward it, to embrace it, and fell back heavily, stone dead. One of the other tirr was still spasming. You could not dare go and put it out of its misery even, that was too chancy.

The two men from the wagon had stopped making a noise and lowered their torches. One, a Xarabian, jumping down, with help from the mix soldier shoved stones under the wheels.

The other man, not Xarabian, but Vis-dark (and Plains dusty), had also swung down.

"Soldiers from the Moih fort, aren't you?"

"Our respects," said Chacor.

"Well, sergeant, you've saved *our* chops this evening. But we deserved it. What a day we've had. First we were robbed—hence our lack of zeebas or any knives, not to mention my employer's irreplaceable samples—then attacked by tirr. Your sublime goddess must have sent you to our aid."

The goddess Corrah, thought Chacor resolutely. But he inclined his head. His men were occupied with carcasses. The one kicking tirr was now lifeless. Chacor dismounted. He went over to the man, and saw he was very tall, and in earliest middle-age, which his agility and energy had perhaps belied. The flaming sky was behind him, then as he, too, came forward, holding out a commodious hand, Chacor received a shock. The man off the wagon was Rehger. Rehger in twenty years' time.

Chacor gave his hand in return.

"Chacor Am Corhl," he said, friendly, feeling clever, feeling slightly drunk.

"Yennef Am Lan. Am everywhere it begins to seem."

About a hundred feet away, the two giant pillars of the Dragon Gate, white, unfeatured, went soaring upward, losing themselves in the coming of the dusk.

"An historic place for our adventure," said Yennef, Rehger's father, glancing toward them. "Don't they say, the first Vis kings came to earth there, carried in the bellies of dragons?"

Chacor shrugged. "That's the mythos of Dorthar. You're in the Lowlands now. Come, share our camp. Maybe we can cheer you a little regarding robbers."

Supper was, again, grilled dust rat and hard biscuit, and some agreeable wine from the fort village, unadulterated by water.

As it got dark, and the stars of the Plains, thick-strewn and effulgent, appeared overhead, they sat talking in the firelight. Yennef gave the impression of being communicative. He was much-traveled—of everywhere, as he had titled himself—Lanelyr, the Middle Lands . . . Vardish Zakoris . . . *and Iscah, too*, Chacor inwardly observed. The man was an accomplished wanderer, what Chacor might have been, or might still become. Yennef, too, had done "some soldiering in youth." For the present, he earned his bread as an agent for a merchant guild in Xarar, and his masters were not going to love him since he had been robbed. Chacor described briefly the plan to raid the bandit nest. Yennef promptly offered his help. "If you can loan me a mount and a sword, I'll eat my luck as I find it. I can still fight, and after today I'd like one." "And to take an order?" said Chacor. Yennef said, "I'll admit, I never served under so young an officer when I was your age. But, of course." The Xarabian, however, Yennef excused. The man was his servant and, as you saw, not tough. He had been brave with the tirr perforce.

It was not yet Zastis, and there was no moon. Chacor sent scouts along the slopes an hour later, where they unearthed some snoozing bandit lookout. He was persuaded into picturing the nest in some detail, which corresponded with prior information. Gathering his men, and leaving the Xarab and two watch in the fire-ringed camp, to make a camplike stir, they set off.

When they got there, about midnight, the raid was quickly accomplished, for the robbers had been smug enough to bed down for the night. Javelins brought the sentries crashing. Next it was hand to hand. The den was in the undershore of a raised embankment with an old ruined wall on it. Some thirty villains came flying and stumbling down from the crest or out of holes. Three or four were mixes. The king himself had light gray eyes. It was an undistinguished fight, with no openings for prowess, for the thieves were used to attacking unarmed civilians. As it turned out, Yennef's robbers were another crew, parasites without the instinct to murder—they and the Xarar goods had gone elsewhere. Nevertheless there was some quantity of loot in the dirty shambles of the warren. Yennef, having acquitted himself very well, got a promise of compensation for himself and his master.

Before sunrise everything was settled, the surrendered foe roped and haltered, having been pressed into burying their own dead. Chacor's detail had only three serious casualties. Since Yennef's wagon was going on to the fort, it proved a convenient vehicle for their transport.

Yennef rode alongside Chacor on the route west. He continued chatty over the evening fires. He seemed perfectly sociable and outgoing. Yet when Chacor, who had a leave due him and now badly wanted to take it in Moiyah, suggested they might go that way together, Yennef put him off. "Even with the peerless zeebas hired from your fort, wagons make slow riding. We'd hold you back." Chacor, who had the northwest Visian's utter abhorrence of homosexuality, wondered if Yennef and his weapon-shy Xarab servant were bedfellows and did not want interruptions. He did not care to regard Rehger's father in that manner, so concluded there was some other secret.

"Well," he said, as they got up to the fort, "do you know where you'll be lodging in Moiyah?"

"Oh. Some inn."

"Don't think I'm prying. But this compensation. I'll be in charge of that. I'll need to have some means to meet you in the city."

"Ah, the compensation. Well, sergeant, isn't there a famous wine-shop called the *Amber Anklet?*"

"For sure. On Amber Street. And I can recommend it. A lot of Dortharians drink there."

"Do they? A Xarabian told me about it. Say you go there and ask for me. When I get your message, I'll call on *you.*"

Chacor, having no fixed abode in the city, and feeling they were now playing a silly game, said, "I tell you what. Be at the *Anklet* the first evening of the new month."

"That's Zastis. Won't you be engaged elsewhere?"

"I'll make sure I'm not."

Yennef gave him an odd look. Did *Yennef* now think he was being propositioned?"

"You're too generous," said Yennef, "all this care about getting me requited for a few ragged blows with a lent sword."

"Moiyan codes," said Chacor. "Even if I hated your insides, my friend, I'd have to do it."

He rode for the city full-tilt, and half a mile off—to increase the drama—the sky soured purple and a summer storm of grandiose violence encompassed him.

Vanek's studio on Marble Street was the first place he went.

There was some flurry there, for they were getting the buckets uncovered on the roof to catch the downpour. (Rain water, when no salt wind was blowing from the sea, was judged the better for the studio's needs than that of the public cisterns.) Vanek was not present. The apprentices were running everywhere at once, the studio offices empty but for desks, and the outer shop contained one attendant and one rich mix idler, poking amid a cupboardful of ivories after a "something." Of Rehger there was no hint. A clerk, hastening to his midday snack, informed Chacor that seeking Rehger meant the house of Arn Yr.

Chacor pelted out, remounted and dashed through the running streets under the pouring rain.

He knew from Jerish, now set up with Annah in the married state on Amber Street, that her father was away with *Pretty Girl*, trading along the Xarabian coast and up to Ommos. The steward in the outer hall of the house told Chacor that Arn Yr's wife was also away, at an embroidery group in the home of a friend. They were approaching the whereabouts of Rehger, when Arn Yr's younger daughter appeared suddenly from a doorway.

The steward fell silent.

Chacor and Elissi, equally silent, looked at one another.

He was like a being of fire, so fast-ridden, so keyed up, and so *drenched* by the tempest that even now straddled the roof and drummed the slates.

She was luminously beautiful, with garden flowers in her hand—she had been arranging them in a vase—scarcely tinted with summer and now extremely pale.

"Thank you," she said to the steward. "Won't you come in here?" she asked Chacor.

For a fact, seeing her had checked him. He had thought of her, been reminded of her by innumerable items on endless occasions. Now a sort of calm flowed over him, as once before in her presence. He thanked her in turn, and walked into the room which gave on a covered corner of the garden.

She laid the flowers on a table. She stood gazing at him. Her whole body seemed expressive of a question.

Intent on his own question, he did not think how it must appear to her. She saw he had ridden there headlong, through the rain, on some impassioned errand. Because she wanted this to be herself, how could she suspect that it was not?

"Elissi—I know you'll pardon the state of me and my hurry, it's on a matter of importance—"

She stood and gazed on him.

Something did then communicate itself, but the impetus of all the past days was not to be turned in a moment.

"I must speak to Rehger the Lydian," Chacor said.

Her face went white. "I—they—told me he was here."
Chacor ended, not hearing what he said. He had just
realized, after all, what she had been thinking.

In a few instants she lowered her eyes and moved to
the table where she had laid the flowers.

"I'm so sorry, Chacor, but he isn't here. Didn't
Jerish say, Rehger has lodgings near the Academy. If
he isn't with Master Vanek—"

"Elissi," said Chacor.

She was arranging the flowers in the vase, with quiet
steady hands.

"Of course, he does visit father. But father is
voyaging."

"Elissi—"

She paused, looked at him, shook her head as if to
say, A silly mistake, no harm has been done.

It occurred to Chacor that, although the prospect of
astoundingly surprising both Yennef Am Lan and Rehger
Am Ly Dis had been his motive for charging into
Moiyah at midday in a thunderstorm, perhaps it was
not all the reason. Of course Jerish must have mentioned Rehger lived by the Academy of Arms, where
he still took Swordsman's exercise. Chacor now seemed
to recall this. And Vanek's clerk had also said that
Vanek himself would return in half an hour. Chacor
might have waited. In fact, the clerk had not, had he,
said Rehger was at Arn Yr's house at all. He had said
Chacor should ask there. Superfluous. Yet here, everything muddled, Chacor had rushed.

Destiny had presented itself to Chacor on the Plains
in the shape of Rehger's father, arrived in accordance
with a psychic prophesy now almost a year old.
Destiny—or call it Anackire—did exist. Maybe he had
always supposed so, or wanted it, that sense of being
held, however lightly, in a vast cupped hand. Whatever you did, whatever befell you, it was possible at
certain moments to cease floundering, to let go. To
float, and to fall, through inner space.

There she poised above the flowers, in the shadow a
figurine of silver.

Chacor said, "What I told you. That isn't why I

came here. Or, it was, but now is not. If I speak to your father, will he cast me through an upper window?"

"Speak about what?" said she. Her voice was colorless. Had she not felt the levinbolt strike the house?

"You. Isn't it the custom here? To get permission of a girl's father?"

She put down the flowers again but did not turn to him now.

"What are you saying, Chacor?"

What was he saying? Before, it was always, I'm dying for you, let me have you. It had even been, now and then, falsely, *I love you*. Before the billowy bed or the warm hillside accommodated them.

To keep himself in order, not to shame himself with sugary words he could not speak, he spoke instead the ancient marriage oath of a prince of Corhl.

"By the goddess, I will take and have you, now and all my days. You shall be mine as my own flesh is mine. As my necessary bones are mine, so needful you shall be to me. And I will spill my blood for you. I will come together with you to make the magic of lifegiving. The goddess is a woman. She hears what I say. Let me be no more a man if ever I deny these words."

It was old, the oath, if not as old as the jungles and the swamps, old as the first speaking men who had known themselves Corrah's. Chacor himself had heard his own father make the oath many times, marrying carelessly this woman and that. In the common mouth of Corhl, the words had become debased. But they remained the Words, and he had given them to her, to this pale girl of the Lowlands. And having said them, burning and proud, astonished and elated, irrevocably fixed now to the course, he added, "By the law of Corhl, I've married you, Elissi. But by the law of Moih we must be betrothed, I know. If your father lets me have you. Beautiful Elissi."

She had waited for him to stop. Now, she picked up another flower and put it into the vase.

The storm was over, and the rain had slackened on the path outside. Chacor sobered. "At least," he said, "say yes."

"No," said Elissi.

*   *   *

Months after, she assured him it was not feminine vengeance. The reverse had been so abrupt, she had not trusted him to know, she said. She had given him doubt's benefit, in case he might at leisure repent. But in a way, which she did not refer to, it was also her insight. He was a warrior, Chacor, a hunter. The prey had been too readily caught, there was no duel. So she gave him one, a chase and a fight. She let him, now he was sure he wanted her, pursue and battle through the whole of Zastis. And to tangle matters further, there came that afternoon an alarm of Alisaarian pirates back up the coast, and a recall to the fort.

The business with Rehger and Yennef tallied with the rest. A deputy sent to the *Amber Anklet* on the correct evening either missed the Lan, or the Lan was not there.

It became an affair of, I will tell Rehger when the alert's off and I catch up to the fellow. Then, alert, over, I'll keep it to myself. Is anything so pat? Probably the likeness was imagined. For by then, thwarted by Elissi, the sense of destiny was wearing thin.

She consented before winter, when the sintal blooms were dropping with a fermenting perfume, making the fish tipsy in Arn's tank. Arn, home from a successful trip, had already acquiesced. Rehger was nowhere to be found. And Yennef—he had been an hallucination, an excuse for allowing oneself to acknowledge love.

"Yes, I love you," she said.

She put her arms about Chacor's neck and he kissed her, kissed her, thinking there was nothing so sweet and alive and holy on the earth, for she had made him suffer long enough for that. Lovers who love are gods, poets said in Free Alisaar. "Of course," she said. "That is Anackire."

And thus Chacor found, despite himself, he had been married to Moih, to the Lowlands, to the Dream of the serpent goddess. A Moiyan wedding indeed.

CHAPTER FIFTEEN

ANACKIRE'S DESIGN

The Raiding Party marched up Amber Street to the thud of drums, clash of cymbals, and whirr of rattles, their torches flapping. All along the sunset avenues, the crowds of Moiyah applauded and donated them fortune, and commented that the bridegroom was a charmer.

Chacor, who had reached the city friendless and lacking occupation almost two years before, was now a captain of one hundred, and included two other captains and a major (Jerish) in his warlike wedding band. They were all barking with laughter and exchanging jests and, as tradition decreed, vowing to put Arn Yr's house to the torch if he refused them. Caught up in the play, intent on his role, crazy to get his girl that wretched custom had also not allowed him near for seven days, the last thing on Chacor's mind was Rehger, absently invited to the feast, or a man once met by the Dragon Gate.

The *Amber Anklet* Inn was busy, and through the open doors, in the courtyard, a host of drinkers saw the Raiding Party and came howling out, offering gratis cups of wine. This likewise was tradition, and while the young men fortified themselves the cries went up: "You make that ruffian give her over! Burn the house down if he won't." An inn girl ran to Chacor and kissed him, and when she drew back, he saw Yennef Am Lan standing five feet away, meeting his eyes, but not eagerly.

Chacor gave a louder bark. The Lan immediately shifted, as if to slip aside into the inn.

"Jerish," said Chacor, "Baed, all of you, there's a man there I asked to my wedding who wouldn't come."

"Must be a friend of her wicked father's!" shouted Captain Baed, entering farther into things. "Get him!"

Yennef was not quick enough to elude a determined sortie of this kind, with the inn drinkers noisily assisting on all sides.

"Not go to his wedding? Thrash the felon!"

Yennef was brought to Chacor. Yennef was all smiles now.

"Well met again. Am I to understand you're going to claim a bride, sergeant?"

"Captain, my dear old friend," said Chacor, embracing Yennef. "So happy you'll be with me."

"To the hilt. What else?"

Chacor said to Jerish: "I mean it. I'm deadly in earnest. Don't let that darling get away."

"Tsk. Your mind should be only on Elissi."

"It is. But this is the matter of Anackire."

Jerish raised his brows. Chacor's use of such a phrase amused him. Nevertheless he said to Baed, "We're to keep him close, that one. We're serious, you understand."

Tiddly and obliging, Baed agreed.

All in communion then, the Raiding Party marched on, Yennef borne in its midst.

"Open your doors! Open your doors!"

Neighbors on balconies and leaning over sills threw ribbons and flowers.

"Open up, or we'll burn you out!"

The doors were opened.

Arn Yr, in elegant regalia, stood with a drawn sword in the hall.

"My daughter you shall not have."

"I have sworn to have her," said Chacor in ringing tones, enjoying it after all. "I have sworn by my gods. By Anackire," he added, to see Arn Yr's face.

"No," said Arn Yr. "My daughter must remain with me. She is my jewel."

"She shall be that to me," said Chacor. "Are you with me, my boys?" he asked the Raiders. They yelled and stamped, and Arn Yr's servants came pounding into the hall, grinning hugely and toting cudgels.

Then the priest spoke from the stair.

"Men, now listen to the voice of the woman."

And down the stair came Elissi.

She wore the Moih wedding-gown that was passed, mother to daughter, sister to sister, aunt to niece, cousin to cousin, for generations. It was a loose garment of woven thread-of-gold, belted by a sash of white silk. On the bride's hair clung a rippling veil of sintal yellow. She was like every proper bride, more lovely than life.

She said, "My father, you are dear to me, but in the natural way I must leave you. Here is the man I choose."

And Arn Yr threw down his sword and made the mock gesture of weeping.

And Chacor, in whose birthplace men were not permitted tears of any sort, having forgotten it, waited for Elissi to cross the floor and take his hand, which she did.

Then the priest came down in his dark robe with its fringes of Moiyan gold, and married them before their witnesses, by the fallen sword, in the sight of something which was not named, a goddess, or their own souls, or only the wakening stars above the roof.

The wedding feast, for which three interconnecting rooms had been opened, the double doors taken off their hinges, sailed like a shining lighted ship into the night.

Master Vanek found, with some interest at his elbow, glamorous and not entirely sober, the bridegroom.

"Master Vanek, where's your apprentice?"

"Which?"

"The very talented one, whose casts for silver work go to Sheep Lane."

Vanek looked lost, then he said, "But we've got farther than that. You mean Rehger Am Ly."

"Don't tell me he isn't here."

"I suppose he is, if you asked him to be. Have one of these salt-grapes."

"Delicious. I must find him. Before I forget him altogether."

"Hmm," said Vanek. He called over another man, very nearly deformed, for his greatly muscled neck, torso and arms dwarfed the two bandy legs beneath. "Have you seen the Lydian?"

"In a cloud of women," said this man, amicably, "discussing the price of bronze with Arn's officer of deck."

He led Chacor across the three rooms, introducing himself as they went as the sculptor Mur. He said his name with such diffidence, Chacor became aware he must be well-known in Moih, and had the social wit to thank him for coming to the wedding.

The last room opened on a stair to the garden. Rehger and two Moiyan beauties, one sable, one saffron, were on the terrace with Arn's deck master, and some others.

Mur stood surveying the scene. He indicated the Lydian, as if Chacor did not know him. "What a Raldnor he made," said Mur, after a moment. His face expressed an absorbed, nonsexual admiration. "He fought professionally at Saardsinmey. By the goddess. He could hardly have made his body better if he'd hewn and carved it." Mur tugged at his lip. "You heard of the mishap?"

"Up at the fort, we get little—"

"The statue was twice life-size, drawn out of the finest marble. I supervised the cutting of the block myself. I worked day and night. With such stone and such a model, it was a dedication, not a labor. Finished, it seemed to me some of my best work was in it, although the expression of the face—with that I could never satisfy myself."

(Chacor fretted at Mur's shoulder. Three rooms distant, Elissi was blooming. Corrah-Anackire speed this anecdote.)

"The features were kingly enough. I had no problem in that way. It's no use taking a body from one and the head from another—a bedding in Aarl that is. But there was some obstacle. If I'd understood it, perhaps I could have surmounted it." Mur made a sign with his left hand, averting dark thoughts. "The statue was completed despite my niggling, and to schedule. It was then moved, under guard, to Xarabiss. A couple of miles from the winter palace at Xarar, from a clear sky, a freak summer storm. A river burst its banks and came down on the riders. The zeebas panicked, awash to their girths. Men were swept under and almost drowned. The platform toppled over. The head of the statue—was smashed off."

Chacor swore swiftly. Even upon his hot impatience this ill-omened thing struck chill.

"Does Rehger know that?"

"Yes. He took it sensibly. The racers say, if a man heeded every stray shadow on the track, he'd be thrown at the first lap."

"What of the Xarab king?"

"Refused the statue and any repair. He said the gods were against it. But he still paid up."

Rehger turned at that moment, and saw them.

Yes, he could himself have been a king. They had said that in Alisaar, with the love-words. Now he seemed no different, the body kept at its vivid pitch by daily exercise, the commanding height, the curious completeness, nothing redundant. He no longer dressed like a lord, that was all. The clothes were those of a well-bred artisan on holiday, no adornment. A king in disguise.

He came over to Chacor.

"The best of congratulations."

"I receive them with pleasure. Fill your cup. I want you to meet another of my wedding guests."

The women on the terrace called plaintively as Chacor took him back into the house.

They had provided the tall handsome Lan with some refreshments, then locked him into an upstairs anteroom. If Arn knew about it was not certain. Jerish and Annah had now and then been seen lingering nearby, or Jerish's fair-skinned, yellow-haired brother and his coppery Ommish wife. Once there had been some knocking on the inside of the door. Through the sounds of the feast it was not much audible. The Ommos lady went to the door, however, and said sternly, "Come, sir, would Yannul the Hero of Lan have behaved so timorously? Shush!"

"He's in there," said Chacor, bringing Rehger to the door.

Conceivably he expected Rehger to know already who this was, since they were operating within the design of the goddess. But Rehger only said, "Who is that?"

"My last wedding guest."

"You've locked the door," said Rehger. "Is he vicious?"

"By now that's a possibility. So I've brought you, Swordsman, to quell him."

Chacor unlocked the door, opened it, and guided Rehger to the doorway. Rehger paused, then moved forward, into the room. Chacor smartly shut the door and relocked it. Having listened a moment for the phonetics of assault and battery—there was only silence—he led his accomplices away.

Yennef was drinking the wine and eating the savory breads.

He looked at the man who had entered, and remarked, "I judge it would be unreasonable to ask for an explanation. After all, this *is* a marriage feast."

The arrival was dark Vis . . . maybe he was an inch or so taller even than Yennef. Powerful, couth—almost a Dortharian demeanor. But when he spoke, it was the accent of Free Alisaar.

"Perhaps you will," he said, "accept both as an explanation and an apology, the fact that you are, sir, my father."

Yennef became fly. He narrowed his eyes and took in more thoroughly what he was seeing. Then he drank from the wine-cup.

"Well, here and there, I've had that accusation made. Usually it's by the woman involved."

"My mother is in Iscah. Or, she may be dead. It isn't an accusation. As I said, a fact."

The Lan glanced him up and down, cool, and guarded.

"But perhaps I was never in Iscah."

"Yes. It was winter. She said robbers had set on you."

"No, no, my gallant," said Yennef, "that was last summer, here. Bandits by the Dragon Gate."

"You seem to have then, sir, a penchant for being robbed. She discovered you near the farm, disabled with a knife-cut in one arm. She persuaded the men to give you shelter, in the dog-house." (Yennef ejected a virulent oath.) "Once you were fit, you went on your way, but before that you had my mother. Her name was Thioo."

"I had her? You mean I forced her?"

"She went to you. She gave herself and you took."

"Did I? It seems a man can get desperate, in the Iscah mountains. If I was there."

"You left her a token."

"Well, one finds one must. Doubtless you've found that, too."

"An Alisaarian drak of bronze-mixed gold."

"Oh. She must have been a spicy lay, then. I was poor in those days."

"You remember those days."

"No," said Yennef, "but from your looks, it has to have been some twenty-five years ago."

"A little more."

"Ah, a little more." Yennef had another drink. "You're from Alisaar yourself."

"The men on the farm sold me for a slave. I was shipped to Alisaar."

"You don't look like a slave."

"I was a Saardsin Sword."

A glint of fascination went under and over Yennef's deliberate facade.

"That I *do* credit. I've seen them fight, and race. Saardsinmey had the best—and lost the best. Anack had you in her hand, if you survived the city."

"They think here Anackire has all things in her hands."

"She has enough hands," said Yennef flippantly.

His mind, in spite of him, was burrowing. Each time he drank the yellow wine, he seemed to sink back

another year, to some other place. Of course, he had
been in Iscah, in Corhl and Var-Zakoris, too. There
had been a mad expedition, anger and youth and some
simpleton's story, hopes of treasure—he could hardly
recollect, only the fruitless venture and the traveling.
There were plenty of escapades, and just as many
girls. Dark women, smoky women, smooth skin and a
smooring of night hair.

"So you had your friends abduct me on the street
because you claim I'm your father."

The younger man said, "No, I'm as startled as you,
to find you here. But they recognized you, no doubt."

"I see. It's that we have a resemblance to each
other. It does make some sense."

"Don't you," said the younger man quietly—he had
stayed even and polite throughout, under Yennef's
attempts to heat him up—"have a knife scar on your
left arm?"

"Two or three as it happens. Shall I strip my sleeve?
You can choose which one's Iscaian."

Yennef finished the wine.

The other man said, "You see, we'd have no business with each other, except that there are questions I
should like to ask you."

"I'm not rich," said Yennef. "And anyway, I have a
legal wife, in Dorthar, and three legal sons."

"The questions have nothing to do with your estate,
sir."

"Yennef. Call me Yennef. I'm not some antique
graybeard. I used to be your age, not a hundred years
ago. My sons have less respect, I can assure you. And
my wife's a ravening shrew." The wine was going to
his head.

"Then I won't ask you," said the other, calm, inexo-
rable, "to strip your sleeve. I'll strip mine." And putting his hand to a plaited leather wristlet—a badge of
the Artisan's Guild in Moih, now Yennef considered
it—he loosed and pulled it off. He came forward then,
and showed to Yennef in the lamplight the lean articu-
late hand and muscled forearm of a professional fighter,
itself with one streamlined scar which ended at the
wrist. Here, where the wristlet had been and the scar

ended, the skin was clasped in a circlet of dull silver scales.

"Aside from the scars of knives," he said, "will you tell me, Yennef, do you have a mark on you like this?"

Yennef felt giddy. It was the final years peeling away. He had suddenly recalled the barren mountain valleys, the blue-white snow piled up like death, and warm beauty slender as a bone that found him there, wedged with the dog among the rocks.

"I don't," he said. "Not I. But my father had a callus like that. As you have it, on the left wrist. It was broader in him, it ran as far as the lower joint of the thumb. He never hid it. He was proud of it. He used to have his sleeve cut slightly short, on the left arm. You know what it is?"

"The snake mark, the sigil of the line of Amrek, the Storm Lord."

Yennef shook himself, trying to shift from one dimension to another, out of the past.

"Who told you? Your mother?"

"Not my mother. A sorceress of the Lowlanders."

"Ah." Yennef stared at his son, and saw himself at long last, in the golden mirror. None of his Dortharian getting—known scarcely better than this one—had returned such a likeness. They took after their dam, and had her stupidity to add burnish. "It's come to me," said Yennef. "I mean, going with your mother. Tibo— that was it, wasn't it?"

"Yes, Tibo. Thioo, in Iscah."

"You say—you don't know if she's dead?"

Still quiet, reasonable: "It was an ungenerous life. She wasn't well-treated. Women in those parts seldom were."

"I didn't think of it—getting her with child. And then those cretinous blockheads sold you. How old were you? For the stadium, it can't have been much more than five or six."

Abruptly Yennef turned away. He walked off and sat down in a hard stiff chair, and put his head in his hands.

He said after a moment, "You embarrass me. I don't know you, or what to say."

"My name is Rehger. They used to call me the Lydian, in Alisaar."

"That's kudos, isn't it—fame by name of the birth-place—*Anack's breasts*, I've heard of you. *I laid a bet on you*—three years—four years back—I was at Jow. I only saw you at a distance, an inexpensive seat. But you won. Blade and spear. A hundred silver draks. I should have risked more—"

"At least," Rehger said, "that repaid your outlay on Tibo."

Yennef looked up. He rose to his feet, straightening himself.

"I don't expect or want your filial regard, Swords-man."

"We're strangers to each other," Rehger said. "But I'd value my history, if you can give it me."

"You want to boast your descent from Amrek Accursed-of-Anackire on the streets of Anackire's Moih?"

Rehger smiled, as Yennef had seen princes do, when they wished to put you at ease. The eyes were like *her* eyes, if Yennef could only remember what she had looked like. For he could not, of course.

Only that she had been beautiful, and a lucky find. Though there was one single image, almost supernatu-ral, flickering between the shadow and the red whisper of a fire—when she had come to him—and he had thought, or only said he thought—the goddess, Cah—

"There's no more wine in this jug," said Yennef. "And that damned Zakorian or whatever he is, the prankish bridegroom, has locked the door again."

But trying the door, they learned another had come at some time to turn the key. They were at liberty.

CHAPTER SIXTEEN

THE CHARIOTEER

Rehger rode out of the city in the black chariot of war, among the soldiery and the banners, under the burnt-blue lid of the sky. And the crowds of the city cried and shouted, and the women threw withered garlands and silks like blood. And the rumble of the marching feet, the wheels, the drums and rattles, were the voice of the storm, going down to battle and to death.

But as he stood there, shackled and scaled by armor, his thoughts had stayed behind in the temple of his gods beside the river.

Drought had shrunk the river up. On the temple steps dead lilies stank and a spiny water-thing had died. A haze lay on the river, a haze of incense in the temple aisle. The gods towered from the mist, their bodies that were nearly human, their dragon heads, glimmering in the light of propitiating flame.

"Have no fear, great ones," he said. "I'll ask you for nothing, as I know quite well you will give me nothing." Yet they did have something to give.

For, out of the shadow stole his mother, Tibo. She was garbed, and even her hair was dressed, in the manner of the queens of Dorthar and the jewelry fashions of Koramvis. But her skin was painted white, as the face of his enemies.

She said, "The Lowlander will kill you, Amrek."

Then she called him names and railed against him. She was terrified. They balanced, as did all things that morning, on the edge of the world. The fall was not to be avoided. But when he turned from her, she stayed him. She was not Tibo, surely, but Val Mala, that woman whose soul was so young it was purblind, half mad. Her existence had been that of a sensual, spiteful and selfish child. Now she was a savage child, frightened even from its child's cunning, abetted by a poisoned knife. "Hear the truth from me," she said.

And she told him then how he had been got on her by her lover, conniving in her bed. He was not the son of the king, no Storm Lord, not Rehdon's sowing—as was Raldnor, who would kill him. He had no identity. An imposter, the gods of Dorthar denied and would cast him down.

When she stopped, he had nothing to say to her.

He did not interrogate her, or reject her words. Nothing in his life, and nothing in that crucial instant, gave him the impetus to do so.

And very soon, borne forward by the chariot of fate, war and death, he rode from the city, off the world's edge, into a country without wars or cities, or rivers, without titles, gods, or names.

The pre-dawn stirring about the cattle-market wakened him, as normally it always did, two hours before the sky lost its Visian darkness. His routines were recurrent but flexible. Breakfast was to be had among the stalls and charcoal braziers by the market gate, with drovers and watchmen. If it was a day for early exercise, he would cross the three streets to the Academy of Arms. For his monthly fee, morning or evening, he could engage Moiyah's best sword-masters, Dortharian-trained, (who in turn vied to duel with a professional, sometimes set him to school others and saw him paid for it.) The standard of the gymnasium courts was not far below those of a stadium. Otherwise one had access to the Academy baths, their staff of barbers, and masseurs, and, if one wished it, the periphery talent of fortune-tellers, betting cliques, commercial telepaths and joy-girls.

Moih being Moih, it was nothing at the Academy to see a rich man's soft sons working out, or gambling, with the garrison soldiers or sturdy porters from the docks. Rehger's personal myth had become known among them and he was greeted there as "Lydian," even by the elite of the Racers' Guild, who spoke of their horses as if they were mistresses, and of not much else.

Usually, by the time the sky had melted to Lowlander pallor, the Lydian was on Marble Street.

But between Marble Street and the Academy, in a small wine-shop known as the *Dusty Flower*, Rehger and Yennef had spent Chacor's wedding night. Until the third, Vis-black hour of morning, they sat either side the table. To the house's sorrow, they drank no vast amount, neither did they talk to any lavish extent. A stilted frankness stumbled between them. There was a kind of distaste, a reluctance to remain and, curiously, eventually, a hesitation at parting.

They had no physical contact. They broke from each other, the two men, like thieves who have planned a crime, or perhaps met to review one long committed.

Rehger did not think he would see the Lan (his father) again.

After all this, there was less than an hour for sleep, but Rehger took it, and dreamed the dream, which the words of Yennef had probably imposed on him.

"The line of descent is easy enough. I have it by heart, for what it's worth. The woman was a prophetess, a priestess. Safca. Amrek's daughter, by some courtesan, who escaped into Lan when the Lowland War reached Dorthar. This Safca might not have been reckoned, except that she had the snake mark on her wrist."

She became holy, Safca, in the upheavals of her time. In the peace which followed, she married into the royal house of Lan, a subsidiary branch. She bore one son late in life, Yalen, a prince, marked as she was, in the same way. Yalen who had his left sleeves cut short to show the brand of Anack. . . . When he was in his forty-sixth year, he fathered a bastard on a serving-girl in a village hostelry. It was on a hunting trip. He used to sport and say, "That spring I acquired the seven wolfskins and Yennef, in the backhills."

The Lan did not relate this with any bite. There had been anger, once, but it altered to irony. The hill girl had walked every step of the road to the capital, and sought out Prince Yalen on Audience Day, with the yowling baby wrapped in her apron. "He was decent to her. He set her up with a tavern in the city, and took me into his household. He had his lawful heirs. Besides, in Lan, the closer the blood-tie the more the offspring are worth. The old man had married his half-sister for that. The slough of the pot-wench wasn't worth anything. But he was fair to me. I was allotted the title it's customary to award, in such a case. They call you the *god-gift*. That was Yennef, the *god-gift*. The trophy Yalen never wanted that the gods forced him to have."

He grew up chafing, could not recall when it started. At thirteen he stowed away on a Xarabian ship. That was the beginning of his travels.

"The year he got the wolfskins and Yennef. I never even had the goddess mark. But the bloodline's simple. Have you memorized it? Amrek to Safca, Safca to Yalen, Yalen to Yennef. Yennef—to Rehger Am Ly Dis." And Yennef had added, "Get a son. Pass the commodity on. Life, I mean. The trade of living."

In the subfusc of the *Flower*, his face blurred and often averted, Yennef seemed, by his coordinated movements, his light voice, the ironic remnant of his youthful anger, a very young man still.

"There is a tale, mind you, Amrek was never sired by Rehdon the Storm Lord. Mala the bitch-queen had him off the king's counselor, in order to hold on to her status—Rehdon couldn't plough her, they said. She scared him so his seed went to water. It might be, or it might not. She was a wicked slut, brainless. She might have miscalculated, or spread lies. She hated her only son."

Surely she had, had hated Amrek. Rehger had felt her hate strike like venomed steel on his bones.

And Amrek had believed her. Or he was beyond caring. In the arena it might happen sometimes, there would be a man like that. Come for an appointment with death.

But Amrek was gone, into the past. Rehger—hearing the sounds of the market, an exuberant, self-important present below his window—felt the huge empty rush

of time that spilled all things away. Aztira had promised that in Moih he would meet his father. This had
taken place, but there was no meaning to it. Rehger
had been a peasant's get in Iscah, he had been a
Swordsman in Alisaar. Those lives were gone, as was
the life of Amrek.

He did not go that morning to the exercise courts of
the Academy. He walked slowly toward Marble Street,
and reaching it, beheld the sun rising over the eastern
slopes of the city. The stone-shops along the lower
concourse were already active. He could see the smoke,
and hear the beat of drums where they were "serenad-
ing" the scored marble to make it split by vibration.
Less than two years, yet Moiyah was well-known to
him, as if he had dwelled here longer. Small, she could
have fit inside Saardsinmey like an egg in a dish.
Yellow amber, for the rubies of the west.

There was a cessation in the drumming. A bird sang
from a garden. He thought of Chacor and Elissi, waking in their love-bed, and, for a moment, of the scent
of a woman's white hair against his mouth, across his
arms and breast.

Rehger turned his head and looked up the street.
The sun was spearing between the buildings, flashing
on some bronze-work in the square before the hall of
the Artisan's Guild. The bronzes were the chosen
pieces of those who, this winter, had earned the guild
wristlet. There were only five of them: There had
been many dozen disappointments. At first, like a
boy, he had gone every day, to look at his success,
there among the four others, the sun gilding it for
glory.

It was the length and height of a wolf, the ancient
prescribed measurements, raised on a five-foot plinth.
A chariot and team, racing at full stretch. You were
warned to work from what you knew. He had had no
model, which was audacious and foolhardy, Vanek
assured him. But memory, he had had that.

The group was faulty, far from perfect. Even the
cast had been too ignorantly ambitious and revealed as
much, after the bronze cooled. Nevertheless, it was
enough to win admission to the guild. It was enough

that, three days after its erection in the square, ten offers had been made for it. And a month later, sixteen more. "You do understand," Vanek said, "some men always bid on principle for the winners."

The Charioteer, among those who had an interest in artistic events, was however much discussed. For all the flaws, it had essential quality. Being static—yet it moved. The hiddraxi, leaping, were one thing, like the shapes of a breaking wave. The chariot had a weightless buoyancy. The man, his hair bound back and clubbed, just the side-locks streaming, leaned into the speed-rush of the team. The reins, like astral filaments, poured from his grip into the animals' hearts, the wheels were wrapped in winds. Grounded on its plinth, the assemblage was half in the air. *Only a racer could have done it,* the connoisseurs had said. Vanek did not say, *They want to buy as they awarded the wristlet, because of what you were.* The guild was not a charitable institution. Vanek had already mentioned that.

Rehger had modeled for the Raldnor statue some weeks before he took up a scoop of warm wax one dusk and pinched out a figure from it.

Mur had left his pumicing and gone into the yard to oversee the oven. The lamps were lit, for it was a stormy evening. Vanek came from his room and looked, and said nothing. Rehger compressed the wax into a blob, and put it down again. Vanek said, "You've made such figures before."

"As a child. There was mud enough. The sun would bake them." He did not add that then his uncle would come and kick them to bits. Vanek went back into his room.

When Mur no longer needed Rehger every day, he obtained similar employment without trouble at other studios and shops in the vicinity. Several of these were less exclusive and more populous than Vanek's, but to stand near-naked, eaten by eyes, was hardly novel to a Swordsman. Only once had it been unacceptable. Arriving at the venue, he had found neither students nor draftsmen, but a small party of wealthy mixes without a stylus or calliper between them. Despite this, he stripped and got on the dais for them, and did nothing else until one of the women came to stand by him and to run her hands along his ribs and thigh. Then he quietly descended the dais, dressed, and left the studio.

Mur, seeing him interested and apt, was by then giving Rehger tasks to do, the rougher portions of rubbing and polishing, the upkeep of the fine utensils in the forge. When Mur rested, never while working, he lessoned Rehger in his art, demonstrating this and that, praising the young man's quickness and ability. Mur noticed that once he had been shown what was done, Rehger seemed able to do it. Mur confided in Vanek. Rehger, coming on this scene, as if in the theater, said with no preamble, "I've been saving my pay. Will you apprentice me, Master Vanek?"

"You're too old for such an apprenticeship," said Vanek. "You've seen my other boys. Lads of ten and twelve." Then he waited, head to one side. He was a cranky man, Vanek. He could use his tongue for a whip or a dousing of cold water, but he rescued flies that fell in the warmed wax, he hoarded sticks and lamp oil, and gave away the limestone off-cuts free for winter fuel to any at the door who asked. Rehger therefore, seeing the tilted head, the waiting, said, "You start them young to build the muscle. I have mine."

"Agreed," said Vanek, "you have at least the back and shoulders for the job."

"But even with what I can pay you, I'll be in your debt over the cash."

Vanek pulled a face. He pointed to the afternoon work benches that the students had not yet returned to claim. "Go and make me something."

It had been clumsy enough, a wax wrestler on one knee. The wire armature was improperly secured and an arm fell off at Vanek's persistent jabbing.

"Fearsome," said Vanek. "We must teach you to do better. But, as I told you once, you've done this before."

"As a child."

"You forget," said Vanek, "we Lowlanders, we believe all men live quantities of lives." He spoke scornfully, as if holding up religion like fouled cloth, between finger and thumb. "I meant you did it in a previous existence, my tall Lydian of Iscah. *Then*. So it will only be a question of remembering. Mur will help you remember. Mur has doubtless also been an artisan over and over. His very soul is warped into that shape."

He did not not consider their religion. Even on the lips of his lover, Rehger had not heeded it. Even so, the craft of the sculptor came to him as Vanek said, like a slow sure remembering, flowing in wild bursts, or shut behind mental walls that must be hewn away. And once, cutting the "skin" from weathered marble, in the yard, with the rubble of marble all around him and the texture of marble in his pores and under his nails, and its flour tasting in his mouth, he recalled how he had fought through the debris, pulling up the blocks and tiles, at Katemval's house on Gem-Jewel Street, finding wrung water-fowl and a girl's body, a favorite chair miraculously intact, the gush of the wave having set it floating, empty. And in that minute, in Moih—but hovering out of place and time—it had seemed to him valid that the touch and smell of the marble did not seem to anchor him to destruction, rather seemed to reach quickly away from it back to some older hour, older that was than his body, heart, and mind.

But the minute passed from him. And he let it go.

Yennef pushed a way through the courtyard of the *Amber Anklet*, to the table under the vine. It was noon, and the Dortharian already there, as he should have been the night before. He looked up, and lifted the corners of his mouth.

"What detained you, Yennef?"

Yennef sat down.

"My own question exactly."

"Really? I'll go first then. I stopped to have a woman on Love Street. She was a very tempting woman. Very blonde and very tender. Despite this, I tore myself from her arms and arrived at our meeting point only half an hour in arrears. You, however, failed me. I kept faith till midnight. A grievous waste of time."

"I," said Yennef, waving over the wine-server, "was

also prepared to wait until midnight. Then I was kidnapped."

The Dortharian watched him, through iron-colored eyes. Apart from short stature, these were his only show of Lowland mix, but unnerving enough in the brazen darkness of his face. (When they unearthed the gray-eyed bandit king on the Plains, Yennef had been reminded of Galutiyh Am Dorthar, but not for long.)

"Kidnapped. By whom?"

"No one important. A wedding party. The bridegroom was a Corhl—that soldier I told you about, who slew my tirr for me on the Plains."

"So then what?"

"Nothing. I joined in the wedding, and couldn't leave until the sun got up. I assumed you'd be gone by that time, and went to sleep it off. Noon was your second choice, and here I am."

Galutiyh sipped his drink, a vintage of Vardath, sweet and rosy. He said, "What a fibber you are, Yennef. Why dissemble? You slunk off with a young man. I never knew you had those tastes, but so what?"

"You followed me."

"I had someone follow you."

"After all these intimate months, you trust me so well."

"Sensible, it would seem."

"Anack's gilt tits," said Yennef. "He's a son of mine."

Galutiyh gave him a prolonged kalinx's stare.

"My, my."

"A by-blow, nothing more. But he'd tracked me down—being a friend to the Corhlan bridegroom."

"Wanted to know why you had dishonored his mother, where the heirlooms were, that sort of thing?"

Yennef shrugged, and drank his wine.

Galutiyh linked his hands behind his head. He said to the sky, "Is it that I'm stupid, or that he thinks I am, or that he is, or that the Dream of the goddess has curdled his brain?"

Yennef did not answer this. He was used to Galutiyh, or had tried to become so. Instead, he responded with, "Down at the dock, I heard some of them discussing a quake in Free Zakoris. The ships brought the word, from Thos. But it may be exaggerated."

"I know about the earthquake, Yennef. A paltry quiver, to a man of Dorthar's capital. It's this other thing I know that's on my mind. Can it be that you're attempting to shield him—this lover-son of yours?"

Yennef called the wine-server again. When he had had his refill, Yennef said, "My sons are in Dorthar. This one—there's no bond between us."

"*Aah.* And that is why you know nothing about him. Did you even inquire his name?"

"I know his name, yes."

"And so do I, Yennef. Rehger the Lydian, a champion slave-Sword of the Alisaarians. Saardsinmey. A rare survivor."

Yennef put down his cup.

"You're aware that I'm less concerned with these supposed sorcerous occurrences. I was hired as a political hound."

"In Dorthar, the political and sorcerous aims of the Amanackire are always considered jointly."

Yennef, who had been to Amanackire Hamos, and got in the walls of ice, and next out again, not much wiser but a deal colder, was conscious Galutiyh had also gone there, and returned with all his superstitions in fresh trim. "The antics of the weather, and the quakes, the volcano and the wave at Saardsinmey— are necessarily alarming," said Yennef appeasingly. "I see them as figments of a general unrest. Omens."

"By which you mean you dismiss the Power the Children of Anackire claim to wield. History displays you are wrong."

Galutiyh was a fanatic. It was useless to protest. It was indeed Galutiyh's proximity which had kept Yennef from resigning his post as Dorthar's agent and spy. You felt that for Galutiyh's partner to renege, however honestly, would be grounds for Galutiyh's cleanest knife in the throat. Most of two years they had been roaming now, paired like felons on a great length of chain. Neither had garnered much, for the Lowlanders of the farthest southern Plains were odd, and the ones in Moih only human, full of business and

family, so if they had secrets they must keep them
even from themselves. As for such bastions as Hamos,
unless you could overhear their perpetual within-speech,
what could you hope to learn?

Galutiyh was rising from the table, sleek and ur-
bane. He was not much older than Rehger, but not so
heroically made, and not as tall as the son or the
father. A devout worshipper of the goddess, there was
still a twig with red paper leaves tucked into his belt—
they were to be had at the Anackire temple here.
Galutiyh made sacrifice once every nine days. Not in
rapture, which was the only reason for offering in
native Moih, but out of dedicated respect. In the wilds,
Galutiyh even would catch rats and snakes and make
blood and burnt offerings. True Dortharian piety.

"Come with me, Yennef, my dear. I'm going to
show you a wonder."

Yennef had discovered that argument must be saved
for extremes. He got up and went after Galutiyh.

"And as we go," added the short Dortharian, "I'll
tell you a tale to knock two inches from your backbone."

The fictitious persona in which Yennef traveled
Xarabiss and the Lowlands was that of a merchant's
agent. Having been partly robbed of his camouflage at
the Dragon Gate, he restocked the wagon in Moiyah
and set off for Hamos. During this short journey, his
nervous Xarabian servant vanished, and thereafter
Yennef did not bother to replace him. Galutiyh meanwhile, entering Moih a season behind Yennef, settled
himself in, in his own way, and built up for himself
over succeeding months a coterie of paid underlings.

It was one of these, lurking at the *Anklet*, who saw
Yennef abducted by a Raiding Party. Much later, loi-
tering at Arn Yr's house, the watcher beheld the re-
emergence of Yennef with a solitary companion, and
dogged them to the *Dusty Flower*.

Something about Yennef's companion advised the
watcher not to try much more. And since he did not
want to get too close, he was unable to decipher any
dialogue. Instead he risked an old strategem on the

wine-shop doorkeeper. "I'm off. There's a fellow in here I think I know. I owe him money."

"Who's that, then?"

"The tall one in the corner. The younger man. He skinned me at Xarar, only I never settled my account."

"No fear," said the doorkeeper. "I know that man. He was never in Xarar. He's the Alisaarian, Rehger."

"No, I tell you it's my beggar from Xarabiss."

"Have it your own way. But I know it's Rehger. He was a gladiator and charioteer, and he lived through Saardsinmey. You go up to the Artisans' Guild and have a look at the bronze he made. A chariot and hiddraxi. They say he's a find, that in a year or so he could be the best in the guild. Go on, you go and see, and then come back and say you owe *him* money."

All this the underling duly reported to Galutiyh.

Galutiyh, who kept abreast of artistic doings, had already visited the bronze-work. As it happened, he had put in a bid for it, for his instinct was developed, and he, too, had caught the fragrance of rogue genius. Applicants to enter the guild did not give up their names publicly with their work. *The Charioteer* was accredited solely to an "Apprentice of the Studio of Master Vanek."

Galutiyh, as he now promised Yennef, had started like a cat-snapped pigeon on bringing the two segments of information together.

Yennef looked at Galutiyh stonily.

"He told me his name last night. And that he got out of Saardsinmey."

"But nothing else? And didn't a distant harp-string twang? Can I trust you, Yennef my dove?"

They were in the square now, before the guild hall, and the five bronzes ranged about them, blinding in the midday sun.

"Here it is. What a group! I *must* have it now. I'll instruct my man to raise the bid."

Yennef looked at the bronze which his son had made. He saw only that it was very fine, then something else cut suddenly at his heart. Flesh of his flesh, which he had met with and parted from, had created this. The knowledge of whatever he had been, and

was, his youth and manhood, his blood, his ancestry—
had gone into it. Yennef reached out one hand, and
the curved necks of the hiddraxi were under his palm,
the chariot wheel, the shoulder of the charioteer. The
metal was hot from the sunlight. It seemed to thrum
and murmur like a hive of bees. It was alive with
Rehger's life. With Rehger's life which in turn Yennef
had created.

"Now Yennef," said Galutiyh, "come out of your
trance. We're going to the studio of Vanek."

Yennef let his hand fall away into the quiet air.

"You're saying my son is connected to that insane
Shansar hocus-pocus you've been suckling on."

Galutiyh beamed upon him.

"Yes, dearest one. And you never *thought* of it till
now."

"Leave him alone," said Yennef.

Galutiyh sauntered away down Marble Street.

As ever, perforce, Yennef would have to go after
him.

The studio shop was vacant, and the cabinets secured. In the offices beyond two clerks were furtively
eating a pie at a desk.

The studio, a huge room lit by braziers hanging
from the rafters and vanes of glass above, had a dim
glaze on it of various smokes and dusts. Only a little
darker than milk, a naked girl model lay on a couch
before the unlit hearth, conversing with some unmoved
students. The farther wall gave on a courtyard where a
large oven was fuming. Slabs of stone stood about
there, but activity had ceased.

Galutiyh mused on the girl who, indifferent by now,
ignored him.

"Rehger," said Galutiyh. "Here?"

One of the students looked around and pointed to a
stair.

Galutiyh, followed by Yennef, ascended. Some doors
ranked along a narrow landing, through one of which
came the soft rasp of pumice.

The Dortharian opened this door and put his head
around it.

"Ah," said Galutiyh, and jumped in.

Rehger looked up, and saw a man had come through the door. He was Vis, there was no mistaking it, yet he had temple leaves in his belt. He leaned on the table, looking at Rehger.

"Tell me, where did you learn to do such marvelous work?"

Rehger remained where he was, beside the small block of whitest marble he had been polishing. From the door it appeared formless, a slender oblong, only breast-high.

"I'm apprenticed to this studio, which is Master Vanek's."

"The Plains?" The visitor was surprised. "A long way surely from home? You're from Dorthar, are you not?"

Rehger had seen the second man, in the doorway.

Rehger said, "I've some Dortharian blood."

"Yes, by all means be quick to claim the High Race of Vis. Where else, then?"

"Alisaar. Anyone who knows me will tell you."

"Saardsinmey."

Rehger said nothing.

"Killing men," said Galutiyh, "it was good commerce? And now you've found your father, too. What exciting days you're having. Would you care to cap the adventure and go journeying?"

"Why?"

"Why indeed. Because I say you must. That's how I earn *my* fame. My unerring sense of the quarry."

There was a bellow of thunder directly overhead. It shook the partitions of the room, and past the window rain broke like a thousand necklaces from a cloudless sky.

In the moment of inattention, Yennef came across the cluttered space, picking up one of the razor-edged tools left lying there. He took Galutiyh around the body from behind, squeezing him close, and laid the flat of the chisel against his throat.

"Unfortunately," said Yennef, to Rehger, "this one means what he says. But if you're swift and stop for nothing, you should be away before his rat-pack dig up the body."

Galutiyh had relaxed against Yennef.

"My body, eh?"

Yennef sensed the slight shift of tendons and said, kindly, "Don't. After all, if you don't force me to do it now, I might relent and spare you, later."

"But *he*," said Galutiyh, "isn't running like you told him to."

"Now," said Yennef. "Rehger. Go. Get on a ship, or get out of Moih at least."

"Shall I explain?" said Galutiyh. "You see," he said to Rehger, "the white Lowlanders, the Shadowless, the *pure* Amanackire—the allied lands believe they are hoping to war with us again. And your special white lady has some part in it, being one of that kind."

Something in Rehger altered.

Yennef said, "Don't listen to his crazy spewings. There's a story out of Shansarian Alisaar that a white Amanackire was killed in Saardsinmey—and rose from the dead. Her lover was a Vis Swordsman. She saved his life by sheltering him in her tomb above the city. To this mathematical cobbler here, if you're a Saardsin Sword and have survived, then you must be a lover of the Amanackire woman. He'll gather his pack and hound you to Dorthar or some Shansar or Vardish holding, and put you to the question. The Shansars call this process the Ordeals. Make your own decision on what that means. Go on, get out. I'll kill this leech. I'll take care of it."

"Your father loves you," said Galutiyh. "He knows our masters will punish him in due course if he does any of that."

Rehger came around the table. He said, to Galutiyh, "I'll take the chisel from him." And with a movement like flight, almost invisible, sheered the chisel from Yennef's grip and undid the Dortharian from his arm.

Yennef stood amazed and cursing. Galutiyh, spun aside, sneered at them both.

"I won't forget your charity, Rehger Am Ly Dis. Nor *yours*, Yennef, you cat-sput." He flung lightly through the door and away down the stair.

"You deserve all he can do then, you bloody fool."

"Perhaps, Yennef. It's not a story, the tomb I sheltered in. Go and ask Chacor, if you like. He was there."

"And no story dead women come back to life?"

"She could heal the dead. No, it may be nothing more than a fact. But I'd like to hear what they say in Shansar Alisaar, for myself."

"You will. On the rack. Over the fires. The yellow Shansarians—Vardath, Vathcri—are as frightened as the Vis, now, of what Lowlanders can do. We've been trying to weed out the opinions of the south, these merchants, because the Storm Lord, who has the peerless blood of the goddess himself, wets his drawers whenever you say *Anackire*. They don't fight with weapons and men, the Lowland magicians. But with earthquakes and storms and tidal waves and cracking volcanoes. They can fly in chariots up to the stars, and murder with a flame from the eye or the fingers. And you played thread-the-needle with one of these. Anack help you. You should have let me kill him."

"He didn't owe his death to me, or to you," said Rehger, absently.

"*Lowlander* talk. Repayments for past lives? Debts for future ones?"

"Yennef, in the arena sometimes, I've recognized the men who came to me for death."

"*She* taught you the philosophy in bed?"

"Or it was blood-lust then. Whatever, I've killed sufficiently. You'd better be on your way before your Dortharian returns."

"Yes, he won't forget, as he said."

"I regret that. Don't think I don't thank you, Yennef. You shouldn't have risked yourself."

"You're my son," said Yennef. He grew calm and said again, slowly, "My son. My first-born, so far as I know."

CHAPTER SEVENTEEN

THE DARK, THE LIGHT

"We're looking for an Alisaarian."

"I have a message here, which he entrusted to me."

Vanek, standing composed and alone in the studio, offered the five mix cutthroats a square of reed paper. "To Galutiyh Am Dorthar, or his captains: I shall await you at the fourth hour of afternoon, in the square before the Artisans Guild Hall. No other will be with me. I am, in readiness to accompany you, Rehger Am Ly Dis."

Could they read? One, apparently. He repeated the sentences to the others. Then, "He's a trained fighter, what about that?"

The most unsightly of his friends remarked coarsely, "There'll be ten or so of us. Let's see him try."

Another objected, "Who's to say he'll do what he says?"

"We'll get him sooner or later."

Nevertheless they wished to search the studio and Vanek allowed it, having earlier sent every additional person off the premises. Subtly controlled by the aura of helpful aloof uninterest which Vanek exuded, Galutiyh's search party did not make much mess, and soon went off again, into the city, whose streets steamed still from their slake of rain.

Rehger's slightly longer letter to Vanek had rendered apology, and enclosed a sum of money (which annoyed, it was the full compensation for terminated apprenticeship.) "If I can ever redeem this, I will do it." But he had seemed to imagine the imperative summons which now called him away might not allow of return. He thanked Vanek, and declared thanks, as apology, were inadequate. "If I might stay, I believe you know I would do so. It's impossible."

Vanek, hazarding between the lines, his latent telepathy questing, arrived at that strange nexus of the random psychic, sensitive of everything without even a phrase to describe it or a shred of proof. Therefore he emptied his studio, and awaited those Rehger regretted might be visited upon him.

There had been a third paper for the Corhl. Vanek, not scrupling, slit the wax and read favorable wishes to Chacor, a farewell, a suggestion that Chacor might be wary of telling anyone the real details of past escapes in Alisaar: It seemed the white Lowlanders were coming to be mistrusted.

The onslaught of rain had unsettled the city. Out on the avenues, the voices were still complaining, and awnings being shaken.

Vanek, having bolted and barred the studio doors, went up the stair.

The unfinished marble was in its accustomed position, and veiled in its cloth as Rehger always left it. More than a year, Vanek's Lydian apprentice had worked on the stone, constantly refining and smoothing, only sometimes prizing a little of the material away. He had selected the piece himself, and split it off under Mur's instruction—not to gain dominion over the stone—but rather to liberate some psyche trapped within.

Vanek, rather as he had slit the wax on the third letter, now raised the veil.

From the door, the marble's progress was not visible. But coming around the slender block, you found the mystery had begun. A face, an exquisite throat, a fountain of hair, had been assisted from their chrysalis.

The silver maidens cast at Sheep Lane had had something of this. Yet they were beings in loveliest slumber. Frozen in her marble, this creature was at the threshold of wakening. A beautiful unhuman girl, drawn from hibernation in the melting snow, all whiteness, skin and hair and eyes, like a woman of the Amanackire, the Shadowless Ones, resurrected out of the winter ground.

*   *   *

The whiteness of Hamos—Yennef had pictured it
extensively that afternoon before the fourth hour.

It was a black city, built of local stone; white marble
came from the north, and they did not use it, there.
The whiteness was in furnishings, the jewels, the garments, the albino pigment of the citizens. It was uncommon to see any Lowlander about in Hamos now
darker than the palest blond. More often, you saw the
golden eyes, but not so often as the eyes of ice. Snakes,
too, abounded in Hamos. They were carved on pillars
and lintels, worn in enamel on necks and limbs and
waists. Or, they were living. They eddied from crevices in the walls and paving to sun themselves. There
was a penalty at Hamos for any Vis killing a snake.
The amputation of a finger from the offending hand.
(This was a witticism. The hero Raldnor had been
missing a finger.)

You saw Vis in Hamos, but they were always traveling. There were only a handful of inns that would
shelter them, and only particular sections of the city
where they might go. For those who wished to worship
Anackire, the temples had an outer court and slab
without a statue. It was the rumor there were no
icons of the goddess any more in Hamos, and her
sister sanctums. They formed the image by power of
will, out of the fires they burned before the altars.

The Plains generally did not seem pledged to the
fears, now rife elsewhere, of Amanackire militance,
and even Hamos did not. Hamos was not of the world.
Though there were said to be occult colleges, they
were concealed, and if sorcery was positively practiced
they gave no sign. Even the Shansar magics and the
Vathcrian magics current in the goddess temples of all
the Middle Lands, and of Var-Zakoris, Karmiss Lanelyr—were lacking.

Having written three letters, Rehger went directly
to his lodging. Yennef walked beside him. They had
agreed, unspoken, to end the discussion of alarms and
tortures. Yennef had plans to avoid Galutiyh, but did
not speak of those either. Rehger had other arrange-
ments to make before departure.

In the succeeding hour then, they exchanged geographies, and a few insights of their separate lives, which was more than had been managed at the first meeting. It no longer seemed stilted to them to remain together, but neither was it natural.

"The artisan's wristlet will be handy to hide the snake mark. They still curse Amrek in the north."

Yennef had drifted into the service of the Council of Dorthar. He had done so many things, none of which had left any milestone. Long lost was the excursion among the mountains above Ly Dis. He had picked up the tale which sent him there in several forms, and repetition more than credence had driven him after it.

"It was suggested an Amanackire flying chariot had crashed there, on some upland valley. You'd even hear this from Vardish soldiers over the border, when they were drunk enough. I know, I served with them. It was a hoary old fable and had got itself adopted. A magician's chariot of the skies, mind you. Winged, maybe. Dorthar has something of that sort, too. The dragons who carried the Vis to earth and made them kings. Well, it wasn't that I believed in it, but it seemed the tree of falsehood might just have a root. I wanted to make my fortune, chance on some treasure trove. Months I went up and down those gods-forsaken crags. Then I found the treasure. Tibo. But never any chariot."

No milestone but one, Yennef thought then. Flesh and blood. All the wandering and the deeds had been self-defeating. Years like dice thrown away. And now the milestone itself—*Rehger*—would throw in his own game. Because he had fancied a Lowlander girl, once, and so been snared in yet another legend, leaky as a sieve.

But they had been through all that. Yennef did not protest again. (His own father had been full of experienced admonitions, on the rare occasions when they spoke.)

The Lan made his exit from the apartment house an hour before the Lydian did so. At parting, each man grasped the other's hand. It was a mockery of gesture, but they could not sustain any other. At least they had done that much. *And his mother's dead. I won't have to account for him to her.* Yennef thought wryly: *To no one, for anyone.*

Rehger seated himself on a bench before the Artisans Guild Hall.

After the rain, the afternoon had redoubled itself and blazed on Moiyah. The sky seemed blasted of color, and white slices of heat and blackest shadow checkered the square.

There was the same feeling of similarity, or re-enactment, which had come on him at Vanek's studio, when the Dortharian pranced into the upper room.

As the brass bell of the guild rang for the fourth hour, Rehger saw a lone figure walking toward him in slow easy strides, and whistling.

But no, the steps were feline, and over there, under an arch, ten or so of Galutiyh's riff-raff were waiting with zeebas.

"Rehger," said Galutiyh, in astonished delight. "Rehger of Ly Dis."

Rehger stood up, and diminished him.

But Galutiyh, having gone about with Yennef, would be used to that.

There was a coast road northward, to the fort and the border. The soldiers used it, you could see both ways for miles.

The mendicant pot-seller therefore, on his skewbald zeeba, did not himself attempt the road until Moiyah's gates were being shut for the evening.

Yennef, who had tossed clues to his fake purposes all over the city, had no idea of trotting over a skyline and smack into the Dortharian's arms. A little before midnight, however, from a coronet of brush and thorn, he did have the charm of seeing the camp-fire only three hundred paces away at the roadside.

"Honey dreams," said Yennef to the twisted soul of Galutiyh asleep. And felt two decades slip from him, as if he could go back.

But there was only forward, up the mountain and

down, and it was a shame that Tibo had grown slack
and dry, had wasted and died, in Iscah.

When the dark came, Vanek woke. He had fallen
asleep in the chair he had brought in, across from the
unfinished marble. It did not seem so very late. Bright
windows shone beyond the window of the workroom,
the noises of the nocturnal city had a soothing con-
stancy. A night like any other.

But the white stone glimmered on the dark, tantaliz-
ing him. Having seated himself to ponder it, he had
slept.

Vanek put himself out of the chair (seducer, not
even comfortable), and lit the glass-topped lamp in the
alcove. Bearing it back with him, he let the light and
shade play upon her, the white girl in the ice. But the
murmur of inner things was gone. He had slept, and
not kept hold of it. How simply the body could divert
the intellect.

And now, only a speck of fire fluttered like a bee on
a marble face.

Vanek drew up the veil again, as Rehger had done,
to protect his work from how much dust now, and how
long a neglect?

The light in the lamp dipped, steadied.

Vanek thought of a nursery rhyme of Moih:

> Blow out the lamp,
> Where is the flame?
> Light the lamp,
> There is the flame.
> Flame, flame,
> How is it so—
> Where do you come from?
> Where do you go?

Elissi would teach that to her children, no doubt.
He had seen her, nine dusks before her wedding, going
with a willing Chacor into the Anackire temple, to
offer.

> Flame, flame, how is it so?

Each life budding forth, withering away. But always, always, struck into another spark, to burn up again inside a lamp.

Flame, flame—

Knowing his stair, and all the house, miserly, not needing any light, Vanek blew out the lamp.

BOOK FIVE

VAR-ZAKORIS TO THADDRA

CHAPTER EIGHTEEN

BARGAINS

On a darkening backdrop, Zaddath was closing the brass-bound doors of her Blue Gate, to the sound of horns. The procedure was carried on at every sunset. Sunrise saw the gate opened with the same ceremony. It was a Vardian way of doing things, for Zaddath, the New Capital of Old Zakoris, was a Vardish city. Now a Guardian sufficed to rule here; the kings had gone home across the seas. The gate, however, stayed a monument to the conqueror, its uprights garnished by mighty fifty-foot Ashkars (the Vardish Anackire), and the surface of the wall torchlit for two miles either side, and faced with tiles of violet glaze.

Missing getting in the gate was not too serious an affair. The suburbs had long since overrun the city, taking in as they went the villas, temples and taverns strewn along the Zaddath South Road. The swamps, too, had been drained, but still the proliferating forest encroached continually on this island of building. Even in the paved streets, whippy tentacles of verdure endlessly emerged, to be hacked and hauled, their roots gouged out with fire. Any house left untended on the outskirts was filled by the jungle and ruined in ten days or less. In the gravid nights of the hot months, in the depths of walled stone Zaddath, frogs chirped and crickets made their sing-song, and large insects dashed themselves against gauze bed-curtains and died there like smoldering jewels.

The riders, who had just missed the gate, showed no inclination to retreat to a handy inn.

Progressing into the gate mouth, the foremost man

seized the chain of a bronze bell hanging there and clanged it.

Two soldiers appeared on the walk above.

"You, what d'you think you're at?"

"Inviting you to let me in."

"Flit over the wall. Or wait till morning. Lay your hand on that bell again, and it'll be a flogging."

"Yours," called Galutiyh Am Dorthar. "I've got business with the Warden and Council."

"What authority?"

"Come and see."

After a wait, three bad-natured soldiers and an officer who had been at dinner, clattered down the stair. Galutiyh displayed some seals. They were impressive. The goddess of Dorthar's High Council, the authentic golden Snake and Rod of Shansarian Alisaar, the Lion-Astride-the-Dragon symbol of Zaddath herself.

The tone of the sentries changed. They cracked a postern, and presently Galutiyh and his riders trotted into the city.

Galutiyh swaggered through the Council Hall at Zaddath, having left his escort of ruffians on the street. The place was mostly empty but for secretaries scribbling in cubbies. For such a career Galutiyh's family had intended him, but he had been more venturesome. He worked and wormed and vaulted his way up. Gray-eyed Galutiyh was not all Lowland-Dortharian. He had a lot of Thaddrian blood on his mother's side. For the Lowland—or other continent—connection, it was somewhere, but no one knew where. He claimed a Lowland grandfather, and had now said it so often he partly believed it himself.

When Counselor Sorbel entered the allotted chamber, Galutiyh was quite gratified. Sorbel, called after the Vardish king, was also the right hand of Zaddath's Warden. Nevertheless, he seemed brisk.

"What do you want, Galut?" (Galutiyh winced at this Thaddrian abbreviation of his name.) "Really a drama, at the gate. No one here would like you to abuse your privileges."

"My lord, I earned my privileges by devotion. It seemed to me speed wasn't inappropriate."

"And why?"

Galutiyh recounted his reason.

Sorbel altered. He looked keener, less at ease.

"This story of an Amanackire woman," Sorbel eventually said, "is a—" he used the Vardian expression, and in Vardian: "Flimsy mast on which to fix a sail."

Galutiyh allowed himself to demonstrate he understood the phrase. "Even so, when the Council of Dorthar sent me to investigate the Plains, I was instructed in this—story. And then it occurred to me the Council here was more in need of my findings . . . they seemed to think it was important. Wasn't it?"

"Don't be insolent."

"Excuse me, Lord Sorbel. Blame the rigors of the journey. Fifty-three days by land and sea."

"Where is the man?"

"Safely shut in a hostelry five miles back down the Zaddath South Road."

"All right. Wait here."

Sorbel went out and Galutiyh sat down. A minute later, a servant brought a tray of cakes and Vardish wine, which boded well.

A great beetle, glistening like a drop of ichor, clung by its pincers to the window-post. One of the three men in the room lurched toward it, raising the pommel of his knife to crush the insect.

"Why not let it live," said the third man quietly. It was the first thing he had said for a long while, and the significance of this, apparently, stayed the man with the knife.

"What do you care?"

"Can't stop him, can you?" said the second man.

The third man was shackled to the table by a iron cuff on his right wrist.

The blond mix, who had been disturbed by an increasing abundance of insect life on their journey west and north, lifted the pommel higher. Beyond the window, the black night tinked and purred.

"In Alisaar," Rehger said, as quietly as before—and

as before the other hesitated—"it was thought unlucky to kill anything before a duel or combat. Since the gods strike in the same way, suddenly, perhaps without cause or care. Like the beetle, you might not see the blow coming."

Galutiyh's blond ruffian stared at the beetle. Grudgingly he lowered his knife.

"Anackire protects," he said, ritually. He worshiped all gods, and none.

He went back to the far end of the table where Rehger's second guard, a swarthy Ommos-mix, giggled. "Scared of the gladiator? Wait till he breaks the chain. No? Isn't he mighty enough?"

Galutiyh first produced a shackle when they came off the Xarab ship at the border port. He had *requested* Rehger to allow this necessity. Rehger did not argue. Once he was cuffed, the other end of the chain was fastened to the wrist of one of Galutiyh's biggest fellows, a dumb, brown-haired man, with crazy eyes. "After all," said Galutiyh to Rehger, when it was done, "you won't mind that. You're a slave, aren't you?" They had ridden the roads up into Xarabiss and there had been some dithering about before they took ship. Galutiyh obviously suspected he was being followed, but had then eluded his pursuer, leaving evidence of a trail continuing on to Dorthar, or at least a more northerly town. Instead, they crossed the Inner Sea at its narrowest point and put in at the edge of Shansarian Alisaar. In a cove on the border a half-rotten fishing skimmer or two lay rubbing her sores on the rocks. One of these hags consented to bear the party up the coast. It was windless weather, and the crew rowed, and Galutiyh's men lounged among the reeking kreels, sometimes casting line themselves for fish or water-snakes off the bows. The Zakor sailors paid them scant attention.

Zakoris ranged herself on the left hand, to all intents impassable country, jungle-forest rising back in stairs that choked the sun, or wading out even into the sea. During the day, Rehger was again unshackled; after dark the chain was fastened to an iron ring in the mast. When this second voyage of twenty airless, mind-

less days and anchored nights ended at the Var-Zakor
port of Ilva, Galutiyh commandeered some scrubby
horses. Then the chain was lengthened and the dumb
man and Rehger rode side by side. At night, when the
travelers halted, Galutiyh would undo the dumb man
and chain himself to Rehger. "May I lie with you,
dearest?" asked Galutiyh. But even then, as always
until then, Galutiyh did not trespass beyond a few
words. He would only chide Rehger in the morning,
"How beautifully you sleep! Not a snore or a nightmare. Teach these others, will you? Their moans and
snuffles drive me insomniac."

Getting on the Zaddath Road, riding through the
villages and into the suburbs, they were looked at, and
Rehger—or it might be the dumb man who shared the
daytime chain—was marked as a culprit. Once some
black-skinned priests emerged from a wayside temple.
They purified the road, when the company had gone
by, both of horse-dung and criminal aura. Generally
the native Zakorians were less interested than the
conqueror Vardians. There was little sign of mixture,
but neither any of oppression. Close to the conqueror
capital, the Zakorians adhered with seeming equanim-
ity to Vardish ways, mostly dressed and carried on as
Vardians, and were bilingual. Here and there you
might see the emblem of a black Ashkar-Anackire,
but never a white-skinned Zarduk or Rorn.

There were laws in Zaddath, too, concerning human
noise after midnight. The hostelry was therefore very
still, and the sound of hoofs approached distinctly
along the road.

"There're our mates, coming back," said the blond
mix. Relieved, he threw his knife quivering into the
wooden wall.

Torchlight began to hit the lintel of the window
where the beetle clung.

When the door was opened, neither Galutiyh, nor
any of the mates, presented themselves. It was a natty
Vardian officer and five Zakorian guard.

The Vardian demanded that Rehger be delivered to
him.

Galutiyh's men obeyed.

In the courtyard, "I see you're a gentleman. If you'll swear by the goddess not to lark around, you can ride free into the city."

"I don't worship the goddess," said Rehger, with the frankness of a good child, the Vardian thought, rather taken with him.

"Well, that's straightforward. By any god you respect, then, or just your word, I think, would do."

"Of course," said Rehger. "You have it."

The chamber was lamplit and windowless. A vane stood wide in the ceiling behind a sieve of linen. Moths still drizzled down. Aside from Galutiyh, and Rehger, there was no man in the room who was not of the peoples of the goddess. Blond hair, the pale summer tan of Lowlander, Shansar, Vardian. Amber eyes. If there was any trace of interbreeding, it was invisible.

The Warden of Zaddath sat in his carved chair, with Sorbel standing next to him.

Directly by Sorbel was another man, tall and strongly-proportioned, garbed like a Shansar prince.

The Warden had turned to him immediately.

"What do you say?"

The Shansarian fixed Rehger with an eagle's look. The yellow eyes scorched and the mouth curled, and his ringed hands moved at his sides in a gesture of some recaptured motion and guidance—Rehger recognized it. He recognized the Shansar. Not his face or name certainly, but his person and the hour of meeting it.

It was Sorbel who spoke.

"He is claimed to be a slave of Alisaar, called the Lydian."

"Yes," said the Shansar. "Your hunting hound was clever." He did not take his gaze from Rehger. "Neck and neck, Lydian. But I didn't tell in Shansar, Rorn was angry. Since it was the anger of Anackire."

The Warden cleared his throat. The Shansarian prince, who owned estates in Sh'alis and Karmiss and, once, had gone to Alisaar to race in the Fire Ride, turned and said, "Lord Warden, we were side by side, he and I, on the cliff above the sea. He remembers, too. That was what he mocked me with, *Rorn*, their nonexistent sea god, when his chariot broke from mine after the earth and the water shook. I would have won the race, but for this *slave*."

"What do *you* say?" inquired the Warden of Rehger.

"He also raced in the Fire Ride, as he says. We were nearer to one another than we are now."

"And you survived the destruction of the Saardsin city?" The Warden, the chamber, both were full of some hesitation, some unwillingness. "How?"

"In a shelter," Rehger said, "on the Street of Tombs."

"You refer to a grave."

"He was at the funeral rites of his beloved," cheeped Galutiyh from his corner. "*Her* rites." At Rehger's shoulder the Vardian officer shifted, but Sorbel remarked, "Be silent, Galutiyh. You think yourself too wise." To Rehger, Sorbel said, in an abrupt harsh creak, "You'll be asked to describe this escape."

Rehger said, "I have to reassure you, my lords. If you're wondering whether I, too, rose from the dead, I did not." It was a perfect hit. Every man in the chamber reacted to it.

"There was a rumor," said Sorbel, "some man of the arena, who was healed."

Rehger said, "The woman you're discussing was Amanackire. In Alisaar, all your blond race are reckoned sorcerers."

"Galutiyh promises us," snapped Sorbel, "that he captured you and forced you here as his prisoner. Please realize, your words and deeds will be scrutinized in the light of that."

"I came with Galutiyh of my own accord."

"Yet you were chained."

Rehger said, "The Vardian officer there still has the chain. Perhaps he would return it to me."

The Vardian, without waiting on response, smartly handed Rehger cuff and chain.

Rehger clasped the shackle on his wrist and taking hold of the other end of the chain, slowly pulled it outward from the cuff. In a few moments the links of the chain had altered shape, as if softening in a furnace. The men in the room regarded this spectacle silently, until the chain crunched from the cuff and Rehger dropped it on the floor. He broke the fastening of the cuff itself more quickly, threw that down also.

It was the Shansarian charioteer who then began uncouthly to applaud.

"This Vis dog brings the stadium to Zaddath. Cheer him. Let us make him a garland."

"Let's first of all discover," said Sorbel, "what this garland is, that he desires. We have questions to put to him. But he has his own questions. Look at him. This man isn't a slave. We think he knows some secret. He disdains our suspicions. Do we stretch him over coals, or whip him, maim him, and expect compliance?" Sorbel glared at Rehger. "Do you have the blood of the Plains People?"

"To my knowledge, no."

Sorbel put his knotted fist to his throat.

"Do you, to your knowledge, have the blood of Raldnor Am Anackire?"

The chamber surged. The lamps flickered and flashed at the uneven breathing of men.

"Do I take you to mean am I descended from the bloodline of Raldnor? My mother was an Iscaian farmwoman wedded to a peasant in the mountain valleys."

"What do you want?" Sorbel cried out shockingly, a sensitive who had lost control of diplomacy in the swirl of empathic vibrations.

"Is it so difficult to guess?" Rehger said. "The woman Aztira was known to me. Like yourselves, I wonder if she could live after death, in the flesh. And if so, where she's gone to."

In the way of the ancient palaces of Vis, the Council Hall at Zaddath burrowed into the ground. Beneath the upper rooms, with their ledgers, clerks, formalities, and clandestine late sessions, corridors descended into the pit of a dry river-course. Down there, even the insect chorus did not sound. There were other noises, sometimes.

The cell was not cramped, lit by a pair of clay

lamps, and with a brazier even, against damp or cold. A clean pallet lay along one wall. The jailer, having detailed the room's appointments, vowed to bring kindling, oil and food, at logical hours. Wine could also be purchased, even women. "Don't get low, sir," said the jailer. "I've never known any man to be left here more than six months."

Rehger seated himself, on the pallet, to wait.

He thought, in flowing, sequential degrees, of the passages of experience which had brought him here. The weave of the cloth, a tapestry of chariots and swords, or shouting crowds, of fire bursting from water and metal from its sheath—and the powder of marble. At the hem, in Iscaian dusk, his faceless mother. Through it all a fragile thread recurring, white as the center of the lamp-flames.

Remember me sometimes. This the Amanackire had written to him, before the city perished.

Alive or dead, she drew him on. He remembered. He remembered her.

And, as he was doing this, another man came to the cell's door and stared in by the grating.

An amber-colored Shansarian eye saw, in the filmy light, the seated statue of a king musing, done in gold-washed bronze.

The Shansarian snapped his fingers, and the jailer made him free of Rehger's cell.

Rehger did not get to his feet, and thus became a king giving audience from a couch. Plainly, he was not fraught. Not doubting or anxious at himself. Nothing could be done to him, got from him. Besides, he was honest. He had said it all.

The Shansarian prince looked down on the seated king.

"So the Fire Ride stays fresh for you, too? I should have come back, the next year, and beaten you, if your city had stood."

"Perhaps."

"Above, in that chamber," said the Shansarian, "you saw a conclave of allies, who distrust each other and all things. They summoned me from the province of

Alisaar. I told them what I'd learned, the famous tale. Will you be told it, too?"

"I came here for that purpose."

"Expect no embellishment. I'm not a paid spy of Vardath, like their Dortharian kiss-foot, Galutiyh. I worship the goddess. My land over the oceans was the first to swear allegiance to brotherhood with Raldnor, and the Lowlands. (Vathcri claims that. They cheat. It was Shansar.) Now, the Lowlands have become two races, and one of these an enemy. The tale is this. Near the end of the months of the scarlet star, a girl of the Amanackire traveled up through the Alisaarian north. She had two or three servants, who served her as the white ones are always served. A lordling of the Shansarian province who saw her on the street, re-called her beauty from Saardsinmey, where he had gone to attend to some affairs. He sent politely to her house to ask if she was the same lady, and if so, to congratulate her on leaving the city before the disas-ter, as he had done. The message was returned that she had witnessed the disaster, or its effect. The prince then sought her doors. They shut. Who aggravate the Amanackire? He came away."

"You were this prince?" said Rehger.

The Shansarian made a flaunting gesture. "I. Kuzarl Am Shansar."

"You'd met her in Saardsinmey."

"Beheld her, after the chariots. She was by then yours. Or so it was said."

"But you saw her, nevertheless, frequently and closely enough, to pick her out this second time, in the north."

"Do I swear to that? The woman on the street went veiled. Yet, you'll know, with a woman one fancies . . . the carriage of her head, the movement of her frame as she walks, linger in the mind."

Rehger waited. Kuzarl Am Shansar studied him, and said at length, "Have you missed that she *boasted* to me? When she sent me a written message to declare she had survived."

"Not missed."

"She boasted also before you of the prowess of her

people? And that they would bring down a proud city of the black races, to make an example of it?"

Rehger did not reply. In his mind, a hawk fell, and Aztira kneeled and wept in hubris and horror. Not only her people, herself: She also had been divided. From that impetus, it had seemed to him, she had—this cunning sorceress—given herself to a murderer.

"The wild tales now spread like weeds all over Alisaar and the province," said Kuzarl. "Perhaps at her instigation. A woman of Saardsinmey had plotted to slay her, done it, seen her in her tomb. After the quake and the wave the Amanackire was reborn, in her own body, which healed of death by her magic."

"The Lowlanders believe life is inextinguishable."

"Yet not the flesh, which corrupts. There are legends in Shansar, of heroes who re-entered their own corpses in time of need. Raldnor is supposed to have done this during the un-war with the Zakors."

One of the clay lamps guttered suddenly and turned red.

As if at some signal, the Shansarian seated himself upon the floor opposite to Rehger.

"Now I'll reveal the second story. There's a marvelous city in Thaddra. Or beyond Thaddra, in the forests farthest to the west. Too far, too lost a land even for the Free Zakors to covet. The Amanackire have built the place. Partly by witchcraft, also by the labor of Vis slaves."

"And who has visited this city?"

"None, maybe. Whispers wend along the rivers. Dorthar says: A makebelieve. Rarnammon's son is a coward and a libertine. For his personal blazon he has a dragon embracing or struggling with a snake. He will sire geese. Still, he pays hounds like Galut to snuff about. But Galut finds the Vis can only vie with each other for crumbs, and the Lowlands are kept blind, or they hide their eyes. No one has seen the city of the Amanackire—save they themselves."

"She traveled westward?"

"It's said so. She was gone like a white smoke. Yet all Var-Zakoris has the tale now, of a resurrected sorceress. In some of the Zakor villages, out in the woods, you come on shrines to her. There's a new plan. To send men to the west, a doomed mission. The forests are impenetrable. The heart of Thaddra is the land of losings. Even gods and heroes vanish into it forever. The westernmost jungles are deeper than the deepest seas. Who enters needs wings. But then, the Amanackire fly," Kuzarl said. "Did she inform you?"

The weak lamp faded. The other also, but with no preface, went out.

In the dark, the Shansarian said, "Spirits are eavesdropping. Or else you have Power. Yes, I credit you do. In the race on the cliff, I felt that."

"The chariots have their own life. Any professional racer would tell you."

"That's Power. But you Vis send it always outward. Your gods are sorry but dangerous things, you put such being into them." Kuzarl leaned forward. His voice was a murmur. "The Vardians might kill you. Such is their fright."

"I was warned of it."

"Yet came here? Then she's called you. At liberty, would you go now to the city—the perhaps-city, in the west?"

Rehger said, after a moment, "If a sorceress called me, presumably I'd have no choice." Then he said, "But what shall I owe you?"

There came the sound of Kuzarl rising, notified by the clink of the jewelry on his wrists and belt.

"There was a second, when we raced the chariots together. Did you think: *Brothers who duel for their birthright.*"

"Yes."

"You have the mind-speech, too. Only a touch. Not enough to send your Vis brain mad. We're dealing now in the dark. Don't haggle, Rehger Am Ly Dis. Some things must be. Sorbel's in a lather up above. But the Warden I'll persuade. You and I. We'll journey west."

The second lamp, which had died, quivered and gave up a hiss of light.

As Kuzarl smote the cell door and was let out, this lamp was again brightly burning.

"He was questioned at great length, and answered openly. The scribes have written down these accounts. But he's Vis. How can he be thought an accomplice of Amanackire?"

Sorbel stood blocking out the dawn in the Warden's high window.

"Not questioned, my lord, under any pressure."

'I've never before known you longing to torture a man."

"We're at war, my lord. You know it. At war with magicians. In the beginning we thought ourselves part of the select, friends to the white race, white as they were. But the Amanackire are albinos, and adopt the sigil of the white serpent. Even their own parent people, the Lowlanders, have been made alien by the Shadowless. So, we discover ourselves at risk along with the dark men of Dorthar and Alisaar, and as little able to protect ourselves."

"I'm lessoned in these things, Sorbel."

"They can attack us when and how they choose. They *will* attack us, because theirs is an inimical and haughty people, possessed of Power. On our side, can the smallest grain of sand be left unsifted?"

"As this Rehger pointed out, you also, Sorbel, would be deemed a sorcerer, south and east and in the Middle Lands."

"And Kuzarl is a Shansar, and mad as they always are."

The Warden laughed a little. He was very tired and wanted the simple comforts of breakfast and sleep.

"Yes, Kuzarl is a Shansar."

"All we know of *him* otherwise, my lord, is that he's a wealthy adventurer. This berserk pouncing of his on the idea of a city in the west—"

"It may exist. He may find it. That may in some sort be advantageous."

"Find with the assistance of Rehger the Lydian."

The Warden said, "Consider, Sorbel. If the man Rehger was her lover, beloved enough that she saved his life—it seems she did—perhaps her kind wish him returned to them, and perhaps our permitting him, unhindered, to reach them, will steady the supernatural balance. You, Sorbel, are aware of the worth of such bargains."

"I dream constantly," said Sorbel. "My wife tells me I call out, till she wakes me. I lie in her arms like an infant, shaken with terrors. I can't ever remember why, where I have been or what I have looked at."

"Kuzarl will go on his journey whatever the Zaddath council decrees. We shall send the Lydian with him. They will never come out of the forests. Nothing may come out of them. In ten years we may still be debating the matter. Perhaps our fears of the Amanackire are only an evil dream. The goddess will wake us, we'll lie in her arms."

Sorbel turned from the window. The gathering sunrise streamed around him. His back to the light, he said, "When they speak to me in the council of these rumors, that there are sorcerers now who can rise from the dead, I dismiss the silly talk. But here, in private, I tell you I believe it. It's as if someone whispered in my ear, at night in the darkness. Against a superior enemy who hates us, and can never die—all struggle supposedly is futile. Isn't it?"

"Struggle," said the Warden, "is frequently useless. And hope, they say, a viper, which entices in order to bite the more viciously. Even so, there is some other state, not despair, not hope, and not struggle. Some belief or knowledge, nameless yet definite. Cling to that, Sorbel. Or, let it fasten on you and bear you up."

The Dortharian agent Galutiyh rejoined his men at the hostelry with a malign flourish, flinging some gold on the table and, as they cursed and scuffled for it, announcing: "Underpaid. The bastards docked our wages."

Galutiyh virtuously resented the mantle of secrecy in which the conclave of allies at Zaddath had gone to earth. Though he had found out, via byways, that Rehger was imprisoned. This did not distress Galutiyh. Now, philosophically, the Dortharian Thaddrian with the phantasmal Lowland granddaddy, switched his vision elsewhere.

He told his company they might make merry in Zaddath tonight. Tomorrow they would be returning along the road to Ilva. There he expected to be meeting someone. This was Yennef. Galutiyh had realized, by the time they made the sea crossing from Xarabiss, that it was Yennef who came after. Yennef had probably reckoned they would go directly to Dorthar, since Dorthar had hired them both. Galutiyh faked his clues accordingly. He had also, wanting something in reserve, left a message for Yennef farther north, in case Yennef did not eventually tumble to the realities. Galutiyh had made sure that in the end Yennef would grope his way into the Vardian west, where the laws of Dorthar would be less helpful and less protective. Galutiyh had not forgotten the Lan's grip and the razor-edged metal at his throat.

While his men whored and got drunk, he made an offering to Anackire-Ashkar in a temple. It was a blood offering, which was permissible here. He asked the goddess to give him his rights and his revenge. This did not seem incongruous to him. Of her eight uplifted arms—each of ivory in Zaddath, with amber bangles, fingers of gold, a topaz in each palm—he gazed on the arm which signified retribution.

She seemed, through the smoke, to smile down at him.

He adored and honored her; she was his god and he gave her what she liked. She would not leave him wanting.

CHAPTER NINETEEN

FIRE, WATER AND STEEL

Forty miles west of Zaddath, all the roads ended. Thereafter, there was only forest, and those things which the forest contained, or let be. Above, sky, sometimes barely seen for days where the canopy had meshed to closure. Southward, from high terraces of ground, once the canopy broke again, mountains were visible, their shoulders half-transparent, their crowns melting into air. In the glades, pools of inky water lay motionless in a mist of gnats and dragonflies. Occasionally a village had hewn a niche for itself. Some had not lasted; their bones showed dimly among the creepers and roots which had eaten them. There were tracks and trails through the trees, the footpaths of men and animals. Along these avenues, where light came in, the summer fires of flowers burned on the earth and dozens of feet up in the boughs. By night the forest was strummed like a harp. Sudden storms hammered the foliage and lizards came down with the rain. This country of the jungle was eternally Vis. It had obtained long before the Vardians, long before men. Treasures might be dug out of it, shafts of ivory, crude masks of deformed gold from Zarduk rites centuries out of date, or the gemmed teeth of travelers. Kuzarl's men, mostly Vardianized Zakors, had not brought maps, or charms for dowsing, and did not grub after such articles.

Along with the ten Var-Zakors were two Shansarians, servants of Kuzarl's household, and a cook from Karmiss. Every man had sworn an oath Shansarian fashion, of loyalty and secrecy, over a sword standing in heated coals. In the old days, they would have had to grasp the metal in the left fist, the subsequent blisters a mark of their intention, a reminder of their faith. Kuzarl had twittingly mentioned this, before requesting the modified version. Rehger he did not ask for the oath. "You're already bound," Kuzarl had said.

There was no time in the forests, except for each day and each night, and, when the going was exceedingly rough, each hour. It was not possible to take pack-beasts through the inner jungles. Each man carried a quantity of what was needful. Sometimes they must also hack their way, every one of the fifteen men, pausing only when exhausted.

Conversation, so often the solace of inactivity, was lacking among them. About the cook-fire by night, the Karmian, who had a fine voice, would sometimes lament his birthland, the Var-Zakors would bet with painted Vardian dice. Kuzarl was given to isolated and thoughtful monologues, concerning Shansar-over-the-ocean, the mythic Lowland war, the gods, Anackire. Into these philosophic examinations he beckoned Rehger, but Rehger never spoke at any length. "Tell me more of Saardsinmey," said Kuzarl one evening. "It was destroyed," said Rehger.

One sunup, two of the Zakors were missing. Their remains were soon found. A huge snake, which had left evidence of its passage through the undergrowth, had crushed them, and devoured one, leaving only his metal ornaments and boots. On the other, birds and reptiles were feeding. Where blood had run into the flowers, they had lowered their calyxes thirstily.

Some of the men were very afraid. The notion of a serpent now was not only physically but psychically threatening.

"Return then," said Kuzarl, straddling the serpent's trail with princely defiance. "Know the way? By Ashkar, I supposed not. Come on, then."

That night Kuzarl said to Rehger, "The Lowlanders burn their dead. This custom is upheld as an acceptance that flesh has been doffed, the spirit flown away. But I detect another origin. They use flames to prevent resurrection."

Kuzarl's band now numbered thirteen. They mounted a strict watch by night.

The Shansarian servants obviously found the dripping molten heat oppressive. Kuzarl, reared, he said, in Sh'alis, was rather more enduring. Maybe a month and a half was gone, since they had left Zaddath.

They crossed a swamp by a Zakorian bridge, partly unsafe. Thrown out on the edge was a massive skeleton, a palutorvus, or some thing even older. Fever stalked the camp, taking up both of Kuzarl's Shansars, three of the Var-Zakors with mix blood. They lay up a day or two. The fevers went down and the oaths held.

Rehger opened his eyes.

"What?"

"Not," said Kuzarl, "more snakes. But I'll show you."

Aside from the dutiful watchman, the rest of the camp slept, not yet troubled by flies. The dawn was starting, back the way they had come.

Kuzarl plucked through the ferns and creepers under a ribcage of trees. At the end, as they had suspected the previous night, was another of the deserted villages. Rather than antique, however, it was quite recent and had not entirely submerged. The huts had become bushes, but a stone pillar-oven, of the oldest type of the shrines of the fire god, braced itself on a step of baked clay. Kuzarl pointed to the foot of the step, where he had previously pulled the creepers aside. A sort of wooden pin had been sunk in the soil, and daubed white. It had something of a face and a veil or mane of bleached human hair.

"A shrine to Zarduk, and a shrine to Aztira," said Kuzarl. "Do you see where the underside of the clay is marked? They were making sacrifice to her. *Burnt* meats."

The sunrise poured past Rehger's body, into the lost village. He looked at the daubed pin Aztira. The night of her burial, he had stood before the altar of the Shalian temple, and promised an offering to the snake-fish goddess, for Aztira's peace. He had never made this offering. Instead, all Saardsinmey had made it, consumed on the altar, flushed by the lustral of the sea.

A slow storm of hatred moved in him. He was now accustomed to this. It had commenced on the ship of Arn Yr, and in the studio of Vanek it had dulled down, aching only now and then, as the scar on his arm never did. But that third life at Moiyah, that had been sundered also, the life of the artisan. As he came west, again the hate burgeoned, deepened, and had by now perhaps possessed him.

"She passed them by here, then," Rehger said.

"Seemingly. These primitives could never have heard of her otherwise."

For myself, I loved you, from the moment I saw you I believe.

The picture returned to him, through the present image of the wooden pin, the image he himself had been forming from marble; and the image of her lovely deadness on the couch, as if she slept.

The hatred engorged him, like desire.

Kuzarl said, "Be wary, Rehger. I told you, the mind-speech isn't quite unknown to you. Your brain thunders, and deafens me."

"And the words?"

"No words. Does a screaming baby have words?"

Rehger lifted his eyes and looked off through the smothering village.

"When asked so surprisingly in Zaddath, if you were of the line of Raldnor," said Kuzarl, "you replied, pedantically, that you took them to mean the line of his sons. Evasion?"

"Mind-read it," said Rehger. "If you're able."

"No need. I put together two blatant themes. You have the appearance of the line of the first Rarnammon, the Dortharian Storm Lords. You are not Raldnor's. You descend then from the seed of his half-brother. Amrek's get."

Rehger turned from the village.

"She told me so."

He had been repelled by her at the beginning. That whiteness. He would harm no woman. But she was

not human. He had cut her from the marble, wrung
her neck in the wax.

Rehger said to Kuzarl, "A Moiyan sculptor used me
as the model for a statue of Raldnor. Taken into
Xarabiss an accident befell the stone. All trace of the
features was splintered from the countenance."

Sword into snake. Snake into woman. A serpent,
which sloughed its skin and crawled out from the black
hole under the boulder . . . something so beautiful—

Rehger leaned down and wrenched the daubed peg
from the earth. He cast it away over the village.

There was a normalcy of sound growing behind
them, in the camp. The cook clattered his pots and
sang.

Kuzarl said, "Tradition dictates, Rehger Am Amrek,
we're enemies. You knew it, and have spoken it."

"A combat then, Shansarian. As and when you
wish."

"The goddess will demonstrate the time and place."

"Your goddess is a demon of the air. Your wanting
it will make the time and place."

Kuzarl bowed, a hint of the codes of Karmiss despite everything.

Not a bird or insect made its noises in the foliage
about them.

They want back easily to the camp, pacted, as if
nothing at all had happened.

The first wilderness ended in the towns and villages,
the cleared and fertile marshes and flax-sumps of the
Var-Zakorian west. There were now consistent vistas,
on one of which the mountains marched away over the
southern horizon.

There had been no route to the Great Sea-Lake in
the days of Old Zakoris. Corhl and Ott had used this
enclosed sprat of an ocean for fishing trade and piracy
upon each other. But now a couple of Vardish roads
rambled to the shore.

Kuzarl's party, again, had been depleted by this
juncture. Five Var-Zakors, despite the desperate oath,
had vanished at the first town beyond the forest. "Tested
in fire," remarked Kuzarl, "the flawed metal breaks.

Such vermin we shan't be saddled with in the depths of Thaddra."

At a fishing port on the rim of the Lake, one of Kuzarl's servants found out an Ottish captain, due to take his twenty-oared galley across to Ottamet and Put. Kuzarl drew a map in the sandy soil with his daggar. "There and here, the Ott-towns, and here, or here, a river which runs off through the mountains northwest, where we are going." So it was settled.

The water of the Sea-Lake gleamed like glass under a high sun, and far out fish were leaping.

The Ottish captain and his men took that for some favorable omen, and trotted instantly to the galley. Kuzarl and Rehger went aboard, but the rest, dawdling in the port, were almost left behind. The Karmian cook railed against the Otts as savages. But their ears were thick with their own dialect and they chose to ignore the faces he pulled, smiling and chattering and nodding in reply.

Ottamet, the capital, was a thatched wooden town, painted scarlet, rose and cream, with brilliant blue jetties of obscure religious meaning, that prodded half a mile into the paler blue of the waves. The sea was tidal but calm, and there had been a strong breeze on the body of the water. The crossing had taken little more than a day. From Ottamet, the galley turned north, flattering the coast. Miniature Ott also had been flinging territorial nets, and advanced in patches up along the Sea-Lake until a wide rivermouth checked her. Here was Put, wooden and thatched, rouged and jettied. Wild parrots nested in the roofs, screeching and squawking. The echoing omnipotence of the black jungle-forest loomed and towered behind. The river estuary, a swamp pillared by colossal reeds, choked up with sand banks, islets and hot springs, sent a quavering fume into the sky. It was possible to get through, carrying a light vessel upended overland, until the main channel of the river won free. No man of Ott wished to go that way, but several were willing to sell all manner of boats.

Lizards the size of two-year-old children sat on stones to watch the bargaining, often conducted in sign language, the tall Shansars and Zakors, the shorter, chunky Otts, with playful wicked eyes. The parrots screeched and scratched.

Before sunset all but one of the Zakors had deserted. One of the Shansarians had gone down once more with fever and been taken in at a hospice by a holy jetty. The Karmian, who was related to this man, became woebegone and was therefore released by Kuzarl to cook for the sick one and save his stomach from Putish "muck." Next morning, when the parrots were barely stirring, the four remaining men of the expedition went out of Put with a slender rowboat slung on their backs.

The river won fifteen miles upstream in a skein of purple lilies that gave suddenly on muscular brown water.

Like a dream the mountain banks of western Thaddra came floating toward them as they rowed.

The mountains stepped down and walled them in. On the sloping plain between the mountains and the river-course, the forests pushed and crowded nearer to the water, and in parts invaded it. Massive trees had rooted in the river, which clashed and hurled itself about them, foaming with rage. But the peaks of the mountains stood in the forest like giants in a meadow, staring away into the past and future indifferently.

Clogged by the jungle, the river had split in strands and narrowed. Conversely it was very deep. They made their journey that day by thrusting off with oars against the boles of trees and great ferns. Overhead, the boughs met to form a tunnel.

From noon onward there began, beyond the noises of their exertion, the boat, the water, the forecast stillness of approaching storms.

The air itself became another hindrance, another block against which to drive the unwilling vessel.

Near sunset a royal sky was erected miles off behind

their sunshade of leaves. The atmosphere boiled slowly over.

For an hour thunder tuned itself among incredible distances, growling like cruel hunger around the valley's hollow belly, striking the mountains and struck aside. From the forests things answered with squalls and cries, brilliant, snuffed-out flickers of wings. Then the silence returned, weighing like lead.

The men let down their oars, laid them over the planks. The water along the channel crinkled, flattened, and grew thick as agate; only where it rocked against the boat did it move, and this seemed half illusion.

Lightning speared across the leaf-eyelets of the sky.

It pierced a distant crag, or seemed to, exploding. Then the thunder boomed as if the heavens fell in masonry blocks.

Wind like a scythe tore through the valley of the river, bending the trees, making the boat jump in the solid water. The men crouched down. The Var-Zarkor was unnerved, agitated, the Shansar servant looked on in a trance.

The wind shrieked unknown words. Lightning passed once more with a tearing hiss.

This lightning hit the top of the tree-canopy, about thirty feet away from the boat.

The world turned inside out as a sheet of living flame threw itself upward. The agate river was changed to gold. A deluge of burning leaves and branches, a fire-howl, enveloped everything.

As the boat ignited, Rehger pitched himself into the river.

Beneath three or four incendiary surfaces, darkness filled the deep narrows. There was no bottom, only here and there blind shelves and obtrusions of the land.

Presently Rehger rose for air. The boat lay some way off, alight and flaring in a cage of flaming elements, wood, reflections. The fire was all around, and above him. Of the other men there was no sign. He dived again.

Red light filtered down to him now, and the river gods sank their fangs into his heels.

He rose a second time, much later. The fire was in turmoil, upstream, but flashing out, catching, hurrying after him.

One of the gods under the river took hold of Rehger by the waist and pulled him, with iron human hands, down again deep under the water.

There, in the opaque reddish dark, he saw the pallor of the Shansar's clothes, flesh and clouding hair. Kuzarl's pale eyes were wide, his paler teeth clenched, grinning, while the scintillant breath escaped grudgingly between them. Letting Rehger go, he hovered before him, like a sky creature resting at midflight, in the levity of the water. Kuzarl had no weapons in his grasp, was revealing the emptiness of his hands. He would use only himself, like one stadium-trained.

To Kuzarl's mind, apparently, the goddess had devised and provided. There was to be combat—

As the Shansar curled over to grapple him, Rehger swung beneath him, lunging up under Kuzarl's body, flinging him off and off and away, a knot of torso and limbs twisting capriciously in the medium of liquid.

Each man shattered the surface once more, perhaps twelve feet from each other, here the limits of the channel. The fire lashed at them, and smoke drifted from their hair as from the water. The atmosphere was spoiled, but they gulped it in. The Shansar laughed, without noise or breath, his eyes blazing like the forest. Tradition: A berserker. He plunged in a vast diving spring, like a leaping fish, straight up and across the channel, falling on Rehger, bearing him down, one of the ringed hands clamped on the Lydian's throat.

As they sank again, Kuzarl's fingers pressed for the life in the neck veins, to bring on sightless confusion, or unconsciousness, but the neck of the Swordsman was armored in muscle, a statue's neck, like the rest of his physique. As Rehger began remorselessly to detach Kuzarl's clasp, the Shansar broke of his own accord and tried to turn to kick his adversary away. But Rehger it now was who secured Kuzarl, forcing back his grinning face, using legs and arms to detain him, and at the same moment angle his body into an agonizing spinal arch.

But the medium of liquid, yet again, advantaged and misled.

The Shansarian abruptly tossed himself backward, a voluntary description of the arch, and hurled both men over in a series of spinning wheels, from which in turn they loosed, and so from each other, to hang suspended there, unappeased.

Certain burning stuff from the forest above, not immediately extinguished, was now arrowing down past them through the river, like flaming comets. Between their lips the silver flames of their breath escaped.

They were not merely flame-breathing sky creatures. Dehumanized, the Shansar was now equally submerged in the fighting-madness of homeland ritual. Nothing was in his eyes but starvation, greed. Buoyed in fluid, his eloquent hands were taut and ready. To Rehger, the blood-lust of Saardsinmey had come back. It was not genuine, or even entire, for through it he thought quite cleanly: This was a substitution, a surrogate, scapegoat for the unbearable itch of hatred.

The crimson comets seared by, going out like old wine in the abyss beneath. How far might they fall?

The two men, strong lungs still lined by a little air, forgetful, eager to renew their contact now as two lovers separated, drove forward, slammed into each other, grasped, would not let go.

Kuzarl, his mouth stretched in a grimace like joy, started to rip, to gouge, to *dismantle* his enemy. But Rehger, speedlessly, with a terrible expressionless power, had commenced to wring, with one arm alone, the last of the air from the Shansar's lungs. The left arm of the Shansar was pinned. He had discovered it to be so, and redoubled the efforts of the right arm—but Rehger now had the right arm also, and propelled it, slowly, graciously, aside and backward—

The awful complaint of this right arm, rotated from its orbit, almost from the socket, penetrated Kuzarl's madness only in order to heighten his murderous frenzy—but a kind of screaming, part berserk fury, and part sheer pain, shot his lungs of the last air. His

ribs caving under Rehger's crushing vice, a helpless
spasm, like a ghastly hiccupping, sucked the water in
instead.

All at once the Shansar was suffocating. Drowning.

He floundered, began to struggle, the gargantuan
vitality of the berserker state beating like gavels—on
the obduracy of bronze.

Rehger, his own vision blackened, his own lungs
seeming to have collapsed flat as the rent skins of
drums, held Kuzarl like a huge, fighting, insane child.
Which grew sleepy, which ceased, inch by inch, second by second, to fight. . . .

Locked together, idly revolvingly, they were gliding
now down and downward.

Rehger felt the heavy head loll against him, the
legs, the jeweled hands flexible as weeds—felt but
could no longer see. And now could no longer feel.

He thrust against the water, to regain the in-jutting
of the channel, the rocks and roots which all this while
had grazed against him, falling. Rehger, holding Kuzarl
now solely by the princely buckle of his belt, hauled
them both, lightly cumbersome, unseeing, unreal, in
a miasma or shadow, against the channel side. Using
its leverage, Rehger launched himself, and the dead-
weight weightlessness of Kuzarl, *upward*—

Darkness. Of water, sight, mind. There was no end
to the dark, or the shadow. To the water, no end.
Subsurface, the channel must have spread. They were
in under the rock, buried, in a stone river.

Whiteness blasted across his face. The air shrilled
into his lungs like knives. He could not make them
take it, and then—could not get enough.

Vision was senseless— They were still inside the water. Vertically now, it lanced upon him. Rain. And the
fire was out.

Under the rain, and the sullen sky snagged on remnants of the forest roof, Rehger rolled the Shansar on
his face and worked the river out of his chest and guts.

The blood-desire had faded as his own life ebbed. It
would have been easy to continue dropping down into
oblivion and night. But only now, surely, did he think

it easy, now when he had brought both of them back from it alive.

Kuzarl, lying breathing on his side, looked at Rehger with inflamed, gentle eyes.

"That's not the last of it," said Kuzarl Am Shansar.

The boat was gone. The Shansarian servant, the Var-Zakor—neither had reappeared. The rain fell. The sky guttered out.

Rehger did not answer Kuzarl.

Kuzarl said, hoarsely, "The Three Ordeals, to find out guilt or innocence, or the victory, or the essence of what must be. Fire, water, steel. Not always in that order. The hero Raldnor passed through them. The steel of the assassin. Tempest. Volcano."

"Save yourself," said Rehger. "We've some way to go yet, I imagine."

"I don't speak of facts, but of truths."

"Shansar truths."

"The Fire Ride— That was the fire, repeated here, you and I. And for you the fire in the sea, like Raldnor, and the wave that had your slave-city—an ordeal of water. And steel, every one of your duels before the mob. But one more time, the steel, with me." Kuzarl was not yet properly returned to his body to be quelled by its discomfort.

Rehger said: "On your terms, I killed you in the river. You're bested. Your reptile goddess gave you to me."

Rehger's eyes, and face, were composed. He spoke without malice or gluttony.

But Kuzarl said, "You killed me and restored me. You kept me for the steel, as she kept you."

"Anackire."

"*Anackire.*"

"If she exists, your goddess, if she is what your people and her own people say, if she is Everything, if she is all places and times, this land, this weather, all men, you, and I, then we're much to be blamed, Shansarian. We botched the world. We made it ill and wrongly, and deserve the disaster and the misery of it. Get up. Let's get on wherever you reckon we're going. If your philosophy's accurate, what does it matter?"

But Kuzarl only nodded and rose to his feet quite steadily. His jewelry had ceased to shine, but his eyes had become once again polished, luminous amber.

"Why do the children play games?" said Kuzarl. "Isn't it unkind and unbecoming to prevent them, even when they bruise their limbs or sometimes hurt their companions. Children must play. And why should we think so?"

Rehger only waited. Kuzarl gestured indolently upriver, westward.

Through the rain, the burnt charcoal fringes of the forest, along the riverbank, westward, they went.

The tangle of trees, miles and days beyond the fire, shut the river. Only the pinnacles of the mountains sometimes showed. They seemed intrinsic not to the earth, but to the sky.

It was possible to snare lizards in the muddy, silty places which the river had left behind. The water which was available was full of salts. In preference, they sliced the stems of ferns and drank their sour vegetable milk.

The now-and-then visibility of the mountains, the passaging of daylight, guided them west.

Aside from necessities, they did not speak.

Their individual endurance and rate of progress was not competitive. They had been welded into a bizarre union. As if by prearrangement, if not the plan of Anackire, all else was removed from them, and there was at last no doubt that a goal existed and would be achieved. Despite the brawl under the river, neither man was impaired, or had given up his wits. The hard common sense of savagery was on them now.

In the middle of a day, conceivably the fifteenth or sixteenth after the fire (or it might have been longer), the Lydian, who was ahead of the Shansar, cut his way through the continuous forest fence into a clearing so wide its farther extremes were out of sight. It was not the conclusion of the jungles for, far off, they lifted up again into the sunlight, like mounds of a blue haze, and ghosts of the mountaintops were anchored over them, southerly, though no longer to the north.

In the clearing was a town.

Having subsisted some time on tasteless and infrequent meat and the resin of ferns, maybe the oddity of the town was simply perspective, transposed.

It had a strain of Ott, of Thaddra, too. The buildings were of mud and had grown together in the manner of a hive. Carving stuck out of the thatches. Wooden birds roosted there, perhaps for good fortune. Then one of these carvings shook its feathers. A flightless fowl was tending its nest. The town seemed to have no proper relation to the jungle-forest. Its people did not stare at the two travelers, only gave them occasional glances.

In a square was a market, where they were able, surprisingly with coins, to get food.

At one side of the square, regardless of other business, a custom of Ott went on, a Death Feast, at a long table. In the seat of honor, embalmed and dressed in its best, the cadaver sat overlooking the feasters with indigo eyelids. The Otts toasted the deathshead and invited passersby to quench their thirst; Rehger and Kuzarl were among these. The beer was potent. Nothing, in any case, seemed truly curious to them, or real.

As dusk came on in a preface of light, a red star appeared in the wide dome over the clearing. It was the first night of Zastis.

"Still the fire," said Kuzarl.

They were seated on a tavern roof, under the awning woven of leaves. An outrider of a night breeze tried the awning, feathering the leaves, the movement of a wing. They might have lived in the town many years.

Down in the square, the funeral had just disbanded. The figure of Death, a man dressed as a woman, and all in white, had appeared to lead the dead away for burial, with happy songs and jests.

Kuzarl's blond head was back, to gaze at the Star. "Your Zastis doesn't trouble my kind. They have no special hunger. All Shansars will tell you so, as they rush for the brothel door. No, no. Transparent lust is the mark of the Vis."

Rehger watched the last of the funeral party. The stirring in his blood was remote, but he had been aware of it for days, realizing the season. He was accustomed to containment, or to the alternatives of action. The combat in the river, even so long ago, had been tinged by some premonition of the Star.

"Zastis is a love-house of the Vis gods," said Kuzarl, "set on fire and burning forever in the skies." Kuzarl might have been drunk. Both men might have been so. "Or," said Kuzarl, "Zastis is one of the mysterious flying chariots of the Lowlanders, or of the Dragon-Kings of the Vis. Combusted, flaming magic, unable to go out, its erotic radiation sprinkling the earth like scarlet snow—"

"If you want a woman," said Rehger, "go and find one."

"See there," said Kuzarl.

Across the rosy twilight roofs, another roof, not far away. There were two women on it, one dressing the other's hair. This apparition gleamed in the gathering dusk, for though the women were smoky-skinned, their long tresses had been bleached. The seated one had noticed Kuzarl's scrutiny. She smiled to herself and looked away. The other continued the hairdressing, but also she began to sing in a low cindery voice.

To get to the women's thatch was no difficulty, since almost all the roofs ran into each other at one point or another.

The women welcomed them courteously, like old friends of the family. They were very modest, nearly bashful. The dialect prevented much verbal commerce.

The younger girl Kuzarl took down the stair. Rehger lay on the roof with the elder, in a nest of straw, under the stars which seemed to expand and spill across the eventual roof of night.

"These people never go north or west, they insist. They don't pry into the limits of the jungle. Somewhere is the sea. But who can reach it? The forest closes on the traveler and eats him up. Only phantoms come back. Mine whimpered me a story of that, and frightened herself so I had to comfort her."

"Nevertheless," said Rehger, "this town uses coins."

"There are other settlements in the mountains, north, and east," said Kuzarl. "So they say. Traders go about from petty kingdoms of Thaddra, lost Zakor and Dortharian outposts."

"And the fabulous city. Have they heard of that?"

"If they hear, they never listen."

They stood at the town's border, where the graveyard was. The tombs were of raised impacted mud. Creepers and flowers grew over them. The stacks looked cheerful and careless, and where they had given way, the flowers only bloomed more exuberantly.

"The city," said Kuzarl, "is lapped in jungle, between this country and the coast. I begin to dream of Ashnesee. Did I mention, that is the name of it?"

Rehger said, "Describe the dream."

"White light ringed by midnight and the fire of eyes."

"You also begin to talk like a priest."

"All Shansars are priests. Priest-warriors. Today, we fight again, you and I."

"And if I kill you," said Rehger, "how will I find the way to Ashnesee?"

"Do you suppose I can lead you there?"

"She gave you directions," said Rehger. "In Saardsinmey, or Sh'alis."

"She? The Amanackire. Ah. You think that."

Past the graveyard, the forest. The sun gilded its facade, then there was blackness.

At length the Shansarian said, "You acknowledge, you are in a sort of dream, a sorcery. You say to yourself, nothing is as it appears to be."

"I understand you'd prefer I thought in this way."

"How are we to duel?" said Kuzarl. "Where shall we get swords? Shall I seek them? I might go into the woods, and take up two serpents. Each would become a blade of steel."

Rehger said, softly, "That was a trick she played on me."

"Who are you?" said the Shansarian. "Do you know yourself? Perhaps you died in Saardsinmey. Perhaps I died in the river."

Rehger turned. *"Now,"* he said.

He jumped one of the tottered grave-stacks and came at Kuzarl. Rehger had drawn the knife the council at Zaddath had given him, to replace that which Galutiyh had had. It was proved. It could hack reeds and vines, and the flesh of lizards. The customs of the stadium were nullified, even the abstaining from sex before a combat. He brought the knife lengthways across Kuzarl's ribs, and blood welled, red as only blood could ever be.

Out sparkled Kuzarl's dagger, Shalian in design, incised with a snake-fish, gems in the hilt. Kuzarl ignored the slit in his side.

Rehger stood back, waiting. When the Shansarian lashed in at him, he blocked the blows, once, twice, and dashed the man from him, disdaining to slice him again.

The sunshine rang on the land. But the fight was heavy and purposeless. Used to the fined reactions of a merciless training, Rehger found his body had become that of a stranger. It did not move as he remembered, and was itself resentful that it could not. There was, above the arena of the graveyard, no murmurous and excited crowd. There was no reason and no prize.

The Shansar rolled and plunged at him again, and again, and Rehger met the advents and the blows, beating him aside, down, and to nothing. Rehger returned the onslaught without emphasis, allowing Kuzarl to shield himself.

From the first and only wound the Shansar bled. This did not seem to disable him, and yet even he did not attack with spirit. He did not strive as he had in the river.

Rehger cast the Zaddath knife from the right to the left hand. He went forward and brought his right fist cracking against Kuzarl's jaw. As the Shansar staggered, Rehger kicked his feet from under him. Kuzarl crashed among the flowers, and the Shalian dagger flew away in a bush.

"You died in a river," Rehger said, "as you told me."

"Amrek," said Kuzarl. "Kill me or let me up to fight you."

Rehger stood over him. "Brothers in Alisaar duel for their birthright. And what's ours?"

"The world. Raldnor's quarrel. Who will possess." He reached to grip Rehger's ankle and pull him down. Rehger snapped Kuzarl's hand away with his foot.

"You're bleeding, Kuzarl. Go back to the women in the town and ask them to see to it."

"Who will possess," Kuzarl repeated. "Your race. Mine."

"Or the Amanackire. If I travel west, I'll find the city."

Kuzarl lapsed against the ground. He seemed suddenly to suffer from the gash in his side.

"I was her servant, in northern Alisaar—Sh'alis. I saw her unveiled. She was Aztira. She'd died and lived again. I lied to you." He closed his eyes against the sun, his face secretive and cunning.

"Did she say her sorcery would act on me to bring me after her?"

"She said nothing of you. She forgot you, Lydian."

"Then she only spoke of the city."

"Something of the city."

"Enough that you could find your way to it."

"Yes, yes. . . ."

"Why did you delay to do so?"

Kuzarl opened his eyes again. His face became proud, arrogant, unknowing. "This thing, and that thing. Or fate elected me your guide."

"But no longer."

Tardily, cautiously, Kuzarl sat up. He leaned on a piece of grave, and helped himself to his feet.

"Ashara-Anack," he said.

He went without haste, quite steadily (as after the river), back toward the town. He made no attempt to reclaim the costly dagger from the bushes. To Rehger, he said nothing more.

The Lydian walked through the graveyard and in under the arches of the jungle trees. The morning light was behind him, the west was represented now by the density of the forest. Soon, as Kuzarl had said that they said, the forest folded in upon him.

It was night. Night in day. There was no day. There was no direction, north or south, east or west. And in the coolness of his anger, the drunkenness of disillusion, and the clarity of the dark, he gave himself then to fate, or to Anackire, or to the will and the after-image of the woman, Aztira.

Nothing seemed alive in the forests now but for himself and the enormous growing trees. Although there was great heat and moisture. When he was thirsty, which was not often, he drank from the sweating leaves.

He went on until an incredible tiredness dragged him to the earth. Then he slept, and when he woke, went on again.

Childishness entered into him. He had towered among men, but here in the endless night of the trees, his identity was valueless.

If he had measured time, it might have been five days later that he came on the pillar.

Its paleness, or some other thing, caused it to glow in the ebony forest. It matched the tallest trunks to their topmost heights, eighty feet, or a hundred. Coming near, you saw the figures of birds and cats, dragons and serpents, carved into the pure white stone.

Beyond the pillar, straight as a knife-cut through the forest, ran an unpaved track, two chariot-lengths across. Nothing blurred the track, or had rooted in it. It went into distance, until the darkness smoothed it away. Without a doubt, it led somewhere. It led to the ultimate hallucination, the Amanackire city. *Ashnesee.*

BOOK SIX

ASHNESEE

CHAPTER TWENTY

DEATH AND LIFE

It was a place of blackness, of untextured night sleeker than water. But out of the black sprang a flame.

And the flame gathered itself, and grew.

The flame became flesh.

Became a woman of unnatural height, white as the snow upon a mountain.

A white body, and eight white arms stretched in rays . . . beneath, the torso ended in the tail of a great snake; the coils like alabaster, scalloped by scales that gleamed faintly, as they ceaselessly stirred.

Far above, framed by a snow-cloud of hair which was also a whirlpool of serpents (twisting, spitting to her shoulders); a pale face, set with a devouring stare of colorless ice. Or colorless fire.

Aztira's face.

Then the sheen of her became unbearably effulgent—and went out.

Only the untextured blackness remained, sleeker than water.

The moon was rising as she left the temple. The Star was already aloft, and west and east the sky was a clear magenta, deepening into night only at the zenith.

From the height of the temple terrace, the young woman had an encompassing vantage of the city, spread around and about her down to its ring of walls. Outside these walls the flattened landscape had swum into nothingness. The city itself had the look of an artifact, a small assembly of carven buildings on the board of some Vis war game. The Star and the stained moon dyed it like a fiery bone.

331

The girl abandoned her height, descending a broad paved stairway between garden slopes of sculpted trees, basins and arcs of water.

Her whiteness glimmered in the hot dusk, if not so emphatically as in the temple. That which she had created there, on the altar, the image of Inner Self symbolized as the goddess, had probably been witnessed, though not a sigh penetrated the sanctum. It was to her a spiritual exercise, a condition of life, similar to the walk she took, morning or evening, through the wide avenues of Ashnesee, or across the plain beyond, where the wind blew sometimes warm and saline from the jungle-forests, or a slinking tirr might come to mouth her footsteps or rub its nightmare head, in abasement, on the dust. She need have no fear of tirr, and in the city of her kind, she was foremost among equals.

At the bottom of the temple terraces, two men of the Amanackire stood beneath a cibba tree, maybe by design, to look at her. Their whiteness, like hers, shone in the umbra of tree and night.

Greetings, Aztira.

They did not speak aloud, but within. And in words only approximately.

In the same fashion, she replied, and walked on, along one of the marble roads without a name, between the pale palaces.

Silence lay on the city. Like the most primal of creatures, these people had no vocal conversation, sounds rarely escaped them. They moved with a deftness nearly noiseless. They seldom inclined to music, and perhaps never sang. Their children, few, for birth was controlled and selective among them, were as quiet as they.

The road was lined solely by palaces, with here and there an obelisk or shrine. These places, some now blooming into lamplight, were interspersed with parks and groves. There was very little else in Ashnesee. Beneath the mansions and the lawns, under the streets, the city was cut by tunnels and chambers, generally manmade, where the maintenance of everyday living went on. Ashnesee was served by slaves, and had been built by slaves. Once dark Thaddrians, Otts and Corhls, and darker Zakors, they were by now a mingled, molded race, some generations bred to their duties and their station.

After walking for the half of one hour, meeting no other, Aztira reached her house. It rose on an eminence, unwalled but moated by a mosaic courtyard. Near the stair was a tall pillared edifice, the Raldnor Shrine. From this proximity the mansion of Aztira was to be identified.

She went up the stair, over the mosaic, and through opened doors. Beyond the unlit vestibule, whose plaster was marked with dimmed pictures, lay the round painted hall of an Amanackire palace.

Ghostly lotus lamps floated on slender chains in the high ceiling. No slave had yet come to kindle them.

Aztira crossed through the hall, climbed more steps, proceeded into the braincase of a tower, a large bare room, with one large window of smoldering glass.

Before this window, which faced east, Aztira stopped. Her stillness was like that of an icon, she did not seem to breathe.

Her entire consciousness was centered at the core of her mind. She was listening, but not for any kind of sound.

In the Lowlands, a village of five huts—this was her birthplace. She was born pale-eyed, and perhaps her mother had misliked her gaze. When the child's hair began to come like silver flax, they knew, and took her to a temple.

Her parents, unremembered, and vanished in her first year, were pure yellow-fair Lowlander, accustomed to mind-speech as to need. Otherwise ignorant, solitary, fixed. From such stock the albino strain normally emerged.

Before she could walk, or talk in the verbal sense (Lowland children from the initial months were capable of a sure if eccentric telepathy), Aztira was in Hamos, that xenophobic city of the south Plains. Here she grew up among her own, those with whom she had no ties of blood, and here she was schooled, as all such children were, a process which incidentally discovered among them the most adept, the most flawlessly *Of Anackire*.

There was no love, and there was no kindness, not in that inner reach. But Aztira did not miss love or kindness, for neither was there any injustice or cruelty shown her. There could be no lies. Though educated to use the spoken language forms of Vis—and, too, of the blond Sister Continent beyond the seas—communication rested on the hundred thousand nuances of mental dialogue. It was learnt early, how to parry and to protect the insights and signals of the mind. For, unlike the merchanting telepaths of Vardath or Moih, these did not give to tactful atrophy any of their supernatural gift. The Amanackire were also children of Truth.

They were a *cold* people, so the Vis had always named them, even at the gold-haired periphery of their tribe. What need had they for warmth? Passion and effusion were the sugar and salt with which the mind-blinded spiced the turning meat of their relationships. What the Amanackire desired they asked, and what they would not render they refused. Now, because they had grown powerful and self-sufficient, because their legend had imbued all Vis, because they were coming to believe that they were gods, they did not hanker after human things.

What was ambition? If wanted, advantage might be taken. And what was love . . . a carnal urge that in the Lowlander was subject to command—or only the product of *fear*—terror of loneliness or death—which states the pure Lowlander had almost eradicated, and which the Amanackire had almost ceased to know.

For the soul continued forever. And (like a mild breeze the other intuition moved upon them), the flesh itself might be sustained.

When she was twelve, a year after she became a woman in the physical sense, Aztira had found herself capable of healing.

One of her fellows had fallen, the skin undone. Aztira knit up the skin again, and drew off the scar like smoke into the air. The motive had been the empathy of startled pain. The fount, herself. To heal was native to her. In fact, she had effected some slight cures before, not understanding what she did.

There were other abilities. In Hamos, especially the inner enclave of Hamos, they were a normalcy.

In the Women's House, which Aztira had now entered, leaving the fostering of her guardians—never anything resembling kin—Aztira practiced the psychic lore of the antique temples. She unbound in herself those arts that—outside, Vis-over—were the tricks of magician-priesthoods, and the substance of myth.

She was aware of the other universe beyond the stones and seals of her Lowland city. Sometimes she saw actual Vis, the beings of this outcast world. They were as alien to her as she to them, in appearance and attitude. She was used to her own kind. The darkness of the Vis perturbed her, even. She had been taught these dark races were the lords of the planet once, in a time which had itself succeeded an earlier unlike era. She recognized the Vis as mortal.

A priestess of a clandestine sanctuary, a scholarly, wise child, she reached her seventeenth year in Hamos, having experienced nothing else. She had had three lovers, perused a multitude of books, unleashed in her body powers that neither alarmed nor distorted her notions of self. She had grasped the fundamental meaning of that which was called *Amanackire*.

Although there was positive sexual differentiation among the Amanackire, there was no submission to gender. In prior history, the Lowlands had upheld a matriarchy. While such as Moih now aped the Vis way, ruled by councils of males, the center of Hamos was a council comprising male and female proportionally.

Before this council, Aztira was summoned. She was just seventeen, having no fears or doubts on the matter of anything.

She was among the most adept of the Amanackire at Hamos, and the moment had arrived when the existence should be made known to her of Ashnesee.

In an amorphous, telepath's way, she had already

intercepted atmospheric currents to do with the City
of the West.

Now they told her, in solid terms of geography and
building and hidden routes. The abstraction was given
dimensional reality. Ashnesee was a city and a kingdom. It was, moreover, an intention. Once before, the
temporal power of the Lowlanders had been thrown
down. Presently Amrek the Genocide would have
crushed all trace of them from the earth. Amrek's
memory, shunned where possible among the Vis, had
survived in black freshness with Aztira's people: He
was enthroned in their mythos beside the messiah,
Raldnor. For where Raldnor had been the life-granting
spring of Anackire, Amrek was the anti-life. They
were, in the being of the Balance, one thing. As the
people of the Plains now resumed a former name on
the tongue of Vis—*the Shadowless*—so Amrek was the
Shadow. And, if he had gone, body and ego, into the
past, yet his elemental presence was retained in the
old hatred, the antipathy between races. In New Alisaar,
broken in all but material dues from the conqueror
Shansars, and in Free Zakorian Ylmeshd to the northwest, and in Dorthar itself, the shining hub of Vis,
which in embracing the godhead of Anackire had de-
graded and corrupted her to an idol—there and other-
where, the Shadow sifted and slunk, and stretched
itself. In every honey skin and skin of bronze and jet,
in every skein of sable hair and every darkened eye—
there, the Shadow was, and waited.

Against this, Ashnesee had been raised.

A fortress. A graven image of another thing, which
only *was*. A sword of snow. The exacting completing
second half of the endless Balance. A serpent all whiteness poised upon its tail.

Into herself Aztira accepted Ashnesee, the voluntary conception of a child.

The idea had a symmetry not one of her race could
deny.

The very name itself, worked a magic within her,
like the melody of that sleeping sea she had also only
heard of. It was the true name of the oldest city of her

kind—Ashnesea—the rusted blade left lying south of
south on the Plains.

Slaves of the Vis race had been herded to the building of this reincarnation of Ashnesee. It lay innermost
in the thick fur of the dark beast's back, the jungles of
the northern west. And close to malignant hating
Zakoris. Yet further particles of Balance.

To Ashnesee then, would Aztira go? It was offered
to her as a quest at the moment her youth itself might
have been craving one.

For Ashnesee was to be sought. As, long ago, some
had sought Ashnesea.

A month later, Aztira left by the north gate of her
city, alone and on foot, which was how the Amanackire
mostly traveled.

In Xarabiss, she was stared at. It was summer, and
there were crimson flowers on the land like a daylong
sunset. The peasants came to offer her fruit or bread,
little basins of broth or wine, with a garland arranged
at the brim. (What she required, she accepted.) In the
cities they made way for her, soldiers pushing the
crowds aside. At hostelries and inns, the best chamber
was at once allocated, but as a rule she chose the
open, where they would place an awning on a roof or
in a garden. She was never disturbed. The busy, loud-
clashing crystal cities of Xarabiss passed as if on wheels.
They were none of them her city of the Plains.

In the narrow land of Ommos, in theory a Lowland
possession, if not much cherished and barely kept, the
journeying girl elicited terror and aversion. In the
towns, no one would look at her, they skulked or ran
away. Ommos itself was considered ugly Vis-over. Coming on a party of mixes on a shore, she took passage in
their ship to Dorthar.

Dorthar she did not amaze.

At the first town she was greeted with ceremony
and gifts, and refused them. Unshaken, they offered
her the use of a traveling chariot, chariot-animals, and
a driver bowing to the street. She had come all that
distance a pedestrian, preferring it, undaunted, having
no need for the security of wagon or servant, her

physical vivacity, that looked so fragile, stronger than
the strength of a healthy man. But she did assume the
chariot for a little of the journey. She was curious to
see the city of Anackyra.

Again, on the open road (now a paved highway), a
delegation accosted the Amanackire. Men in gold trim
and heavy ornaments who asked, under their goddess-
banners, if she desired escort, who inquired if she
wished to meet with the Storm Lord—he would, they
promised, receive her with pomp. She put them right,
there. She had no interest in their High King, the
mixed-blood bastard descendant of Raldnor, and though
she did not speak of it in that way, that was the way
they took it from her, without a flicker or a risen
brow.

Under a dragon comb of mountains, Anackyra demonstrated streets of hammered marble, many Anackire
temples of bare-breasted golden harlots, bleached-hair
Dortharians, prosperous Vathcrians, and tall, brazen
Vis.

Having to address her, from the princes in their
chariots to scrabbling rabble by the gutters, it was with
the title *Priestess*, but now and then, *Goddess*.

She lived a year in Dorthar, up in the hills between
Anackyra and the ruins of ancient Koramvis. A lord
had made over a villa to her, the nobility had been
jostling to do it. Mix slaves waited on her. Tame
pigeons nested in the feather trees, but the kennel of
hunting kalinx the lord had removed—the Amanackire
Goddess had no inclination to venery.

If any white Amanackire were her neighbors in these
regions, they did not reveal themselves, and were not
spoken of.

There was an importance to Dorthar, and to the
dissimilar twin cities—the ruin above, the rebirth below. One adjourned here, to absorb the psychic smol-
der, or to pay some obscure respect to it.

This spot was a well of Power, deep and unstable as
the earthquake-faulted strata of the land.

Aztira compared it to the being of the other spot,
the gamepiece of the Amanackire, which by then, like
a tiny muffled light, was a beacon in her brain. Ashnesee

had been erected solely upon *ground*. There was no
reservoir of mystic and violent energy beneath. In
itself, that was significant enough.

All this time, the time of traveling and resting, no
part of Aztira had faltered. None of her beliefs was
shaken or changed. These mortal Vis were alien, and
interested her less than their monuments. Fearing nothing, knowing herself mightier, and awarded everywhere homage, she did not query her supremacy. And
when she glanced inwardly toward the beacon of the
City of the West, it did not trouble her any more than
the sea and the forests which coiled it round.

After that year of pause breathing in the airs of
Dorthar, Aztira traveled again. She went down the
coast in the other direction, south by ship from Thos,
and crossed to Shansarian Alisaar. (She found Shansarian reverence like that of other countries, and their
unease also quite comparable.)

She was approaching the age of nineteen, in Sh'alis,
when the slow mental breakers from the west altered
their tempo.

Her leisurely meandering was leading her always to
Ashnesee, and thus in a manner Ashnesee had already
claimed her. She was only a filament straying from
and to the kernel of its thought and plan. Otherwise,
having no necessity to reach outward, she had fed her
eyes and ears, her moods, but never explored analyti-
cally anything of the real and ordinary life of mankind
which everywhere fermented. Yet suddenly, for no
apparent reason, as if she had put her hand upon a
pulse in the body of some statue—she felt the genuine
aliveness of the world and of its mass of peoples,
surging and whirling on every side. And only then she
learned how Ashnesee had also felt this surge and
whirl.

Like a beast rousing from fathomless sleep, Ashnesee
had lifted its lids and distended its nostrils—

The white serpent, waking. . . . As Aztira sensed
the terrible invading threat of living mass pulsing,
boiling against her, Ashnesee long ago had sensed it.
And Ashnesee the serpent was gathering itself.

For the first hour in all her days, Aztira was over-

come by a featureless, awful doubt. She did not see
what it was, for it was so unusual.

In the burning starlit nights of northern Alisaar, the
goddess-girl, unable to compose herself for sleep, paced
up and down the courts and passages of a house some
Shansarian aristocrat had given her. Her own instinct,
feeling the ambivalent clutch of external life, was to
thrust it off, trample it. The woken instinct of Ashnesee
was like her own.

The sword-snake yearned to strike a warning, ward-
ing blow.

As she comprehended her own skin on her bones,
the flowing hair that clothed her head, so with Ashnesee, now.

What Ashnesee willed, she must will, for the will
was corporate, indivisible.

Linked with this power, some sensation never before experienced entered her marrow. It was both
physical and spiritual. It had no name, but it shamed
her, and this led her at length to suppose it was, itself,
shame.

A Shansar prince with Karmian graces, who had
religiously sent her wines and flowers and jewels, was
going down to the south, to vaunting "Free" Alisaar.
A chariot race, famous and notorious, drew him there.
Most of his Shalian household would go with him, and
quantities of horses.

Aztira informed the man, Kuzarl, she would travel
with him but without display. Falling on his knees, he
told her such a commission was an honor.

She did not know why impulse drove her south, to
Saardsinmey, a city by the ocean. Infallibly, her psychic's prescience thrust her forward. She obeyed herself, for in the past she had always been able to rely on
what she was.

New Alisaar loathed white Lowlanders and demanded
money (Kuzarl's), and sneered behind its fingers, but
was also afraid.

Aztira subtracted funds but only one servant from
Kuzarl, a mix girl with tawny eyes. Aside from this,
Aztira, in the coastal city, broke free of Kuzarl en-

tirely. He was cleaving to her, although she had not
lain with him, as if he were her lover—protective,
possessive. He brought pearls to lave her feet and she
directed him at once away.

During the last piece of journey out of Sh'alis, riding in a curtained litter, Aztira had given herself,
doubtfully, to inner conflict.

It came to her she traveled beneath a shimmering
blade. It came to her that, like a cipher of vengeance,
she herself would be the precursor of the storm.

Saardsinmey was the target of the Amanackire sword.
An upsurge of Vis arrogance was typified in it. What
could be more suitable than to destroy such a thriving
boast. Nothing need be threatened or claimed. The
message of the act, even if received without knowledge would, on other levels, be understood exactly by
every consciousness of Vis. And the Sea of Aarl swept
the beaches of Saardsinmey, an oceanic earthquake
zone with cellars of somnolent fire. . . . Walking about
the streets of the ruby-tiled metropolis, the urge was
on her repeatedly to smite them with hand or mind—
For this she had come, to revel in aversion and foresight.

She dressed in white and veiled her white hair in
whiteness. And surrendered herself to the flaming sweet
tumult of pride, going up and down a city of the living
dead.

The racial hysteria grew in her like a poison until it
almost seared her out. She had not thought to resist or
to question. She went on watching and waiting on the
first intimations of destruction. Only then could she
take her own departure. She must see it begin.

And in this heightened state, this sort of ecstasy, she
started to hear a name, over and over. Even Kuzarl
had uttered it. It was the name of a god—that was,
one of the mortal gods of the mortal Vis.

The Lydian, they said. The Lydian, Lydian, Lydian.

Everything had been elevated or compressed to symbols by now, in her delirium of Power. So she regarded the virtue of this name, and said to it: The city
makes you its soul. Then, the Lydian *is* Saardsinmey.

And she thought, *He will die in the doom of the city, this man.*

And she started to seek him out, but in a dream. She did not, in fact, set eyes on him. Nevertheless, suddenly, in some supernatural manner, she found him. In the slang of Vis she was a sorceress. She "looked" at Saardsinmey's Lydian, and "saw."

Scattered across the world, probably, there might be others, the brood of palace women and freed slaves. Yet here, at this node of history, an ultimate of symbols had occurred. The death of the boastful city could encompass a death of the bloodline of the Genocide.

Saardsinmey, the Lydian: Amrek, the Shadow.

She witnessed only a moment of the famous race, from a balcony near the end of Five Mile Street—the chariots tore down the night in a molten river, torchfire and screaming, and were gone.

He would be the victor. She had already judged that.

Purchased outside an inn, by an alley, two birds slain for a supper. Galvanized from corruption by her white hands, she sent them where she had learned they would be noted, for the Lydian.

Victory is transient. Since he is, tonight, your city, tell him this.

Earthquake had spoken before she did, out at sea, a promise. The sword in the starry sky and she its messenger—

That had been the apex of her flight.

Immediately after, she plunged to the nadir below.

She, too, was to die in Saardsinmey.

Not in the cataclysm. For her, it would be sooner.

She woke in a lucid dawn, aware. (The pink petals of sunrise glimmered on her couch, as she lay in the old house behind the lacemakers, by the street they called Gem-Jewel. . . .)

The unheard bellow of the city's gathering death had obscured the lower crying that was her own.

She was not yet nineteen. She struggled and beat death away, there in her mind, in dawn and silence, alone. But the huge black hawk came down again

upon her heart, and settled there, folding its wings.
And she accepted.

She beheld then in a bright fragment, how it was to
be, and that it came through him, her ending—the
Lydian, the Shadow. He was her death, and, strangely
she was his—but his *life*, also.

In a trance she rose and went about her day as ever,
and when the evening stooped on the streets she walked
out unguarded, on foot, and chanced on the means.
As she had known she should.

The means was the carriage of a stadium dancer, a
coal-black Zakorian. (The Balance, always that, dark
with pallor.)

"The Lydian . . . tell me how he's to be come at."

The Zakor girl fenced a while. Her brain snarled
and veered, and with no effort Aztira read it.

"Thank you," said Aztira, like a killing snow.

And under the columned midnight arches near Sword
Street, she lingered, and saw him stride out into the
eye of the lamp. Rehger, the Lydian.

In him there was a completeness, to her gaze obvious at once. The savagery of leopard and lion, the
gentleness of doves, the calm of deep water, the edge
and might of fire. Yet, something unfinished too, something awry. The life had begun—but not moved in its
allotted course. Like a star wrenched from its sky. Oh,
the star blazed— She was pierced by the brilliancy of
him, burnt.

Amrek—Vis—mortal—bronze almost to black—out
of the Shadow, the light.

*For myself, I loved you, from the moment I saw you
I believe*.

Though he denied her, he would come to her.

And though she conceded it was now inevitable, she
had forgotten death.

*(Aztira stood like an icon before the glass window in
the tower at Ashnesee. The moon had ascended to the
roof. Beyond the city and the walls, the plain was a sea
of night.)*

They were lovers then, life with death mingling. She
has won him to her by priestly trickery, in the childish
wickedness of her delirious desire, herself half-hypno-

tized by the acceptance of fear. She had won him by death-dealing. (She saved Chacor, their victim, that she should owe the Corhl nothing. She had brought the boy back from the blow of Rehger's sword as she would have led an animal from some crumbling pit into which it had strayed, frightened by her voice.) She was in three conditions—shame, hubris, love. She was flung from each height into another or into an abyss, and all this she showed Rehger plainly, not in the telepath's way, but in the woman's.

Finally, she was able to become with him only that, a woman. A blissful peace enveloped her. The battle was done. Fatalistically, she dismissed the destiny of the city, and did not listen to the footfall of her own particular death.

Even so, she detected it.

Then—she saw how the pattern might be resolved, and how—in the jaws of a whirlwind—her dying should stay Rehger for life.

She bought Panduv's tomb. (Black for whiteness.)

Panduv would survive; Aztira knew it, just as she knew the milk that day had venom in it. She had paid well for her own murder, coins for lilies and bane. She had consented.

And even as she penned her letter to him, to her lover and her love, she had gloried in her Amanackire Power, which held pain far off. She had exalted that she no longer dreaded to die. And, lying down softly on the couch, she had cast herself adrift, as it seemed into a tremendous nothingness, like slumber, sensuous and enfolding.

He would live through her, he could not forget her, now. She had left behind a shrine of gold and silver and could go to sleep.

But, ah—what came after—

"*No,*" she said aloud, the woman at the window.

The horror which had been, there in the black tomb, empty and swilled by water, this she resisted, would not recollect. Her exclamation, charged with her will, started a soundless vibration in the tower room.

Now across the night, beyond the window, the terraces of the city, the walls, the slopes of earth and darkness, her lover hunted her. It was not that she had called to him, or even that he could have heard her, the beating of her heart, the susurrus of her mind, here in the forests at the land's western brim.

They were perhaps condemned to meet again because of what they were, because each furnished for the other a spectral landmark in the chaos.

To the traveler, the track, beaten so flat and lacking obstacles, was the business of a couple of days. During the midafternoon of the second day, he came to a clearing, unlike any other clearing previously encountered. The forest, primeval, architectural, seething with profound animation, was curtailed as a shore would end against water. To the limits of keen vision, this curtailment stretched. While beyond the brink there was a plain.

To any who had seen them, the plain resembled, here in the womb of the jungle-forest, the bare rolling flanks of southernmost Vis: The Lowlands, south of Moih. They had weathered, it was true, rather differently in an altered climate, these alter-Plains. Their tones were more sonorous, richer, and here and there an island of ripe vegetation rode on them, or postings of the forest itself.

Where the surge of the forest and the line of the track stopped, and the lake of the plain commenced, was an arch on pillars, seventy feet in height, carved as a game-figure, white as the straight blade of the road, five chariot-lengths in width, that ran away beneath.

The road was paved with large dressed blocks. In a city of Dorthar, Karmiss, Xarabiss, Alisaar, the road would not have been a phenomenon.

Marching beside the road at intervals were obelisks of white marble, with crests of gold-leaf, catching sun.

There was not a mark on the road. It was new-made, an hour before, it seemed. Nothing had ever gone over it. Not a wheel or a hoof, not a footstep, a lizard, a bird, a leaf, a wind.

Narrowing in perspective, it pointed to a low mountain rising from the plain perhaps seven or eight miles

away. In the manner of mountains, the top of the crag
was lit by snow: The city.

The city.
It had been raised on a platform of rock, and the lit
snows of its crags were towers and the heads of walls.
The sun struck down on it, and crystals flashed from the
mirrors of huge windows. In size, it was itself not vast.

The road roused up into a high causeway, but where
the causeway came against the platform of the city,
there appeared, from the plain below, to be no gate or
entry. The face of the platform was sheer.

A wood of trees, also like the arboreal stations of
the Plains, had collected at the roadside, before it
gained the incline to the causeway. Here Rehger left
the paving, and from this area he watched as the
westering sun got over the platform, and a brass sunset turned the whiteness of the city black.

The city did not seem real. It had about it, or
appeared to have, some of the imagery of legendary
Dortharian Koramvis, which Raldnor had broken in
bits.

A wind blew east over the plain, once all the day
was out. It was warm and silken-heavy, smelling of
farther jungles where the sun had fled and fallen. The
wind brought no perfume and not a note or murmur.
Zastis was rising.

The Star had also sprinkled red lights along the
surface of the plain. They blinked and flickered, like
luminous nocturnal roses. But it was a black wave of
red eyes which was blowing now, as the wind had
blown along the earth.

It would be possible for a man to climb a tree of the
wood, but they, too, could— Besides, their dreamlike
slowness checked him. Their odor was not as he remembered it from the menageries of Alisaar. In Moih,
Chacor, but not Rehger, had hunted them. And once,
as a child in Iscah, he had been snatched up by Tibo,
as Orbin sprinted before them, and his mother's braids
stung against his neck as she ran with him for the farm.

Tonight, on this surreal plain, it was a pack some

fifty or sixty strong, gliding as if wafted above the ground, without stench or cry.

They washed against the wood, entered it, and turned tens of heads to look up at him with the fire-drippings of their eyes.

One put its forelimbs on a trunk, the slaughterous claws retracted.

The evil shape of the head of this single beast caused Rehger a curious puzzlement, that it should in its form prefigure so exactly what it was—

He was not especially alert, had gained none of the ebullition of danger. He had not drawn the knife, it was sheathed still, like the talons of the tirr.

Aztira. Her name had a likeness to theirs.

The Tirr that had put its forefeet on the tree dropped down again.

The wind's breaths rustled the leaves of the wood, but there was no other noise. Then there came a noise without any sound, a sort of whistling purr, in the ears, or in the skull.

The tirr pack responded. They gathered themselves away, pressed back into the trunks of trees, where their eyes did not cease glittering and winking.

Two men walked out between the tirr and the trees, shining like nacre. By mind-speech, evidently, they controlled the pack.

Rehger did not speak, or think. If the Amanackire attempted to scour his brain, he would not make it easy.

One of the two men parted his lips.

"You are approaching the city."

The other said, in the same pithless, unused voice:

"Your kind do not enter Ashnesee, except they enter as slaves."

"Ashnesee," said Rehger. Sensitized to it now, it seemed to him he felt his thoughts shoot out a bolt of anger, or great heat. "I'd heard that was one of the words for your city."

Their snake stares turned on him like sightless stones.

Outside the wood, the moon now was rising, white kindred of theirs at any time but Zastis.

They must scent his ancestry, rage—his, theirs, weaving its lines of force between them.

The first man said, "Follow."

As they walked along the road, the tirr were melting into the night, as if night had constructed them and lent them movement, and kindled their eyes like stars, and now put them out again.

CHAPTER TWENTY-ONE

THE HEARTH

The gate into Ashnesee was, for Rehger, a shrine or sarcophagus located at the base of the rock platform, below the causeway. The white men breathed on it and it opened—you heard of such devices in their temples. The aperture closed behind them.

A stair went underground, and led into a warren of man-hewn passages, dully and oddly lit both by distant torches and some faltering luminescence that seemed to have no source.

The route, at first level, then lifted itself in ramps. They emerged into a shut courtyard like a well, where the hot moon streamed in at one corner of the shaft.

The city stayed mute.

Another covered passage ran from the court, finishing at a slender door of cibba wood. The plashing of water had suddenly become audible. When the door—managed this time by touch—slid wide, rosy moonlight burst out again, crushed into the juice of a vast fountain. Its curtain, in cascading down, seemed to bar the way. But there was an interval of dry space, and through this one passed into a garden.

The white men moved ahead, ascending, not glancing back, as if mislaying the barbaric animal they had brought in with them.

Rehger, however, hesitated, to view the city of the Amanackire. It lay on three sides, rinsed by the moon and made of the moon. . . . Tiers of pillared buildings, ruled by roads like frozen rivers—and, among clusters of trees, slim groves of towers whose heads were shaped like the masks of beasts—things not quite viable. And though small cells of illumination rested there in pools, humanly lifeless, too, a necropolis, so exquisitely formed it was, and devoid of motion as of sound.

The white men had halted at the top of the garden, under the vertical of a mansion there. A tower rose here, also. It had a serpent's head burning coldly with the eye of an enormous moonstruck window.

Rehger followed the terraces up to the men under the wall.

"This is her house?"

They looked at him.

He said, "You've brought me to her. Aztira."

It was not that he had begun to read their minds. There could be nowhere else they would bring him.

One of the men pointed. (Rehger saw another gate, this of decorative iron, ajar in the white wall.) They disliked to speak aloud, when it could be avoided.

And they would let him go on alone. They did not, then, mistrust him. Or she did not. Or, whatever his scheme or temper, they had valued themselves at more.

When he made no instant move to enter through the gate, they left him, and descended the lawns.

Then, standing on the grass of her garden, in the Zastis night, he remembered the house behind the lacemakers, and how he had gone to her, there.

But Ashnesee had even a different smell, an arid and vacant air, like that above a desert ruin, tinged merely now and then with a ravenous cloy of orchids.

He put his hand on the iron gate.

He would come into the mansion by way of the door beneath the tower, where the vine clung to the stones. From this entrance, the corridor would lead him into her hall, the great blanched oval with a floor of mosaic tiles, on whose walls were paintings of low hills, and pale-robed maidens who danced, immobile, in a field of grain, all lit now by the glow of the lotus lamps above. On the hearth, which in the evenings of the cold months would sometimes blossom fire, flowers lay sprinkled, giving off a dusty sweetness. A huge coiled snake of silverwork guarded the hearth, with eyes of creamy amber. There were few other furnishings.

Aztira waited, by the hearth snake. She wore a dress the color of the girls' robes in the mural. She had no jewels.

In the quiet Rehger's progress through the house, light-footed as the padding of a lion, was audible. And that, not once did he pause.

The girl's eyes flame-flickered, but only like the eyes of the inanimate snake. If she breathed, it had remained invisible.

The heavy drape at the doorway was swung aside with a jangle of rings.

He did not stop even then, but crossed into the room, over the patterned floor. His eyes were on Aztira, and on nothing else. Even the snake did not seem to divert his attention. He strode under the lamps, and they turned him, one after another, to gold, until, perhaps ten feet from her, the advance ended.

He had arrived in the city of gods a vagabond. The glamour and the shackles of Saardsinmey were done with, two years had run away, forests had resisted and torn at him. More than ever, in the torrent of this, he had stayed, become, a king. And his black eyes fixed on her with all she remembered of their beauty, and their strength and cleanness. Such clarity was itself a power.

The girl before the hearth of flowers held out her hand to him, palm uppermost. There on its whiteness lay a triangle of tarnished metal.

"The coin your father left your mother," she said to him, "the drak which you gave me to divine. My proof, in case it is wanted."

"Proof of what?" he said.

"That I live."

"Oh, lady," he said, standing in the golden shadow, "I know that you live."

"But that I died, also?"

"Yes. That you died and woke up, and here you are. The Goddess Aztira."

She continued to extend to him Yennef's drak. He did not come to her to accept it.

She said, "I took it with me to my grave, to comfort me." But her hand sank down, closed now on the coin.

"Your kind," he said, "live forever. Why did you need comforting?"

"Since I was without you," she said.

He said nothing. He was completely still, as she was, now, and as the city itself.

Aztira said, "Hear and believe this. I foresaw my death, but that was all. I predicted murder and terminus. I entreated you to my funeral rites because I reasoned the tomb of black stone would withstand the shock and the water. There was some measure of choice for me. But I was glad, in dying, trusting you would survive."

"Thank you then for that, madam. You get no thanks from Saardsinmey."

"No," she said, "I won't bow my head and cringe before you. If I am ashamed, it is my affair. If it was evil and my sin, that, too, is mine, not a matter between us. I thought I would die—oh, the soul, yes, the soul is eternal. But body and soul are strangers to each other. I—there would be nothing more of me. You think that to return out of bodily corruption is a simple thing? You said—that I *woke*. No, Rehger. This isn't how it was. I hope you will let me tell you of it, but not yet."

"Perhaps never. Did you call me here by some witchcraft?"

"Not by any sorcery. Not by the energy of the will or mind. Only my memory of you. That perhaps did cry after you. But I see, you would not have listened."

"I was instructed to remember you. I've done so. No day or night, since Alisaar, that I failed to think of you. You stayed alive for me, Aztira, like the stink of mutilated flesh and sea filth, and a hundred sights of rubble."

"Enough," she said. "You can't kill me to blot out the crime of my race."

"It seems not."

"Would you have done so?"

He said, "In my thoughts, lady, I've slaughtered you many times. The way a Vis would crush a snake. That picture would come to me. To break your neck."

"And in these thoughts did I never in return blast you with lightning?"

Her voice had risen. She looked indeed as if she burned coldly, her whiteness livid. And suddenly, she glanced toward the wide hearth, partly lifted up one hand. And there were flames on the stones, not flowers, shooting upward to send a crash of light into the chimney, and limn her pallor (and that of the silver serpent), as if with blood.

He felt the scorch of the fire on his body, then—it cooled. Flowers scattered the hearth; the only light came down from the hanging lamps.

"And since you can never kill me, Rehger, and since apparently I'll spare you, what next?"

"In Var-Zakoris and Dorthar," he said, "the chance of this city is a cause for debate. They would like someone to go back, and tell them."

"A paid agent. As your father was."

"Did you divine that also from his coin?"

"In other ways. I had no time to tell you all I learned. But you have met with your father."

"It was the meeting with him which put me on the road to Ashnesee."

"My regrets you could," she said, "get nothing more from it."

Aztira turned. She went to the wall, to where a tree of pale ruddy leaves was painted on the plaster. She touched one of its branches, and a faint murmur passed through the wall, along the floor. In seconds, a figure came in at the hall's other doorway. Rehger had seen a goddess of the city, now he saw one of its slaves.

She was a dark woman, umber-skinned and small, clothed in a linen smock, her hair bound closely to her head. She bowed from the hips, drooping down like a thirsty plant.

Aztira said, "Here is the lord I told you of. Take him to the prepared chamber, and serve him as you were instructed."

Her tones were distant. It was not the address of mistress to slave, but of a sleepwalker to a phantom. Though chattels, the servers of Ashnesee were not, then, considered to be actual. They were only specks of a commanding brain.

The Amanackire said to Rehger, as if in another language, "Go with her. You will not be uncomfortable. Tomorrow you may depart by the same hidden route. The two men who brought you, one or other of them will come here at first light. Be ready. You have seen the City of the West has substance. Perhaps they will reward you for the discovery, in Var-Zakoris. Or say you lie. Or in returning you may be forfeited to the jungles. Understand, it was your bond with me, Rehger, that drew you here, against all odds. Not my outcry, or any magic. Your fantasy was of finding me alive and of killing me, knowing that if I had lived, to kill me would be impossible. You undertook this sullen quest because there was nothing else for you to do."

He stood and gazed on at her, unspeaking, a statue with somber, considering eyes. Behind him, shadow on shadow, the black slave-girl waited, head still bowed.

"You mourn Saardsinmey not only for its destruction, but for its false purpose, which you borrowed. Gladiator and king, your freedom would have come with death. You would have perished inside five years."

He answered then.

"So I believed."

"You had made a pact with it. But your true life, which you had chosen and begun in Iscah, was interrupted by the man who bore you away. He declared he gave you a gift of brightness, days of glory, Katemval the slave-taker. But he cut the thread of the life you planned, that which your soul had wanted—"

"I don't credit the soul's life, Aztira. You know as much."

"It was too late to recapture in Moih the ghost of that beginning," she said, paying no heed, it seemed, to his denial. "Or else the *making of things* was not the only task you had set yourself. How willingly, therefore, you abandoned that last great victory you won over the stones, in the Lowlands, your apprenticeship. To hunt instead the ghost of *me*." She moved back, slowly, drifting as if weightless, to her hearth. She said, "Go with the slave."

"Aztira," he said.

"What now?"

"If your race believes in many physical lives, do they ever fear rebirth as some man of Alisaar or woman of the black Zakorians?"

Startling him, she laughed, lightly; all her youngness was in it.

"Yes," she said, "they do fear that. They say it would be self-punishment. Why else must we maintain one body against death, but to elude this truly awful fate?" Laughter and irony faded from her. "Leave me now," she said. "You have had enough of me."

When he turned, the crumpled slave straightened somewhat and went ahead of him, into the mansion.

CHAPTER TWENTY-TWO

THE CITY OF THE SNAKE

Across the ceiling of the room, clouds had been painted on a ground of milky azure. They had no look of fundamental sky, yet, in the dusk of dawn and evening, seemed to float, while the blueness swam upward and changed, if not into ether, at least out of the condition of paint. The walls were incised with a coiling design which resolved into a serpent's head beside the door. A tap on one of its eyes caused the door to open. On the other, and there would come at once one of the slaves with expressionless faces like dark brown wood. There were high-up grills which let in air and some quantity of light, but nothing more, and there were no furnishings beyond a bed, assembled for the guest, and wound with curtains. But the insects of the jungles of Vis seldom found their way into Ashnesee. Adjoining the chamber was a room for bathing and a closeted latrine, both of which outdid the best of the rich houses in Alisaar. At night an alabaster lamp was lit on a stand of marble.

He did not make ready to leave, the morning after his arrival.

He lay in a vast cavern of sleep, such as had sometimes come on him after a race or a fight. They had known this, the creatures of the house, and let him alone. Waking at noon—the sun was up above the grills—he saw they had removed the choice, uneaten meal offered the previous night. Later, when he had brushed the serpent's eye-socket, a breakfast was brought in.

Rehger did not interrogate the slaves of the city. Like their overlords, they seemed to have no inclination to verbal speech. When one had made to taste his food, he shook his head at her and she went away. He had not supposed the sorceress would resort to drugs or toxic substances. Conceivably it was her pain or anger, or her scorn, to imply, through the slave's action, that he would think so.

The bedchamber being large and uncluttered, he took exercise there, as if he were a prisoner and had no rights to the rest of the mansion or the garden below, which they had shown him were accessible. The streets of the city were another issue. He was not forbidden them—simply, they were not alluded to in the mannerisms of the slaves.

The second night was sleepless, the gate of the vast cavern fast shut against him. Wine-red Zastis tinctured the grills. He did not ask the house of the sorceress for a girl. He did not want one of their bed-menials, however pleasing or acquiescent. He recalled the blonde Ommos-Thaddric woman, in the roof-thatch of the last village. He considered her, and when desire became unbearable, he turned his memory to the image of death in the square below, the white she-man, joking and applauding a corpse to its grave.

When the sun rose he went after all down from the upper floor of the mansion, into the outer court, and into her garden, where the city was to be seen. The inanimate bleached buildings rocked at anchor in a soft morning mist, through which beast-headed towers seemed to lift their snouts to snuff the air.

All the flowers in the garden were white, or of a diluted pastel. White pigeons were cooing in a tree, and he was able to hear the rush of the fountain that concealed the garden's lower entrance. No other sounds came up the hill. However, a quarter mile off, erected on a level with the tree of pigeons, one of the pillared buildings had put out a branch of smoke. A temple to the Lady of Snakes, maybe, where the altar fires were still kept alight, from politeness, by gods no longer needing to worship.

A voice blew quietly against his ears. Rehger did not react to it. This was how she had communicated first with him, Aztira, calling his name in his mind. Now he only felt the pressure of her attention, like a slight pressure of fingers, yet for several moments. After which, she withdrew from him like a sigh.

He continued down to an edge of the garden, where there was the girdling of a low, steep wall. Far beneath, on the misty boulevard, between the monuments, and great houses, he beheld some men and women walking, without haste, two by two, or alone. Like the city, they were all one in whiteness. Zircons flowed over a woman's wrists, a silver clasp was struck on the shoulder of a man's tunic. None of them looked up to see if any watched them from the garden's vantage. Had they done so, they might have taken him for a slave, a brawny servant of Aztira's mansion who, for some reason, was not moving in the rat-tunnels under the lawn. But doubtless they would not probe his brain to learn why this was, for he was subhuman and did not count.

(He had garnered a notion of the undercity from the invisible coming and going of the slaves, and from once or twice seeing their emergence or retreat through apertures in the plaster, pillars and stairs.)

But for the Amanackire citizens, they progressed unhurriedly over the surface, along the boulevard, and two by two or alone, vanished in adjacent thoroughfares.

Further on in the morning, on the lush hill of a park, he saw another group of them. They seemed at a kind of slow and measured play, a ritual, or a dance even. There was no music and no song.

He could recount these scenes in Zaddath, if ever he returned there.

Rehger thought of Amrek, who had meant to wipe this people off the earth's face. He stared across the city.

He had admitted, as far away as that last village in the forest, that he had no purpose remaining to him. Purposeless, he had known therefore he would reach this place.

The feeling was similar to something he had experienced in his childhood, brought out of Iscah by the man Katemval. It came back to Rehger sharp as a knife. How the child he was had wept suddenly—losing something. It was the black bitch-dog—it was the black hair of his mother—all he could properly remember, save her name, pronounced differently.

The hurt, so small and incoherent, swelled and battered under his breastbone now, trapped and bemused in his man's body.

Not Yennef, not Katemval, nor Tibo. The stadium had been parent to him, creatrix, and Daigoth, deity of fighters, acrobats and charioteers, Daigoth was his god.

But his mother had reverenced Cah, squat, bloody, and blacker than all other things. . . .

What had driven him was not pride or hate, or rage, or love. If he examined himself, it transpired that he had never validly undergone any of these states, these justifiable emotions of humankind. What motive then, for any of it?

And as he balanced on that height of the unreal yet extant city, he knew that he had lost himself forever. Rehger, like Amrek, was gone into the past.

*   *   *

She sat, almost all that long second day, her hands folded, overhearing the ebb of the struggle within him. It was her Power which made her able to do so, and made her able to endure it.

Then, when shadows had covered all her floor, she put that from her, and rising, sought him.

She loved him, but beside her love for him there was her own destiny, and that of her race. *Anackire*. She must be two women, the lover, and—his conjuration—the sorceress.

She reached the threshold of the chamber in the scattering sunset.

He stood, arrested, in the center of the room, as if he had been pacing about. He wore the clothes the slaves had brought to him, on her orders. The garments were white, as every piece of good raiment was, here. And in his thoughts a picture lay discarded, of another man in Moih, a dark Vis clad in white for his wedding. (Who this man was she could not tell.)

"Zaddath, or Dorthar," she said, "will want to hear all you can tell them of my city."

Were his eyes empty, now? Their blackness seemed to have no depth—like two shutters of burnished iron.

"Come with me," she said mildly. "Tonight something may happen in Ashnesee that will be of interest to the councils of Zakoris and the Middle Lands."

"You know so much of me," he said. His voice was empty, surely. "Everything."

"Nothing, my dear. Nothing at all. I don't know if you revile me still."

All she could decipher now, there in this room of her palace, was the sea-change in his perception. Rollers poured and thundered on the beach. Below, his meditation had become unformed but constant, and like that of a child grown very old.

"You're inviting me to go with you into the streets of your city," he said presently, gravely. "If that's your wish. Yes, goddess."

"Goddess. You haven't been tainted by the superstitions of fools."

"Now I have."

"Rehger," she said.

"But I don't recognize that name you give me," he said, "that man, that Lydian. He was done for in Saardsinmey. Your lesson, which I have learnt."

"You misunderstood—" she cried, blindly and suddenly, the liar and lover, now. And at that he moved to her and gently put his hand, curving, quiet, against her face. She remembered so well the warmth, the strength and self-restraint of his formal caresses, the peerless grace of the lion taking her up like a leaf, not to damage her—

She thought, woman's thought: *What have I done?* She said, "You suspect you will not return to Zaddath with your news."

"It seems unlikely. But I'll go with you now, Aztira."

She put her own hand against his, and drew away. She closed her heart, and said, "You must walk a step or two behind me. Pardon me, that I ask you to do it."

"Of course." He smiled at her. She saw that he was serene. He had surrendered. This was the dignity of the king borne to the public scaffold—again it was she who must rein in wildness and lament.

"No one," she said, "will think you a slave. We seldom keep secrets in Ashnesee. Some are already aware of the guest of my house. Even to his bloodline. Seeing you, the knowledge will run like fire among them. This isn't dangerous in itself."

"No."

"But you may feel the lash of it. You're able to shield yourself."

"I know that, too."

"An unusual ability in a Vis. The line of the first Storm Lord, Rarnammon, boasts a Lowland strain. Now entirely debased among the Dortharians."

She walked before him down through the mansion.

At the higher grills and windows, the sunset massed hard, glistening scarlet. Yet, emerging from the vestibule, the west lay over behind the city, more suavely dyed, a flush of amber soaked on silk. The shrine exactly below the house snared the sun on its lid of gold. The rest was darkened like a cloud.

The woman descended the terraces and turned east.

Her whiteness blazing on the dusk, she preceded him
along the nameless roads of Ashnesee.

A stairway of stone led into the shallow valley.
Night had already gone down into it, and filled the
bowl of grass and trees as if with smoke. The towers
rose out of the dimness, gleaming, their peculiar cupo-
las, which were the heads of kalinx and tirr, the slender muzzles of dogs or the hooked visages of birds,
blushed like copper. These staring masks had pairs of
eyes, crystal windows, each balefully holding the dying
sun.

White among the groves, the Amanackire had gathered. There were perhaps two hundred of them, which
might be the sum of their numbers in the city. A
minority were children, or adolescent. Mostly they
looked to be between twenty and thirty years, at the
commencement of long adult life for a Vis, the peak
maturity of the Lowlander. There were no old ones.
Men and women mingled, as the children mingled
with the rest, no person or group adhering to another.
And their faces, which were, every one, flawless and,
if analyzed, beautiful, were as blank as the cut marble
faces of the beast-towers, or even of the bred slaves
with skins of wood and eyes of mud.

Lamps shone from some of the trees, and stars were
coming out, and the big Star itself had got over the
rim of the valley sky, red in redness, like a ruby in
wine.

Aztira reached the top of the stairway, and Rehger,
behind her.

And all the Amanackire, Children of the Goddess,
lifted their heads to see, reminding him of the tirr that
guarded the plain outside the city.

He did not need mentally to hear the inquisition
that washed murmuring through the groves, like ur-
gent ripplings over a pool. Nor how it brimmed against
the girl who had brought him here. What answer she
gave he did not know. He let the fluttering, saturating
needles furl in about him, bore with them, a rock in a
tide. *Amrek*. Perhaps this was the demon they summoned, or it was more subtle, more dreadful. If they

were conscious of him as a man he did not guess. He
was All-Vis, to them. But to himself, only granite, and
their sea of intellect and magic, sweeping over and
about, was unable to do more.

After a while the sea furled away again and left him
alone.

Then Aztira started to go down the stair, and he
followed her.

He had begun, since he had let go, to be aware of
her love. And, as long before, her impossible might.
(It was these elements, twinned, that had caused him
to smile.) Somehow the desperateness of such power
awoke compassion.

When she came to the foot of the steps, the people
had parted to let her by. There was an aisle of flesh
and robes and trees. They walked along it, he and she.
It ended against the column of a tower. Thirty feet
above, the dog's head was growing paler on the deepening dark, the eyes had relinquished their rabid glare
and turned chill.

The way into the tower was an oval door of white
lacquer. Aztira leaned her hand against it, and it opened
inward.

The room had been made round, and on its walls
were the expected frescoes, pastoral visions, dancers,
a beaming solar disc of gold. As in the palaces, lamps
had been lit, all up the vault of an inner stair.

By its positioning, the groves and fanciful decora-
tions, he had by now deduced what the area was. A
graveyard, and this, one of the tombs. The assembly
was not, however, a burial party.

Aztira glanced at him. She moved on into the round
hall, and up into the stairwell. He, and he alone, went
after her.

At the topmost level of the tower, the marble ended
in a coal-black chamber. Here, on a pedestal, flames
burned in a black bowl, in the manner of their temples. By the flame-light, nothing was revealed but for
a silver bed, and lying on the bed, a man.

He could have been anyone of the Amanackire who
waited below. Their unflawed faces had by now be-

come all one face, males and females, duplicated over and over, saving only hers.

The man on the couch was breathing. Once, in every minute, his shoulders, the sharp line of the ribcage, were disturbed with motion.

Again, Aztira glanced at her companion. She put up her hand, as she had done in returning his caress. Now the hand was to stay him.

She approached the bier, and stood over it. To all appearances, she was a sister to the breathing corpse, so physically alike they were.

"Urhvan," she said, aloud.

Her lids dropped over her eyes.

She was speaking within. Yet the chamber rang with the litany of her inner voice—entreaty, reassurance, *insistence*.

The man's eyes opened without warning. They bulged. He let out a braying scream.

It was a noise of the arena. A sword had gone between the bladed armour of the bones, into the belly. A death cry, panic and disbelief, fury and denial.

"Urhvan." Aztira said, again out loud, while the whirlpool of thought and energy soared and smote against the black room, and the glare of the flame-bowl flattened, flared.

The woman bowed over her struggling brother. Her hands settled to his forehead and his throat. His body shuddered and relapsed. He lay along the bed of death, as if dead once more, but now he breathed with a defeated regularity.

After a little while, Aztira drew back. As she did so, the man sat up sluggishly on the couch. His face was stupid. Then that slipped from him. He was in possession of himself. He was Amanackire. They gazed on each other and spoke with their minds. And the room sang.

The flame had steadied in its agate cup. In the eye-windows of the dog, the darkness was complete.

Soon, the Amanackire male got up from his couch. He looked about him, once, his eyes passing across the image of a dark man clothed in white without any attention. Before Aztira, the Amanackire made an obeisance of the Lowlands, the flight of one hand to brow and heart. Without any other show, he then went by her and down the inner stair.

The man and woman left behind in the tomb's upper chamber confronted each other, also quite wordlessly. Until there thrust out of the nighttime groves of the burial garden beneath the thud of one huge atmospheric pulse—deafening as any shout.

"But you," he said, "were alone."

"I was alone, and in Alisaar."

"Is it always an act of such violence?"

"Was it ever easy," she said, "to be born? Urhvan canceled his own life twenty days ago, on the agreement of return. That has become the final ordeal. Those who dare to do it, and restore themselves, become the elect of Ashnesee. There are at present only ten of us, but eventually each will have met with and outwitted death. In nearby towers, some are lying who have couched with death a year, and longer. Their flesh stays pristine. Thus, the pledge. They will return. At the flickering of the life-spark, we go to them, to minister, those of us for whom the testing is already past." Her eyes strayed to the blackness in the windows. "I suffered renewal alone, but I was spared the deed of suicide. A tavern-girl slew me to save you from my bane. I had only to accept her pitcher. She had even dressed it for me with lilies."

He said, "Didn't you think to ask that other favor of me. To wait for you."

"Ah, no," she said. "No."

"Since you say you reckoned only on death."

"Yes, maybe I am dishonest there. All my kind are warned. Any adept of my people might return out of the night. But then." She looked down at the vacant bed of silver. "How unlikely it is, such a thing."

He waited now, if not in Alisaar. At last he said to her, "Did you also want privacy for your return in anguish?"

She said, "I shrieked and rent myself with my nails. I didn't know my name or who—or *what* I was. I thought myself an animal, a fish, a serpent. I thought that life was death, I was dying, and blood ran from my mouth and in absolute horror I attempted to tear free of the snare. No, no, I did not want your witness. The body weighs like lead. The seeing eyes are like sightlessness. To call out is to be dumb and to breathe is to *suffocate*. Anguish, agony. To die is better. And one day, I may die completely and be gone. But now—how shall I ever be sure? To live. That is our chastisement and our blessing. For you accused me truthfully. We are gods, my kind." She put back her head and her hair spangled about her and her eyes were bloodless fires. The Power that streamed from her was like the rays of a winter moon. It was no more than a fact, what she had said to him in the inadequate language of men. "Eventually we will be as we were, as our history has us to be. There is a memory. It's said we were winged. I nearly think it may be so. We have also traditions among us of lands above the sky, and that we rode from such places in chariots like stars, and will go back there, to reclaim many kingdoms. We dream of it. I, too, have done this. And when I dream—there are other colors there, which I— But I can describe none of them. And all those worlds will be ruled by my race. Without mercy or pity, until we fall or are pushed down again from our heights, and our wings are broken and our season finished. We heal of death. But there will be a death born from which even the Shadowless can never heal. For we shall be feared very much, and hated equally. Until the dawn of that death, then, the path lies upward. The cups of flame will burn before our untenanted altars, and those names we worship will be our own. We are gods. But Anackire is not a god. Anackire is everything, and of this the gods are only part."

A twilight had come into her eyes, seeming to tint them, but not with colors—or with those indescribable colors of which she could not tell him.

"We are to be envied and despised," she said. "You know it."

He inclined his head.

"Vis will tremble," she said. "But it will be worse, at last, for us. In the end, we shall be lost." She held

out her hands to him over the bier of her risen kindred. "So, we are alike, you and I, after all."

When he went to her, she laid her head against his
breast, as if she were tired and yearned to sleep.

"Before sunrise, you must be got out of this sorcerous unclean city. Rehger, I will send you by a safe
road. To the sea. Nor far, my love. Will you trust me
to do it?"

"Yes. But that's for the morning."

She said, in a whisper, "You have read my thoughts."

The dry pond of the plain had gathered to itself a
fragrance on that evening. It was the perfume, lacking
all the myriad smudgings and stenches of humanity, of
the distances of a starry sky and the ground swell of
the metamorphosed foliage of Ashnesee.

They walked the ridges and defiles of the city.

She discovered for him, as they went by, the massive monuments, and gilded shrines, the fair diadem of
the temple, with its bloom of inner fire. Where the
palaces were aglow, sometimes the silhouettes of beings
moved on the lights. (Often, the noble buildings stood
void.) In a garden, now and then, like statuary alive,
the pale Amanackire went up and down. They were in
constant union and almost always separate.

Twice, Aztira came upon her fellows on the road-
way. Some greeting was exchanged, naturally in total
silence.

The allergy of all that place, directed toward him
like an instinctive music—this he could not fail to
sense. She had said he must be gone before the new
day. He had beheld them in their sanctum, and he had
been allowed to judge the rite of reincarnation. And
he was Amrek, and All-Vis.

But their antipathy was nothing in the peace of that
evening. Beside her lawless and boundless beauty,
nothing. The Star exalted in their celibate heaven.

As they walked, they spoke occasionally of Alisaar,
of Saardsinmey, as if still it throve, sparkling with
torches, and the races in the stadium due to begin.
They laughed together once, thrice. The old stigmas

had been sloughed, with the meanings of time and sentience.

In the oval hall of Aztira's mansion, slaves had laid out a princely supper. The plates were silver chased in gold, with a design of sea-monsters—assuredly a gift from Sh'alis.

The wine was red: From Vardath.

Their conversation, which had become untrammeled, melted into the pauses of reflection, and of desire.

Her bedchamber, reached by a little low stair, warmed by a dozen tapers, had no windows, was enclosed as the womb of a shell.

Her nakedness, when he encountered it, the whiteness of her, like ice or marble, had, too, its inner fires, which he had forgotten. They took each other like leopards, famished, the commerce of a minute. And then again, the earth revolving and flung away.

It was the house behind the lacemakers. He heard the far shamble of the traffic on Five Mile Street.

Or it was Moih, and at his prayer the statue had become flesh.

"Rehger, forgive my use of you."

"We seemed evenly matched."

"That was not the use I meant."

"I will forgive you anything, Aztira Am Ashnesee. You will outlive me, anyway. What does it matter?"

"Once you leave me here," she said, "I shall become again a ghost, to you."

As they lay on the pillows, through the final hour of darkness, she had begun to plait her hair. When he moved from her arms, he found it all in fetters round him. He lifted three or four of the plaits, shook them, and let loose the showering hair.

"You smell always of blossom and clear water."

"But you will forget me, nevertheless."

He made to begin loosening another of the plaits. She stopped this.

"In Iscah," she said.

"In Iscah, what?"

"The sign of a married wife."

He stared then deeply into her eyes, frowning, curious.

"What mystery is this?"

"Never mind it," she said.

He put his mouth to her breasts, their pale and velvety buds, but lust was done with, hers and his. She had called him by his Alisaarian name, but he might forget that also, when he left her. He knew as much, indifferently.

"The dawn has begun," she said softly, in a while. "A man will be standing in the garden, under the tree where the doves gather—do you recall? He led you into the city, and will lead you out of it. A hidden river runs away through caverns toward the coast. Where it breaks from the ground, there will be a boat, provisioned and ready. But then there is the wide western sea. Oh, Rehger," she said.

"Zastis is good sailing weather," he said.

She did not weep. Her eyes, as the Lowlanders said, were formed of tears.

They made love an ultimate time, swimming and slow, drowning, and cast ashore apart.

Transparent sunrise flooded the bedchamber when its door was opened.

He went between the bars of light, each falling behind him like a dreamer's sword.

Not till he had traveled the corridor's length, did he hear her say, "Don't turn. There's an ancient rhyme which warns against it. Forget me and prosper. I think you will know me still, when next we meet."

He raised the curtain at the corridor's end, and going on, let it fall again, between them.

The white man met Rehger Am Ly Dis under the tree of doves. They went together, not a phrase exchanged, to the lower tract of the garden, by the fountain there, and into the tunnels beneath Ashnesee.

So then the Vis wanderer saw Aarl-Hell, out of the legends of his own people. It was glimpsed, inadvertently almost, at a turning here, in a passage there—Laval fires burned in it and toiling figures lurched hither and thither spawning nightmare shadows. The slaves of the Chosen Race were busy. They oiled the clockwork of paradise above and could not afford to idle.

The undercity was an ant hill.

Rehger passed through it unchallenged on the heels of his guide, and came at long last into a luminous cave. Flat and thin, the river wormed along its rocky channel.

The Amanackire observed Rehger's progress down the bank for less than a minute before retracing his steps into the warren of hell.

Alone, about an hour after, Rehger encountered a group of slaves on the river rocks. But they did not appear to see him, though he went by within three feet of them. They were fishing in the steely water.

And later again, when daylight had started to be ahead of him, he saw another detachment of slaves, squatting on the bank. They were actually laboring at nothing, perhaps resting. (Their faces were mindless yet controlled.) They might have been the very ones who had put ready the boat—and stacked in it the store of food and barrels of water and wine—that presently he came on.

It perched in the shallows, and beyond, the river yawned wide and the cave frayed into air and sky and leaning granite. And on the clifftop, the black thatch of the jungle-forest flourished like giant weeds.

Rehger pushed the boat into the main course of the river, brown and lazy water veiled by insects and heat. He rowed, and in the forests the sun beat and birds squalled.

The city had disappeared, and soon an angle of the river-wall closed away the exit from the caverns.

The day and the river, the boat and the man, went on toward an assumption of the sea.

But as he rowed, the man sensed upon him the eyes of a goddess in the sky. Eyes of tears, without pity, sorrowing.

He would reach the ocean. Sailing in to shore, he could then proceed gradually south. It was a prolonged voyage, but finite. Winds would rouse and belly the slanting sail, fish leap in an offering of sustenance.

Huge plated beasts would wallow from the beaches of the jungle, but not dare attack the oar-finned wooden animal with its one snapping wing.

Even the pirates of Free Zakoris did not often try the water here. There was nothing for them to steal, and they had besides religious qualms concerning these coasts.

South, should one reach it, the very land itself pointed toward Alisaar. The world commenced again, and the circle of the ring was sealed.

In the serpent-headed tower, Aztira gazed within herself, seeing a life adrift in waters. But it was not Rehger's life.

Perhaps I did not even need to ask your forgiveness.

His generosity would have allowed her what she asked, and had done so.

A covenant, between your race and mine. Between reality and hubris.

Among the Shadowless, on the pure white banner of their pride and her own, she had branded darkness irrevocably. Created now, and fixed, the genes of her descendants would carry it to eternity. A rogue flowering, it would fruit when seldom looked for. From the albino tree, a black viper. A constant, and recurring, theme. With every generation, bronze skin, black hair, black eyes, would spring from the core of the snow.

Inside her body, implanted, the seed of her lover, his child. Rehger's son. But grown in the ocean of her adept's Power, like herself, he would be, this boy, this man, a magician and a god. A god of the blood line of Amrek, with the mark of the snake on his wrist.

It was the Balance. It was *Anackire*.

But, also, it was only love.

For love must have something.

She pressed her hands against her side, seeing what was yet invisible, unknowable, and known.

Westward she did not gaze. She did not think of it, or stretch out the psychic tendrils of her will. Nor did she entreat. She had no superior left to hear her prayers.

But she felt the drum of her heart like that of a stranger, as in the tomb she had felt it, when terribly as death, it called her to return.

That was all.

When the drumming smoothed and quietened, and coursed back into her own breast, she knew the circle was complete.

At dusk, when the Star rose, an enormous soundlessness claimed the sea, under the mutter of its waves and the vagrant shiver of the wind.

The boat drifted between land and liquid and atmosphere. Tidily, the sail had been secured, and the uneaten stores of food set out to tempt the birds. The wine, poured in the sea, had long ago been drunk away.

No other thing was in the boat.

Where the Star pierced through the water, it revealed, as if fathoms below, disorientated meanderings, the wreckage possibly of a sunken ship, or merely shoals of fish foraging.

Later the moon was birthed out from the amphitheater of the forest.

Maybe the moon did finger a sudden glitter on the sea. But it was the dance of water-things, which flirted in a diamond rush of spray and dived again to the depths.

The reflection of the boat stayed black on the lunar ocean but faded when the moon swung over. By morning, when the gulls came to feed on the viands of Ashnesee, the vessel was already listing.

The birds fought and screamed over the feast, to have it all, before the boat should go down.

BOOK SEVEN

ISCAH

CHAPTER TWENTY-THREE

CAH THE GIVER

A child about two years old was sitting by the fish pond, carefully undressing a wooden doll. With the dull start of surprise that sometimes assailed her, Panduv recognized this apparition as her own daughter, Teis.

She was a pretty thing, her skin deep-toned but Iscaian still, yet with Panduv's jet-black horse's mane, hair that hung almost to her ankles when she stood up, and now spread all round her on blue tiles of the pool's rim. Spring sunshine struck fiercely along the roof terrace. The pool crackled light like jagged glass and the fish hid under their stones. In the shade of the awning, the nurse-woman was stringing beads and crooning to herself.

Teis had finished undressing the doll. She lowered it into the pond. The doll floated a moment, then turned over and sank straight down.

The child gave a sudden wail.

Panduv sprang forward and seized her up.

"No. Bad kitten. You must *never* lean into the pool."

The water was only two feet deep, which would have been enough. Panduv found herself, as so often, occupying simultaneous roles. In a swift succession of voices and actions she hugged and scolded her child, berated the nurse, and rescued from the pond the doll.

"Next time it will be three taps of the rod. (Here is your doll.) Don't tell me your eyes were fixed on the child, plainly they weren't. (Am I to wait to have her drowned?) Why did you throw it into the pond in the first place?"

The nurse mumbled and groveled. Teis regarded

her mother with an intent all-knowing gaze, and inserted the doll's left foot between her lips.

"Now, Kitty, don't bite the wood. The splinters will get in your mouth."

The child, all-knowledgeable, eyed Panduv who, an adult, had unlearnt the original wisdoms.

Panduv shook Teis. Teis laughed. The black woman liked her child and was inclined to believe she would become interesting as she grew. As yet Teis had few words. The passion of the baby—most babies—for self-injury and, thereby, potential suicide, Panduv had long since accepted. There was an antique saying of the Iscaian hills, (the nurse had repeated it frequently), *Fresh from the womb of Cah and wants to get back there.*

The nurse was a capable creature, only sluggish sometimes. But then again, the young leopard mother, who spent three quarters of every day willfully absent from her daughter, might have reacted too wildly.

Panduv saw the fat old witch was looking at her under crinkled lids, divining her thoughts and sensing forgiveness.

"Teis, go to nurse," said Panduv, setting her fruit once more on the blue tiles.

"Nurse," said the child. "Teis," announced the child. She waddled toward the beads the nurse was now waving to entice her.

Panduv stretched herself, and strolling to the balustrade, looked down from the hilltop toward Iscah's afternoon capital.

She had the view by heart now, as she had the rooms of Arud's villa, the blue walls and tiles, the average number of fish in the pond—which varied as they bred or ate each other—the routines of the domestic season. She was Panduv, the Priest's woman. That was her official title. It was not without kudos. The acolytes of Cah, even here in the more sophisticated capital, did not marry, but their doxies were kept openly, and, where cared for, with some show. The men of the city did not treat Panduv impolitely. And though she must address even the oil-seller as "master," he in turn nodded to her, and provided of the best.

As to walking a certain number of paces behind her lord, Panduv had a litter to bear her about the streets. Veiled she would not go, however, and not a single soul did not know the Black One.

For Arud, though he now and then lay with other girls, Panduv had remained his fancy, and the overseer of his home. He allowed her, by Iscaian standards, incredible liberties, and left her much to herself.

But Teis he loved. Aside from bringing her expensive toys, he would even, in the privacy of the house, play with her, chasing the child so she pretended fear, or crawling about the chambers carrying her on his shoulders.

For status, he would have wanted a son, which was what Panduv had promised him. She had been very sure, and after a night of grueling work, to see a sister of the female sex had emerged from her loins, provided her the first startlement of motherhood. Following the birth, care with herbs and specific exercises of the stadium, precautions taught every girl of Daigoth's courts, ensured Panduv kept barren.

The early heat had distilled hallucinatory glimmers from the roofs. Along the hillside, feather trees lifted their slim plumes. In the courtyard below, a slave was scrubbing the household altar.

Panduv offered now to Cah the goddess, since women were granted this boon, here. Alternative ethics of worship, like those Arud had exposed in the mountains, were unmentioned.

Yet she was aware that Arud was a powerful member of his temple, part of an inner elect, and had risen effortlessly in the past three years to the high office of Adorer. His priestly robes were heavily fringed with silver, and vessels of gold, and thin glass, had appeared as if by magic almost overnight in the house. Content and sanguine and no longer sent about on the tasks of a Watcher, Arud also gained in weight.

Panduv supposed she, too, had thickened. Child bearing, and the somnolence of her days, would have padded her satin flesh. Despite that, she was to all the women of the capital, where plumpness if not obesity stayed the vogue, a bone. She ate sparingly, even in boredom, and had continued her dancer's athletics in the concealment of the villa.

Arud, partly anxious for his exotic pet Zakr, half eager to display flashy lack of convention, gave her the handling of a light chariot. She was not, by Iscaian law, able to drive on the streets, but once up among the hills, she discarded the driver. The sight of his merry back, bounding for the nearest tavern, had come to symbolize to her a holiday. The hiddraxi were imported, another evidence of Arud's wealth. She trained them to flight on the sidelong paths, hurtling into the upland valleys, where she would herself break loose to swim the streams and sleep in the grass. When the child was older, she should be taken, too. Arud would not object. Approached deviously, he was nearly always compliant. He had come to see his generosity to a woman as an aspect of free thinking, and sometimes referred to it impressively before colleagues.

Already, Panduv paid heed to the diet of Teis. (The nurse was a problem, endlessly slipping her sweetmeats.) Panduv lessoned the little girl in embryonic moves of an acrobat and dancer. Teis had natural ability, but her attention was inconstant. It would be an extravagance besides, to bank upon any future for a girl. Had it not been hard enough, letting go all plans for herself?

Only torches twined now in the dance of fire.

Panduv turned. Like two spiders, the nurse-woman, and her daughter, were weaving a web of beads.

"Be wary, nurse." Panduv was harsh. "I'll leave her with you until sunset. Remember your duty to the Master's child."

Infallible words.

The child laughed again, seeing her mother desert her.

In point of fact, Panduv got no farther than the market place.

Tomorrow was a holy day, the festival of Cah the Giver. (Arud had set off for the temple at sunrise and would not leave its precincts until tomorrow's midnight. Another motive for Panduv's restlessness; when he was in the house, at least he was a cause of occupation.)

By temple law, all buying and selling must cease before this evening's sun went down, and the market was a madhouse.

After a negligent try or two, Arud's chariot driver stalled the vehicle at a herd of orynx. The hiddrax stood trembling.

Panduv would have wished to call the man a fool and cuff him.

Instead, "Master," she remarked, in tones of burnt honey, "Arud's animals are distressed. Please do turn into that side street there."

"Impossible, woman," said the driver. In her instance, "woman" was title rather than dismissal, uttered quite deferentially. Panduv gritted her teeth, waited. "See, the pigs're almost past."

And past the orynx continued, thumping with their bristly sides the wheels and left flanks of the unhappy team, while men leered and grinned at the Black One, and mere women scurried by like ticks across a dog.

Superfluous to protest. Emblem of everything now. She had accepted. Like the ageless fire-sorceress in the mountains, Thioo . . . Nothing matters. Here we are. Here, it's the custom. A Lowlander philosophy: We have all time and in time anything can be accomplished. The waste of one small life is nothing.

Why think of such things? Life was radiant and absolute.

But maybe it would be more comfortable to accede. Not only in her outward values, but through and through. What then? Eat confectionery, render to Arud a tribe of male brats, grow lush and portly—

Panduv surfaced as if from under a river, returning gasping into the scalding heat and the market noise.

Across the humps of jostling pigs, a rabble of drovers, the sweetmakers' booths and the towering jars of the sugar-sellers, Panduv saw into the enclosure of the slave-market. The fence was scanty, a rope run round between posts. On to the auction block had been

pushed a gang of five men, wrist-chained together.
They were all but naked in five skins of metallic darkness foreign to Iscah. On this dark, appalling scars and
lacerations indicated their former employment. They
were off a slave-galley, men of abnormal strengths,
but actually useless in terms of service. It was well-
known, they could be bent to nothing else having
outlasted the oar and the whip of an oars master. The
fifth man was the Lydian. Rehger.

The floor of the chariot seemed to evaporate and
leave her adrift in the air. Even as this happened to
her, reason grasped her firmly and set her down again
on a solid surface. No, it was not Rehger, not Saardsinmey and living life. No.

Yet, if not Rehger, a man so like him—

Though lean and muscular—how else would he have
survived?—he did not have the distinctive build of the
professional Swordsman, a Son of Daigoth. This man,
too, was older than Rehger would have been, had he
lived. But handsome, and in manner off-hand, princely
almost, divorced from the chain and the company. He
stood and looked about, while the other four crouched
snarling.

"There," said Panduv to her driver. "Lord Arud
lacks a bodyguard."

"No, woman," said the driver, slightly offended and
reproachful—she had forgotten in her desire to joy her
lord her proper address of *master.* "No good. Those
are off some Zakr pirate the Vardians trounced. Such
muck can only be put in the mines."

Panduv braced herself.

"Master, your leave to tell you. Lord Arud has said
to look out for such a slave."

Dismissing female stupidity, the driver did not re-
spond. While, from the auction, Panduv could hear
the other men saying much the same as he had. Certain of the capital's priestly factions held a stake in
mining concerns of Shansarian Alisaar. Presently there
would come a bid of this sort.

Even though a mirage, it was imperative to save
him.

Panduv left the chariot. Her driver gawped at her.

Women did not behave in this way. Only the lowest
went about here on foot and unescorted. Leopard-
black, veil-less, slender and upright, Panduv stalked
upon the enclosure, stepped over the rope and trod
forbidden ground.

Outrage was immediate, but tended more to ridicule
than brutality. In the silence which succeeded the oaths
and sneers, Panduv approached the auction block.
The men made way, affronted beyond words. The auctioneer was stone.

"Your pardon, master," said Panduv, head lifted
and eyes cast down. "It is the business of my Lord
Arud the Priest, the Adorer of Cah."

Someone yelled, "Yes, we know who keeps this
black bitch."

But the auctioneer, a traveled fellow, aware that
times and etiquette might change, prudently murmured,
"What then?"

Panduv whispered in turn, "He would buy that fifth
man. Keep him for Lord Arud. Money shall be sent
inside the hour. Don't fail. You'll make a profit."

The auctioneer drew a long breath. "All right. Now
for the sake of Cah, get out, *out!*"

Panduv, on the first occasion in her years at Iscah,
drew up a corner of her gauzy sleeve, and masked her
face. She crept away through the crowd of masculine
essence, making tiny moans and sighs, to appease it.
As she went, she felt the astonished stare of the fifth
slave going after her, molten or icy on her spine. She
was not sure which.

When they had fed him, they de-loused, scraped
and bathed him, washed and trimmed his hair, shaved
his face, salved and bound an open wound or two,
dressed him in the linen garment of a house-servant,
and sent him up the stairs.

In a blue chamber that gave on a terrace, the gorgeous black girl from the market sat in a chair and
looked at him.

He presented her with a bow straight from some
court of the Middle Lands. He sensed she might care
for it and be amused.

"Your kindness, lady," he said, "is beyond thanks. But you took a risk. Didn't they warn you, my type absconds, or murders his owners inside two days."

"The ship was a pirate," she said. "They caught you somewhere."

"No, I was legitimately sold to them, bartered, more correctly. By a friend of mine."

"And before you were a galley slave, what were you then?"

"A free man. And sometime agent of Dorthar. By birth? A Lan, with connections to the royal line there. My name's Yennef."

"Yennez," she said. Then, crisply, throwing off the slur, *"Yennef."*

He smiled. His teeth were white. All of him seemed sound and vital. But his eyes were luminous and curiously dreamy, rather as Rehger's eyes had been. Groomed, he looked more like Rehger than ever. It was bizarre.

"We're strangers then, lady, in an alien land. Is that why you had compassion for me?"

She did not intend to tell him why. To him it would mean nothing, and for herself, she did not want to chatter of it.

"My lordly master," she said, "has need of a bodyguard."

Yennef grinned. "You find me suitable."

"On reflection, not. It would be better, I think, to manumit you and let you go."

The grin fell from his face They gazed each other out. It was fine to have before her a man prepared to do this, eye for eye.

"Why?" he said. Then, remembering Iscah, "You paid your lord's cash for me. What will *he* say?"

Recklessly she answered, "It's a feast of Cah. Gifts are exchanged, sometimes they free slaves and prisoners. I'll tell him this was an offering on his behalf. He's a priest. It will look pious, and also display that he's rich."

"*Oh,* no," he said. "He'll have your silky hide."

"Oh, *no,*" she repeated. She said, without pride, "I can usually make him do what I want."

Yennef considered. He said, "But you still look made of silk."

She stared back.

"If you need a woman," she said, "I've no objections to your having one of the kitchen girls, before you leave."

"Those little rounded wobbly stuffed cushions? That will be nice."

Panduv said, briskly, "I've already sent for the clerk. The deed of manumission will need to be written and sealed quickly. At sunset all business stops, for the festival."

"And you have use of his seal, as of his coffers, this malleable master of yours."

"The Lord Arud is sometimes away at the temple two or three days together. I regulate his house."

"And after the clerk, what?"

"You'll be given provisions and set on your road."

He said, "I've forgotten which road that was."

Suddenly the attractive nonchalance and swagger went from him. His broad shoulders bowed and he hung his head. For an instant a look of bitterness and frustrated gnawing grief got hold of his face. Then these, too, seemed to drain out of him, as if he no longer had the stamina to effect them. She recalled, he was older than Rehger, almost twice his years, maybe, and had been cooped for six months or more on a Zakorian pirate galley.

"Sit there," she said, and when he had done so, she brought him wine and served him, as if he were a master of Iscah and she a dutiful woman.

A minute later (they had not spoken any more, except that, unIscaian, he thanked her again), the clerk was sent in with his papers and case of ink and wax.

Panduv was sorry. She was more sorry than was comfortable at the swift curtailment of this interlude.

He had lost all track of time, nearly of all things, on the galley. That was normal. To survive, less so. It was Galutiyh the Dortharian who had rendered him to the pirates. Yennef had not been thrown from the trail of

Galut and his dross, and of Yennef's son riding with
them. Yennef had sensed the false leads in Xarabiss,
but not been able to get over the water in proper
order to keep up. That was luck proving flighty, as it
always had. Then a series of mishaps occurred on the
way to Zaddath—which was where he knew, by then,
they must be heading. Some of the delays might have
been fashioned by Galutiyh—lame mounts, felled trees,
obliterated paths. Or not, depending on the dedication
of ill-fortune. Then again, maybe it was only bloody
Anackire, working out her scheme-dream of the world.

Galutiyh's men ambushed Yennef in the rough country around Ilva. Galutiyh had his score to settle. There
were beatings and other games. In the end, dizzy and
carefree from swamp fever, Yennef beheld himself,
from some distance up in the air, being traded to black
men with smashed faces, whose long low ship flew a
tattered doubled-moon and dragon. They were not far
from old Hanassor, one gathered from the talk. Free
Zakorian reavers. He gave himself over as done for.

He had already, somewhere or other, apologized to
Rehger for non-utility. Well, his son would expect
nothing of him. His son. In the gut of the stinking
black galley, Yennef had visions of Rehger—torn apart
on a machine of torture, poling upriver between mountains, in a jungle, a king in a chariot riding to war,
standing among white towers of marble.

Finally, Yennef believed that Rehger was dead, and
believing it, most of the anguish dimmed. How could
you mourn and rage over something to which you had
no rights? Besides, it might all have turned out otherwise. Yennef, condemned to die in the pit of the
galley, need not trouble.

But nourished on the gangrenous meat and vermin-
nous bread-slabs and diseased water, rowing in the
boiling ship belly, men perishing around him, endlessly cut by fire—the tongues of whips—expecting
always no tomorrow, his fever abated or was amalga-
mated into him, and Yennef lived. And then came a
night of furious rowing, the Zakor seeking to evade a
Vardian patrol with a Shansarian captain out of Sh'alis,
sea-wise and angry. Chased up the lawless coast almost

into Hanassor's rocky cliffs, the Zakorians discovered themselves trapped between their pursuer and another waiting Vardian. The pirate was rammed.

As she was sinking, blond men came down into the howling hell of the rowers' deck and broke the shackles.

It transpired Yennef was now the property of Vardians. They knew him for a Lan, but were not overwhelmed by former ties of friendship. They shipped him across to Iscah in the intestines of a merchant vessel, not rowing, simply bolted fast to the planks. From the port, his gang and a couple of others were marched to the capital. They were not worth much, and the mix now in charge of them had no patience. When men died they were tossed off the road into ditches. This was Iscah. And there were plenty of crows.

Gaining the market, Yennef was cheerful. He had gone by most other emotions, save contempt—of self and every other.

He knew of Cah—of course, his past had taught him, a million years before, in a mountain hovel in the snow. And all at once there Cah was, gliding through the slave-auction. Crow-black herself, wand-slim in her gauzes, with a silver wristlet and necklaces of ivory.

And Cah spoke to the auctioneer and Cah brought Yennef to this house on the hill. Cah, quite properly, was the lover of a high priest and would make the man do what she choose. Cah had let Yennef free. In her presence then, the backbone of indifference crumbled.

The Lan was not wholly sane, she saw that now. It was not a rowdy or pernicious madness, gentle, rather. Perhaps it would subside. But the cause seemed deeper, older than the reavers' ship.

Best, would be to send him out in the early morning, before the sun rose on Cah's festival. He could bribe the city gate, and Arud's seal would settle any argument. She could not give Yennef a mount, but with the provided coins doubtless he could come on one. She believed what he had said, about the Lannic royal line. Rehger had had this princely look about

him, too. She could have supposed them related, the
Lan, the Lydian, but Rehger had been birthed from a
witch girl and an itinerant in the jumble of the Iscaian
mountains.

The business with the clerk was slowly got through,
in Arud's name. In law no woman could do anything,
and the clerk, seen to with a double fee, conducted
the affair as if an invisible Arud were at his elbow.
When everything was accomplished, Panduv sent the
Lan to one of the guest cells that opened on the
altar-court. It was a ridiculous excess of hospitality, as
buying and freeing him had been. This did not seem
important, nor Arud's reaction to the news, which she
could hardly deny him, seeing the legalities were for
public record, and meanwhile the entire house was
primed.

Arud's return (tomorrow's midnight, drunken and
slack from the temple mysteries which involved both
blood sacrifice and carnal orgy), felt far off, as if to be
located in another decade.

She had given instructions to the villa servants concerning the man Yennef's comfort. At the correct
hour, one of the boys should go to rouse him for
departure.

Panduv crossed to her apartment, to see Teis put to
bed. The sun was a red ball rolled almost all the way
down the hill, and by its flushed glow the child lay on
her mat giggling, as the nurse told her stories and
tickled her. Panduv's presence was noted by both and
dismissed. Panduv stayed only a minute in the room.

She paced the roof terrace until the sun set. A
religious stillness had descended on the city so that she
heard a night bird begin to sing in a garden at the foot
of the hill. The stars were sown. The evening was
beautiful. The black woman stood high up in the sky
on the priest's roof, yearning for things forgotten or
never known, until the breeze blew cold. She chided
herself then, and went in again to the house.

There was a spring star which, a while before midnight, shone in through an upper window.

It woke Panduv, pointing down between her eyes.
Or she thought it did.

She was aware immediately of a presence in the
chamber, and stiffened, imagining snakes. But then it
came to her the intrusion was not physical. Nothing
was to be seen, or heard, yet, as if a voice had spoken
in her head, she received the phrase: *Go offer to Cah*.

She was rebellious. *Who tells me so?*

In that moment she woke in earnest.

The apartment was undisturbed and silent and void,
but for the dry chirrup of the cricket which dwelled
behind the hearth stone.

Presently Panduv got up and drew on her mantle.
She covered herself only with that. Leaving the bedchamber, she walked out into the passage, barefoot—

Starlit air hung from the window-places. At the
corridor's end, a flight of steps led into the altar-court.

On the house altar of Cah, freshly scrubbed and
spilled with an aromatic, a dish of oil had been left
burning for the festival. The drowsy flickering light
showed only the lumpen stone of the goddess, faceless, and breastless, even. Yet it had been awarded a
crown of flowers.

In her mind's eye, Panduv saw herself, a dancer in a
garland. She saw the Lydian wreathed after combat's
victory.

Although she was now awake, at least in part, another question welled through her, words she did not
even understand. *You want your hero's glory back
again?* And, like the question not understood, a reply,
Only to live.

The court, open to heaven, let starlight, too, in at the
doorway of the guest's cell.

He lay alone, motionless, but awake, she knew. He
also had had his training. He could kill empty-handed
if he judged her some thief or mischief-meddler.

"Hush," she whispered, to let him recall her voice.

Then she heard him laugh, very low.

"This time," he said, "it *is* Cah, coming through the
shadow to me."

Somnambulist, she kneeled down by him. It was

dreamlike. As he reached out to her, her narrow hands slid about his neck.

Their mouths and bodies met recognizing some unnamed landfall, aphrodisiac as Zastis.

It was not only that he was Rehger—Saardsinmey—but that he was for her all regretted things. He had become not merely a young man, but her own youth, the male alter-demon of her flesh.

His hands found out her skin, her breasts, her thighs, as if, sightless, he must learn her by touch alone. When he possessed her, the strength of him was like the heart of fire. Always quiet in love or lust, she knew she must cry out. It would not matter, the house expected him to be with some girl. . . .

As the rhythm of the life-dance bore her up, she did not remember who he was. She did not know his name. She forgot she was Panduv.

Like a coiled flower of the chaplet of the goddess, (black Cah the Anackire-eyed), the pulse of her womb, the bud spreading its chalice, stretching to be filled.

She clung to him and he to her. The crying sang from her and she must smother her delight with her fist for fear it be heard—

The spring of liquid light pierced through her.

The flower-womb cupped and clasped and closed upon it.

Night and silence resettled like a fall of dust. In the silence, they were stilled together, saturated in the warmth of each other, and the starlight ticked across the floor.

"That was a welcome gift you gave me," he said.

"It's a time of giving."

When she moved to the mattress' edge, pulling her mantle once more around her, he said sternly, "Will you be quite safe here? I don't know what's in store for me, but if—"

He stopped, and in the space she did not say anything more.

She saw the shine of the stars on his eyes as he watched her go, on his gentle, madman's eyes. And out in the court, the wick was guttering before the goddess.

Panduv did not look back. She went up the stairs, along the passage, to her couch, and lay down there and slept at once.

About an hour and a half before dawn, fragmentedly, she discerned the noise of the yard gate, and knew that he had been let through, on to his unsure road, into his different future.

She woke again late in the morning, languid, not remembering. Then she thought it a dream, until the evidence of her own body put her wise. The craziness of what she had done thrust her mind forward in a senseless progression. Arud must suspect. He would cast her out into the streets and they would stone her there—such things went on, even in the sophisticated capital. Perhaps she should at once remove herself from the house. Why had she ever remained? How many occasions she had been on the point of an exit from this life. Something had stayed her. The child, maybe, or sentimental fondness for the paunchy priest who, by her wiles, she had so much changed, setting him at liberty also from the mores of masculine Iscah, to her benefit.

And she had grown comfortable. Her roots had gone down into this unsuitable soil. She bloomed here. She would not run away.

How should he know anything? Who had spied? The holy stillness of the night had been nearly un-canny, and in the hour of her excursion to the court-yard, the villa had seemed deserted, or its inhabitants under a spell—

She fell asleep again, and opened her eyes at last to a sound of brazen cymbals. It was the festival proces-sion clashing over the afternoon.

A deep lassitude was on her, but she rose and went through certain bodily contortions now habitual with her after sexual union. For spring, the day had turned hot and heavy. She found her muscles intensely reluc-tant. She was debilitated, and left off.

There was the other way, to be sure. The herbs she had had the merchants fetch for her, the leaves of the plants she nurtured in her apartment. Their scent was pleasant, all but one. She gave for its excuse the pretty speckling of its leaves.

She brewed the drink in some distaste. The remedy was decided but unkind. There might be sickness, then she would bleed, which would not be to Arud's liking, for, after the orgies of the temple, oddly, he was often hungry for her.

Well, it served her right. Since she had been so lavish with her greed and was now too lazy, and besides so very nervous. . . . For the Lan was not as young as her priest, therefore probably not as virile. Yet the single embrace—a burning— Best drink the herb. A day or two of malaise and Arud peeved would be a suitable penance and punishment for silliness.

The cup was ready. She held her breath against its smell, the actual look of it. And as she raised the goblet there in the afternoon storm-light—a terrible wailing cut through the sky.

It was a sound dehumanized, supernatural. It seemed to overpour the basin of the atmosphere and bring down the house.

She was in Saardsinmey, inside the pillar-drum, flung every way as heaven fell. The roar of crashing stone and of huge waters, the screaming of a single gargantuan throat.

Panduv spun about and the cup of abortion whirled from her fingers and the exquisite glass shattered on the tiles with the drink like lizard's blood.

Panduv raced upward through the villa.

Stairs passed under her and walls tumbled down.

On the roof terrace, the sky had indeed unreefed itself, a rent blue-black sail. Peaks of the city were stabbed out in a weird yellowish glare against its dark.

Two female servants collapsed on their noses before her.

The awning flapped with a horrible loudness. The nurse woman began to wail again.

Panduv reached the fish pond and looked into its cloudy eye. There in the pupil lay her child, face down under a spurling ink of hair.

A prophecy fulfilled. A circlet joined. Be rid of the unborn, and the born also you were rid of.

Panduv did not think. She reached into the pool and gripped the form of Teis, which no longer had the texture of anything fleshly, or familiar. Panduv pulled forth this object, and turning it over her knee, squeezed the water out. Then she tossed the child, like the unreal thing it had become, on its back. In the avenue of the child's throat a fish had lodged. Panduv, like a magician, brought it forth and threw it into the pond. Miraculously, the fish began at once to live and swam swiftly under a pebble.

She was a Daughter of Daigoth's Courts. She knew many clever tricks. She slammed her child across the breast an appalling blow, hateful, that set the staring women off into hysteria once more. Then Panduv, leaning to her child's face, kissed her mouth, a hoarsely sighing kiss of love after the blow of hate. (So it appeared to the women, who described it afterward in superstitious awe.) A kiss. And the beaten chest of the little girl lifted.

The child's lids parted and Teis was there, in the eyes. She crowed and choked and howled, clutching her mother. Panduv held her fast, and the storm cracked like a goblet and water swept over them all.

The harvested plant would not provide sufficient maleficence again for some days. She could then re-make the brew, but perhaps too late. She would not bother. Holding her child, Panduv was conscious that she had accepted also the second child, the spark of fire lodged gemlike in the girdle of her belly. The sly goddess of Iscah had outwitted her, and what Cah willed you could not go against. The pregnant mother was sacred to Cah. Then, let it be.

"All this to come home to! You're nothing but trouble to me, you Zakr wench."

Arud ranted, quartering the chamber with a prowling plod. After the storm the night was massive and fragrant, limitless and cooled with stars. His litter had arrived two hours after midnight. He was not so sodden as the general rule, but discontented over some

minor slight, for the more weighty his spiritual domi-
nance the more he valued himself, and the more he
knew himself envied.

His holy robes swung around his thick body, their
richness dazzling. On his breast the insignia of the
Adorer, a pectoral in which two golden figures revered a disc of jet and topaz, clicked and wriggled
with its own irritation. He had about him, all over his
smooth surfaces, even in his splendid hair, the tang of
incense.

It would have been the clerk who sent a cautious
message to Arud, arranged for it to be waiting at the
temple porch. The message reviewed the buying and
manumission of a galley-slave, in honor of the festival.

Ready for sleep, Arud had awakened. He had come
directly to her, this fly-brained Zakr wretch, the curse
of his house. He discovered her seated in her chair,
polished ebony in a silk mantle, her black mane man-
tling over it. Her glamour only set him off worse.

She bore the tantrum. She was used to them and
had learned the best mode for their duration. Allure,
a modest downcasting of eyes and head, hands meek,
palms opened and upturned, as if to slake a rain of
slaps, In fact he rarely struck her, and then never
murderously. Only once, in the mountains, had he
been prepared to do that, and not to her.

He would not hit out at her now. He would never
guess the truth. She was in the arm of Cah, though he,
the priest of Cah, had not yet realized.

He exhausted his invective. Then he bellowed for
wine, and she brought it to him, softly as a dove.

"And what do you say, woman? Is it a lie?"

"No, my lord." (She only called him *Arud* when he
was reasonable, sober, and blithe. She foresaw it would
be less and less that she might call him *Arud*.)

"*Not* a lie? Then explain yourself."

Panduv kneeled. She put her hand lightly as a leaf
on to his instep. The touch stirred him; his feet, she
had long ago found, were sensitive.

"A woman in Iscah may own nothing, my lord. But
I have put all my jewelry there, on the table by the
lamp. The jewels were your bounty to me, but if you

take them back, they'll repay you the cost of the
Lannic slave."

He gave a growl of scorn.

"You don't say why, still."

"An offering to Cah."

"Freeing a slave is man's business."

"It was done in your name, my lord. The city will be
jealous of your wealth and impressed by the pious
gesture. It's something you would have done yourself,
had you been here—"

"*Would* I—you Zakr—"

She chanced an interruption. "Because I was desperate, and you've always been charitable to me."

His face thundered down at her. Yet, she had caught
his interest. She always could, and perhaps for a handful more years. His desire, his curiosity.

She said, "When you took me in, I vowed I would
give you a son. I disappointed in that."

Abruptly his features relaxed. Teis was a talisman.

"Cah gives as she gives. Teis is female, but I love
the child. She brings light into my house."

"I've prayed to the goddess to allow me a son. You
know, I've been barren."

Annoying her, as he sometimes did, with inconve-
nient sharpness, he said, "I thought that was how you
preferred it."

Panduv raised her eyes now.

"I want only your gladness. I want to keep my vow
to you."

Then, gracefully, dancer in all her movements though
dancer no longer in the Dance, she rose and leaned on
him, gazing into his face. "The man was my offering
to Cah, in exchange for fertility."

Arud peered at her. Fatigue and excitement mingled in him. The drugs of the mysteries, the cavorting
pale brown wodges of the temple girls, the memories
of the day itself, would always bring him to this leopard-
being, this night-woman. He put his hands on her
waist, thin, supple as oiled rope, slipped to her flanks,
the fierce sheer buttocks, under the wave of hair, silk
over silk over silk.

"And do you think she heard you, Panduv?"

She let her own hands rise along his chest. With a
sudden bewildered pang she acknowledged the Lan
had been nothing to her, that all the past was gone.
And that this man who still, with one able smiting of
her own she could have killed, this limited and anger-
ing man, inflated with self, running to fat, this *priest*,
had grown into her as the seed of the child would
grow. "It's with you," she said, "if she has."

As he began to work upon her, with the finesse of
the arts she herself had taught him, she thought,
Suppose—another girl. But she knew this would not
be.

Later, tomorrow, when he was well-rested, she must
speak to him about the nurse. The house buzzed with
events and it would be difficult to persuade him from
slaughter, there. But the old ninny, asleep under the
awning as Teis drowned, was too old to turn out and
too useful to be beaten to death. They wanted to go
back, the newborn and the very young, and plotted
and cheated to do it. For they soon detected the world
was a harsh country. Until the recollection faded of
some better land from which they had come, they
must be guarded. Panduv would assume the post. Cah
had ensured she must.

Arud was struggling upon her, reining himself that
she, too, should be satisfied. Having learnt the manner of it, she arched herself against him and cried out,
the two long disembodied cries with which she had
answered the Lan before. It was only fair that she
should act them out for Arud. He was to father this
child, this gift of Cah.

Groaning, he spent the unnecessary worth of his
loins, and Panduv held him in her arms.

In the third month, as was customary, Panduv was
borne in her litter to the Women's Court of the fane,
to give thanks.

The Mother Temple of the capital was raised on a
tall whitewashed platform with a stair of red obsidian.
The pillars of the temple were painted carmine and
black, and the cornice was gilded. This house of Cah

did not reek of offal, only of the sweet gums and
alcoholic oblations of the faithful.

The door into the Women's Court was small and the
Court itself not large. Only females of the moneyed
class could afford to approach the goddess, the spot
was infrequently packed. Panduv gave the prescribed
coins to the portress and passed inside.

The Zakorian had come to the Court twice before,
treats Arud had donated. The area comprised a bare
lidless box of walls and flagged floor, with, at the
farther end, a group of citrus trees, the altar standing
among them.

Panduv was alone with Cah.

The statue was modern, of a woman, voluptuous
but not gross, veiled as fashion preferred by a smoldering gauze. Through the film, her eyes of tawny
topaz would sometimes flash like flame. She was black,
so black it was not possible to trace her countenance
or read her expression.

The black woman confronted the black Cah, and
laid on the altar some cakes, baked, in accordance
with tradition, by her own hands. Panduv's baking was
indifferent. She had no talent for such chores. But,
though she had come to credit Cah, Panduv was not
uneasy. Cah had got from Panduv what she wanted. A
cake was only a cake.

When she left the Court, bees were gathering in the
citrus trees and among the flowers on the wall. Summer was advancing. Pleasingly, the Red Moon of Zastis
fell early this year, she could enjoy Arud before she
grew too big.

The temple was also busy with its bees. About the
offices and sanctuaries the lesser priests were hurrying. Across the platform there came the chant of boys'
voices, gaining mathematics, and beyond, the drub-
bing of mallets from the mason's yard. A respect for
learning and the arts had begun to invest the capital.
A sculptor of the temple school had created the Cah
of the Women's Court. A theater was being built.
Only men temple-trained would be licensed to act, as
to carve, study the stars, or take positions of temporal
authority. But a son of Arud could expect such school-

ing. For Teis, there were other means, a subterfuge Arud had condoned: His daughter would be granted her letters. But for his son, what might he wish he would not have?

Arud would be High Priest in ten years, or twelve. It was almost sure. Unadmitted to the secret connivance of the temple's inner clique, yet she had glimpsed its dexterity. The new thinking of Iscah, the very statue in the Women's Court, these in themselves evinced the nature of change, and of the men behind it.

At home Teis was sitting placidly with the current careful girl. But seeing her mother, the child came gamboling forward.

She put her hand on Panduv's belly, where she had been told the other child was sleeping.

"How he?"

"He's well."

Teis pressed her ear to her mother, to hear if he was yet saying anything. Her own ability with words increased daily. She did not want to be usurped.

The summer climbed its golden stair into a palace of drenching heat and powdered dust. Its descent was jarred by rains. The winter swooped across the sea, white-winged, and snow came down again as the year before on the Iscaian south, a happening scarcely known in previous history.

There were reports of earth tremors north and east. In Dorthar a lightning bolt was said to have sliced the cupola from a temple of Anack—in Anackyra, or perhaps only at Kuma. Farther east yet, a fleet of fifty ships of Shansarian Karmiss had gone down in a tempest, not a man saved. There were scares of plague in Corhl, but the entry of the snow ended such tidings.

Wildest of all, maybe, a tale stole out of Thaddra of a white dragon lurking in the jungle wastes of the west.

It was a bad winter for many, rife with portents and false alarms, cruel with freezing.

But in the villa of Arud, the fires were lit, they dressed in furs, and roasted nuts, and the cricket still chirped in the hearth.

*   *   *

Her pains began in the middle of a winter night. Teis had been dilatory. This one was early.

Panduv had been dreaming. Her children were grown. The girl, in a bright gown, was up on the roof. A parasol of tree stood in a tub beside the pond now, and hanging there in a cage was a chattering bird, which Teis was feeding. She seemed aged about eighteen. Her hair, though woven back in a ceramic band, reached almost to the ground. At its very tips, the shining mass was divided into brief little plaits, twelve of them, each ending in a gleaming golden ring. Panduv deduced that her daughter had married.

Her son was unmistakable.

He was black, as she was, but although he had the beauty of a god to her eyes, it was not like her beauty. Not even, as she considered it in the dream, Rehger's beauty, quite. But he had the eyes of Rehger the Lydian, and coming up to her smiling and calm, he put into her hands a gift. It was a living leaping breathing burning dancer—of somber wood.

"For the Giving Feast," he said, "Cah's festival." Then, without demand or unease, "Do you like it, mother?"

He was happy. It was not in the smile. But in the substance of the inner depth behind his visionary seer's eyes. He was entire.

She turned the dancer in her hands, amazed, and Teis leaning on her shoulder said, "Mother, that's you."

And suddenly her whole body sloughed from her and her *soul*, yes the soul of her, was dancing the fire dance, with all the nonsense of the body scorched away— But in that second a shriek of pain ran through her core.

He began early and he hurried to the world.

In the agony she remembered to call out the appropriate sentence: "Cah aid me!"

Cah aided.

The head of her son, black as charcoal, pushed into

life. Once the torso and the limbs came out, Panduv saw she had birthed a perfect living creature.

Arud when—against the tenets—he entered the room and took the boy, lifted him up and swore.

"Your color, you Zakr woman. But he has my eyes. Look, do you see? My eyes and my race—male, by the goddess."

Exhausted, Panduv drifted on her pillows. Arud put earrings of gold into her hand, just as, in a dream, some other present had been placed there—but the idea of it had gone from her in the toil of labor.

Then they gave her the baby and she suckled him.

He had the Lydian—the Lan's—eyes, but it was benign that Arud should mistake them for his own. He would be a generous father. In all but flesh and blood, this would be his son.

She would convince Arud that the child must have an Iscaian name, an old name of the uplands, which in Iscah was mostly given as Raier.

Against her breast, the child slumbered. His face was composed and couth. Within its pliable contours she beheld, clear as moon in cirrus cloud, the serene and sleeping face of a man of sixteen or twenty-five years. But that was still to come.

DAW

TANITH LEE

"Princess Royal of Heroic Fantasy"—The Village Voice

THE NOVELS OF VIS
☐ THE STORM LORD   (UE2273—$3.95)
☐ ANACKIRE   (UE2274—$3.95)
☐ THE WHITE SERPENT   (UE2267—$3.95)

THE FLAT EARTH SERIES
☐ NIGHT'S MASTER   (UE2131—$3.50)
☐ DEATH'S MASTER   (UE2132—$3.50)
☐ DELUSION'S MASTER   (UE2197—$2.95)
☐ DELIRIUM'S MISTRESS   (UE2135—$3.95)
☐ NIGHT'S SORCERIES   (UE2194—$3.50)

THE BIRTHGRAVE TRILOGY
☐ THE BIRTHGRAVE   (UE2127—$3.95)
☐ VAZKOR, SON OF VAZKOR   (UE1972—$2.95)
☐ QUEST FOR THE WHITE WITCH   (UE2167—$3.50)

OTHER TITLES
☐ DARK CASTLE, WHITE HORSE   (UE2113—$3.50)
☐ DAYS OF GRASS   (UE2094—$3.50)

ANTHOLOGIES
☐ RED AS BLOOD   (UE1790—$2.50)
☐ THE GORGON—AND OTHER BEASTLY TALES
     (UE2003—$2.95)

TRADE PAPERBACK EDITION
☐ THE SILVER METAL LOVER
0-8099-5000-6   ($7.95)

NEW AMERICAN LIBRARY
P.O. Box 999, Bergenfield, New Jersey 07621

Please send me the DAW BOOKS I have checked above. I am enclosing $_____
(check or money order—no currency or C.O.D.'s). Please include the list price plus
$1.00 per order to cover handling costs. Prices and numbers are subject to change
without notice.

Name _____

Address _____

City _____ State _____ Zip _____
Please allow 4-6 weeks for delivery.

DAW

A New Superstar in the DAW Firmament!

Mercedes Lackey

THE VALDEMAR TRILOGY

☐ **ARROWS OF THE QUEEN: Book 1** (UE2189—$2.95)

Growing up in a repressive, puritanical environment, young Talia dreams of serving as a Herald—one of the Queen's elite special guard, who act as lawgivers, peacekeepers, and even warleaders. Chosen by one of the mysterious and powerful Companions, Talia is awakened to her own unique mental powers and magical abilities, and assumes a vital role in the attempt to save the kindgom from disaster.

☐ **ARROW'S FLIGHT: Book 2** (UE2222—$3.50)

Talia, a full Herald at last, must face new and greater challenges as she rides forth on Patrol, dispensing Herald's Justice throughout the land. But in this realm, beset by dangerous unrest, enforcing her rulings will require all the courage and skill Talia can command—for if she misuses her special powers, both she and Valdemar will pay the price!

☐ **ARROW'S FALL: Book 3** (UE2255—$3.50)

As Talia, the Queen's own Herald, undertakes a dangerous diplomatic mission, she is plunged into a sorcerous trap . . . a trap which may keep her from ever warning Valdemar and the Queen of the marching armies and sorcerous destruction which are even now reaching out to engulf them.

DAW

DAW PRESENTS THESE BESTSELLERS BY
MARION ZIMMER BRADLEY

THE DARKOVER NOVELS

The Founding

☐ DARKOVER LANDFALL	UE2234—$3.95

The Ages of Chaos

☐ HAWKMISTRESS!	UE2239—$3.95
☐ STORMQUEEN!	UE2092—$3.95

The Hundred Kingdoms

☐ TWO TO CONQUER	UE2174—$3.50

The Renunciates (Free Amazons)

☐ THE SHATTERED CHAIN	UE1961—$3.50
☐ THENDARA HOUSE	UE2240—$3.95
☐ CITY OF SORCERY	UE2122—$3.95

Against the Terrans: The First Age

☐ THE SPELL SWORD	UE2091—$2.50
☐ THE FORBIDDEN TOWER	UE2235—$3.95

Against the Terrans: The Second Age

☐ THE HERITAGE OF HASTUR	UE2079—$3.95
☐ SHARRA'S EXILE	UE1988—$3.95

THE DARKOVER ANTHOLOGIES
with The Friends of Darkover

☐ THE KEEPER'S PRICE	UE2236—$3.95
☐ SWORD OF CHAOS	UE2172—$3.50
☐ FREE AMAZONS OF DARKOVER	UE2096—$3.50
☐ THE OTHER SIDE OF THE MIRROR	UE2185—$3.50
☐ RED SUN OF DARKOVER	UE2230—$3.95

DAW

A WORD FROM THE PUBLISHER

Collectors and friends of DAW Books will be interested in learning that DAW has arranged with Starmont House, Inc. (P.O. Box 851, Mercer Island, WA 98040) for the publication of certain DAW titles in hard-bound, full-size editions.

The first titles, which will appear in 1987, will include THE RETURN OF THE TIME MACHINE by Egon Friedell, THE YEAR'S BEST HORROR STORIES: IV edited by Gerald W. Page, UNDER THE GREEN STAR by Lin Carter, and DON'T BITE THE SUN by Tanith Lee.

These books will be available only from Starmont and certain selected bookshops. DAW Books will not be selling them directly. For further information and prices, write directly to Starmont.

This notice is for the benefit of our readers and is not a paid advertisement.

—*D.A.W.*